GUILTY
KNOWLEDGE

Legal thrillers by Michael Monhollon

Criminal Intent

Guilty Knowledge

Trial by Ambush (Robin Starling Courtroom Mystery #1)

Juggling Evidence (Robin Starling Courtroom Mystery #2)

Dog Law (Robin Starling Courtroom Mystery #3)

Laughing Heirs (Robin Starling Courtroom Mystery #4)

Gone Ballistic (Robin Starling Courtroom Mystery #5)

GUILTY
KNOWLEDGE

A Legal Thriller

Michael Monhollon

Reflection Publishing

Abilene, Texas

For Seth and Joshua

ONE

_____

BEFORE THE FACT

Chapter 1

As he opened the door, the phone began to ring. He hesitated, looking back into the house, decided he wasn't going to answer it, and turned away, pulling the door shut behind him. *Whump*, there she was, right up against him. His arms went out reflexively, her arms went out, and each of them stepped one way and then the other, trying to get clear.

He managed a shaky laugh as he stepped back. "I'm sorry. I haven't been dancing..." He broke off when he saw the gun, black in the early twilight. Her arm was extended, the gun raised, the barrel pointing just to his right, but moving.

"Hi, Alan."

He recognized her and backed up further, his heel catching on the threshold and his back hitting the closed door. She extended her empty hand toward him as if to steady him, and he shrank from her touch as if she were a corpse risen from the grave. The gusting wind played with her dark hair.

She laughed. "Oh, the gun," she said, and she moved away from him, reaching behind her to tuck it into the waistband of her short skirt. But it wasn't the gun that alarmed him; it was her.

He managed to recover his balance, but his heart was pumping.

She held out her hands, palms up. "It's just me. Tracey. Say something, okay?"

He swallowed. "What are you doing here?"

"I was thinking maybe 'hello.'" Lightning flashed silently behind her. Her eyes were in shadow, but he remembered that they were, for someone with her dark hair, a disconcertingly light shade of blue.

"Hello," he said. From far away came the low rumble of thunder.

"Can we go inside?"

"I was just going jogging." He glanced down at himself, inviting her to note the evidence of his running shoes and gym shorts.

"Yes, but then I turned up, and you invited me inside."

She reached past him to turn the knob and push. The door, unlocked because he didn't carry a key when he jogged, swung inward.

"It's about to storm," she said, looking back at the street as lightning brightened it again. "You don't want to go jogging."

"I can get wet."

"You can get fried by lightning, too. That doesn't make it a smart thing to do." She took a step toward the open door, and he stepped to block her. The movement brought them together, so that she was standing against him, looking up into his face. Five years telescoped to nothing. He had held her only yesterday.

She stepped around him, her eyes not leaving his face until she was past him, inside the house.

As she turned away, he hardly saw the gun in the waistband of her skirt. He did see how the ends of her dark hair brushed her slender shoulders as she walked. She hadn't changed at all.

Outside, the first drops of rain spattered the sidewalk. He closed the door and leaned against it, his hands behind him on the knob. Tracey Coleman turned and looked at him.

"You look scared to death. I didn't think trial lawyers were scared of anything."

He didn't know what to say to that. He shrugged.

"You knew you'd run into me again sooner or later," she said.

"Yes. I thought it would be in a public place, though."

She laughed, and the sound was as familiar to him as an old song. She took out her gun and set it carefully on the coffee table. Dread rose in him like the tide, but he left the door and came into the living room.

"Why the gun?" he asked.

"Force my way in. Make you talk to me." She'd had her navel pierced. He could see the gleam of the gold ring beneath her short blouse.

"Why did you want to talk to me?"

She dropped onto the sofa. "Same old sense of humor. I'm kidding, okay? I wasn't planning to come here at all. I was out walking, and a couple of creeps started following me."

"And you had a gun?"

"I always have a gun."

She had changed after all. "How did you know where I lived?" he asked.

"I've kept track. You were a pretty big part of my life."

He himself had not kept track.

"I live in your old apartment complex, you know," she said. "It's only about a mile from here."

He dropped into a chair and put his head in his hands as time telescoped on him again. He was twenty-seven, two years out of law school. Fists banged on his door in the night, police visible through the peephole, her father standing behind them on the landing, the wind whipping a pale raincoat about his legs. Thunder. Flashes of lightning brightening the scene like a flashbulb. It had been storming that night, too, and he could hear rain on the roof.

Tracey said, "I didn't get your old apartment, of course. Daddy would have freaked. Could you check the door and see if anyone's out there? I only lost them about a block from here."

He had been too focused on the threat posed by the 110-pound girl on his sofa to think about any external threat. To him, the creeps she'd said were following her seemed more phantasmal than real. He went back to the front door and put his head against the glass of the tall, narrow window to the left of it. It was getting dark, but the street lamps provided sufficient illumination for him to see past his own reflection into the yard and the street beyond it. There was no one. He turned the thumb latch to lock the door.

When he turned back to the living room, he found that Tracey had changed position. Her empty sneakers were on the floor, and her legs were curled beneath her on the sofa. He hesitated, then went back to his recliner and perched there. "There's no one," he said.

"You sound like you don't believe me."

He felt his mouth stretch. "Why else would you show up on my front porch with a gun in your hand?"

"Thank you."

"Who are they?"

"I don't know. I was walking around the high school track when I noticed two guys watching me."

His eyes went to the gun on the coffee table. It had a short barrel, no more than three inches or so, but it was too big for easy concealment.

"I have a little derringer I usually carry in my pocket, but tonight I couldn't find it. This is a Walther. Walther PPK? You know."

6

He shook his head.

"James Bond."

"Is that what he carried?"

"Duh. Astin Martin? Vodka martini, shaken not stirred?"

"I've heard of the vodka martini thing."

She rolled her eyes. "It's hard to believe I ever slept with such a cultural illiterate."

"James Bond is culture?"

"Such as it is. The guy who gave me the gun was a Bond fanatic."

"So he was culturally literate."

"Oh, good grief. I didn't sleep with him, if that's what you're thinking." She paused. "Well, it was no big deal anyway. Do you want to touch it?"

He started.

"I mean, I see you eyeing it and all."

She was talking about the gun. He shook his head, smiling weakly.

"Pick it up if you want to. Just be careful. There's a cartridge in the breech, and the safety's off."

He didn't pick it up. Her easy familiarity with firearms reminded him that she had changed, just as he had. The world was different.

"I wouldn't say no to a glass of water," she said.

His mouth twitched. "If it were offered, you mean?"

She smiled at him.

Oh, that face, he thought, and he got up.

She didn't stay put, but trailed him to the kitchen, deeper inside his house. He opened the cabinet door, glanced at her sitting at his little kitchen table, and said, "We can't do this."

She raised her eyebrows. "Do what?"

"Just pick up again like nothing happened."

"Pick up again. You mean sleep together? I thought you were just going to get me a glass of water."

He sighed as he got a glass out and set it on the counter. Rather than fill it, he dropped into a chair across from her. "What we did cost me everything, you know — my job, my friend and mentor, and really my self-respect."

She studied him. "I'm sorry. Of course, I was just seventeen."

He nodded. "I know. You had a lot to deal with yourself. For what it's worth, I'm sorry, too."

"Don't be."

"I can't help it. Guilt has been a big part of my life these last five years." He shrugged. "I've actually become religious again, trying to deal with it."

"I thought the church was better at making you feel guilt than helping you deal with it."

"We've got the confessional."

"Oh, God. You've been talking about us to a *priest*?"

He shrugged. She rose and got the glass from the countertop. She looked at him. "How did he take it? The priest."

"He seemed able to deal with it."

She shook her head. "'A sexual experience so profound it will change your religion.' I ought to put it on billboards." She opened the refrigerator and looked in. "Can I have grape juice?"

He said she could, and she poured, twisted the cap back on, and put the jug back in the refrigerator. When she picked up her glass, she stood leaning against the counter and looking at him. Finally she took a large breath and expelled it.

"Okay, I think I get it," she said. "It doesn't make me feel real great, but I think I get it."

"Get what?"

"Sleeping with me was evil; it was bad; it was the worst thing that ever happened to you. Does that sum it up pretty well?"

His mouth twisted. "Let's just say it was illegal. That's enough."

"I was eighteen."

"When they caught us."

"I'd been eighteen for two days." It was something her father hadn't acknowledged. She was his seventeen-year-old daughter. It was why the police were there, why Alan had spent the rest of the night in the county jail.

"We'd been at it for six months," he said.

She rolled her eyes and took a long drink from her glass. The dark juice stained her mouth like a child's. "At it," she said. "No, we hadn't been at it. My eighteenth birthday was our first time."

A wave of unreality washed over him. "What?"

"That's what we told them, remember? We wouldn't have had to tell them that much if I'd been able to find my underwear."

In the mad scramble that started with the pounding on the door, it was amazing that they'd been able to find anything. When he opened the door to the police and her father, almost the first thing anyone had noticed were the striped panties lying across the back of the loveseat.

"That's all we had to tell them. That's all that happened," she said.

He gave an uncomfortable laugh. "I always thought of reality as something given, not something we adjusted to suit ourselves."

"Why not?" She put down her glass. "Listen to me, Alan. Only two people were there. The only thing that keeps reality from being whatever we want it to be is the pattern of electrons spinning around in there." She tapped his forehead with her index finger. "Get with the program."

His mouth opened, but not to speak. He had a sense, suddenly, of looking out at the world through her eyes, and what he saw was an alien landscape.

"Oh, lighten up! It's not like you went to prison."

"I lost my job."

"Well, you couldn't expect Daddy to keep you around after he'd caught you diddling his daughter."

"Diddling?" Alan said. "Is that what they call it now?"

"No. That's what my grandmother called it. I thought it might offend you less than some of the alternatives, but I guess a person with your commitment to reality isn't going to deal in euphemisms. What would you prefer? Screwing? Fornication? Statutory rape?"

Angrily she picked up her glass and pushed off the counter. Grape juice sloshed onto her blouse, staining it like blood. She froze, her head down, watching the stain spread slowly.

He stood up.

"I'm sorry," she said in a small voice. "I guess we do have a lot of baggage between us."

"It'll come out."

She started to cry, standing with her head down, her slender shoulders jerking. He hesitated, then laid a hand on her back. She turned toward him and rested the top of her head against his chest. After about a minute, her shoulders grew still, and she looked up at him with eyes a pale, watery blue.

She said, "I'm sorry about that, too."

"It's all right."

"Can I use your bathroom?"

He nodded. "Back across the living room. Turn right."

She was gone. For the moment, at least, he could breathe.

Chapter 2

When she came out, he was in the living room. The wind had started moaning in the chimney, almost drowning out the sound of rain on the roof. The French doors into the back yard creaked and groaned.

Tracey was wearing one of his T-shirts. "I soaked my blouse trying to get it clean. Skirt, too. I hope it's okay to wear one of your T-shirts while they dry a bit."

The T-shirt was one he wore in lieu of pajamas. During the day it lay across the footboard of his bed, and he tried to think when he had last washed it.

She crossed to the sofa and sat down, the pink of her panties showing through the T-shirt's thin cotton. "I see you've finally hung those old movie posters you had sitting in your closet."

He nodded. He'd had them framed when he moved into the house.

"Your dad gave them to you, didn't he?"

"When I graduated from law school." All the posters were original release prints of courtroom dramas: *To Kill a Mockingbird*, *Twelve Angry Men*, *Witness for the Prosecution*.

"Even though he's not a lawyer."

"No. Economist."

"And you've never seen any of the movies."

"I have now. Not long after..." He stopped. "I went through all of them in the course of a week about five years ago."

"Ah. Make you feel close to dear old Dad?"

He shrugged. "Last I heard he was at the University of Chicago."

"Like that, huh?"

He nodded, looking at her from halfway across the room.

She held up a bare foot to wiggle her toes at him.

"Got your socks wet, too?" he asked her.

"Yep. Soaked your floor. Don't worry, I used one of those ratty looking towels in the cabinet to mop up after myself."

He would have just called them his towels.

"I'm sorry. I barge in, drink your grape juice, spill it all over myself, and help myself to an old T-shirt. You don't mind about the T-shirt, do you?" She sniffed briefly at the underarm. "It may not be too clean."

He felt a faint flush of embarrassment in his face and neck. "It probably isn't clean. If it'd been clean, I'd have had it in a drawer or something."

"I don't mind, really. Actually, though, I'd have expected a dirty T-shirt to be in the laundry basket. I figured this was a clean one you'd taken out of the dryer a little too soon."

The storm outside had fallen silent, at least momentarily. Alan glanced at his watch and was surprised to see that it was just past nine.

Tracey said, "That's flattering."

"The storm seems to have stopped."

She tilted her face toward the ceiling. "So it has." Her eyes met his, and a strangely appealing, lopsided smile pulled at her mouth. "Storm's over, it's getting late, and I'm keeping you up. I'll go check my clothes."

She disappeared into the hallway and came back a minute later still dressed in his T-shirt. Her blouse was in one hand, her skirt draped over her arm. "Still a little damp," she said, almost apologetically.

"I'm not saying you have to rush off," he said. "It's just..."

"You mean I can stay?"

"Stay?"

"Here. Tonight."

He had a sudden vision of them together in his bed, his arms around her, his face in her hair, and he could feel the heat of her bare skin.

"On the couch," Tracey said. "It doesn't make out into a bed, does it? Huh. No, I see. Just an ordinary couch. But it's comfortable, and it's long enough for me. Okay? Hang on, I want to hang these back over the shower rod."

He started after her. "Tracey—" He stopped short as she popped back through the archway, almost into his arms. She laughed, smiling — but a little desperately, he thought.

"We've already had our dance. On the front porch, remember?" She gave his ribs a pat and bounced past him. He turned after her, feeling comparatively slow and ponderous, like a ship coming around.

He said, "You're not afraid to go home, are you? I'd be happy to take you."

"I guess I am afraid, a little." She positioned a throw pillow on the arm of the sofa and plumped it. "I don't know how long those guys had been following me. They may know where I live."

He tried to think. For family, all she had was her father, and he couldn't face Roger with his daughter in tow, not on another rainy night.

Tracey said, "This will be fine if you've got some kind of quilt or blanket I could borrow."

"Would you rather I take you to a friend's place?"

She met his eyes then, and her shoulders fell. "No, that's okay." She brushed by him on her way back toward the bathroom.

He followed. "It's not that I'm trying to get rid of you. I'm just trying..."

As he turned the corner behind her, she shucked off his T-shirt, giving him a glimpse of a long, slender back and, at its base, twin dimples about two inches above the top of her panties. He jerked back out of sight.

"I know," she called. "You're just trying to be helpful. You're just trying to take me and leave me almost any place but here." The bathroom door banged shut.

When she came out, she was back in her own clothes. The juice stain was lighter, but the wet fabric was largely transparent where it stuck to her skin. "You don't need to take me," she said. "I can walk."

She retrieved her gun from the table. "There aren't too many guys who will mess with a pissed-off chick armed with a semiautomatic."

As she opened the door, cool, rain-scented air wafted into the house. The wind had died, but a steady rain was falling.

"I think it's letting up," she said.

"Tracey."

She took a deep breath and stepped outside, pulling the door shut behind her.

"You can stay if you want to," he called.

She was gone. He took a deep breath, then let it out with a shudder. He took another breath, and the doorbell rang. He went and opened the door.

"Do you mean it?" she said.

He hesitated, then nodded. "There's a bed in the guest room. You don't have to sleep on the couch."

"I wouldn't stay," she said. "I really wouldn't, but I am worried about those two guys."

Chapter 3

Barry Royal was on a padded table in the third bedroom. The injection Dr. Mullins had given him was beginning to take effect. As he struggled to sit up, he no longer worried about putting weight on his injured arm. He no longer felt his arm much. He no longer felt anything much, except for a surging sense of euphoria that made no sense in light of the night's failure.

"Help me keep him down," Dr. Mullins said, and Tony, one hand holding layers of gauze against his cousin's shoulder, applied the heel of his other hand to his cousin's forehead.

Barry lay looking up at the wonder of the textured ceiling. The doorbell chimed.

"Ding dong," Barry said.

"Geez, doc, what have you got him on?" Tony asked.

"Think of it as pain killer," Mullins said. "I'll get the door. You keep him down, and keep pressure on that shoulder. He's lost all the blood he can afford to."

At the door was Hugh Royal. Behind him in the circular driveway, his Bentley gleamed in the blowing rain. "Is he okay?"

"He's lost some blood. The bullet's still in there, and he'll lose some more before I get it out." Mullins turned, and Hugh followed him into the house.

Barry's voice was audible in the hall. He was singing, possibly in German.

"But he's okay," Hugh repeated.

"He'll live, if that's what you mean, barring complications. This isn't a hospital."

"Hallo, hallo," Barry said as they entered the bedroom. "Guten abend. Did you see it, Dad?" His eyes were on the ceiling.

Hugh hesitated. "See what, son?"

"The ungrateful wretch betrayed me." Barry laughed, then added in confidential tones, "I didn't realize he was Leporello."

"What's he talking about?" Hugh asked Tony. "Who's Leporello?"

Tony shrugged.

"Who's Leporello?" Hugh asked Mullins.

"Nobody we need to worry about. We're limited on our choice of anesthesia. I can't put him under in this setting, so I've given him a psychotropic. Do you know what his blood type is?"

Hugh shook his head. "I don't know what my own blood type is." He stood looking down at Barry. Barry's shirt had been cut away, and his belly rose in a pale, hair-matted mound. A stainless steel bucket stood near the table, the sleeve of Barry's shirt trailing out of it. Inside, the sodden fabric stood in a pool of darkening blood.

"What happened?" Hugh said to Tony.

Mullins gestured, and Tony moved to give him room.

"She shot at us, is what happened," Tony said.

"Shot at you! Who?"

"Who do you think?"

"So what's happened to her?"

"Nothing. She got away from us."

Hugh's mouth tightened, and he shook his head.

Mullins pulled a low stool under himself. One hand on Barry's shoulder, Mullins positioned the stainless steel bucket between his knees. Then he reached for the steel probe and the forceps that lay in a metal tray at the edge of the table.

"Are those sterile?" Hugh asked, as Mullins began to probe the wound.

"As boiling water can make them," Mullins said. Blood poured from Barry's shoulder, some of it splattering into the steel bucket, the rest of it washing over Barry's chest and the table and dripping to the floor.

Barry was twisting his neck to look.

"Got it." Mullins held up what looked like a clot of blood, but was evidently the slug. He dropped the forceps and slug into the bucket between his knees and applied a fresh mass of gauze to Barry's shoulder. "Hold this. I've got to get my sutures."

He came back with needle and thread, and a large, dark bottle of iodine with a stained label. "Okay."

Tony moved back again. Mullins moved the gauze, poured iodine liberally into the bleeding wound, and handed the bottle to Tony. "This isn't going to be pretty," Mullins said as he started to sew. "But it will get the job done."

Hugh said, "And then what?"

"He should take it easy for a few days, avoid using the arm. I don't think the slug hit the bone — I didn't see any fragments in there — but without an x-ray we can't be sure. Our biggest risk is infection."

"Infection! No!" Barry exclaimed from the table. "This fortress built by Nature for herself against infection and the hand of war."

"Optimism springs eternal," Tony said.

"Hope," Barry corrected.

No one paid any attention to him.

"Alexander Pope," Barry said.

"How long's this going to go on?" Hugh asked.

Mullins said, "Another hour, give or take."

Holding his uninjured arm high in the air, Barry said, "Hope springs eternal from the human breast. Man never is, but always to be blest."

"Super," Hugh said.

"He's not just some pasty-faced, hollow-chested, long-dead European poet, you know," Barry said.

"Who's not?" asked Tony, still grinning.

"Pope," Barry said.

"He's out of his head," Hugh said. "Don't encourage him."

Barry said, "Of ALL English authors, the most quotable. The least we can do is get him right."

"Okay," Mullins said. "I think I'm done here." He trimmed his suture with a pair of scissors and rolled back on his stool. "It's in God's hands, now."

Barry began singing in a deep, rich baritone that was surprisingly good, "Ehre sei Gott! Ehre sei Gott! In der Höhe! In der —"

"Oh, geez," Tony said.

"That girl's got a lot to answer for," Hugh said, speaking loudly enough to be heard over Barry's singing. "I don't know how much of this we can take."

Chapter 4

Sometime in the night a noise woke him. Alan's eyes opened, and he lay staring at the pale expanse of his ceiling, quietly listening for whatever sound he had heard to be repeated. When the sound came, it was so faint, so stealthy, that for several moments he failed to recognize it.

The sound came from the front door, pushed slowly closed, the lock engaging with a click that might have gone unheard in the ordinary bustle of the daylight hours, but which carried clearly in the still air of — he glanced at his clock — 3:17. Alan rolled to the edge of his bed and got carefully to his feet, aware of the unnatural tempo of his heartbeat as he crept to the door of his bedroom.

There was a light on somewhere in the main part of the house. As his eyes focused on the open door of his guest room, he remembered Tracey Coleman. Tracey was in the house. He moved down the short hall to the guest room and looked in warily. Even at night, enough light filtered through the plantation blinds to show the empty bed with its covers thrown back.

Something bumped somewhere in the house, then bumped again. Alan moved softly in the direction of the living room, where he stopped at the archway and inclined his head just enough to see into the room.

Tracey was kneeling in front of the sectional bookcase, a small penlight in one hand.

"Tracey?" He flipped the switch, and a floor lamp came on.

She jerked upright, spinning toward him. For a moment she didn't speak — just stood staring at him with wide, startled eyes.

"Oh!" she said then, putting a hand to her chest. "You scared me." She was wearing a navy pocket-T that came down just to the tops of her thighs. It was another one of his, a fresh shirt to replace the first one she'd borrowed.

"Is something wrong?" he asked.

"I couldn't sleep. I was hoping to find something to read."

He went to stand beside her, his eyes following her gaze to the books behind the glass on the bottom shelf. He said, "Which were you leaning towards, *The Catholic Catechism* or *The Catechism of the Catholic Church*?"

She grinned up at him sheepishly. "I was thinking *Voices of the Saints*. You're taking all this religion stuff seriously."

"I —" He nodded.

"Was it that awful?"

"The sex part wasn't awful at all, if that's what you mean. It was the aftermath." The sex part had been like the answer to the meaning of life, though this probably wasn't the time to say so, standing alone with her in the middle of the night, her T-shirt riding up and her panties showing because of her arms crossed under her breasts.

"Daddy busting in on us," she said.

"Your father. The police. Getting hauled down to the station. Getting fired from my job and not even being able to go in to clean out my desk."

"It was a bad aftermath, I guess."

"I guess," he said. "I thought I heard the front door."

"Just now?"

"Before I came out here."

"That was me. I thought I heard something, too, but nobody's out there."

He studied her, then went to the door, checked the deadbolt, looked through the window. Everything seemed as it should be. He turned the thumb latch and opened the door. A small lamp burned at the end of his sidewalk, illuminating a fine mist and reflecting in the wet sidewalk. Alan closed the door.

Tracey had moved up beside him. "Okay?" she said.

"I guess so."

"Good night then." She put a hand on his arm and stretched up to kiss his cheek. Then she left him, going through the archway and turning toward the guestroom.

He stood looking after her, hardly aware of his heartbeat's accelerated cadence.

Chapter 5

The next morning, Saturday, he thought of her as soon as his eyes blinked open. She'd inhabited his dreams so much that it seemed as if she had been with him all night. He rolled over to look at his clock-radio, got up, and went out into the hall.

The door to his guest room was closed. "Tracey?" He knocked, but there was no response. "Tracey?" He heard the shower in the hall bathroom come on.

He went to the kitchen to pour himself a glass of the grape juice that had stained Tracey's mouth and blouse, then went to the front door to retrieve his paper. The sky was clear, and the sidewalks nearly dry. The air, in contrast to that of the previous evening, was crisp and cold. The storm had ushered in a cold front.

He kicked back in his recliner to glance over the headlines. It was the first Saturday in a month that he had no reason to go into the office.

Just as he turned to the editorial page, the doorbell rang. He stood up with the paper, folding it, and he glanced in the direction of his hall bathroom. The sound of the shower had stopped.

Before opening the door, he looked through the side-window. There was a girl on the porch, a tall one, wearing jeans and a polo shirt.

He opened the door, his pulse beating in his neck. "Jordan?" he said.

She had a hand behind her back. "Hi, Alan," she said, smiling. "I've brought breakfast." She brought the hand out from behind her back to show him a pan of sweet rolls covered with a thick glaze of melted sugar.

"Great," he said.

"So may I come in?" The navy shirt made her eyes look as blue as sapphires, and there was grace in her hip-shot stance.

He hesitated, trying to think with a brain that had gone numb.

Tracey called from behind the closed door of the bathroom, "Alan? Alan, have you got a blow dryer?"

Jordan's head turned toward him. "Uh oh," she said. "I should have called first." Her pan of sweet rolls was pointing to the porch floor, all but forgotten as the glaze began a slow slide toward the lower end of the pan.

"No, it's all right," Alan said to her, grabbing at the pan and restoring it to horizontal. "It's not what you think." To Tracey he called, "I don't have a blow dryer. You'll have to make do."

"How do you know what I think?" Jordan said.

"What else could you think? But it's not like that. She's just spending the night."

"Oh, just spending the night."

"Yes. She —"

"She what? No, forget it. I don't even want to hear it." She turned away, but he reached out and clasped her arm, drawing her through the door into the house.

"Jordan. Listen."

In the bathroom Tracey dropped something, and it clattered in the sink.

"Okay, I heard it. Look, I'm just going to leave these sweet rolls and go. You can return the pan some time when it's convenient." She pushed the pan at him and pulled her other arm free.

The bathroom door opened, and Tracey came out. She was wearing yet another of Alan's old T-shirts, and her hair was wrapped in a blue-and-white striped towel. There was no makeup on her face, and she looked about fourteen years old.

"Good grief," Jordan said softly, looking at her.

For her part, Tracey was clearly startled by the sight of Jordan. "Oh, hi," she said. "What's up?"

"You're Tracey Coleman," Jordan said.

Tracey didn't answer. Both sets of eyes turned to Alan.

"Look," he said. "What it is..."

Jordan held up a hand. "I don't want to hear it. Enjoy the sweet rolls."

"Jordan..."

She shook her head at him, then she was through the door, pulling it shut behind her. The door closed on the edge of the throw rug and rebounded several inches, leaving Alan to watch as she ran swiftly down the sidewalk to her car, her long legs scissoring gracefully. At her car, a Mustang convertible, she pulled open the door and, without glancing back, swung down into the low bucket seat.

Tracey had come to stand beside him. The Mustang pulled away from the curb, and she said, "Who was that?"

He took a large breath and expelled it slowly. "Jordan Conway. A lawyer at our firm." He glanced at her, then turned back into the room.

"Is she your girlfriend?"

He shook his head. "I don't know. She's interested, or she was until five minutes ago. She'd heard about the thing with you, of course. Who hasn't? But she seemed to be willing to overlook it."

He went and dropped into his recliner, then noticed the front door, still standing open. The day, which had seemed crisp and pleasant only minutes ago, was now merely cold. Tracey still didn't have any pants on, just his T-shirt.

"I feel terrible." She took the towel off her head and bent forward to shake out her hair, then flipped it back as she straightened. "You should have explained things."

"If it had been anyone but you, I might have been able to. Or if you'd been wearing clothes."

She looked down at herself, then up at him. Her lopsided smile was apologetic.

Chapter 6

They ate the sweet rolls at the coffee table in front of the TV, only half-watching the antics of Elmer Fudd, who was armed and armored with a spear and magic helmet. Tracey sat on the floor, legs extended under the table. Alan sat on the couch, leaning forward as he ate.

"Jordan's a good cook," Tracey said at one point, licking her fingers.

Alan nodded, glancing from the TV to her as he chewed and swallowed.

"Any thoughts about how you're going to get her back?"

"No." He took a sip of his milk.

"No?"

"Well, we work together. We may or may not have a sort of date tonight."

"May or may not? A sort of date?"

"We were both going to the East Texas Symphony's Boot-scootin' Ball tonight." *Boot-scootin'*, as he understood it, meant he was supposed to wear boots and jeans with the rest of his tuxedo.

"Together?"

He shrugged. "In tandem."

Her eyes narrowed. "Does that mean 'in a line'? That doesn't make any sense."

"It can mean 'together.'"

"Why not say together?"

"I don't know. Why not say in tandem?"

"Never mind. Are you riding together?"

"I think so. I assumed so."

"Who's driving, you or her?"

"We hadn't really worked that out yet."

She rolled her eyes, pausing to lick the glaze from her fingers. "Look. If you like her, then you need to act like you like her. Get on the phone, or, better, go over there."

On TV Elmer Fudd was carrying off Bugs Bunny's limp carcass.

"What should I say about the Boot Scootin' Ball?" he asked.

"Whatever you want. Offer to drive. Ask her to drive. Propose another activity altogether. Actually, I may be there myself. Daddy's got a table."

"Oh, that won't be awkward."

"So go with another activity all together. Spending time together is the important thing. The rest of it's just background music — which in this case is going to be a lot of swing music from the thirties and forties."

"With jeans and cowboy boots?"

"It's how you know you're in Texas." Stretching, she picked the cordless phone from its cradle and held it out to him. "It seems like you used to be better at relationships."

On the television a cereal commercial ended, and the local news anchor came on. In the corner of the screen was the photograph of a girl who looked a lot like Tracey. "A local woman kidnapped from her Southside apartment," said the anchor. "Get the full story and up to the minute developments at six."

"Was that you?" Alan asked Tracey.

She was on her feet. "I need to use your phone."

"You're holding it."

She looked at it, dazed, then punched in a phone number. "Hi, Daddy? It's me. No, I'm all right. I just saw it on the news five seconds ago. I spent the night with a friend of mine, and I guess I left my cell phone at home. What ... You're kidding! When was that? Was anything taken? Oh, my gosh, and everybody's been ... I'm so sorry. I had no idea, how could I? Alana... No, I don't guess you've met her. She went to UT." Tracey and her father went round and round the same bits of information a few times before Tracey said, "You don't have to do that. I'll see you at the ball tonight. I'm fine, Daddy. My apartment was burgled, but I'm fine. Well, sure, I feel a little shaken up, but I'm all right. I wasn't there." She listened. "Okay. Okay. As soon as I can get there."

When she hung up, she said, "I gotta go."

"What—"

"Somebody broke into my apartment last night. Shots fired, apparently, and somebody called the cops. Everybody's been working themselves into a frenzy."

"Do you need to call the police to let them know you're all right?"

"Daddy's going to have them meet us at the apartment. He says they're going to want to talk to me."

"I imagine so."

"I need to see what's been taken and everything."

His eyes shifted as he considered. "If we leave right now, I could drop you out and be gone before anybody else gets there."

"You don't have to be gone."

"Your father's going to expect Alana to be the sort of person who might be wearing a dress."

"A cross-dresser?" But she was grinning.

"If I show up at your place with you in tow, he's going to know we spent the night together."

"You're feeling guilty now for things you didn't even do, but all right. I take your point."

Chapter 7

The passenger door of Alan's old Corolla squeaked as Tracey opened it and squeaked again as she pulled it shut.

"That door doesn't get much use," Alan said by way of apology. "I need to oil it."

"You need to replace it."

"I think that would be overreacting." He braced his right hand on the back of her seat as he turned to back out of the driveway.

"This is the same car you were driving five years ago. The whole door needs to be replaced with one attached to a shiny new BMW."

His mouth twisted, but he didn't answer. When he saw the block of three-story buildings approaching on his left, he slowed the car. "Which one is it?"

"Third one past the entrance."

He let the car drift past the entrance and across the lane of traffic to a spot along the curb. He was parked facing traffic, which was probably a violation, but he didn't plan to stay long.

"It's the third-floor apartment," Tracey said, pointing.

There were no blinds or curtains on the window. "It has kind of a deserted look," Alan said.

"I had miniblinds. I don't know what's happened to them."

She opened the car door, and the hinge screeched as the door swung outward, screeched again as she pushed it shut. Alan winced.

She came around to his door. "You coming up?"

"I better not."

"The Wrath of Coleman?"

"Your dad's been under a lot of stress the last twelve hours. I don't think seeing me would do much for his disposition."

"You're probably right. I shouldn't have said Alana. Wait for me."

She pushed off the car before he could respond, and he watched her cross the strip of grass separating the apartment building from the road and circle the building toward the entrance.

"Crap," he said suddenly. He pulled away from the curb and across the road in a wrong-way U-turn. He turned in at the entrance to the apartment complex and turned again toward Tracey's building. He didn't see a police car, nor the sort of high-end luxury car he would expect Roger to be driving. Nor Tracey's car, for that matter, assuming she still had the Porsche she had had five years ago. He backed into a space in front of the building across from Tracey's and ran across the lot.

When he got to the landing in front of her apartment, he stopped. The door gaped open, splintered and broken, with more than a dozen holes punched through it. Broken strands of yellow tape, printed with the legend *Police Line - Do Not Cross*, hung from the doorjambs.

"Holy hell," he breathed.

Inside the doorway, plaster covered the floor, the fine, white powder marked with innumerable footprints.

"Tracey?" He pushed at the door with the toe of his running shoe, and it swung further inward. A floor lamp lay on its side, sofa cushions were scattered about, and a small stereo system was smashed and on the floor. There was no sign of Tracey.

He took a breath and stepped into the apartment. A jumble of books lay at the foot of an empty bookshelf — paperbacks, mostly, among them *Catcher in the Rye* and Truman Capote's *In Cold Blood*. Tracey came out of the bedroom, and their eyes met.

"Housekeeping doesn't seem to be your thing," he said.

Her lip curled. "Bastards wrecked it, didn't they?"

"One of them was bleeding." Alan pointed to a spattering of dark splotches right at Tracey's feet. The trail of blood arched toward the bedroom. "I wonder what happened."

She shook her head. Walking more gingerly, she stepped to the doorway of the tiny kitchen, and Alan moved up behind her.

The white trash liner had been pulled out of the trash can and tossed to one side, littering the floor with soup cans, candy wrappers, banana peels and yogurt cups. The kitchen had a faintly organic smell to it.

"It looks as if they were looking for something," Alan said.

"Well, duh."

"I mean, not the usual something. Your TV's still here, and your Blu-ray player. They smashed the stereo rather than take it..."

"I think a bullet did that."

"Okay. They shot the stereo rather than take it."

"Accidentally. If they were standing on the landing when they put those holes in the door, the stereo would have been in the line of fire."

She was right, but he wasn't going to allow himself to be distracted from his main point. "Nobody looks underneath the trash can liner for valuables," he said.

"Maybe they weren't looking for valuables. Maybe they just wrecked the place out of spite." She took a breath and exhaled noisily. "Daddy said the police will want to know what's missing. I hardly know where to start."

A sound came from out on the landing, a shoe scuffing the cement. Tracey moved to the door, and Alan stepped into the bedroom, where drawers were hanging from the dresser, the mattress was tilted onto the floor, and clothes and suitcases and all sorts of stuff were lying everywhere.

"Hi, Daddy," Tracey said. "It's a mess, huh?"

"Tracey."

There were running steps and a soft grunt.

"It's good to see you, kid," Roger said. He had a big, deep voice that reminded Alan of a tuba sometimes, and he had the build to match. At five-ten, he was of average height, but he was so broad and square that he seemed short. With his thick neck and heavy features, he would look more like a construction worker than a lawyer were it not for the cut and quality of his suits. In the courtroom he had something of the aura of an Al Capone.

"Where's my car?" Tracey asked him. "I didn't see it out front."

"Police lot somewhere. There was a window broken out of it."

The sound of footsteps on the stairs announced the arrival of others. The footsteps came into the living room and stopped. After a moment — Alan imagined the shaking of hands — Roger said, "Hal, this is my daughter Tracey."

"Glad to see you in good shape, Miss Coleman."

"Tracey, this is Hal Green."

"Pleased to meet you."

"Any idea yet what's missing?" Hal asked.

There was a pause. "Could you give me a minute?" Tracey said.

"Sure," Hal said, and she popped into the bedroom, almost running into Alan.

She pointed to the walk-in closet, which was standing open, and Alan hesitated. Any confrontation with Roger was likely to be bad enough, even if it didn't start with Alan crouched among his daughter's shoes in the closet.

She gestured more vigorously, pushing at him with her other hand.

"This is going to be the kind of report I like to write," Hal said. "You say she saw herself on the news? Beats all."

"Spent the night with a girlfriend," Roger said.

"Lucky thing."

Alan stepped into the closet, and Tracey closed the door on him, leaving him in darkness. He could hear her moving around in the bedroom, shutting drawers and scooting things around.

When she spoke again, the sound was muffled. It sounded like she said her guns were gone.

Alan turned the doorknob as far as it would go and eased the door open a couple of inches.

"I think I had four handguns underneath the clothes in the dresser's bottom drawer," Tracy was saying.

"You think?" Hal's voice.

"One of them might have been in the trunk of my car. It's not out there, or I'd check."

Hal said, "We searched your Porsche. No handguns in the trunk."

"Okay. Four guns taken, then."

"Do you know the makes and models?"

"Kel-Tec P32," Tracey said. ".25 caliber Davis derringer."

"Hang on, let me get this down."

She waited. "Sig Sauer P232," she said. "And a Ruger. I'm not sure of the model number on that one, but it shoots .22 long rifles."

"Quite an arsenal."

"I like messing around with guns, or I used to. It was kind of a phase I went through."

"I suppose you've got a carry permit." Such a supposition was no big stretch. Nearly anyone in Texas could acquire such a permit by paying a fee and taking a one-day course in gun safety. "I rarely carry a gun myself," Hal said. "Too much trouble."

Roger asked, "And you get away with that?"

"So far. Anybody know about your guns?" Hal asked. "What you had, where you kept them?"

"Sure," Tracey said.

"Who?"

"Just about anyone who knows me."

"You got the serial numbers somewhere among your paperwork?"

"If the paperwork's still here. It may take me awhile."

Roger said, "It may take her awhile to find anything in this mess."

"Uh huh." There was a pause, a few aimless footsteps, then Hal's voice again. "Mind if we move on into the bedroom for a few minutes? I had a couple of questions."

Chapter 8

They were coming. Carefully, Alan backed away from the closet door, leaving it ajar.

After some movement and shuffling of feet, Tracey said, "I'd offer you a place to sit, but there isn't one."

"Unusual thing to have at the head of your bed," Hal said.

"It's kind of a trophy thing. I won a USPSA tournament. I've got the ribbon somewhere, but..."

"This is more dramatic," Roger said.

There was a pause, perhaps for a nod of the head or a shrug of the shoulders. "You said you had a couple of questions," Tracey said.

"That chain-ladder you just stepped over — is it yours?"

"Yes."

Roger said, "It's a fire escape. I got it for her when she moved into the third-floor apartment."

"Did you hang it out the window last night to get away from the intruders?" Hal asked.

"Unh unh."

"The burglars seemed to have gotten out that way as the police were coming up the stairs. I wondered if maybe you used the ladder first, going out the back-way while they were coming in the front."

"I wasn't here."

"That's right, you were visiting your friend...Alana? Could you spell that for me?"

She spelled and said the last name was Flanagan. It was an Irish name, like Alan's own. He rolled his eyes.

Tracey said, "I wasn't planning to spend the night, but the rain started and I didn't want to get out in it."

"That's right. Your car was here, wasn't it?"

"Alana picked me up."

"So until you saw yourself on TV, you didn't know anything about the burglary of your apartment."

"Right."

"How'd you get back this morning?"

"She dropped me."

Hal grunted as they moved out of the bedroom. The voices faded to silence. After a minute, Alan pushed at the door of the closet, and it swung open with a long, slow squeak.

Hanging on the wall at the head of Tracey's bed was a pistol target, mounted and framed, evidently the trophy they'd been talking about. It showed the silhouette of a man with a series of concentric circles marking his chest. There was a tight cluster of shots over the heart, and, where the bulls-eye had been, the red backing showed through the torn paper.

He pushed at the upended mattress, and it fell back onto the box springs. Between the bed and the window lay a jumble of chain and pipe — the fire escape the burglars had used. Alan pushed thoughtfully at it with his foot and noticed a small, braided purse lying half under the bed. He knelt and pulled it out, then hesitated. Most women he knew had strong expectations of privacy when it came to their purses. His eyes cut to the door, but there was no one there.

He flipped open the purse. A wallet, a key chain, a small brush, and a tampon. Nothing else. He pulled out the wallet, saw the currency, and pulled it out.

Twenties, six of them, along with a ten, two fives, and a one.

He put it all back, closed the flap of the purse, and slid it back toward the bed. His left knee popped as he stood.

His hands in his pockets, he turned slowly, scanning the room. There was a smear of blood on the windowsill. Outside the window stood a large, gold-leafed sycamore, largely blocking the next apartment building, though not the third-floor window immediately opposite. A heavy-set woman stood at the window, looking at him.

He drew back instinctively, even as the woman herself stepped out of sight.

In the living room, he could see 45th Street through the French doors that opened onto a small balcony. There were no windows facing the parking lot on the other side of the apartment. He let his gaze wander. The apartment had been ransacked, but not robbed; from all accounts, ransacked quickly and thoroughly.

Stepping out onto the landing in front of the apartment's mangled door, he could see the parking lot, but he didn't see Roger or Tracey or anyone else. He went down.

Not far away, a guy about his own age was waxing a cherry-red convertible. Alan started across to his own car, hesitated, and looked up at the building next to Tracey's. He turned toward it.

On the third-floor landing, he rang the bell. He waited. As he reached for the doorbell again, the door swung open violently. It was the woman he had seen from Tracey's window.

"You're that man who was watching me from that window across the way," she said. "What do you want?"

Alan gave her what he hoped was a disarming smile. "I was going to say you were the woman who was watching me."

She glared at him, then made a face. She shrugged. "Okay, maybe I was. I'm sorry."

"I wanted to ask you about last night."

"Are you the police?"

He smiled again, shaking his head. "I'm a lawyer."

"A lawyer!" She stepped into him. In a lower voice she asked, "Who're you after?"

"No one. Actually, it would be more to the point to say I'm a friend of the girl who lives across from you. They found her, by the way. She's okay."

"This is the young woman who was climbing out the window last night?"

His eyebrows went up. "Do you know her?" he asked.

"I've seen her around. Last night there was some noise from across the way —quite a lot of noise. Turned out to be gunshots. I looked out my window to see what the commotion was, and there was this girl of yours, climbing out onto a fire ladder that was hooked over her sill."

"Did you see her throw out the fire escape?"

She shook her head. "When I saw her, she was just coming out the window. It was dark, you realize. I just saw a bit of her before she climbed down behind that tree that grows outside my window."

"But you recognized her?"

"Sure." After a pause she said, "Am I going to have to testify about this?"

"I don't see why. What else did you observe? Anything?"

"The two men climbing out after her."

"Climbing out the window?"

"Yeah. I thought one of them was going to fall. It looked like maybe he was hurt or maybe he was climbing one-handed because he was holding onto something. Maybe he did fall. I heard a shout, and then the other man was coming out the window pretty fast-like. Course, 'cause of the tree, I couldn't see anything except right at the top."

Alan waited, but it seemed she was done. He couldn't think of any more questions. "Thank you for talking to me," he said.

"So what happens now?"

He shrugged, smiling. "I don't know. This isn't a court case."

She nodded, but her mouth was screwed up in dissatisfaction.

"Yet," he said.

The thought seemed to cheer her.

Chapter 9

He was crossing back between the buildings when he heard his name. "Dougherty! Alan Dougherty."

It was a man's voice. Alan stopped and looked around, but he couldn't see where it was coming from.

The driver's door of a dark Lexus parked on the street pushed open, and a man got out. It was Roger Coleman, wearing jeans and a button-down. He made a gesture with his hand: Come here.

Alan hesitated, then walked over. "Hi, Roger."

"I wondered," Coleman said. "You're Alana, aren't you?"

Alan's face twitched in a quick grimace. "It was getting dark. She was scared, and she needed someplace to stay."

"Scared! Scared of what?"

"I don't know. She told me there were men following her."

"What men?"

Alan shook his head, shrugged.

"She didn't tell you?"

"She said she didn't know."

"That's a hell of a story."

"Yes."

Roger didn't say anything, and Alan didn't elaborate.

"She's twenty-three now," Alan said. "And she slept in the guest room."

Roger grunted. He said, "Alana's just something she called you, right? You haven't started dressing up in women's clothes or anything."

Alan gave him a weak smile and shook his head.

"Don't screw with her, Alan. I mean it. Don't you screw with her."

The injunction seemed ambiguous, but Alan was willing to obey it in all possible interpretations. "I won't," he said.

Coleman fished the ever-present Marlboros from his shirt pocket and tapped one out. "Everything's been a mess since that night I pulled her out of your apartment. You know that, don't you?" He lit the cigarette, and the lighter disappeared back into his pocket. "Sheer chaos," he muttered. He turned back to his car, opened the door, and swung down into his seat.

"Roger?"

Coleman squinted up at him through the tobacco smoke.

"I am sorry."

"Sorry doesn't put Humpty Dumpty together again, does it, big guy?" He pulled his door shut.

When he was gone, Alan trudged back to his car, walking with his head down. Tracey stepped away from the building and laid a hand on his arm. "How'd it go?"

"Not as badly as I expected."

"Meaning..."

"Meaning he didn't leap on me and beat me about the head and neck."

She smiled. "Poor Alan. Look what's happened since I turned up on your doorstep."

"I'm okay."

"I just talked to the apartment manager. It'll be Monday before they can get my door replaced."

He felt dread blossom in his chest. "So you want me to take you to a hotel?" he said.

She looked genuinely startled. "No. I was thinking..." She trailed off.

He smiled, or tried to, and she slapped his arm.

"You're playing with me," she said.

"Go pack some clothes."

He watched as she ran lightly up the first flight of stairs. Her slim, bare legs were enough to make him cry.

Chapter 10

On the way back to his house, he had a claustrophobic moment when his heart raced and he felt suddenly he couldn't breathe. He pulled against the curb and stopped, unrolling his window to let in the crisp fall air.

"Are you all right?" Tracey asked him.

He nodded, focusing on the gold leaves of the sycamore trees that lined the street. His heartbeat slowly returned to normal. He put the car back in gear.

"What in the world was that all about?"

"I don't know. I—"

"I'm getting to you, huh?"

He shrugged, feeling apologetic and not sure that he should.

"You hungry? Maybe you need something to eat."

"I don't think it's hypoglycemia."

"My treat." She held up the little braided purse he had found in the bedroom, and he remembered the fan of twenties. The burglars had taken four guns, but no TV, no Blu-ray player, and no wallet.

"Okay," he said.

He had about finished putting himself on the outside of a half-pound burger when Tracey said, "One more favor, if it's not going to make you feel trapped or anything."

His eyes went to hers. "Okay," he said.

"I don't have anything to wear to the Symphony Ball tonight."

He kept forgetting the ball. "Why do you want to go to that thing?" It would make his life easier if she didn't, assuming he and Jordan would be there.

"After last night I've got to, okay? I owe Daddy that much."

"So we need to swing back by your apartment?"

She shook her head. "I don't have much in the way of party dresses. Would you be willing to take me to Macy's or Dillard's?"

"Or Macy's and Dillard's?" He felt like he was trapped in an affair with her again, this time without the sex.

"What is it with men and shopping? You're all alike, aren't you?"

"I was going to say the same thing about you women."

"So the answer's no."

"I didn't say that."

"The answer's yes."

"It's just that you're asking me to participate in three of my least favorite activities."

"Which are?"

"Shopping for clothes, shopping with a woman, and shopping with a woman for clothes."

"That sounds like something you've said before."

He sipped his drink. "Maybe it is," he admitted.

"It won't take thirty minutes."

"You can pick out a party dress in thirty minutes?"

"Well, maybe not to keep. But if I find I don't like it, I can always take it back tomorrow."

"I guess I can stand anything for thirty minutes. There's always Friedrich Nietzsche."

"What?"

"He was a nineteenth century atheist philosopher."

"I know who he is. I just don't know what the hell you're talking about."

"He said, 'That which does not kill us makes us stronger.'"

Her forehead creased. "And that's applicable to shopping?"

"To shopping with a woman for clothes."

She rolled her eyes, balling up her napkin and tossing it onto the table as she got up. "Let's go, big guy."

He started, because it was what her father had called him.

It took her forty-five minutes rather than thirty, but he found that his suffering was not acute. In fact, the whole experience was rather pleasant, and he was impressed with Tracey's methodical approach. It helped that she had the slight sort of figure that women's clothing seemed to be made for.

She modeled four dresses for him, then went back to a dress with an outer layer of gold lace over a slightly darker lining. The cut of the dress was simple, and it stopped above her knees. She made the dress look good, and it returned the favor, showing off her legs to good advantage.

"This is my favorite of the bunch," she said. "What do you think?"

He nodded. In contrast to the dark hair tumbled about her shoulders, bare but for golden spaghetti-straps, her skin seemed pale as milk.

"I spotted some pumps and a purse to go with it. I think I ought to put my hair up." She pushed up her hair with both hands. "Why are you looking at me like that?"

"I like the dress. It looks good on you."

"Yeah, well this thing costs close to four hundred dollars. If some dentures don't hit the floor tonight, I'm bringing it back."

Chapter 11

Hugh Royal, already wearing his tuxedo with a pleated shirt and onyx studs and cufflinks, stopped in front of the narrow doorway and looked around. He stood on the sidewalk in front of The Cured Leaf, an upscale tobacconist and cigar lounge in downtown Tyler. He didn't smoke, and the narrow doorway led, not into the retailer's establishment, but to a narrow staircase that served the loft apartment above it.

Hugh sighed, then took his hands out of his pockets and pushed open the door. At the top of the narrow stairs, he knocked.

"It's open."

He put his hand on the iron lever, took a deep breath, and went in.

The apartment consisted of a single open room with gleaming heart-of-pine floors. The kitchen area was to the right, easily identified by the copper pans hanging from the ceiling. Beyond it was the dining area, where the sideboard gleamed with pewter cups and serving dishes. A living area was ahead and to the left, structured around a large, cream-colored Turkish rug. Beyond the white-leather sofa, the sleeping area had an art-deco motif.

My son has the heart of a decorator, he thought.

Barry was in the sleeping area, sitting in a massive upholstered chair, a patent-leather shoe on one foot and the other shoe in his hand. He had on tuxedo pants and a shirt with a wing collar, though his black tie hung loosely around his fat neck.

Hugh stopped just beyond the sofa and looked at him.

Barry looked up, his bandaged shoulder giving him a hunched appearance.

"Your jacket going to fit over that hump? Makes you look like Quasimodo."

Barry's face took on a curiously furtive expression. "Ah, Esmeralda, my gypsy beauty," he croaked.

"What?"

Barry looked into the shoe he was holding and addressed it in mournful tones. "Why was I not made of stone like thee?"

His father's lip curled, showing his teeth. "Why do you always have to be such a fruitcake?"

"That didn't sound like Charles Laughton? I thought it was a pretty good impression." Barry lifted his leg far enough to grasp his ankle with his free hand and pull it onto his knee.

"Are you all right? Any pain or anything?"

"Nope. Those pills the doc gave me have me doped to my eyeballs." Barry put on the remaining shoe. "Last night was even better, of course. I'd have watched him cheerfully while he took off my arm."

"Ben's all right." Ben Mullins and Hugh had been friends since high school days.

Barry stood up. He swayed and had to take a step to keep from falling over.

"Maybe you shouldn't go," Hugh said.

"I'm all right. What's Tony been doing?"

"He found the rental car she drove in from DFW."

"And?"

Hugh shook his head. "Nothing. It was clean."

"He going to be at the ball tonight?"

"He's bringing Carlotta."

"You think those two are getting a little close?" Barry asked.

"Tony's a good man."

"Sure, but is Carlotta's father going to share our high opinion?"

"Get your jacket on. Let's go."

Chapter 12

Alan had blue jeans. Though his tux dated from his first months with the Coleman law firm, that had been only seven years ago, and the jacket still fit him. He'd gotten his boots when he moved to Tyler and hadn't worn them more than once or twice since. The leather on the outside edge of the vamp had cracked, but the boots would serve him as long as he didn't have to wade through any puddles.

An hour before the Symphony Ball was to start, he sat with Tracey in the living room of his house, both of them dressed up, neither with anywhere to go, at least not yet. His car key, which he had taken off his ring, lay on the coffee table. Both sat looking at it.

After several minutes Tracey asked, "This is your plan? Sit here in your party clothes just in case Jordan turns up? Suppose she's sitting in her party clothes waiting for you to pick her up?"

Alan glanced at his watch. "In thirty minutes or so, we'll cruise by her place to see if her car's in her driveway."

"And if it is?"

"I'll run you out to the party, then come back and get her."

"And how do I get back here?"

"I don't know. I guess you'll have to work that out."

She sighed. "Okay, then. I've worked it out."

"How to get home?"

She nodded. "I'll drive."

"Drive what? I thought you said your Dad had your Porsche taken to a glass place to get the broken window replaced."

"He did. He also got me a rental. It's sitting in front of my apartment." She stood. "You can drop me on your way to pick up Jordan."

He looked up at her in disbelief. "How long have you known you had a car back at your apartment?"

"A while. Daddy texted me while we were at Dillard's. I was in the dressing room."

He got up. "I've spent the afternoon worrying about how I was going to juggle two women, and all the time..."

"Alan."

"What?"

"You don't have to worry when I'm around. I'll take care of you." She patted his cheek. On the way into the garage, she added, "Don't bring her home with you, though. That might be awkward. I can't stay at my place until they get the door fixed, you know."

Jordan Conway wasn't at home. He was standing on the stoop in front of her Cape Cod house, considering the dark, multi-paned windows on either side of the door, when his cell phone rang. He fished it out of his jacket pocket.

"Hello?"

"So where are you?" It was Jordan's voice.

"Standing in front of your house, wearing jeans and a tuxedo jacket and feeling foolish."

She laughed.

"So where are you?"

"Standing in front of your house, wearing a party dress and feeling foolish."

"It's almost like we deserve each other."

"Almost."

He waited, but she didn't say anything else immediately. "What do you want to do?" he asked.

"I'll wait here. You come get me."

He nodded, though there was no one to see it. "On my way," he said.

She was sitting on his front porch swing when he got there, but she stood as he pulled to the curb behind her Mustang. She was wearing a black, sleeveless sheath dress that made her look both elegant and professional. She smiled at him as he walked up the sidewalk.

"It's like you're the one who lives here," he said.

"Not yet."

He stepped onto the porch and held out his arm. She slid her arm through his and they walked back down the sidewalk. "Whose car shall we take?" he asked.

"I'll let you drive me."

"Happy to. It will foster my sense of manliness." He beeped the lock, then opened the door for her with a screech of hinges.

"That is one manly sound," she said.

She sat and swung her legs in.

He smiled as he walked around the Corolla. There was something about watching a woman in a tight, short dress get into a car, especially a woman with such long legs.

The radio came on as the car started, Mick Jagger singing about his lack of satisfaction.

She reached forward and clicked it off.

"You don't like the oldies?"

"I love the oldies, but I need to clear the air."

He sniffed tentatively, and she slapped his arm. "I didn't mean that. It's about this morning. I behaved badly. I'm sorry."

"Don't worry about it. The whole situation was a disaster. Besides—" He flashed a smile at her. "You brought cinnamon rolls."

The Harvey Convention Center was a sprawling one-story, flat-roofed building of pale brick with a few concrete accents, its most interesting architectural feature its fifteen-acre parking lot. Jordan drew up under the porte cochere, where a young woman with a nose ring and two young men sprouting unusual configurations of facial hair waited in red blazers. "I'm not sure I want to trust these people with my keys," Alan said, but she was already getting out and straightening her skirt. She leaned back in.

"Alan, you're the one person in town who can trust anyone with his keys."

"Is that another crack about my car?"

"People wouldn't give you a hard time if they didn't know you could afford better."

Alan got out and handed his keys to a man with a plug of hair growing from each cheek. The man slipped into the driver's seat, and the Corolla pulled away.

Jordan took his arm, and they walked up the red carpet rolled out for the occasion. In the convention center, the band was already playing Glenn Miller's "In the Mood." In the vestibule a high school girl in a long red dress looked at their tickets and pointed out their table on her clipboard. As they moved past her into the subdued lighting of the big hall, the volume of the music increased by an order of magnitude. Only a few couples were on the dance floor, but the table areas were packed with people talking, laughing, touching, exchanging hugs and air kisses. Most held a drink — a wine glass, a tumbler, or a bottle of beer.

No one was at the table assigned to Alan and Jordan, though there were napkins in several of the chairs and a purse in one of them. Jordan picked up the tokens at two of the vacant places, each set in a tiny drawstring bag.

"I'll get us something from the bar," she said, speaking loudly to be heard over the music and the noise.

"I'll go with you." But he hesitated when he spotted Roger Coleman only a couple of tables away, and Jordan was gone. Coleman, who wore black jeans with his tuxedo and lizard-skin boots that added a couple of inches to his height, was standing with an older man and a woman. Though his head remained tilted toward the woman as if he were listening intently to her amid the hubbub, his eyes had fastened on Alan.

Alan smiled mechanically and looked away. He'd already had his confrontation with Roger today. Hands closed on his arm, and he jumped. It was Tracey, wearing her new gown, her arms and legs and shoulders bare and on prominent display.

"Hi, Alan. Is this your table? I'm right over there." She gestured in the direction of her father. At the table nearest Roger Coleman was the purse she had purchased to go with the gown, hanging from the back of one of the chairs by a long spaghetti strap. A man tripped on it and staggered.

"Oops," Tracey said. "I should have left it in the chair."

"I guess so," Alan said.

The man picked up the purse, fumbling with it, and hung it back on the chair. His gaze met Roger Coleman's, and he drew himself upright. He then gave Coleman a sharp nod and walked off, weaving only slightly.

"That's Charles Danvers," Alan said.

"Duh." Like Alan, Danvers had been working for Roger Coleman five years ago. Since then, he had been ousted from the firm for mismanaging a trust fund. "I know him and all about him," Tracey said.

"I guess you would." Coleman's gaze had returned to Alan. "Look, I've got to go find Jordan."

"Okay." But she stayed beside him as he worked his way through the crowd. He stopped.

"What are you doing?"

"Going to get a drink."

"After this morning, how do you think Jordan's going to react if she sees us together?"

"She's the one you brought to the dance, isn't she?" She smiled in the direction of a fat man who had stopped a half-dozen paces away. The man turned his head and moved away from them.

"What's with him?" Alan asked.

"With whom?"

"That guy with the hump on his back." He gestured with his chin, but the man had disappeared into the crowd. "Never mind."

"Jordan must have gone to the bar on the other side of the dance floor. I don't see her." Tracey had maneuvered him into the line at a window where drinks were being served. "I've got extra tokens if you want something."

"Jordan's getting me something." He looked up the line for Jordan, but didn't see her.

"Alcoholic or non?"

"I didn't specify. Non, I suspect."

"How about I get you a whiskey sour? It'll make hair grow on your chest."

"I have hair on my chest, thank you."

"Yes, you have that line of hair between your pecs there." She poked at his tie. "I noticed it the last time I had you naked. You needn't go on about it."

He put his hand over hers, moving it off his chest as he looked past her, expecting to see Jordan approaching at any moment, but it was Roger Coleman he saw, watching them from a new perspective not far away.

"Ah, heck," Alan said softly.

Tracey caught the direction of his gaze. "I really don't understand Daddy's objection to you."

"I diddled his teenaged daughter?"

"That was five years ago. I'm talking about now. Not only are you one of the gray-flannel-suit crowd, but you don't drink, you don't smoke, and your idea of a cuss word is lands-a-mercy."

"You have never heard me say lands-a-mercy," he said.

"You know what I mean."

"I guess I do. I'm a younger and only slightly more masculine version of your grandma. Your father should be delighted."

The man in front of them turned around. "Alan!" He was a slight, blond-haired man wearing steel-framed glasses. Harvey Couter, yet another lawyer with the Coleman firm. "It's good to see you. Gosh, I don't guess I've said two words to you since..." He broke off, and his eyes cut to Tracey. "Well, hello!" he said.

"Hello, Harvey."

Harvey recognized her then, and his eyes cut back to Alan. He had been with the Coleman law firm five years ago, so of course he knew all about Tracey and Alan.

"I guess I look different with my hair up," she said.

"I'll say!" Harvey said. "You look good enough to..." He broke off again.

Alan saw Jordan coming from the other side of the room, a wine glass in one hand, a tumbler in the other. "Gotta go," he said.

The tumbler was for him. "Orange juice," Jordan said, handing it to him. She took a sip of her wine. "They have a good cabernet, if you want some."

"I wouldn't know a good cabernet from a glass of cranberry juice."

"You are a sophisticate."

They went back to their table. Three of their tablemates had showed up, two men and a young woman, maybe twenty-five or so.

"Hello," Alan said.

The older man nodded, and the younger man stood. "Tony Royal," he said, shaking hands. He was about six feet tall, with dark hair cropped close on the sides and worn just long enough on top to hint at its natural curl.

"Alan Dougherty. This is Jordan Conway."

"Pleased to meet you. This is Carlotta Basoalto."

Her hand felt small and delicate in Alan's.

"And this is my uncle Hugh."

Hugh Royal wore a double-breasted tux with pointed lapels. Alan reached across the table to shake the hand that was only indifferently proffered, noting the gold bracelet that seemed to stay in Hugh's palm as he shook hands.

Jordan touched Alan's arm. "Let's get a dance in before they present the debutantes."

"The whats?"

"Haven't you ever been to one of these before?" She took his hand and led him onto the dance floor. "I love Duke Ellington," she said, "don't you?"

"Mm," he said.

"That's what I call golden oldies." She moved against him and laid her head against his chest. Her feet were moving, and clearly she had begun to dance. Alan, for his part, did his best not to step on her feet as he tried to figure out the pattern.

"I played baseball in high school," he said.

"Thanks for sharing."

"I mean, I was an athlete. I ought to be able to do this."

"You just need a few lessons. I'd be happy to teach you. Ow." He had dosied when he should have doed and stepped on her foot.

"Excuse, please." He felt a hand on his arm. It was the young Hispanic woman, Carlotta Basoalto. "Where is Tracey Coleman? Do you know this?" Her voice had a Spanish lilt.

"Tracey Coleman?" he repeated stupidly.

"You were together a little while ago, were you not? She and I arrived back from Mexico City yesterday."

"Yesterday?"

"Yes, yesterday. We have a little unfinished business. She is still here, is she not?"

Alan glanced at Jordan. "Yes, she's here somewhere," he said.

Chapter 13

A series of eighteen-year-olds walked from one end of the room to the other on their fathers' arms while the MC intoned: "Bailey Walker, the daughter of Wade and Rhonda Walker, has been with the Belles three years. She plays tennis and is president of the Yearbook Club. She enjoys horseback riding and playing videogames with her brother. Next year she will be attending Texas A & M to major in pre-veterinary science." There were a lot of Bailey Walkers, and they slowly lined up across the dance floors on the arms of their paunchy, balding, or otherwise superannuated fathers.

Alan and Jordan watched from their table with Hugh and Tony Royal. Carlotta Basoalto had disappeared, but she had been replaced by the big guy with the hump on his back. Actually, it was his shoulder rather than his back; the jacket of his tuxedo was tight on one side like a hand towel had been stuffed in there with him. Tracey's chair was still empty and her purse now was gone: Perhaps someone had tripped over it one too many times and had moved it to the seat of the chair — maybe Harvey Couter, sitting beside the empty chair and eyeing it hungrily.

People were on their feet and clapping before Alan realized that the processional was over. The applause faded, and the MC announced that the buffet lines were now open, serving brisket, prime rib, asparagus, and twice-baked potatoes.

"You can never get too much beef," Jordan said as band started up again and the crowd surged toward the tables. They moved with it until Alan stopped her with a hand on her arm.

"Let's eat our salads first," he shouted. "The line's already halfway around the room."

"It's not going to get any shorter."

"It will eventually. Trust me."

One corner of her mouth rose. "If you mean that the line is moving and the number of people in the room is not infinite, of course you're right, though I'm not sure what practical significance it has."

Despite her doubts, she came back with him to the table. Only the hunchback remained. Alan nodded to him as he sat and picked up his salad fork.

"Nice party," the hunchback called across the table.

"Yes."

"A very merry, dancing, drinking, laughing, quaffing, and unthinking time," the hunchback said.

Alan glanced at Jordan, looked back across the table. "What?"

"I was trying to compensate for the lameness of my original observation."

"Which was what?"

"'Nice party.' Though orange juice probably wasn't the sort of drinking and quaffing Dryden had in mind." He nodded at Alan's tumbler.

Alan sat looking at him, salad fork in hand, nonplussed at the direction the conversation was taking. "Dryden?" he said.

"Nobody reads anymore. You're an educated fellow — lawyer, aren't you? Four years of college, three years of law school, and still you're an ignoramus."

"I haven't read Dryden."

"High school diploma, myself," Barry said. "No education, though apparently unlike a lot of people, I did learn to read."

"Good for you."

"I don't guess we've been introduced. Barry Royal." He held out his hand. Alan half-stood and reached across the table for it. The hand proved dry and meaty, with fingers so short that he didn't even try to close them around Alan's hand. "I'm here with my father, Hugh Royal." He pointed at the chair that had been occupied by the older man with the double-breasted tuxedo and the gold bracelet. "Tony Royal." He pointed at the chair next to it. "He's my cousin, but we've grown up together ever since his father died in a car crash. Race car driver. His father, I mean, not Tony."

"And who's the girl?" Jordan asked, nodding at the remaining chair. "I think her name is Carlotta."

Barry nodded. "Carlotta Basoalto, Tony's date. Actually, she's sort of my father's ward when her own father's out of the country. Lives in the carriage house at the end of Dad's driveway."

Alan said, "I heard she's just back from Mexico."

Barry's glance was sharp. "Yes, she is. She's Columbian, though, not Mexican."

"I heard she was traveling with a girl named Tracey Coleman." He was still having a hard time accepting the busy day Tracey had had the day before: international flight to Dallas, then through customs and on to Tyler and home, where she unpacked, grabbed a gun, and walked a couple miles to his house.

"The girl you were with just a little while ago." Barry nodded.

Alan glanced at Jordan, who had an eyebrow raised. It seemed everyone in the convention center had been watching as he talked to Tracey.

"I don't guess you've seen her anytime in the last few minutes, have you?" Barry asked.

Alan shook his head.

"Who?" Jordan asked. "Tracey or Carlotta?"

"Either one. They went out into the lobby together when everyone else was getting up to join the buffet line. Neither one's been back."

Alan put a forkful of salad in his mouth and considered, chewing.

"You're thinking," Barry said.

Alan swallowed. "What, can you smell rubber burning?"

"Did I offend you by calling you an ignoramus? I didn't mean it personally."

"The *Chicago Tribune* once called Henry Ford an ignorant idealist, and Ford hit them with a million-dollar libel suit."

Barry's lip curled. "Are you threatening me with a libel suit?"

Alan smiled and shook his head, taking another bite of salad.

"Who won?" Barry asked.

Alan followed the salad with a sip of orange juice. "Ford won, nominally," he said, "though a lot of people said that when the *Tribune*'s lawyers had him on the witness stand, they went a long way toward proving their point."

"So how much did Ford get?"

"Six cents."

Barry laughed.

"I take it you hadn't heard the story."

"No."

"Which goes a long way toward proving a point Will Rogers made once," Alan said.

"Which was what?"

"That everybody's ignorant, only on different subjects." He went back to his salad.

"You're good, aren't you?" Barry said.

Alan shook his head, standing. "I just look good within my own sphere of competence."

"Your father a lawyer?"

"Economist."

"I wondered whether your earliest memories are of being cross-examined over the breakfast table."

"Not exactly." He looked at Jordan. "Ready for the buffet line?"

Her gaze followed the perimeter of the room, still lined with people. "Okay," she said.

"Well," he said when they had stood in line awhile, "the line may be long, but at least it isn't getting any shorter."

Her face twitched, which was perhaps all the reaction his witticism merited.

"Who are those people at our table, anyway?" he asked. "Do you know?"

"The Royals? Hugh Royal is a businessman, owns and manages most of the skating rinks and bowling alleys in this part of Texas. I don't know what his boys do. Work in the family business, maybe. Look." She nudged him and jerked her head. Charles Danvers, the man who had tripped over Tracey's purse, was slumped over one of the tables, his head resting on his folded arms like that of a small child taking a nap at his desk.

"Drunk, do you think?"

"I think," she said.

So did he. His mother had often finished the evening in just that condition, usually on the sofa with her head thrown back and a glass tumbler still clutched in her hand, half its contents spilled onto the cushion beside her. He had always blamed his father for that, but his mother bore her own share of the blame.

Jordan said, "There's not much left of him, now that Roger Coleman has finished with him."

"No."

"I wonder how Coleman lives with himself."

"He's a hard man to work for."

"To stay working for, you mean."

"Jordan..." He glanced behind them, but a gap had opened in the line. "You can't blame him on my account. How could he keep me around after...? Every time he saw my face, it would have made him sick."

"And Danvers?"

"He did it to himself, too. A trustee who engages in self-dealing — from what I heard, he misdirected more than half-a-million dollars his way. Coleman had to let him go."

"And had to sue him on behalf of the client."

"Yes."

"So I guess Roger Coleman is really the victim in all this."

"The lawyers who work for him have put him through a great deal of unpleasantness."

"They've suffered a good deal of unpleasantness themselves."

Standing and looking at Charles Danvers, Alan could not deny it.

"So why do you think everyone in the Royal group is so interested in talking to Tracey Coleman?" Jordan asked.

"On another topic..."

They eventually made it to the front of the line, got their food, and returned to their table. Barry Royal had left it, and none of the other Royals had returned, which left Alan and Jordan to themselves. There was still an empty seat at Roger Coleman's table between Coleman and Harvey Couter, too. No sign of Tracey.

Neither she nor any of the Royals had returned by the time they had finished their meal, which they ate mostly without conversation, each engrossed with his own thoughts. It was hard to talk over the band anyway as it worked through Count Basie and the Andrews Sisters, Tommy Dorsey and Louis Armstrong. Alan didn't listen to much music from the Big Band Era, but he found he liked it and thought he might download some to listen to at home.

When he put down his fork and leaned back, he saw that Jordan was looking at him.

"What?" he said.

"So how about it? Shall we dance?"

Chapter 14

The night had turned cold. Alan stood with his hands in his pockets for warmth as they waited for the valet — this one a girl with blue hair and a tattoo on her neck — to bring his car. "Assuming it's still here," he said.

"Give it up. I'm done insulting your car."

"Okay." Jordan had her arms folded across her chest, hugging herself. He shifted his weight and moved his feet. Their breath was white in the cold air.

"If you'd danced like that, we could have kept at it," she said, nodding at his moving feet.

"Sorry about your foot."

"My feet. Both of them, but it's okay."

"I dodged them as long as I could."

"So it's my fault for having big feet."

He grinned at her as his car rolled to a stop in front of them and the valet got out.

They got in the car, and he leaned across the console to kiss her. Her mouth was cold.

After a moment, her hand went to the back of his head, her fingers sliding down to the nape of his neck. She held her face against his.

"Heat," she said.

"Yes." He kissed her again, longer and more fervently.

"No. Heater," she said when the kiss ended. She released him and gestured at the console.

"I was hoping we could generate our own heat."

"I have more faith in a combustion engine."

"Well, thanks." But there was a smile in his voice as he started the car.

The blower threw an icy blast of air at them, and he cut it back until the car could warm up. The radio became audible, a man's voice talking about Star Honda.

"Ooh, ooh," she said, "I've got a present for you."

She fumbled with her purse and came out with a CD, which she pushed into the stereo. She punched a button to skip ahead a few tracks, and the electric guitars and the pulsing synthesizer of the Edgar Winter Group's "Frankenstein" began to vibrate the car.

A couple of weeks ago he had told her he thought it was the greatest rock instrumental of all time, and now here it was. "Wow," he said. "Thanks."

"I knew you'd never get around to buying it."

As they were leaving the parking lot, the sound of drums began to jump back and forth across the car, and the synthesizer started going off like popcorn. Jordan had settled back in her seat to enjoy the audible light show. He was almost to her place when it ended.

"Where are we going?" she said, sitting up.

"Your place. We're almost there."

"What about my car?"

He'd forgotten about her car. He turned right instead of going straight at the next intersection, heading toward his house.

Chapter 15

A light was on inside his house, imparting a soft glow to the curtained windows. Instead of circling around to the alley and his garage, Alan drifted to a stop against the curb.

"Did you leave the lights on?" she asked him.

"I don't know. I wouldn't have thought so."

"So someone's inside."

He noticed the eyebrow. "She doesn't have a key," he said, shaking his head. Probably, he should have given her one, but he hadn't even thought of it.

"Who does have a key?"

"No one."

Both eyebrows were up now. "I'll call 911." She reached for her purse.

"Don't do that. I might have left the lights on."

"But you don't think so."

"No, but I could be wrong. Let's not overdramatize the situation."

"Someone's broken into your house and may still be inside. I'm not sure it's possible to overdramatize the situation."

"No one's broken into my house."

"How do you know?"

"Well, I don't know. I just can't imagine it."

He got out of the car and walked around it, aware of her muffled voice repeating his last words: "You can't imagine it."

He pulled open her door.

"Okay, fine," she said. She pushed her phone back into her purse as she swung her legs out, her dress sliding up her thighs. "We're both going to get shot, and it will all be due to the paucity of your imagination."

He took her hand and pulled her to her feet.

"You're going to let me go in with you, aren't you?" she said.

"Would you rather just get in your car and go home?"

"I'd rather go in with you. I'm not too keen on having an unpleasant and possibly fatal encounter with some masked intruder, though."

He grinned. "So now he's wearing a mask. Don't worry, I'll protect you."

"I have no doubt you'll take the first slug for me, but then you'll fall to the ground and where will I be?"

He put his hand to the small of her back as they went up the sidewalk together. "I'm touched by your concern."

"I'm just trying to penetrate that thick skull of yours."

"You've achieved penetration. You can leave off now."

She made an exasperated sound and shook her head.

The front door was locked, just as it should be. Alan reached into his pocket for his key ring.

She put a hand on his to stop the jingling of his keys. "Listen," she whispered. After a moment she put her head against the door, and he did likewise. He looked at her.

"Voices," she mouthed silently.

He nodded. Holding his keys against his palm to muffle them, he sorted out his house key and pushed it softly into the lock.

Her hand closed on his again, stilling it.

He looked at her. She jerked her head toward the street.

He shook his head.

She rolled her eyes and let go of his hand. He took a breath, held it a moment, and pushed open the door.

What was immediately apparent was that the voices belonged to Johnny Galecki and Jim Parsons, or rather, to their alter egos Leonard Hofstadter and Sheldon Cooper. They were accompanied by a laugh-track.

The Big Bang Theory. Alan exhaled gently, relaxing his shoulders. The shifting color of the light from the living room confirmed the source of the voices. It was the TV: Johnny Galecki and Jim Parsons weren't really in his living room. He disengaged himself from Jordan, whose fingers were pressing into his upper arm like four spikes and an opposing rivet, and he picked up the heavy onyx elephant from the table in the foyer. Holding it by the trunk, he stepped to the edge of the living room with Jordan crowding him uncomfortably from behind. He stopped.

Someone was lying on his sofa: A jean-clad leg was on the back of the sofa, a tuft of dark hair on the cushioned armrest.

"I'd better know you," Alan said, loudly.

The face of Steve Booker appeared above the back of the sofa. "Oh hey, Alan." His eyes went to Jordan, and he twisted on the sofa to get to his feet. "You've brought home a date. How awkward for me."

"Jordan Conway," Alan said, stepping back to introduce her. "This is Steve Booker, a friend of mine from Dallas."

"I was with him in Nuevo Laredo when he got that elephant he's holding," Steve said. "He didn't really

72

want it, but he was fascinated by all the bargaining that was going on, and he wanted to see what he could get it for."

Alan held the elephant up, still holding it by the trunk. "Thirty dollars," he told Jordan. "The asking price was seventy. I got up to thirty, the shop owner got down to thirty-five, and we flipped for the difference."

"Alan won the toss. We were in college then, four of us taking turns at the wheel of Alan's beat-up Ford on our way down to Puerto Vallarta. An entire week spent drunk as lords."

Jordan was looking back and forth between Alan and Steve as if seeing, unexpectedly, an entirely new facet to Alan's personality.

"I'm glad to know he hasn't always had the Corolla," she said.

"If he hadn't stayed halfway sober," Steve said, "we'd have all wound up in a Mexican jail somewhere. How many policemen did you bribe down there anyway?"

"I didn't bribe any of them. I gave them money to take back to the courthouse in payment of any fine we might owe." Going back to the front door and looking out, he said, "Did you drive? I didn't see your car." There was nothing out there other than his car, Jordan's, and a late-model Mercedes parked against the curb on the far side of the street.

"You should have heard him: 'No need to take us to the courthouse, officer. Please instruct the judge we wish to plead guilty and to pay our fine.'"

"I was very clear each time as to what the money was for. So is it around in the driveway?" Alan put down the stone elephant.

"No, it's out there." To Jordan: "I knew he was going to be a lawyer someday."

"How did you get in the house?" Jordan asked. "Do you have a key?"

"Steve doesn't have a very high opinion of lawyers," Alan said.

"I didn't need a key," Steve said to Jordan. "As for lawyers, I'm like most Americans. I rank them right above prostitutes and drug dealers."

"You rank them higher than prostitutes?" Alan said.

"Huh. Come to think of it, no. Maybe I'm not that much like most Americans."

"So why didn't you need a key?" Jordan said. "Are you a locksmith?"

"Bank examiner. Mine's the Mercedes coupe. You ought to get you one. Give people some clue you're a successful attorney rather than an aging grad student or something."

"You don't drive a Mercedes," Alan said.

Jordan asked, "So how does a bank examiner get into locked houses?"

"He uses a key."

"Since when do you drive a Mercedes?" Alan said.

"Since last week. I test-drove one as kind of a lark, and when I realized I could afford the payments, I thought why the hell not?"

"You said you didn't have a key," Jordan said, beginning to hyperventilate.

"You'd be amazed how the chicks go for it," Steve said to Alan. "Women are so shallow."

"So did you have a key, or didn't you?"

"What? No, I didn't need one. This is Alan's place: First possibility, molding over the door. Second, the hanging plant. I found his spare mixed in with the potting soil."

Jordan's eyes went to Alan.

"I know," Steve said. "Kind of trusting for a lawyer, isn't he?"

"I'm going to leave," she said. "The two of you are driving me crazy."

"No," Steve said. "Stay and have a drink with us."

"Alan doesn't drink."

"No, he gave it up. That doesn't mean we can't drink, though. I've brought provisions."

She smiled sweetly at him. "Bye, Steve."

"I'll walk you out," Alan said.

Steve followed them to the door. "You'll be forcing me to drink alone," he said to Jordan. "Very unhealthy for me."

"If I stayed, I'd be an enabler."

"A what? Don't tell me you read tabloids like *Psychiatry Today*."

Alan stopped him with a hand in his chest. "Bye, Steve," he said. He pulled the door shut between them, and he and Jordan were alone on the porch.

For a moment they looked at each other.

Jordan's face twitched, and she abruptly started laughing.

"Sorry about messing up your plans," Steve said when he came back in.

"I didn't have any plans."

Steve snorted.

"Well, we are meeting for breakfast on Monday."

"Which can't be as good as her being here for breakfast on Sunday."

"She wasn't going to be here anyway."

"Who's sleeping in your guest room, if not her? The bed's not even made. I gotta say, I've been wondering where you're going to put me up. You've got a house now, but still no place to put an extra guest."

"No one's sleeping in the guest room."

Steve stood up. "Just a minute," he said. He came back with Tracey's skirt and her bra and her pink blouse, left there when Tracey changed into her party clothes. He stood holding them, his eyebrows raised.

"It's a long story," Alan said.

"I like stories."

"You might have noticed that the bed in my room isn't made either. We slept in different rooms."

Steve went to check. When he came back, he was shaking his head. "I don't know about you. Sometimes I think you're some kind of pervert. Was it Jordan?"

"Tracey Coleman."

He frowned. "Wasn't she...Holy moly."

Alan nodded. "And then some."

Chapter 16

Tony Royal stopped the Bentley under the porte cochere where his uncle Hugh stood with his hands jammed in his pockets, the vapor of his breath bright in the floodlights.

"Has Carlotta turned up?" Tony asked.

"No. And you've been gone long enough."

"Sorry." He'd driven around the convention center in a widening spiral, but he'd seen neither Carlotta nor Tracey. He'd even been to Carlotta's carriage house apartment and to Tracey's apartment.

"I can tell you one thing. She's not anywhere inside that building." He tossed his hand at the convention center. "Not in the women's room, not anywhere."

Tony got out of Hugh's car and closed the door. "She has to be here somewhere. The car we came in is still here."

"What about Tracey's car?"

"I don't know," Tony said. "As of this morning, her Porsche had a broken window, but she could be driving it anyway."

"That or a rental. In which case it could be any of those." The sweep of his arm took in the smattering of cars scattered across acres of parking lot.

"We'd better check them. Where's Barry?"

"Inside."

They reentered the foyer. On the other side of the glass doors, two men were putting chairs on tables, and a woman was vacuuming. All but a few of the party-goers had gone, as had the members of the Guild who had spent two days decorating the place. Where the photographer had been, Barry had pushed three chairs together and was lying across them, his feet on the floor, his forearm shielding his eyes.

Tony nudged him with his knee. "Wake up, Beautiful," he said.

Barry shifted his arm and squinted up at him. As the evening progressed, he'd had increasing difficulty finding a balance between pain and the stupefying effects of his narcotic pain medication.

"We've got a few cars to check, then we're going home," Hugh said.

"Best news I've heard all day." Barry sat up with some difficulty and sat for a moment with his forearms braced on his thighs. "Okay," he said, and surged to his feet.

They went out to the Bentley. Hugh took the driver's seat, and Tony took shotgun. Barry stretched out in the back.

Hugh drove them across the parking lot to the first cluster of cars. "There's a flashlight in the glove box," he said.

"No one's in any of these."

"Go shine the flashlight into them anyway."

Tony got out with the flashlight. When he got back in, Hugh drove them to a Toyota Solara sitting by itself. Tony got out, shone the flashlight, got back in. They drove to the next car.

"Okay, we're done," Tony said finally. "Drop me at my car and let's go home."

Tony's car was a Touareg SUV. Hugh pulled up next to it, and Tony got out.

"I think someone's in there," Hugh said.

"What?"

"Someone's in your SUV. Give me that flashlight." He took it and got out as Tony got out on the other side.

The flashlight revealed a woman in the passenger seat, though she'd slid down so far that she was sitting mostly in the knee well. Hugh jerked at the door handle. The door opened, and the woman fell out, her legs remaining caught under the dash, one arm and her head hitting the asphalt. Hugh shone the flashlight on her upturned face.

It was Carlotta, Luis Basoalto's only daughter. One eye had been obliterated, and a thin line of blackened blood ran from the crusted socket.

Hugh turned away abruptly and, before he could take more than a couple of steps, bent forward and vomited between his feet.

TWO

ARREST & COMMITMENT

Warrant of arrest: A written order from a magistrate, directed to a peace officer or some other person specifically named, commanding him to take the body of the person accused of an offense, to be dealt with according to the law.

—Tex. Code Crim. Proc. art. 15.01.

A "commitment" is an order signed by the proper magistrate directing a sheriff to receive and place in jail the person so committed.

—*Ibid.*, art. 16.20.

Chapter 17

The next morning Alan woke to a ringing telephone. He reached for the receiver and rolled onto his back with it pressed to his ear. "Hello?" he said.

"Alan. Have you seen the morning paper?" It sounded like Roger Coleman.

Alan pushed himself up onto one elbow, squinting at the clock. The time was six-fifteen. "Did I see the paper?" he repeated, still feeling mentally foggy. "The Tyler paper?"

"You haven't seen it."

"No, I've been asleep."

"Carlotta Basoalto was shot and killed last night."

"Who?" He sat up, shoving a pillow between his back and the headboard. Then he remembered. "The girl with Hugh Royal and his boys. She was supposed to be at our table."

"The police called here a couple of hours ago. They wanted to talk to Tracey."

"She's not here."

"I'm not playing the irate father here. I just need to talk to her."

"I understand that, but she isn't here." Alan glanced toward the open door of his bedroom just as Tracey Coleman, wearing the same T-shirt she had worn the night before, wandered into the doorway. She leaned against the doorjamb, yawning.

Roger said, "Do you know where she might be? She isn't at her apartment."

"Could you excuse me?" Alan said. "I'm going to have to hang up, but I'll call you right back." He put the phone in its cradle. "Where the heck did you come from?" he said to Tracey.

"I came from the East Texas Symphony Boot-scooting Ball. Thanks for looking out for me by the way."

"You disappeared."

"You didn't see me talking to Carlotta Basoalto?"

"No," he said carefully, his pulse quickening.

"You didn't see me talking to Harvey Couter?"

He tried to remember. "Maybe."

"Alcohol doesn't affect him the way it does normal people. He was just letting me know in case I drank too much to get home safely."

"At least he's willing to use his powers for good rather than evil."

She snorted. "Oh, yes, the human octopus. Still, before the night was over, I was wishing I'd taken him up on it. I had to walk home. Lost one of my pumps in a sewer grate in the first block and had to limp along like Cinderella."

He would have said Alice in Wonderland. Somehow Tracey always seemed to be on the wrong side of the looking glass. "Why in the world did you have to walk home?"

"Those creeps who were after me Friday night were there at the Ball — sitting at your table, in fact. When it became clear they weren't going to leave me alone, I had to leave."

"Sitting at my table," he repeated. "The Royals?"

"Yes. Barry and Tony Royal."

"What did the Royals want with you?"

"They're a couple of sociopaths. I don't know."

"Even sociopaths do things for a reason. What did they want from you? Money? Sex?"

"I don't know."

"What time did you get here last night?"

"I wasn't wearing a watch."

Nonresponsive, he objected silently. He'd been in too many trials not to notice when somebody failed to answer a question. "Was Steve up?"

"Is he the one who's sleeping in your guest room? I had to choose between crawling in with one of you and making a place for myself on the couch."

He could only assume she had chosen the latter. "We were up until nearly one," he said. "Where were you?"

"In transit. You try walking four miles in your stocking feet, getting off the road every time you see a pair of headlights."

He studied her. "Tracey. What's all this about? Really."

"I wish I knew." She propped her right foot on her left knee, exposing the creamy skin on the inside of one thigh. The posture was as provocative as all-get-out, but entirely uninformative.

"I've got something to show you," he said. He tossed back the covers and reached for his pants. He was wearing nothing but jockey shorts, and her eyes cut downwards.

"Oh, look away, will you?" he said. "It's not that."

Chapter 18

Except for some biographical data, the Sunday edition of the Tyler Courier-Times contained little information. Carlotta Basoalto, age 26, had been found shot to death late the night before in a vehicle outside the Harvey Convention Center. She was survived by her father Luis Basoalto and her brother Carlos Basoalto, both of Teaselville, Texas. She was a student at Tyler Junior College and a dancer with Theater IV. There were no details relating to the murder itself.

Alan and Tracey sat side-by-side at the kitchen table, the newspaper open in front of them. When they had read all there was to read, Alan pushed the paper back. He looked at Tracey, and she looked back, expressionless.

"Do you want to tell me about it?" he asked her.

"Tell you about what?"

"Carlotta was looking for you last night. I don't suppose she found you."

"What if she did?"

"That's not an answer."

"No, and I'm not on the witness stand. What if Carlotta did find me?"

"Then you may have been one of the last people to see her alive. Your father said the police want to talk to you."

"Why?"

"How should I know?" he said, suddenly exasperated. "When they find you, you can just tell them that you're not on the witness stand and you don't have to answer their questions. They're bound by law to respect that, and they may even tell you as much."

"You think I'll be a suspect in Carlotta's murder?"

"How the hell should I know? You haven't told me a damn thing about it."

She studied him. "That's a bit stronger than lands-a-mercy."

"The way I feel, lands-a-mercy just doesn't cover it."

"What do you want to know?"

"Tell me about this trip to Mexico City, the one you went on with Carlotta."

"You know about that."

"The world knows about that."

"We didn't actually go to Mexico City, or not together. Carlotta was in Bogota, which is where her family's from. Her father lives there part of the time, and she has other relatives there."

"This is Bogota, Colombia?"

"Is there another one? Last weekend, Carlotta called me from there and suggested I meet her in Mexico City."

"Why?"

"We're friends. She thought we could hang around a few days and do some shopping."

"How do you know Carlotta?"

"Daddy used to do a good bit of work for her father and Hugh Royal. Daddy and Hugh went to Robert E. Lee together. They still play golf."

"What's the connection between Hugh Royal and Carlotta's father?"

"The two of them own all the roller rinks and most of the bowling alleys in this part of Texas. Right now

Carlotta's living in Hugh's garage apartment, what he calls the carriage house."

"How well do you know the younger Royals, Tony and Barry?"

"Not well."

"But they've been harassing you. They broke into your apartment."

"Well, I know them well enough to know they're not very nice."

"What do they want?"

She hesitated. "Let me back up. I went to Mexico City to meet Carlotta."

"And you got back day before yesterday. Friday."

"I'm telling you this as my lawyer, right? You can't repeat any of it."

Alan nodded his head in assent. "Sure. Privileged communication."

"The short version is, I met Carlotta in Mexico City. We shopped. We partied a little bit. Two days later we came back."

"I think I need the longer version. What happened in Mexico City?"

"Nothing that matters, except that we bought matching cosmetics cases."

"Uh oh."

"Yeah. Have you ever gone through customs? After you get off the plane at DFW, you pick up your checked luggage and carry it through."

"Okay."

"Friday I lost Carlotta going through customs. She picked a shorter line, I think. I plopped my cosmetics case on the counter and handed across my passport and declarations card. As the woman was stamping the card, I realized I had Carlotta's cosmetics case. Not mine." She paused.

"Okay," Alan said again.

"Her cosmetics case was a lot heavier. I got through customs and found Carlotta hadn't waited for me. Apparently she'd taken the train to the next terminal for the connecting flight."

"What did you do?"

"First, I checked the women's room. No Carlotta. I went into one of the stalls, and I sat down and went to work on the lock of that cosmetics case. I bent it all to crap, and then I found out my own key opened it. You know what was inside?"

He shook his head.

"A package wrapped in black cellophane, a bunch of cosmetics piled on top of it. It was right in the bottom of the case where anyone would have seen it."

"What was in the package?"

"About five pounds of white powder. It made me so mad, I decided not to make my connecting flight. I rented a car instead and drove it home."

"What happened to the white powder? You take it with you?"

"Yes. Then Barry and Tony broke into my apartment Friday night, and I had to escape out the window."

"And that's when you showed up here."

"Yes."

"Having left the white powder behind in your apartment for Barry and Tony to find," Alan said.

"Yes."

"Did they?"

"I have to assume so. I left it in plain sight on the kitchen table."

He remembered the garbage strewn over her kitchen, the soup cans and yogurt cups. He would have said that if they'd found what they were looking for, it was in the last place they'd looked. "So why were they still after you last night? Why did Carlotta want to talk to you?"

"I'm afraid to think what Tony and Barry wanted. Revenge, maybe."

"What interest did they have in the white powder?"

"Cocaine. We might as well call it what it is."

"What interest did they have in the cocaine?"

"They put up the money for it, evidently. Carlotta told me at the reception."

"So you did talk to her."

She nodded. "Outside in the parking lot. Carlotta said the Royals were giving her five grand for picking up the cocaine and bringing it in for them. She apologized for not telling me before, but to make it up to me she was going to give me half."

"Give you twenty-five hundred dollars?"

"I took the risk."

"Some of it anyway."

"We went back inside and separated in the lobby. Carlotta had to go to the ladies room. I waited for her because Hugh Royal was standing just inside the door, and I thought she could provide me cover."

"And then?"

"Carlotta didn't come back. I went down the hall to the women's room, but she wasn't there. It kind of freaked me out. I mean, I knew she hadn't gone back to the ball. I was standing where I could see both sets of doors."

"And you never went back inside."

"I started back, but there was Hugh Royal standing in the lobby just where I'd been not five minutes before."

"What was he doing?"

"Waiting. Glancing around. He didn't see me because at that point I was peering through the leaves of a big, potted ficus tree. Eventually, he went inside, and I scooted past and out the main door."

"And went to your car."

"No. Tony Royal was in the parking lot. I was driving a rental, and he couldn't have known what it looked like — I don't think he could — but he was out there patrolling the general vicinity. I ducked around the building. I didn't know what to do. I lurked around for a bit, but then all three Royals were out patrolling the place. Eventually I decided to try walking back."

"Four miles."

"Don't think I was happy about it."

"How did you get in when you got here? You didn't ring the bell."

"No need. I just used the spare key in the hanging plant out front."

He was beginning to think he might as well leave his door unlocked.

"How did you know what was in the paper?" she asked. "Who was on the phone just now? Daddy?"

"That's sweet," said a new voice. "But you can call me Steve until you get to know me better." It was Steve Booker, standing in the doorway.

Tracey and Alan exchanged glances, but neither spoke.

"Somehow I get the feeling you weren't talking to me," Steve said. "To tell you the truth, I've never been too comfortable with girls calling me Daddy."

Chapter 19

Tracey was still in the shower. Alan laid six strips of bacon across a cold skillet, enough, he thought, for the three of them. Six eggs were nestled in a dish towel on the counter by the stove.

"So that's Tracey Coleman," Steve said. "I never met her, you know." He sat at the kitchen table in a short terry cloth bathrobe complete with hood. "Seeing her, I have to say I understand. Five years ago, she must have been steppin' dynamite."

She hadn't lost a thing, in Alan's opinion. "Which bank you doing this week?" he asked.

"First Tyler." As a bank examiner with the Federal Reserve Bank of Dallas, Steve Booker had a job that brought him to Tyler one or two weeks a year.

Alan said, "Isn't First Tyler Susan's bank? Does she know you're coming?"

"Not yet." He took a sip from the glass of orange juice he had settled on after complaining at some length about Alan's perpetual failure to stock coffee.

"Is she seeing anybody these days?"

"Don't know."

"Are you?"

"Of course." The fatty strips that laced the bacon became translucent and began to glisten in the heating skillet. Alan turned down the heat and got out an eight-inch omelet pan for his eggs. When Steve failed to expand on his answer, Alan turned to look at him.

"Who?" he said.

Steve flashed a grin. "Everyone I can." Tracey came into the kitchen dressed again in her dark skirt and sleeveless blouse.

"I don't want any eggs," she said. "Just bacon." She picked up two of the eggs and opened the door of the refrigerator to put them back.

"I could make French toast with them," Alan said.

"Bacon will be fine."

"Nervous?"

"Not really." Her eyes scanned the counters. "Where's the coffee?"

"Alan doesn't keep coffee. It wouldn't be in keeping with his boy scout image." Steve sat with his legs stretched in front of him and crossed at the ankles. His bathrobe, which covered him only to mid-thigh, exposed long, bare legs covered with dark hair.

Tracey eyed him incredulously. "What are you, some kind of gigolo?"

Steve looked at Alan. "With the great ones, it always shows."

Alan, one corner of his mouth rising in a faint smile, crossed the kitchen and knelt in front of one of the cabinets.

"Great ones!" Tracey echoed with a note of contempt.

Steve said, "Even at a glance, you yourself perceive that women would pay to be with me."

She rolled her eyes, pulling a chair out from the table and dropping into it. "Pul-lease," she said.

Alan came up with a coffee maker in pristine condition. Inside the glass carafe sat a gold brick of vacuum-packed coffee.

"Hello, Mama," Steve said.

Alan set the coffee maker on the counter and plugged it in.

"Is that new?" Steve said. "You might want to run some white vinegar through it to clean it out."

"I haven't got white vinegar. You want coffee or not?"

"Coffee," Steve and Tracey said together, almost in unison.

Alan cut open the coffee and reached into a drawer for a spoon.

"I don't get it," Steve said. "When I wanted coffee, you didn't have any. When *she* comes in, suddenly you have a spanking new coffee maker and gourmet coffee."

"It was a gift. I'd forgotten I had it."

"Who gave it to you?"

"Mom, last birthday."

"Doesn't she know you don't drink coffee?"

"Evidently not."

Tracey was looking at Steve's hairy legs, her expression showing some distaste. "Can you put those things under the table so I don't have to look at them?"

His face showing hurt surprise, he swung his legs under the table. "It hardly seems right," he said. "I'd be willing to sit and look at your legs."

"Why is that not a surprise?"

When they had lingered over breakfast as long as they reasonably could, Alan said, "Let me get this stuff in the dishwasher, then we'll go."

"Go where?" Steve asked.

"Nowhere," Tracey said.

Alan looked at her.

"I've decided not to talk to the police."

Steve's eyebrow jumped, but to his credit he didn't say anything.

"I'm not sure you've got a choice," Alan said.

"They can't talk to me if they can't find me."

94

"Unless you're planning to leave town immediately, they're going to find you."

"So I'll leave town."

"How?"

"I don't know, I'm making this up as I go. I wish..." She was interrupted by the doorbell. "Crap," she said.

She wished she had her car, Alan felt sure, or even the rental, which was somewhere in the parking lot of the Harvey Convention Center unless the police had moved it. He pushed back his chair and got up.

"You're not going to answer it."

"I've got to, Tracey."

"Why have you got to?"

"Because we can't hide forever. We're going to have to talk to people."

"We can talk to them later."

He made a face and left the kitchen, heading for the front door.

"What's wrong with him?" Tracey asked Steve. "Why does he have this compulsion to answer doorbells?"

Alan didn't hear Steve's answer.

Chapter 20

He opened the door and found Roger Coleman on his doorstep. Why *do* I have this compulsion to answer doorbells? he wondered suddenly.

"You didn't call me back," Roger said.

"I got distracted. Sorry."

"Heard from Tracey?"

He hesitated.

"I need to talk to her, Alan."

"I know. Come in and have a seat."

He left Roger standing in the living room and went back to the kitchen. Steve was standing in the open door to the garage. "She's gone," he said. "She just got into your car and drove off."

He felt sudden panic. A murder investigation was underway, and Roger Coleman was in his living room. "Why didn't you stop her?"

"If you didn't leave spare keys hanging on pegboards everywhere, there would have been no need to stop her. Anyway, it didn't seem my place."

Alan didn't leave spare keys hanging on pegboards everywhere, just one key hanging on one pegboard by the door to the garage. One, unfortunately, was all it took.

"Well, crap," he said. He went back to the living room.

Roger Coleman turned toward him.

"Where is she?"

"She isn't here. I was just talking to a buddy of mine from college who's spending the week with me."

"Why did you have to leave me in here to go talk to him?"

Alan inhaled. "Tracey was here," he said. "When I was talking to you on the telephone, she showed up suddenly in my bedroom doorway. I had no idea she was in the house."

"Where is she now?"

"I don't know. She just took off in my car."

Roger dropped onto Alan's couch, deflating. After a full minute, he looked up at Alan and said, "They found a gun in the car with Carlotta, a little two-barreled derringer."

Alan sat down himself.

"Tracey had a derringer," Roger said. "She reported it stolen after her apartment was burgled the other night."

"The same one?"

"I don't know. My informant couldn't tell me the model." A smile twisted Roger's mouth. "This is going to sound strange, coming from me, but I can't tell you how much better I'd feel if I knew you and Tracey had left the ball early, and she'd spent the night with you."

Alan shrugged uncomfortably.

"I know, a college buddy's staying with you. What a night for you to have a chaperone." He levered himself up off the couch. "Tell me, how did she get in your house without you knowing about it? She have a key?"

"She found the spare."

"An answer for everything."

Alan turned his hands palms up.

Roger, looking down at him, nodded once, then went to the door. He left, and Steve came in. After studying Alan a minute, he said, "Tracey's father?"

Alan nodded dumbly.

"Not your day, is it?"

"He seems to think Tracey's going to be charged with murder."

Chapter 21

The next day was Monday. Alan called Jordan Conway before seven. They'd talked about meeting for breakfast, and, anyway, Tracey still had his car.

Jordan drove them to IHOP. When she had ordered oatmeal, and he'd ordered bacon and eggs, she said, "It wasn't entirely clear to me what was wrong with your car."

"Nothing's wrong with it."

She raised an eyebrow.

"Except that I haven't got it."

"Who does?"

He hesitated. "Tracey Coleman."

Jordan rolled her eyes.

"I didn't lend it to her or anything. She just drove off with it."

"Why would she do that?"

"She's hiding from the police."

"Are you wanting me to throw this coffee on you?"

"Do you remember Carlotta Basoalto from the party Saturday?"

Jordan nodded. "The knock-out with the sexy accent."

"You knew she was dead."

"No she's not!"

He wasn't the only one who didn't keep up with the local news. "Evidently she was murdered with a derringer, which might have been the same derringer that was stolen from Tracey's apartment the night before."

At least it gave them something to talk about over breakfast. It also gave him a chance to think through what he knew about the events of Saturday night and about what Tracey had told him. He felt a little more on top of things, a good feeling that lasted right up to the moment the elevator doors opened on their floor, and they saw a police officer talking to the law firm's receptionist.

"Here he is," the receptionist said nodding at them.

"Here who is?" Alan said, though he thought he knew the answer.

"This policeman is looking for you."

"My name's Curtis," said the cop. "Are you Mr. Dougherty?"

"Yes."

Alan glanced at Jordan, who looked from him to the police officer and back again, before heading reluctantly down the hall toward her office.

"Could I speak with you for a few minutes?" Curtis said.

"What about?"

Curtis's eyes cut to the receptionist, who immediately turned her attention to the computer screen on her desk. He looked back at Alan.

"Come on back," Alan said.

He stepped aside for Officer Curtis to go ahead of him into his office, then he shut the door behind them. As Alan went around his desk, Curtis took a seat in one of the client chairs.

"So what's this about?" Alan asked again.

"I understand that you were at the East Texas Symphony Boot-scootin' Ball on Saturday night."

Curtis's teeth seemed unnaturally white, and they gave him a predatory look.

"I was there."

"With Tracey Coleman?"

"No, with Jordan Conway, the woman who got off the elevator with me just now."

"You were seen talking to Tracey Coleman."

"That's got to single me out."

"Evidently you have a history with Tracey Coleman."

It was one way to put it. "What are you after, Officer Curtis?"

"We're looking for Tracey Coleman."

"She lives on 45th Street, I think. The Cornerstone Apartments."

"We have her address."

"She isn't there? Have you talked to her father?"

Curtis wasn't there to answer questions. "Are you saying you don't know where Tracey Coleman is?" he said.

"I don't."

"You haven't seen her since Saturday night?"

It was a question Alan wasn't ready to answer. "Why did you say you were looking for her?" he asked.

"I didn't say. I'm just asking questions, which you seem reluctant to answer."

"I might feel more comfortable answering questions if you said what you're after."

"Information. What would I be after?"

"Evidence that would tend to implicate me in some crime," Alan said, his heart beginning to pound.

Curtis gave an involuntary snort. "Are you referring to the murder of Carlotta Basoalto?"

"Isn't that the crime you're investigating?"

"What makes you think you're a suspect?"

Alan lifted his shoulders. "A police officer in my office asking questions?" he suggested.

"I haven't asked you any questions about a murder. I've only asked about Tracey Coleman."

"You've asked me where she is."

"That's right."

"And I've said I don't know."

"Yes."

"And yet here you sit," Alan said.

For a moment Curtis was silent, and Alan focused on steady breathing.

"We're not getting very far, are we, Mr. Dougherty?"

"Since neither of us knows where Tracey is, I don't know how far we could expect to get."

"Why so evasive? You're acting almost as if she were your client."

"You give me too much credit. Mostly, I'm trying not to incriminate myself in a murder that seems to have occurred at a party I went to."

"If you do come to represent Miss Coleman, remember that only communications she's made to you as her lawyer are privileged. Not anything you might have done or witnessed."

"I haven't invoked attorney-client privilege."

"Because she's not your client," Curtis said.

"I don't think I said that."

"So she is your client?"

Alan shrugged. "Does she need a lawyer?"

Curtis unbuttoned the breast pocket of his uniform and extracted a sheet of paper that had been folded twice. He unfolded it and leaned forward to place it on Alan's desk.

The document was a warrant ordering the arrest of Tracey Coleman for the intentional murder of Carlotta Basoalto. It was signed by a Donald

Donaldson, municipal court judge of Tyler, Texas. Alan read it and pushed it away.

"I guess she does need a lawyer," he said.

"But you're not it." Curtis refolded his warrant and put it away.

"I don't know. In the circumstances I think I might be."

"That might prove awkward if you're a material witness to the movements of Tracey Coleman."

"Yes, it might," Alan agreed. "That's unfortunate. I don't like awkward."

Curtis took a breath. "Let me see if I can help you. We'll say you are representing her. I'll try not to ask you about anything she's told you. We'll stick with what happened."

"At the Symphony Ball?"

"Yes. At the ball and afterwards."

Alan shook his head.

"You've said you were there."

"I don't think I've admitted to anything except talking to Tracey Coleman."

"That's a start."

"And a finish. A murder's been committed. Before I start making admissions, I want to consider in what way anything I say might be used against me."

Curtis's mouth twisted in distaste. "Tell me, counselor. Are all lawyers such weasels, or is it only the ones I run into?"

Alan returned his gaze. "It sounds like you're trying to intimidate me into giving up my constitutional rights."

Curtis shook his head. "You've seen the arrest warrant. As an attorney you're an officer of the court. If you know where Tracey Coleman is, I expect you to tell me. If you find out, I expect you to call me."

"If Tracey Coleman contacts me, I will inform her that she is wanted by the police and that she should go to the station to turn herself in."

Curtis stood. "Fine," he said. "You can warn her, but I suspect we'll get her anyway."

Alan was at his desk when his iPhone began to play "The Bridge at Khazad Dum." He dug it out of his pocket and slid his finger across the screen. "Alan Dougherty."

"Hi, Alan." It was Tracey.

"Where..." He trailed off.

"Where am I?"

"You're not in custody, are you?"

There was a long silence.

"Are you?" he repeated.

"So that's why a patrol car's parked in front of my apartment."

"Yes," he said. "That would explain it."

Chapter 22

Tracey's only options were surrender or flight. Flight seemed like a bad idea, but then, he didn't really know what he was dealing with. Twice, he started to call Roger Coleman. She was his daughter, and a man who had practiced law for nearly twenty-five years was going to have better instincts than a man who had practiced law for seven.

But he didn't want to be the one to communicate bad news to Roger Coleman. If Roger had had his way, Alan himself would be disbarred and in prison.

His next thought was to talk to his own senior partner, but his steps slowed as he approached Jim Angley's office. Angley's motivation for hiring him five years ago had been to affront Roger Coleman (Alan suspected) as much as to acquire the only attorney in Tyler to have graduated from Yale Law School. But Angley might not be willing to take on the representation of Roger's daughter in a murder case. It could get ugly — malpractice-suit ugly — especially since no one in the firm had any real experience in criminal law.

He turned around in the middle of the hall and went straight to the elevators, taking out his cell phone as he walked.

Twenty minutes later he was a half-dozen blocks from his office, reasonably certain that no one was watching him. His own car pulled up to the curb next to him. He pulled open the door on the passenger side and got in.

"Hi," Tracey said.

"Hi."

She swung the car away from the curb.

"You've changed," he said.

"You seem just the same."

"I mean your clothes." She was wearing black slacks and an open blouse over a white, ribbed shell.

"Everybody has to sometime."

"Turn right here. The police station's just down from the town square."

He pulled open one of the double glass doors, and they went in holding hands. A man in uniform sat behind a sheet of heavy glass that was so thick as to have a bluish tinge. He was reading a dog-eared copy of an investment book called *The Money Masters*, his wooden chair tilted backward so that only its rear legs were on the floor.

Alan tapped on the glass, and the cop looked up. The legs of the chair came down. He closed his book and laid it carefully on the counter. "Help you?" he said.

"My name is Alan Dougherty. I'm an attorney."

"Richard Witte," the policeman said. "Cop."

Alan smiled perfunctorily. "A Lieutenant Curtis came by my office this morning to inform me that an arrest warrant had been issued for Tracey Coleman. Is Lieutenant Curtis in?"

The cop looked at Tracey. "This her?"

"Yes."

"Just a minute." He disappeared through a door at one end of his glassed-off enclosure.

They waited. After about a minute, Tracey said, "We ought to just walk out. Teach 'em a lesson about customer service."

Alan nodded.

It was a full five minutes before Lieutenant Curtis came out of a side door. "You did know where she was," he said to Alan.

"She called shortly after you left. When I told her about the arrest warrant, she insisted we come down immediately."

"Save it," Curtis said. "It's wasted on me." He led them to a large metal door and pressed a buzzer. "I assume you'd like to stay with her?" A black man in the khaki uniform of the sheriff's office opened the door. He stood in a short corridor that ended in another door. Curtis and Alan and Tracey crowded in with him, and the door closed behind them.

The deputy sheriff rapped on the inner door. A flap opened on the other side of a tiny window of reinforced glass.

"You're not carrying a weapon? Either of you?" Curtis asked them.

Alan shook his head as the inner door opened.

"Miss Coleman's going to have to be searched."

Alan looked down at Tracey, whose hand had tightened on his arm. Inside, she followed a young, uniformed woman into the next room, and, when she came out several minutes later, there were tears on her face. Another cop directed her to a wall with ruled markings. When he had her where he wanted her, he took her picture: head-on, left profile, right. He fingerprinted her, then directed them into the center of three cells.

"In here. Lieutenant Curtis will be back for you."

There was a bench along one wall. Alan sat with Tracey on it, and the heavy door boomed shut. There was a clang as a bolt shot into place.

There were several minutes of silence.

"Where's your gun?" he said finally. "The Walther you had at my place."

He thought that she wasn't going to answer him.

"Under the driver's seat in your car," she said at last.

"Oh." He himself didn't have a carry permit.

Time passed with neither saying anything. Eventually he spoke again. "You know, there's something that bothers me about your trip to Mexico City."

She looked at him with eyes shot through with crimson threads. "This is tougher than I expected."

He made a face. "I know."

"So what bothers you?"

"What would have happened if customs had searched that cosmetics case?"

"Huh? I'd have been arrested, I guess."

"Would you? The claim check on your ticket wouldn't match the tag on the luggage."

She looked wary. "I guess that's right."

"Probably they're less likely to search it, because unlike Carlotta you hadn't been to Colombia, and you didn't have any Colombian stamps in your passport."

"Okay."

"Still, a lot of drugs come from Mexico. A search was certainly possible."

"Sure. That's what made me so mad."

"You'd have realized immediately that it wasn't your cosmetics case, of course. When they dumped the cosmetics and you saw the cocaine, you would have known exactly what had happened: Carlotta set you up as her mule without a word to you, giving you all the risk for none of the reward. When customs or the DEA or whoever arrested you, what would you have done?"

She shrugged. "Snitched on Carlotta, I reckon."

"That's what I reckon. I can hear you now: 'Hey. Hey! That's not my case. That belongs to Carlotta

Basoalto. Look at the luggage tag. Look at the claim check here in my ticket folder. They don't match.' You'd tell them Carlotta switched bags on you, and you'd tell them where to find her."

Again the shrug.

"Not much protection for Carlotta there," Alan said.

"I guess not."

"That's what doesn't make sense to me."

Several minutes passed without Tracey saying anything. Alan said, "On the other hand, if you were in on it, if you had agreed to carry the contraband through customs for a share of the profits, then Carlotta could count on you to protect her. She'd already be clear of customs. When you denied ownership of the bag, and customs discovered that the tag on the luggage didn't match your claim check, you'd play it differently. 'I must have picked up the wrong bag. Somebody else checked this one, not me. No, I don't know who, how could I?'"

"Wouldn't they just look it up on their computer?"

"Do they record baggage numbers in Mexico?"

"Probably."

"Yeah. When I was a kid, the only record of who checked what was the claim check attached to the passenger's ticket. Probably the system's tightened up everywhere now."

Tracey moved away from him on the bench.

"Either way, if you're in on the deal, you can buy Carlotta some time," Alan said. "Carlotta can't be waiting for you right there outside of customs. She doesn't want to be arrested immediately if the cocaine is discovered. So if you wanted to, you could leave the airport with the cocaine, double-crossing both Carlotta and the Royal boys. Barry and Tony burgle your apartment to recover their cocaine;

then, at the party, Carlotta confronts you with what you've done..."

"You believe I killed her, don't you?"

"I don't know what to believe."

They were silent for a time. Finally, Tracey said, "What do you want from me?"

"A better story. Preferably one that's true."

She didn't say anything.

"Maybe I can help," he said.

"You can't help me. You're too much of a goody two-shoes."

"You're in the maw of the criminal justice system. You need a goody two-shoes."

He waited.

"Okay," she said at last. "I was in on it. Carlotta gave me a fake luggage tag, one that couldn't be traced to her. I cut off the other one, and slipped the new one on. Carlotta carried the old tag through with her."

"What did you use to cut the tag?"

"A car key filed sharp. After that, it was just like you said, except that Carlotta was in on the double-cross. When I left the airport, we were double-crossing the Royals. Our share was supposed to be five grand for carrying the stuff through customs. Carlotta and I talked about it and decided I should take the stuff and ask for twenty-five. We were going to split it."

"But it didn't work."

"Nope. Tony and Barry broke into my apartment and got the stuff back before I could ask for anything." She shrugged. "It was probably hopeless from the get-go. Hugh Royal wasn't going to let himself get rinky-dooed by a couple of girls."

"Hugh Royal?"

"He was the one bankrolling the thing."

"Come on." Hugh was a wealthy man. He had made his fortune building and operating roller-skating rinks and bowling alleys in Tyler, Longview, Marshall — pretty nearly every town of any size in East Texas.

"All I know really is what Carlotta said."

"So what happened at the reception?"

"Carlotta told me everyone was still pissed at me, but not to worry, it would all die down eventually. They didn't know about her involvement."

"And then?"

"Then she went down the hall to the ladies' room and never came back."

"And you started dodging the Royals."

"I didn't have much choice. Not only did I try and steal two kilos of their cocaine, I shot Barry — I guess it was Barry —"

"What?"

"He had something on under his jacket. It could have been bandaging."

"Go back a minute. What did you do?"

"Shot Barry through the door of my apartment. At least, I know I got somebody. You saw all that blood trailing through the apartment. It sure wasn't mine."

"Why did you..."

"They were going to do the same thing to me. They rang the doorbell just like a friggin' Jehovah's Witness."

"And that meant they were going to shoot you? When's the last time you got shot at by a Jehovah's Witness?"

"I look through the peephole to see who it is, they see the peephole darken, and *blammo!* They let me have it through the door."

He stared at her. "Just because someone rings the doorbell..."

"If I was Pollyanna, I'd be dead. They returned fire almost instantly, blew holes in my door, shot my stereo all to crap..."

"You couldn't have known they were going to..."

"Like heck I couldn't."

"Did you see them coming? Had you seen a gun?"

"By the time I saw a gun, it'd have been too late. These are bad people, Alan. Bad people do bad things."

"But they don't necessarily shoot you through the door of your apartment."

"It stood to reason. It's what I would have done."

He shook his head, disbelieving.

"Let's say they weren't going to shoot me. What am I going to do, invite them in to beat the snot out of me? Maybe sexually assault me while they're at it? I didn't expect to hit anyone, for heaven's sake. I was just trying to get them to back off a minute, give me a chance to get out the window."

"What did you shoot him with? Not the derringer they found with Carlotta."

"Unh unh. The Walther I had when I got to your house. I fired one shot, and it bought me the time I needed."

Alan was silent as he processed the new story.

"If they'd gotten hold of me right then, I think they'd have killed me, cocaine or no," she said.

He nodded slowly.

"You understand then?"

"Uh, no."

She rolled her eyes.

"How is it you know Carlotta?" he asked.

"I've known her since we were little. We kind of grew up together."

"How did she come to be so tight with the Royals?"

"Hugh has some business dealings with her dad. She's been staying in the garage apartment out by his pool."

Again, Alan was silent.

"What are you thinking?"

He shrugged. "I don't like it."

"I knew you wouldn't believe me."

"I didn't say I don't believe you. I said I don't like it. You're in the position of saying, 'I shot my Walther at one of Carlotta's accomplices on Friday, but I didn't shoot my derringer at Carlotta on Saturday.' It makes you part of a criminal conspiracy gone bad."

"It's the truth, though. And you see what it means — either Tony killed Carlotta or Barry did. They had the derringer. They took it along with the other guns when they broke into my apartment."

"Why would they shoot Carlotta?"

"They overheard us talking and realized she was in on the double-cross? I don't know."

"You can't say anything about any of this to anyone."

"Why not? You don't believe me, so you don't think anyone else will either?"

"No. Your story about a criminal conspiracy hurts you more than it helps. It gives the prosecution the one thing it may be lacking at this point, which is motive."

"So what do I say?"

"Nothing. The police ask you any questions, you say, 'I want my lawyer.' That's it. Don't explain, don't get into any conversations. Your answer to any question they ask you, your response to any comment they make, should be just that one phrase."

"'I want my lawyer.'"

"Exactly."

"Okay."

It was nearly an hour before the door opened. Lieutenant Curtis said, "We're going to walk over to the courthouse now. The D.A. wants her presented in justice court."

Alan stood.

"I'm willing to take her without handcuffs, if you are."

Chapter 23

Alan and Tracey walked with Lieutenant Curtis along the sidewalk that skirted the town square, where benches surrounded an obelisk dedicated to Smith County peace officers killed in the line of duty. Fallen leaves from the sweetgum trees lay scarlet on the grass and sidewalk. A dozen cars were parked in the diagonal parking spaces.

The courthouse was a rather ugly tan-brick building across the street from the square. Curtis directed them to a side door that led directly into the basement, where the hallway ceiling was too low for psychological comfort, and Alan's leather-soled shoes made gritty sounds on the dingy green tile.

Alan had appeared before Justice of the Peace Emmett Martin several times before, though never in a criminal matter. Justice Martin was a fat, jowly man who never seemed able to find his glasses, and today was no exception. As Alan and Tracey stood together for the reading of the complaint, Justice Martin scanned his desktop and patted file folders and stacks of papers. His court reporter, her fingers poised over the Stenograph, looked straight ahead, her face impassive. Justice Martin picked up his gavel and whacked it hard on the bench three times. After a few moments of ringing silence, the court clerk opened the door from the outer office.

"Kathleen, my glasses," the J.P. said to her.

Kathleen rolled her eyes as she walked through the courtroom to the opposite door, which led into Justice Martin's chambers. Kathleen came out again with his glasses. She laid them on the bench and went out again, having never said a word.

The J.P. peered through his glasses at the complaint and cleared his throat. As of yet, no one had arrived from the district attorney's office, but Justice Martin, not a lawyer himself, made a practice of never waiting on them. The complaint he held was the affidavit sworn to by Lieutenant Curtis on which the arrest warrant had been issued. The J.P. read it aloud in a clear, thin voice, charging Tracey Ashton Coleman with the offense of intentional murder as defined by Section 19.02(a) of the Texas Penal Code and describing the evidence that established the probable cause necessary for her arrest.

"A .25 caliber Davis derringer was found at the murder scene, and a slug recovered from the body of Carlotta Basoalto. Ballistics comparisons established that the slug was fired from the derringer, which was sold and registered to Tracey Coleman on November thirteen, two thousand ten. The decedent, Carlotta Basoalto, was last seen alive leaving the Harvey Convention Center, at which time she was in the company of one Tracey Coleman."

The J.P. finished reading and took off his glasses. Holding them in one hand, he leaned across his desk to peer at Tracey. "Do you understand the nature of the charge made against you?" he asked.

Alan nudged her.

"Yes, sir. Your honor."

Justice Martin wagged his head at her. "Now, just because you've been charged with a crime doesn't mean you don't have any rights. You do, and I'm required to tell you about them. You have the right to remain silent. That means you don't have to make any statement to the police or to answer any of their questions. If you give up your right to remain silent, anything you say can be used against you later in a court of law, and it probably will be. You have the right to an attorney..." When he had gone over her rights under *Miranda v. Arizona*, the seminal 1966 Supreme Court decision, he asked her if she understood those rights. She said she did. He went on to tell her of her right to an examining trial, where the prosecution would have to establish probable cause to believe her guilty or, failing that, let her go pending the grand jury's return of an indictment. While he was explaining that, the door pushed open, and a man came in carrying a briefcase high against his chest.

The J.P. broke off and raised his eyebrows. The man was wearing a light gray suit, a white shirt, and a striped tie. He was young, perhaps only in his mid-twenties, his scalp showing pink through the close-cropped hair on the sides of his head. "I'm Dan Rascoe from the district attorney's office," he said.

Justice Martin smiled at him, showing too many teeth for the smile to be entirely pleasant. "I'm very pleased to meet you," he said. "My name is Emmett Martin. I'm a justice of the peace here in Smith County. Over there we have Mr. Dougherty..." Alan nodded. "And Officer Curtis. Standing on the other side of Mr. Dougherty is the accused in this case, Tracey Coleman."

Rascoe bobbed his head once at each of them.

"Are we all straight?" the J.P. asked him.

"Yes. I'm here in the matter of Tracey Coleman."

"Oh, you are," the J.P. said. "Unfortunately, we've about concluded with that matter. Would you like to stay and participate in another one?"

"You've already set bail?" Rascoe asked, fumbling for the clasp on his briefcase.

"Are you just asking to be polite, or would you like to address the question of bail?"

"I'd like to address the question of bail."

"Well, perhaps that's possible, even now. I know how busy your office must be. You want to participate in a hearing, but you hate to sit through all the formalities with the rest of us. It's hard to blame you. Can you blame him, counselor?"

"No, your honor," Alan said.

The animus that had threatened to explode from Justice Martin seemed to subside suddenly. "Very well, Mr. Rascoe. I'll hear your argument. What do you suggest in the way of bail?"

Rascoe wet his lips with his tongue. "Five hundred thousand dollars," he said.

The J.P.'s eyebrows went up. "That sounds like bail for a capital crime."

"Not necessarily. For intentional murder she could get life imprisonment. She's young, and her father is a successful attorney. If bail is set too low, there would be insufficient disincentive for her to flee the country."

"Her father," the J.P. repeated. He looked at Tracey. "Young lady, is your father Roger Coleman?"

"Yes, your honor."

He turned back to Mr. Rascoe. "Are you suggesting that because of the identity of her father, Ms. Coleman requires a higher bail than would otherwise be the case?"

Rascoe nodded. "Yes, your honor."

"Where is Roger Coleman?" the J.P. asked Alan.

"I don't know. We haven't been able to get in touch with him." Tracey glanced at him, but Alan kept his own gaze on the J.P.

Rascoe cleared his throat. "Surely, your honor, you'll agree that the financial resources of the defendant's family are relevant to the question of bail."

The J.P. glared balefully at him. "Young man, Roger Coleman is a respected lawyer in this community, not a wealthy member of some criminal syndicate."

"He's got money, and it's his daughter. You have to look at that, your honor."

Alan winced. *You have to* was not a phrase to address to a judge.

"Mr. Rascoe, how long have you been a lawyer?"

"I sat for the bar in July."

"What does that mean?"

"Pardon?"

"I don't want to know when you took the bar exam, I want to know how long you've been licensed to practice law in the state of Texas."

Rascoe tilted his head uncertainly. "I'm supposed to hear back from the examiners any time now."

Justice Martin blinked at him. "Do you mean..." He broke off. "Do you mean to say that you don't even know whether you've passed the bar exam?" He pointed a fat, fleshy finger in the direction of the door, shaking his head as he spoke. "Get out of my courtroom, Mr. Rascoe, and don't come back until you have a license to practice law. You can tell your boss Mr. Larson that I expect him to do me the courtesy of sending licensed attorneys to represent the state of Texas in my courtroom, and furthermore that I expect them to arrive on time. Do you understand me?"

Dan Rascoe didn't answer. He had begun backing toward the door, holding his half-open attaché case in front of him like a shield. He reached the door just as Justice Martin asked his question, and he pushed through. The door banged shut behind him.

Justice Martin looked at Alan. "What bail do you suggest, counselor? I don't err, do I, in assuming you've been to law school?"

"No, your honor."

"That you've sat for the bar exam, passed it, been sworn in before a judge of this state, and received a license to practice law? Good." He sat, clasping his hands in front of him on the bench. "I await your recommendation."

"I think she should be released on her personal bond," Alan said.

The J.P. threw back his head and laughed. "So I've heard half-a-million dollars and nothing at all. Counselor, you've got balls, I'll give you that." He shook his head. "Bail is set at fifty thousand dollars. The hearing is adjourned at two-fifty-five." He whacked the gavel on his bench and stood up. "Half-a-million dollars and nothing at all," he muttered as he went out. "Lawyers."

Tracey looked up at Alan. "What happens now?"

Alan looked past her at Lieutenant Curtis. "I'm afraid you go to jail."

"What?" She looked suddenly sick.

"It won't be for long. I'll get hold of your father. He'll post bail before you turn around in your cell two times."

He and Tracey followed Lieutenant Curtis down the hallway to the cage, a barred area where a deputy sheriff sat at a scarred wooden desk. Only Tracey and Curtis went in, and the bars closed behind them.

A female deputy disappeared into a back room and came out carrying a pair of slip-on shoes and a yellow jumpsuit, which she handed to Tracey.

"You can change in there," she said, gesturing.

"Change?" As she took the clothes, Tracey looked back through the bars at Alan.

He tried for an encouraging smile, but managed no more than a pained expression. Tracey Coleman disappeared through a doorway, and he turned away.

Chapter 24

Roger Coleman wasn't at his office. "He said he'd be out for a couple of hours this afternoon," the law firm's receptionist told Alan, glancing at the clock on her desk. It was just after three o'clock. "I expect him back any time now."

He hesitated. The receptionist — Pam Owens, according to her nameplate — hadn't been there when Alan worked for Coleman Anders.

"I guess I need to wait for him. It's about his daughter."

"What did you say your name was? Alan..."

"Dougherty."

"Oh. My. God."

He made a face. "No, just me. Alan Dougherty."

"You're...you used to work here."

He thought sometimes he was the most famous person in Tyler. "Yes," he said.

She picked up the phone and punched a couple of buttons. After a moment, she put the phone down again. "His secretary doesn't answer," she said.

"Should we..." He moved his finger in the direction of Roger's office.

She pushed back from her desk. "Let's walk down there."

Roger's door was open. His desk was clear but for that day's *Wall Street Journal,* laid out on the gleaming cherrywood in front of his high-backed chair. On the wall opposite the desk, a sofa, a coffee table, and a couple of upholstered chairs were arranged in a little sitting area.

"Alice, do you know where Donna is?" Pam Owens asked the woman at a nearby desk.

Alice didn't know. Nor did she know when Mr. Coleman would be back in the office.

"This is Alan Dougherty," Pam said, dropping her voice. "You know, the one who..."

Alan didn't turn his head to see what gesture or eye movement accompanied the words. He stood looking at Roger's high-backed chair, thinking about all the times he had sat in front of it, going over this case or that one, about Roger's patience and his perpetual good will. I've got a lot to answer for, he thought.

"Why don't you have a seat?" Pam said at his elbow. She nodded her head toward the desk, indicating one of the client chairs. "Can I get you anything? Coffee? Coke?"

He shook his head, smiling, thinking that he was no doubt the last person in the world Roger would want shown into his office when he wasn't there. "No," he said. "Thank you."

She left him alone in the office, possibly because he'd once been a lawyer with the firm and was now a minor celebrity. Minutes passed. Alan's eyes passed over the titles on the shelves running along the wall by the door. Roger's law school text books: *Torts, Cases and Materials; Constitutional Law*. Any number of legal treatises on subjects ranging from banking to Texas probate. On the bottom shelf was a row of corporate minute books, the name of a corporation embossed on each spine.

One of the corporations was SupeRink, Inc., which sounded like the name of a company that owned and operated roller rinks, possibly Hugh Royal's company.

Alan's eyes cut to the door. A man wearing a tie walked past, glancing into the office. As their eyes met, Alan nodded, but the man continued on without acknowledging the nod. Alan's gaze returned to the shelf.

Hugh Royal, he thought. Roller-rink magnate, small-time drug smuggler. It didn't make sense. If Hugh were smuggling drugs, it would be on a larger scale. Instead of bringing cocaine into the country in the bottom of a cosmetics bag, he'd have dozens of couriers swallowing tiny balloons of the stuff, heavy duty balloons made from the fingers cut from surgical gloves and tied off.

He got up and took a few steps away from the couch, swinging his arms and glancing at the empty doorway. He made his decision and reached the bookshelf in two quick strides. Kneeling, he pulled out the minute book for SupeRink, Inc., and flipped it open.

The first document was the Articles of Incorporation, dated April 16, 1998. He turned one page, then another, his eyes scanning. Only one hundred shares of stock had been authorized, twenty of them going to Hugh Royal, eighty going to a Luis Basoalto. Carlotta's father?

He continued to leaf through the minute book. The annual reports listed the directors of the corporation — Hugh and Luis and a Carlos Basoalto — and the officers. Hugh Royal was president. Roger Coleman was secretary/treasurer.

The cadence of Alan's heartbeat increased a notch. He closed the minute book and slid it back onto the shelf.

"Alan?"

Still in a crouch in front of the bookcase, he started so badly that he spilled backwards onto his buttocks. He found himself looking up at Roger Coleman.

"What in the world..."

"It's Tracey," Alan said, getting to his feet. "She's in the Smith County Jail."

Roger dropped his briefcase into one of the client chairs and sat down in the other one. "Go on."

"She was arrested for the intentional killing of Carlotta Basoalto. Bail's set at fifty thousand dollars."

"So she's been presented."

"Emmett Martin. About an hour ago."

Roger looked dazed.

"I can give you a copy of the complaint."

Roger's eyes focused slowly, and he nodded. Alan got it out of his briefcase and handed it to him.

For a long time Roger stared down at it.

"No mention of the burglary of Tracey's apartment," Alan said. "She reported the murder weapon stolen on the day of the murder."

"You think they haven't made the connection?"

"It's possible. I haven't connected the dots for anyone."

"Maybe they have made it, but they don't believe the weapon was really stolen."

"No one can doubt the apartment was ransacked."

"But as to what was missing..."

"You're right. They only know what their murder suspect told them on the afternoon of the murder."

Roger's eyes shifted away from Alan, but he nodded.

"A bigger weakness in their case may be the lack of any apparent motive."

"They were friends," Roger said. "Tracey and Carlotta."

"Exactly. Without motive, the prosecution hasn't got a case, or at least not much of one."

"But if they come up with a motive..." He didn't finish the sentence, and Alan didn't finish it for him. There was no need to.

"As I said, bail is set at fifty thousand dollars. I told Tracey you'd have her out before she'd turned around in her cell two times."

Roger turned back to Alan, but he didn't seem to be seeing him.

"Roger?"

Roger nodded.

Chapter 25

It was almost four o'clock when he got out of Roger's office, and Alan hadn't eaten since breakfast. He thought maybe that was why he felt so bad. He drove through Whataburger and ate his burger on the way home. It helped. At least he found he had enough energy to change clothes.

He was sitting in the recliner in the living room when the doorbell rang. He glanced at his watch, but the room had grown too dark for him to see it. The doorbell rang again, but Alan remained where he was. It was a good evening to not be home, he thought.

After several minutes, a key scraped in the lock, and the door opened. Steve Booker set his suitcase inside the door and went back out to return the spare key to the soil of the hanging plant. He came in and picked up his suitcase, shutting the door behind him.

As he headed past him toward the bedrooms, Alan said, "Hello, Steve."

"Holy —" Steve dropped his suitcase as his arms came up. "Who the...Alan?" He flipped a switch, and a floor lamp came on. "Why the devil don't you answer your door? Why are you sitting in the dark?"

"What happened to Susan?" Alan asked. "When you left for her place last night, I didn't expect to be seeing a lot more of you this trip."

"I don't know what happened to her," Steve said. "She just started flying apart over dinner. I took her to Omar's, thinking that after six months a little extravagance was called for: white tablecloths, red candles on the tables, a bottle of good wine... It went really well until dessert, when she told me the three things she liked best about me."

"That started an argument?"

"I think the argument became inevitable at that point."

"What did she tell you?"

"That I was witty, that I knew my wines and other interesting stuff, and that I was a snappy dresser."

Alan raised an eyebrow.

"The trouble started when she asked me to return the compliment. What did I like best about her, she wanted to know."

"And you said —"

"Dimples in her cheeks, a great ass, and legs to China. Tell me, who could possibly be offended by that?"

Somehow it struck Alan as hysterically funny. "Maybe she was hoping you'd come to appreciate her more spiritual qualities," he managed at last.

Steve was glaring at him. "Snappy dresser is a spiritual quality?"

"It goes deeper than legs to China. And the rest of what she said clearly had to do with qualities of the mind."

Steve shook his head. "Women," he said. "You can't live with them. You can't douse them with kerosene and set them on fire."

"Let me ask you about something."

"Are we changing the subject?"

"Yes."

"I'm not ready to change the subject. I want to talk about me a little longer. Do you have any advice for me?"

"Sure. You won't take it."

"What is it?"

"You could send her a card. Or better, if you're willing to spring for about half the price of that meal, a card and a dozen roses."

"What kind of card?"

"One that says 'I'm sorry we quarreled.'"

"I'm not going to apologize. I dropped a hundred bucks on her, and I said three nice things about her, and for that she blows up. I think she's insane."

"I didn't say you had to apologize. You can be sorry you quarreled without admitting the quarrel was your fault."

"Oh, I get it. I'm not saying I'm sorry for a single thing I did. I'm saying I'm sorry she's such a neurotic bitch."

Alan smiled. "But much more diplomatically."

"Well, she'd take it as an apology. I'm not going to do it."

"It's your life."

"You're a big help."

"I tried. Can we change the subject now?"

"Okay. I guess."

"I need a favor. You're examining First Tyler this week. I want to know if either Hugh Royal or SupeRink, Inc., has a loan with the bank."

"Why? Does this have something to do with that woman that was killed?"

"I don't know. What I'm interested in are tax returns, financial statements — anything in the loan file along those lines."

"You want copies? That'd be illegal as hell."

"Not necessarily copies."

"What then?"

Alan sighed. "What I'd like to know is why an apparently wealthy man would engage in small-time smuggling."

"Did he?"

"His sons did, or Tracey says they did, and she thinks Hugh was bankrolling the operation."

"You think so, too?"

"I don't know what to think."

"How small time?"

"She thinks five pounds of cocaine. If cocaine smuggling operates on the metric system, that's what? Two kilograms."

"I'm not sure two kilos are small time. Might well have a street value in six figures."

"Whatever. It's a hell of a lot of risk for a legitimate businessman to take."

"Maybe it's a turn-on for him. Or maybe Tracey's wrong; maybe his sons were doing it on their own. Earn themselves something above and beyond whatever allowance Pop gives them."

"Maybe."

Steve opened his mouth to say something else, but just then the telephone rang. Alan held up a finger.

"Hold that thought," he said.

It was Roger Coleman. "Alan," he said. "I just talked to Tracey."

"She's out of jail?"

"No, not yet. I —" He hesitated. "I don't think I thanked you properly for being there for her today."

"Sure. Is there a problem with the bail?"

"Let's just say there're complications."

"Can I help?"

"No, I'm handling them. In fact, that's what I wanted to talk to you about. We appreciate what you've done for Tracey, but we don't need you anymore. I'm going to take over her case from here."

Alan was silent.

"Alan?"

"Well, sure. If Tracey doesn't want me..."

"She may not know she doesn't want you, not yet. That's the reason for this phone call."

"What?"

"If she contacts you, just let her know that you've turned the matter over to me."

"Roger, Tracey's the client. I'm attorney of record. I can't just stop returning her calls."

"I didn't say stop returning her calls. Talk to her. Tell her you've withdrawn from the case."

"That's her call. A judge isn't going to switch lawyers on her against her will."

"He will if you and I are together on this."

Alan thought about it. "I can't do it," he said finally. "If Tracey wants to change her lawyer, fine. If she doesn't—"

"Haven't you done enough? Why do you want to insert yourself in the middle of her life again?"

"I'm not inserting myself. I'm there. I understand that you're not happy about that. I don't entirely understand why Tracey wants me, but ethically I'm bound to stay until..."

"Ethically!"

Alan flinched.

"Look, Alan. Tracey is charged with a serious crime. I know you've done fairly well in some civil trials, but this is out of your league. Tracey needs an experienced criminal attorney, not a thirty-two-year-old neophyte who's still figuring out how to wipe his own butt in the courtroom."

Alan felt a surge of anger. "That's hardly fair."

"I've told you what I called to tell you. You're off the case. If you try to force your way back into it, I'll see to it that you're sorry."

He hung up, leaving Alan looking at the receiver. He put it down.

"Alan?"

He held up a hand. He needed a minute. "Okay," he said finally.

"Tracey Coleman's in jail?" Steve asked.

"Yes, and it looks like she'll be spending the night."

"In a cell?"

"She's charged with murdering Carlotta Basoalto."

"Who was on the phone? Her father?"

Alan nodded.

"What did he say?"

Alan shrugged. "Evidently experienced trial lawyers like to wipe their butts in the courtroom."

Steve looked puzzled, but he let it go. "I can't believe it. The girl we ate breakfast with only yesterday is in jail on a murder rap — and it takes a call from her daddy for me to find out about it."

"You wanted to talk about you, remember?"

Chapter 26

Alan fell asleep easily enough, but woke just after three and couldn't go back to sleep. Three o'clock became four o'clock, then four-thirty. At five he got up and put on shorts, a T-shirt, and running shoes. From the hall he could hear Steve snoring.

Outside it was colder than he'd expected, maybe mid-forties. Too cold for shorts, but instead of going back inside to change, he took off at a brisk pace, and he held it until his chest was heaving, unable to keep up with his body's demand for oxygen. He dropped back into a slow jog and turned for home. His skin was clammy, but he wasn't sweating.

At seven, when he was ready to leave for work, Steve was still asleep. Alan left him a note on the kitchen table: "You're sorry she's a neurotic bitch. Tell her."

He drove straight to the county jail, which was on the top floor of the courthouse. There was an interview room at the intersection of the two cell blocks. A deputy sheriff, a woman with frizzy red hair, opened the door, and Tracey walked past her wearing a bright yellow jumpsuit. Alan stood with his hands in his pockets, eyeing her. The door closed.

"You look like a lemon drop," he said.

She managed to smile at him. "You mean good enough to eat?"

"Are you okay?"

She shook her head.

He pulled a chair out from the table and straddled it, nodding at the chair across from him. She sat.

"Your father called last night," Alan said. "He wants me off the case. He says I have no experience in criminal cases, and the place to start isn't a murder trial involving his daughter. He's right about that."

"So you're calling it quits?"

"Not necessarily, but it's something we should discuss. I've had ten jury trials, all of them civil trials. It's not the same thing as criminal defense work. Criminal defense is its own specialty."

"How many did you win?"

"The civil cases? Seven of the ten."

"What happened to the other three?"

"Nobody bats a thousand."

"Not a lot of people bat four hundred. You're doing better than that."

"Trial work isn't baseball. A lawyer once said, I think it was G. Bennett Williams..."

"Who?"

"He used to own the Redskins. He said that no matter how good a lawyer was, he was only going to win about sixty percent of his cases, and, no matter how bad he was, he was always going to win about forty. That twenty percent in the middle was where skill made a difference."

"And you're winning seventy."

"I have won seventy. Ten cases isn't a career. The point is that your father has more experience than I do and a lot more legal resources. Speaking objectively, he probably ought to be running the case."

"Let me ask you this: Why hasn't he made bail for me? Fifty thousand dollars is a lot of money, I know, but I also know he's got it. Why am I still sleeping in a cell?"

Alan hesitated. It was something he'd been wondering himself. "Have you asked him?"

"He says I should be patient."

"Patience is a virtue."

"It's not one I'm interested in cultivating right now."

"Maybe he's afraid you'll run off, and the prosecution will use it as evidence of guilt."

"I'm not going anywhere."

"Does he know that?"

It was her turn to hesitate. "I don't know."

"Do you have another theory?"

"About..."

"Why you're still sleeping in a cell?"

She shrugged. "I guess I've been wondering whether he's afraid of Luis Basoalto."

"What's caused you to wonder that?"

"I don't know. I just think there's something he's not telling me."

Alan thought about it, frowning.

"You're not going to abandon me, are you?"

"No."

"You won't let Daddy bully you?"

"No. I let you down once. I don't know how much of this is my fault."

"*Your* fault!"

"You were seventeen. What did you know?"

"Well, thanks."

"Up until that time, you were a sweet, conscientious high school student."

"Who seduced a lawyer in her daddy's firm."

"You didn't seduce me."

She smiled wearily. "You were like a deer in the headlights," she said. "You didn't stand a chance."

Chapter 27

That afternoon Alan was at his desk reading the chapter on examining trials in a book called *Criminal Trial Techniques*. When he glanced up, he saw a man in the doorway, and he jumped.

Jim Angley, his law firm's senior partner, came in. "I'm sorry," he said in his deep voice. "I didn't mean to startle you."

"That's all right."

Angley shifted one of the client chairs in front of Alan's desk and dropped into it. "You'd never guess who I just talked to," Angley said.

Alan waited a beat, then said, "Roger Coleman."

Angley's eyebrows rose toward a full head of silver hair. "Good guess."

"Do you want me to tell you what he wanted, or do you want to tell me?"

"You are good."

Alan put a business card in his book to mark his place and slid the book away from him on the desk. "It's my last trick," he said. "You've decided something, and I have no idea what it is."

Angley jerked his head at the book Alan had been reading. "I take it you want to proceed."

"It's what Tracey Coleman wants. I'll just say I'm willing."

"Do you have any experience at all?"

"Ten civil jury trials."

"Any criminal experience."

"I helped a friend with a traffic ticket once."

Angley pursed his mouth. He said, "Criminal law is its own area, you know. The rules are different, what you have to prove is different..."

"And the stakes are different. I know."

"You want to do this? You don't have to, you know."

"I want to do it."

Angley smiled. "The last time Roger called me about you, it was to ask me not to hire you. He wanted you out of town."

"I would have been. I was packing when you called."

"He and I were in the same fourth grade class. We were neck-and-neck in a reading contest, competing for the right to ride in a limousine. We've been extremely competitive ever since. Not quite friends, not quite enemies."

"Who won the reading contest?"

"I won that one, but he's won his share since. A lot of the fun went out of it for Roger when his wife died — if it ever was fun for him, the way it was for me — but the competitiveness is still there."

"Old habits die hard," Alan said.

Angley nodded, turned a hand palm up.

"Did you know Hugh Royal?" Alan asked him. "Was he in your fourth grade class, too?"

"I don't think so. I remember him from some classes in high school."

"Roger know him?"

"For a couple of years they were best friends, I think."

"Luis Basoalto?"

Angley gave him a look. "He came later."

Alan nodded.

"What about Luis Basoalto?" Angley asked him.

"It was his daughter who died."

137

"You could be getting in over your head."

That was something he could figure out on his own. "What can you tell me about Luis Basoalto?" he asked.

"Not a lot. Nothing definite anyway. But if we have any organized crime in Tyler, he's the one behind it."

Alan was silent.

"Examining trial tomorrow?" Angley asked him.

"Thursday."

"You know not to put on any evidence, don't you? This is your chance to look at the prosecution's case, not to give them a look at yours."

"I know."

Angley nodded. "Okay, then," he said.

Chapter 28

The battered counsel tables in Justice Court were made of yellow pine. Alan chose the one on the left and put his briefcase on the floor against a table leg. Carved on the table was the legend 'R.H. + T.P.,' circumscribed by a heart. Alan got out a yellow pad and a pen, and he placed them on the carved initials. He straightened and stood for a moment, letting his eyes wander over the courtroom: the judge's bench, separated from the rest of the courtroom by a low wooden rail; the wooden armchair where the witnesses would sit; the two rows of empty chairs in the jury box. Alan was thirty minutes early, and but for him the courtroom was empty.

He sat and picked up the pen, but didn't doodle. It seemed to him as if time were suspended, though the courtroom clock ticked with a sound like dripping water. He waited.

The door opened, and Roger Coleman came in, stopping when he saw Alan. The door snicked shut behind him. Alan raised his eyebrows, waiting for Roger to come out with whatever unpleasantness he was going to come out with.

"I told you not to come," Roger said.

"I know."

Roger took a breath and released it. He went to the wall opposite the jury box and took one of the few chairs available for spectators. Justice Court didn't have a big draw. He put his briefcase on the floor beside him.

When the deputy sheriff brought Tracey in, she was still in the bright yellow coveralls of a prisoner. Roger stood, and she went to him and hugged him, her eyes going to Alan as her cheek pressed against her father's chest.

Alan stood up, drawing Roger's gaze. A few seconds passed.

"He shouldn't be here," Roger said.

Tracey looked up at him. "I need him."

"No, you don't, honey."

Tracey didn't say anything.

The deputy sheriff who had brought her in went to an empty chair and sat in it, crossing an ankle over his knee and both arms across his chest. Dan Rascoe, the young law school graduate who'd been routed so badly just three days before, came in with Lieutenant Curtis and another police officer. Rascoe glanced at Tracey and her father, gave Alan a nod, then went to the other table and put his briefcase on it.

The door to the J.P.'s chambers opened, and Justice Emmett Martin, immense in his black robe, entered the courtroom. Everyone who was not already standing got up. When the judge sat, Tracey walked over to sit beside Alan.

Justice Martin's glasses were on his desk this time, either as a result of his own foresight or that of his court clerk. He picked them up, fixing them on his nose as he opened the case file. He looked up and focused incredulously on Dan Rascoe. He took his glasses off again.

"Mr. Rascoe?" he said.

"Yes, your honor," Rascoe said, standing.

"Mr. Rascoe, I thought I told you to stay out of my courtroom until such time as you became a licensed attorney."

"Yes, your honor. I got the bar results yesterday." There was a slight tremor to his voice, and in the circumstances Alan couldn't blame him.

"I take it you passed," Martin said.

"Yes, your honor."

"Have you been sworn in?"

"In Judge Mitchell's courtroom."

Justice Martin smiled. "Congratulations, Mr. Rascoe."

Rascoe nodded. "Thank you, your honor."

"I've read the complaint, so there's no need for an opening statement," the J.P. told him. "I know what you hope to prove. Put on your first witness."

Roger Coleman got to his feet, and everyone looked at him.

"Your honor, you know me. I'm Roger Coleman. My daughter is the accused in this case."

The J.P. nodded. "I understood that."

"She has been represented so far by Alan Dougherty of the Angley law firm, but he's withdrawing from the case. I'll be taking over."

Beside Alan, Tracey stiffened.

The J.P. looked at Alan. "Mr. Dougherty?"

"I'm remaining on the case, your honor."

Justice Martin frowned. "With Mr. Coleman as lead counsel?"

"With me as sole counsel."

Martin glanced at Roger, then addressed himself to Tracey. "Ms. Coleman, who is your lawyer?"

"Alan Dougherty." She looked at her father. "Sorry, Daddy."

Roger let out his breath in a long sigh. Then he shook his head and sat down.

In the courtroom, there was a long silence.

"Mr. Rascoe, your first witness," Justice Martin said.

As his first witness, Dan Rascoe called Officer William Jenkins, who moved from his seat beside Lieutenant Curtis toward the railed-off chair against the left wall. There is no jury in an examining trial, which is nonbinding in any case. At issue is whether the police can hold the defendant pending indictment by the grand jury, a relatively brief span of time.

The court reporter stood and raised her hand. "Raise your right hand," she instructed the witness. When Officer Jenkins was sworn, she resumed her seat in front of the Stenotype.

Jenkins sat down, too. His uniform fit him snugly. He was a small man with a red, round face and protuberant eyes.

"Counselor?" the J.P. said to Rascoe.

Rascoe stood. "State your name and occupation," he said to Officer Jenkins.

Jenkins' voice was unexpectedly deep and resonate. He was, he said, Corporal William Jenkins of the Tyler Police Department.

"Corporal Jenkins, we're interested in the events of October twenty-fifth of this year. Were you on duty that night?"

"I was. Dale Gardner and me — Dale Gardner's my partner — we were on motorized patrol. We got a call from the dispatcher at approximately 12:50 and, as a result of that call..."

Alan stood up, and Jenkins stopped talking. Alan said, "I believe the question was, 'Were you on duty that night?'"

Justice Martin nodded. "Just answer the questions asked, Officer Jenkins," he said.

Jenkins nodded.

"What did you do as a result of the call from the dispatcher?" Rascoe asked him.

Jenkins cleared his throat. "Dale and myself proceeded to the Harvey Convention Center where two men were waiting for us in the parking lot, Hugh and Tony Royal. They —"

"What about Hugh and Tony Royal?" Rascoe interrupted, glancing at Alan.

"They said there was a dead woman in the Volkswagen Touareg that was parked there."

"Did they say who?"

"They said Carlotta Basoalto. Actually, she was pretty much hanging out of the vehicle. Still, with the lighting and all it was hard to see much. We —"

Alan, on his feet again, said, "The question was, 'Did they say who it was?' I believe he's answered it."

Testimony was supposed to proceed by question and answer to give opposing counsel the opportunity to object to inadmissible material. Justice Martin nodded.

"So you found a woman in the car?" Rascoe asked Jenkins.

"A dead woman," Jenkins said, nodding.

"Carlotta Basoalto?"

"Carlotta Basoalto," Jenkins agreed.

"How did you determine her identity?"

"There was a purse there with her in the car. The driver's license had her picture."

"How did you know she was dead?"

Alan stood up, ready to object if Jenkins offered a medical opinion.

"There was a hole where the woman's eye should have been," Jenkins said.

Alan said down.

"Your witness," Rascoe told him.

The brevity of the direct examination was surprising. Alan stood. "Whose vehicle was this Touareg?"

"The vehicle where the body was found? It was registered to Hugh Royal."

"Hugh Royal? One of the men who discovered the body?"

"The deceased lived at his place, evidently. This was a car he had given her to drive."

"How do you know she was driving it?"

"Well, partly from what they told us, partly from the key to the vehicle being in her purse."

"Did anyone else have a key to the Touareg?"

"I guess so."

"Who?"

Jenkins shook his head. "Don't know."

"Did you inquire, did you look?"

"We didn't."

Alan reached for the stapled pages on the table in front of him. "Corporal Jenkins, I want to show you an inventory of the crime scene that was given to me by the prosecution." He stood. "Your honor?"

Justice Martin nodded, giving him permission to approach the witness. Alan did so, uncomfortably aware of Roger's gaze as he went to give Jenkins a copy of the inventory.

Alan said, "This inventory purports to show what clothing the decedent was wearing, and what items of jewelry. It indicates what items were found in the seat and the knee-well with the body, and what items were found in the rest of the car. Do you know whether this inventory is true and correct?"

"Yes, sir."

"You do know?"

"Yes, sir."

"And it is true and correct."

"I said that."

The key item on the list was, of course, the murder weapon, the .25 caliber Davis derringer, but Jenkins wasn't the one to ask about that. "The decedent, then," Alan said, "was wearing a pearl necklace?"

"Yes, sir."

"Genuine pearl?"

Jenkins shrugged. "You could ask my wife," he said. "She'd know." He glanced around smiling, but no one in the courtroom responded.

"You don't know," Alan said.

"I don't know," Jenkins answered, his face reddening.

"She was wearing earrings," Alan said. "Valuable ones, or do you know?"

Jenkins looked across the courtroom at Lieutenant Curtis.

"I'm asking you," Alan said.

"I don't know."

"There was money in the purse you found. How much exactly?"

Jenkins eyes scanned down the page in his hand. "It says here two hundred sixty-four dollars. And a dollar fifty-six in change."

"Nothing had been taken."

"No."

Rascoe stood. "Your honor, the witness can't say what, if anything, had been taken. He can only testify as to what was there."

Alan said, "Your honor, I object to Mr. Rascoe instructing this witness in the middle of my cross-examination."

"You have to admit that he has a point."

Alan shook his head definitely. "No. The witness has testified that nothing was taken. If he's testifying to things outside his knowledge, then the prosecution can make that point on redirect or argue it in his closing."

Justice Martin looked back at Rascoe, still on his feet behind his table. "Very well," he said. "The answer will stand."

Alan moved on to another topic, having eliminated robbery as a possible motive for the crime. As far as he knew, the prosecution didn't have anything else. He hoped it didn't.

When he had finished with his cross-examination, Rascoe stood. "Just a few questions on redirect, your honor," he said. "Corporal Jenkins, the inventory you have in front of you lists a necklace, earrings, and a pair of gold bracelets on the right arm. As far as you know, all of those items were costume jewelry, they were fake."

"Objection," Alan said, half-standing. "The question is leading." Every lawyer had the opportunity to prepare his own witnesses prior to trial; therefore, at trial he was not permitted to lead them through their testimony. Leading questions, those questions that suggested an answer, were limited to cross-examination.

"Can you tell this court how valuable these items of jewelry were?" Rascoe asked.

"No, sir."

"Or whether they had any value?"

"No, sir."

In the long run, none of this mattered. The prosecution would have the jewelry appraised well before the main trial — or, failing that, the defense would. What Alan had been trying to do was to inflict damage on the prosecution's at-this-point only partially prepared case — enough damage to get Tracey out of jail until such time as the grand jury might choose to indict her.

"I see a wrist watch listed as well," Rascoe said. "Can you tell us how valuable that was?"

"No, sir."

"I don't see any mention of rings. Was the decedent not wearing any?"

"Not that I saw."

"No further questions."

Roger Coleman stood up. "Your honor, could we have a few moments recess?"

The judge looked at Alan, who looked at Roger. Alan shrugged.

"Very well. Ten minutes." The judge slapped his gavel on the bench and stood up.

Alan met Tracey's eyes and gave her what he hoped was a nod of encouragement, but Roger was already heading out through the clerk's office to the hall.

Chapter 29

When the door closed behind them, Roger turned on him. "Just what do you think you're doing in there?"

"Attacking the prosecution's case."

"The examining trial isn't the place for that. I thought you knew that. The examining trial is where you see what the prosecution has. You save your traps for the main trial, where they can have some effect on the jury."

Alan considered. "All right," he said.

"All right? You don't know what the hell you're doing. You need to admit that and get yourself off this case."

"I'm not here because I'm Clarence Darrow. I'm here because Tracey wants me to be."

"We can't always get what we want."

"Rolling Stones," Alan said, and Roger looked at him as if he'd lost his mind.

He said, "If you can't take this seriously..."

"I know. Withdraw from the case. If I need to take a leak, withdraw from the case. The judge overrules one of my objections..."

"You're not funny."

"I'm not trying to be. I'm just trying to focus on the task at hand, and you're a distraction."

"Evidence of robbery would actually be a good thing," Roger said. "It provides a motive not specific to Tracey. Anyone might have killed Carlotta in order to rob her."

"That's true, but it's a gamble. If Tracey's convicted of intentional murder, she can get as little as five years. If it was murder in the course of a robbery, it's a capital crime. The penalty is either death or life imprisonment."

Roger opened his mouth.

"No other options," Alan said. "Look, I've got to get back in there." He pushed open the door and walked through the clerk's office, aware of Roger following immediately behind him.

The prosecution's next witness was a short man with milk-pale skin and several long strands of blond hair swept across what would otherwise have been a bald head. He settled himself into his chair and cleared his throat.

"Could you tell us your name and occupation?" Rascoe asked him.

"Dr. Michael Quillen. Assistant medical examiner, Smith County."

"What is your educational background?"

"I have a B.S. in chemistry from the University of Texas and a medical degree from Baylor. I'm board-certified in pathology."

"How long have you held your position as assistant medical examiner, Dr. Quillen?"

"Five years."

"And in that time, you have performed how many autopsies?"

The doctor pursed his lips. "Perhaps one hundred twenty."

"Were you employed as assistant medical examiner on the night of October twenty-fifth of this year?"

Of course he was, or he wouldn't have been on the stand. In response to a telephone call he received at his home, he had gone to the Harvey Convention

Center, where police officers had directed him toward a car parked at one end of the lot.

"And what did you find in the car?"

"A woman who had been dead perhaps three hours at the time I examined her."

"How did you establish the time of death?"

"Body temperature. And the very early stages of rigor mortis, which usually begins in the eyelids and the muscles of the jaw some three to six hours after death. Also the absence of any postmortem lividity, which would begin some four hours after death. There were undigested peanuts in the stomach and very little of anything in the small intestine, suggesting the decedent died very shortly after eating, but of course I have no independent knowledge of when she last ate."

"How long after eating the peanuts would you say?"

"Less than an hour."

"But based on body temperature..."

"Allowing for variations in possible cooling rates and for uncertainty as to the decedent's baseline temperature, I can only estimate that at 1:25, the time I took her temperature, she had been dead between two-and-a-half and three-and-a-half or three-and-three-quarter hours."

"So you're saying she died between when and when?"

"Between nine-forty and ten-fifty-five."

"Could you determine the cause of death?"

"Gunshot wound. The bullet passed through her left eye and embedded itself in the bone on the inside of her skull at the back of her head. There were no other wounds."

"Was she killed there in the car?"

"Based on the amount of blood in the car, I would say so."

"Did you remove the bullet from the decedent's skull?"

"Not then and there, but later, during the course of my autopsy."

"What did you do with the bullet you removed?"

"I sealed it in an envelope in the presence of Lieutenant Curtis of the Tyler Police Department. We both signed the flap, and I turned the envelope over to him."

"Thank you, doctor. Your witness."

Alan stood, aware of Roger's disapproving gaze. "Dr. Quillen, can you tell us anything about the angle at which the bullet was fired?"

Dr. Quillen cleared his throat. "It was fired at a slight upward angle of perhaps thirty degrees. The bullet hit the top of the skull at an oblique angle and was deflected into the back of the skull."

"When you say 'upward angle of thirty degrees,' are you assuming that the decedent was sitting upright?"

"Yes. I'm assuming she was sitting upright."

"Though you don't have any reason for making that assumption. As far as you know she could have been leaning over at the time she was shot."

Dr. Quillen shrugged.

"Isn't that right?"

"It is. But the more she was leaning, the lower the origin of the shot. You lean her too far, and the gun would have to be fired from the direction of her navel."

"What was the range? How far away was the muzzle of the gun when it was fired?"

"A couple of feet. No more than three feet."

"How can you tell?"

Quillen puckered his lips for a moment, then said, "The entrance hole was split, and there was scattered tattooing caused by the powder. Neither condition would have been present had the shooting taken place at a distance of greater than two or three feet. On the other hand, the wound wasn't scorched or blackened, and there was no bruising beneath the skin, which tells us that the range was more than two or three inches. It was not a contact wound."

"So the range was from two to three inches to two to three feet. Is that correct?"

"That's correct."

"The gunshot could have been self-inflicted."

"I don't think so."

"Why not?"

"There were no gunpowder granules embedded in the skin of either hand."

"You performed a paraffin test?"

"Yes."

"The presence of powder granules would suggest that the decedent had recently fired a gun?"

"Yes."

"Is the absence of powder granules conclusive?"

Dr. Quillen hesitated.

"The absence of powder granules is not conclusive, is it?" Alan said.

"No, not conclusive. It would depend largely on the condition of the weapon."

"And on whether the decedent was wearing gloves?"

"She wasn't."

"She wasn't when you saw her."

"That's right."

"Thank you, doctor."

Chapter 30

Dan Rascoe called Lieutenant Curtis to the stand. At Rascoe's direction Curtis identified himself for the record. Coincidentally, he, like Dr. Quillen, had a B.S. in chemistry. His first job had been with the police force in Lufkin, Texas, and he had been in Tyler eight years. The questions about his educational background and professional experience were directed toward establishing him as an expert witness.

"Lieutenant Curtis," Rascoe said. "Dr. Quillen has just testified that he removed a bullet from the skull of the deceased and that he turned that bullet over to you. Is that correct?"

"It is."

"Did you perform any ballistics tests on that bullet?"

"A lab tech named Jeremy Douglas actually performed the tests," Curtis said. "But he did so in my presence, and we noted the results of the tests together."

"What kind of bullet was it?"

"A .25 caliber bullet weighing eighty-two grains."

"Was a weapon of any kind found at the scene?"

"There was. A .25 caliber Davis derringer."

"Did you perform any tests to determine whether the bullet Dr. Quillen gave you was fired from that gun?"

"We did. We used the gun to fire a test bullet into a wax slab, then used a comparison microscope to compare the test bullet with the fatal bullet."

"What did you find?"

"About half the circumference of the fatal bullet was too damaged for comparison, but from the undamaged portion we were able to establish that the class characteristics — that is, the marks left by the lands and grooves of the rifling — were identical on the two bullets, which means that both were fired from a .25 caliber Davis derringer. In addition, we could establish enough individual markings on each bullet to determine that each was fired from the same gun. The derringer we found was the murder weapon."

"Did you find any fingerprints on the gun?"

"No. No prints, no smudges. The gun had been wiped clean."

"Did you make any attempt to trace the gun?"

"We did. The gun was registered to Tracey Coleman roughly two years ago." Curtis opened a folder on his lap. "Copies of the registration papers were faxed to me this morning."

Rascoe distributed copies to Justice Martin and to Alan, then moved to have the papers admitted into evidence. When it was Alan's turn to question Curtis, he said, "Dr. Quillen told us that a paraffin test was performed on the decedent Carlotta Basoalto in an attempt to determine whether or not she had recently discharged a firearm. Was a similar test performed on Tracey Coleman?"

"No."

Alan waited. When Lieutenant Curtis failed to elaborate, Alan asked, "Why not?"

"We didn't take her into custody until Monday, two days after the murder. It seemed unlikely that the results of a paraffin test would be meaningful."

"If there had been gunpowder granules embedded in the skin of her right hand, you don't think that would have been meaningful evidence?"

"After two days, I wouldn't expect to find any. It's the absence of granules that wouldn't have been meaningful."

"Then why not perform the test? You find powder granules, and you've strengthened your case. You don't find any, and you can label the test unmeaningful."

"There was no chance that the results of a paraffin test would have helped to clear Ms. Coleman. In my opinion, it is unlikely such a test would have made any difference either way."

"Who made the decision not to perform a paraffin test on the defendant?"

Curtis shook his head. "I don't recall that the matter was even discussed."

"Who had the authority to order the test?"

"I did."

"Did you make any attempt to connect the murder weapon to the defendant at any time more recent than two years ago?"

"No."

"Are you aware that the night before the murder, Tracey Coleman's apartment was burglarized?"

Rascoe objected. "Your honor, he can't ask that. It isn't proper cross-examination. I didn't ask Lieutenant Curtis any questions about a burglary. If the defense wants to go into a reported burglary, it needs to call the lieutenant as its own witness."

The J.P. looked at Alan.

"He asked about tracing the gun, your honor. What Mr. Rascoe wants you to infer from the registration papers he introduced is that the murder weapon was in Tracey Coleman's possession and control from the day she bought it until the night of the murder. It isn't so. And he's objecting now because he doesn't want you to hear that the gun —"

Rascoe interrupted. "Your honor! He's trying to introduce evidence before you've had the chance to rule on whether or not it's admissible."

"I'm not introducing evidence," Alan said, speaking directly to Rascoe. "I'm making an argument. What I say isn't evidence unless I've been called as a witness and put under oath."

The J.P. brought his gavel down on the desktop, reclaiming their attention. "Remember to direct your arguments to the court and not to each other." He said to Alan, "I take it Ms. Coleman's apartment has been burglarized?"

"Reported burglarized, your honor," Rascoe corrected. "Reported burglarized the very day of the murder."

The judge glared balefully at Rascoe, because of course he had been talking to Alan. "I'm going to allow the question," he said.

Rascoe dropped down into his chair, exhaling sharply in disgust. Martin banged his gavel and, flipping it a half-turn to grip it by its head, pointed the stem at the prosecutor. "Mr. Rascoe," he said.

Rascoe froze where he was, not moving even the muscles of his face.

Keeping his eyes on Rascoe, the J.P. said, "Continue, Mr. Dougherty."

"Isn't it a fact that on the evening of October twenty-fourth, the day before the murder—" He looked at Rascoe. "—the defendant's neighbors called the police, and the police found evidence of forced entry and a ransacked apartment?"

Curtis said, "I can't tell you anything about that of my own knowledge. I can tell you what I was told."

The J.P. shifted his gaze to Alan and raised his eyebrows.

"Hearsay," Rascoe said, softly. With a few exceptions, witnesses were not allowed to repeat out-of-court statements that had been made by others. If facts were being asserted, the law wanted those who asserted them to appear in court.

"It does look like you're going to have to call your own witness on that," Martin said.

The ruling meant that the court wasn't going to hear evidence of the burglary. In an examining trial, the law required the prosecution to put on witnesses, and the defense benefited from learning something about the nature of the prosecution's case well in advance of the final trial. But a defense lawyer would rarely want to confer similar benefits on the prosecution.

Alan nodded, his mouth compressed. To Curtis he said, "You've told us about a Davis derringer. Where was this gun in relation to the body of the deceased?"

"Just under it."

"Under it?"

"Yes, on the floor of the knee-well."

"Suggesting that the gun hit the floor before the body of the deceased?"

Rascoe stood. "Objection. Calls for a conclusion."

Alan said, "The prosecution itself established the witness's credentials as an expert."

"As to ballistics."

"As a police officer with extensive experience in examining crime scenes," Alan said.

Justice Martin said he would permit the question.

"Is it your opinion that the decedent's body, when it slid forward into the knee-well, came to rest on the gun?"

"It might have. The gun could have been tossed into the floor as the decedent's body was sliding down in the seat."

"Or pushed beneath the decedent's body after it had come to rest?"

"Possibly."

"In either case the gun registered to Tracey Coleman was left deliberately at the scene."

"She could have panicked."

"True. She could have dropped the gun in a panic. Would she have done this before or after carefully wiping it clean of fingerprints?"

Curtis was silent, and Alan didn't press the point. This was, after all, merely the examining trial. He said, "The prosecution has resisted the idea that no items of value had been stolen from the decedent. Did you find any property belonging to Carlotta Basoalto in the possession of the defendant?"

"No, we did not."

"Did you look?"

"Yes."

"You searched both her person and her apartment," Alan said.

Curtis nodded assent. "Yes."

"Did Tracey have a key to the Touareg?"

"Not that we could find."

"Again, you looked?"

"We did."

"Whose fingerprints were in the vehicle, other than the decedent's?"

"Tony Royal's."

"Tony Royal?"

"I understand they went to the party together."

"Were his prints on the steering wheel?"

"No. There were no prints on the steering wheel."

"None? Isn't that unusual?"

"Not if it had been wiped clean."

"What else was wiped clean?"

"The door-handle on the driver's side."

Alan thought for a few moments. "Lieutenant Curtis. Are you telling me that Tracey Coleman's prints were found nowhere in or on that vehicle?"

"They were not."

"Not even on the murder weapon."

"No. As I said, the murder weapon was clean."

Alan paused for some additional reflection. "No further questions," he said finally.

Rascoe stood. "That's our case, your honor. We ask that the defendant be committed to the jail of Smith County and a bail set more consistent with the seriousness of the crime charged."

"Counselor?" the J.P. said to Alan.

"We move that the defendant be discharged. The prosecution has failed to establish any motive for the crime. It has failed to establish the defendant's possession of the murder weapon at any time more recent than her registration of it some two years ago. The evidence is most consistent with the theory that somebody else deliberately implicated the defendant by using her gun to commit the crime and leaving it at the crime scene."

Justice Martin shook his head. "You're right, I think, that the prosecution hasn't proved its case beyond a reasonable doubt, but at an examining trial it doesn't have to. Probable cause exists to hold the defendant for trial in district court."

It was to be expected, but it hurt all the same.

"Do you wish to put on a defense?" the judge asked Alan.

"No, your honor."

"The bail will remain at fifty thousand dollars."

Chapter 31

Justice Martin retired to his chambers. Rascoe walked out with Lieutenant Curtis, and Tracey left the courtroom in the custody of the deputy sheriff. Roger Coleman and Alan found themselves alone in the courtroom.

"I've got a question," Alan said.

Roger stopped on his way to the door. "Okay."

"Why is Tracey still in jail?"

"Because you just lost the examining trial."

"I'm talking about bail. Fifty thousand dollars doesn't seem like that much money. Are you afraid she's going to get into trouble if she's out there on her own?"

"Maybe."

"So this is your version of a pumpkin shell?"

"What?"

"'He put her in a pumpkin shell, and there he kept her very well.'"

Roger studied him. "Luis Basoalto has just lost his daughter. You know who he is, I suppose?"

"I've heard stories."

"They're true, all of them."

"What does that mean?"

"What, am I speaking Farsi? The stories are true. Luis Basoalto is a dangerous man. The safest place for Tracey right now is in the Smith County Jail."

Roger left. Alan remained standing, his briefcase resting on the table, his eyes on the rail in front of the judge's bench. There were too many things he didn't understand. Roger knew more than he was telling, certainly more than Alan did, which might mean he ought to rely on Roger's judgment.

The trouble was, he wasn't sure he trusted Roger.

The clerk stuck her head into the courtroom. "Are you all right?"

He looked at his watch. He had been alone in the courtroom for ten minutes.

"Where do I go to make bail?" he said.

He was sitting on a bench outside the cage when the elevator opened and Tracey came out dressed again in her own clothes. Alan stood up. His eyes met Tracey's through the bars as a deputy sheriff put a key in the lock.

"What happened?" she asked him as they walked down the hall. "Where's Daddy?"

"I don't know. Back at the office, probably."

"So who made bail?"

He moved his head uncomfortably. His recent house purchase had soaked up all his traditional savings, and the fifty thousand dollars had come out of his 401(k). "Your father didn't think it would be safe," he said. "He's afraid for you. Afraid of Luis Basoalto, I think."

"So you got me out?"

"Yes. I don't know if it was the right thing to do or not. What do you think?"

"Oh, it was the right thing to do."

"You're not afraid?"

"Should I be?"

He shook his head. "I have no idea."

"Well, thanks anyway. I owe you."

"No, you don't. I gave them a certified check. They're just going to hold it until all this is over."

They were at his car, and he put down his briefcase to open the door for her.

"Where are we going?"

"My house."

"You're going to protect me?"

"No. We're going to get that Walther PPK of yours out from under the car seat, and you're going to protect me." He closed her car door and walked around to the other side.

"I can do that," she said as he swung into the driver's seat.

"There's one other thing. You used to have a key to your father's law firm."

Her face became guarded. "Yes," she said.

"Do you still have it?"

"I might. Why?"

"I'm thinking I might want to borrow it."

Chapter 32

"Are you talking about breaking in?"

"No." He shrugged. "Yes. Hugh Royal is one of your dad's clients. Luis Basoalto is a shareholder in SupeRink, Inc., the company that owns all the skating rinks and stuff."

"So?"

"I'd like to know more about that."

When they got to the Loop, she said, "What now? Are we going by my apartment for some toiletries and a few clothes?"

"It depends. Where's your purse?"

"That's why you bailed me out, isn't it? To get you into Daddy's firm."

"No. Okay, it was a factor. Do you have the key or not?"

She rolled her eyes. "Yes, in my purse." She reached down and pulled it out from under her seat. He'd forgotten that she'd been in possession of his car until just before her arrest.

"Actually, I have a lot of my stuff in your trunk," she said. "Enough to get by. I picked it up after I left your house on Sunday."

"Ah."

He turned into the alley that ran behind his house and from there into his driveway. As the garage door rolled upwards, Tracey said, "This is kind of exciting."

"Hiding out?"

"Moving in with a guy. I've never done that before."

He decided to leave that one alone.

Steve, having finally apologized to Susan for her being a neurotic bitch, had moved out again the day before. Their reconciliation had solved the problem posed by the one spare bed, though it did make the living arrangements more intimate for him and Tracey.

It took them fifteen minutes to empty the trunk of his car, another fifteen for Tracey to hang up her clothes and put them away, then to lay out her things in the hall bathroom.

"I can't find my toothbrush," she said. "I think I left it in the motel."

"Is that where you spent Sunday night?"

"Yeah. I paid cash and wrote down a phony name."

"You can use my toothbrush."

"Gross."

He gave her a half smile. "I'm kidding. I'll run to Wal-Mart for you."

"I'll go with you."

"You need to stay out of sight."

"So I'll stay in the car and you run in. Can we get some dinner first? I've had nothing but carryout fast food for a week. And eating with a toilet in the room takes some getting used to."

"I could rustle us up something here at the house."

"Like what?"

He hesitated.

"How about Miguel's? It's kind of dark, and it's got those high-backed booths, so no one's likely to see us."

He thought about it and nodded. "Okay."

He had just put the car in reverse to exit the garage when his cell phone rang. He braked and dug in his pocket for it.

"Hello?"

"Hey, Alan. Steve. It's only four o'clock, bud. Why aren't you still at the office?"

"It's been a full day. What's up?"

"Two things: One, Susan's apologetic enough about blowing up at me that I doubt I'll see you again before I head back to Dallas."

"That good, huh?" It was just as well, he thought. He wouldn't have to explain his new living arrangements.

"Two," Steve said. "Neither Hugh Royal nor SupeRink have any loans with First Tyler."

"I thought you weren't going to check."

"I'm just reporting a nullity."

"Well, thanks," Alan said.

"Sorry I came up empty."

"It was a long shot."

"I guess it was. Hup, gotta go. See you."

Chapter 33

After enchiladas and rice and refried beans, Alan parked the Corolla on the street around the corner from the office building that housed the firm of Coleman, Anders and Davis. There was no one at all on the downtown streets, just a lone pickup parked against the curb two blocks away. It was 10:30 and had been dark for more than two hours.

Alan drew a breath, and Tracey looked at him.

"You know we have to go past a security guard," she said. "What's your plan for that?"

"Sign in at the desk."

"They'll know we've been here."

"We're not going to trash the place. No one's going to have any reason to check the register."

He got out of the car, then reached back in for the tie and suit jacket he had worn in court. He had refrained from changing clothes for just this moment. They walked around the corner to the entrance of the building. Ignoring the revolving door, Alan pulled at the door next to it, but it was locked.

He looked up at the security camera. The speaker above the door emitted a burst of static. "Yes?" said a voice.

"Ben Mullins," Alan said. "Coleman Anders."

The door buzzed, and he pulled it open. As he signed them in at the guard's station, Tracey made small talk with the security guard.

"He's going to remember you," Alan said when the elevator doors had closed on them.

"It's you we don't want him to remember. Who's Ben Mullins?"

"Guy I went to law school with."

"Who's Carmen Sternwood?"

Carmen was the name he had put down for her once he realized the guard didn't know her by sight. "Fictional character," he said. Carmen was the wild younger daughter of old General Sternwood in *The Big Sleep*.

The elevator stopped moving and the doors opened on a dim hallway.

"I didn't know you read fiction," Tracey said.

"There's a lot you don't know about me."

The law firm of Coleman Anders took up the entire floor. Double glass doors to the right marked the entrance, and the large receptionist's desk was visible beyond them. To the left was an unmarked, solid door that served as a back entrance for those who had a key. Tracey fished in her purse for hers.

"Unplumbed depths," Alan said.

"You?"

He smiled at her, and she shook her head and fitted the key to the door. "I've never seen anyone so proud of having read a book." She pushed the door open on a slightly narrower, slightly darker corridor, and they went inside.

"What are we here for, exactly?" Tracey asked as they walked.

"Whatever files we can find on SupeRink."

All the office doors were closed, and the nameplates gleamed dully. Alan stopped at an unmarked door. "This is the file room, or it used to be."

"Daddy probably knows all about SupeRink," she said, putting her key in the lock.

"Your daddy and I don't talk much."

"Good point." She pushed the door open, and he reached inside for the light switch.

The file room was double the size of a normal office, and it was filled with row after row of open shelving filled with file folders. It was here that inactive files tended to gravitate over time. While Alan had been with the firm, the office manager had made an attempt to color code various sorts of folders, and there were blue, green, and red folders mixed in with the plain manila. The lawyers hadn't cooperated, and eventually she'd given up. Scanning the shelves, Alan saw that the folders, though legal-sized and letter-sized and erratically colored, were still alphabetized by client.

"We're looking for R and S," he said, walking down the rows.

There was no file for Hugh Royal in the R's. In the S's there was a single accordion folder for SupeRink, and he pulled it out, scraping back the elastic band and opening the flap. Two manila folders, neither all that full. That was it. "Crap," he said.

"What is it?"

"Not much here."

He pulled out the thicker of the two folders and set the other one aside. The pages that he turned through were dated about two years before, and all seemed to relate to some kind of pension plan Roger had been setting up.

"It looks like SupeRink is a holding company," he said as he paged through the documentation. "It owns TyleRink and PaRink and MaRink..."

"PaRink and MaRink?"

"They're in Paris and Marshall, evidently." Paris, in addition to being the capitol of France, was a small town up near the Oklahoma border.

"Is there a HendeRink?" she asked.

He shook his head. If Hugh Royal had a roller rink in Henderson, either there was no documentation for it here, or it was part of MaRink or one of the others.

"What do they do for towns with no R in their names?"

"You mean, is there a LongRink?" Longview was a county seat east of Tyler. "I don't know. I've haven't seen one."

He closed the folder and picked up the other one. It was a good deal slimmer. The top sheet of paper was a notice to SupeRink of an I.R.S. audit. The page behind it was an assessment for additional taxes. Behind that was a lengthy memo drafted by Harvey Couter, who, when he wasn't chatting up women or making like a human octopus, was a pretty good lawyer. The I.R.S. had claimed that the salary paid to SupeRink's president, Hugh Royal, was excessive and that half of Hugh's salary should have been paid out in dividends. Corporations could not deduct dividends from income as they could salaries, and the I.R.S. was always on guard to make sure that high salaries weren't used as a way to escape the extra layer of taxation.

Couter's memo disputed the I.R.S.'s contention. Nine hundred thousand dollars was not excessive compensation for running a corporation that controlled, through its subsidiaries, nineteen skating rinks and five bowling alleys with combined annual revenues of nearly 8.5 million dollars. The memo summarized the case law identifying the relevant considerations: company size as measured by revenues, success as measured by earnings growth and return on capital, and so on. SupeRink seemed to be comparable to a number of companies that had been allowed their deductions.

Alan flipped back to the front page and noted again that the memo was addressed, not to the I.R.S., but to Roger Coleman. He flipped to the last page, page 22, and read the memo's conclusion: The I.R.S. was wrong in disallowing SupeRink's deduction; SupeRink should contest the assessment.

There was nothing in the file to indicate the result of the contest, or whether there had even been one. There was nothing else in the file at all. Alan didn't know what he had expected to find, but he felt disappointed.

"Well?" Tracey said.

"Nothing. I don't guess your key will get you into individual offices."

"We could try."

But the key didn't work on any of the offices. In addition to the back door and the file room, the key unlocked the copy room and the supply closet, and that was it.

"Well, that's a bitch," Tracey said.

"It is that," Alan agreed.

Chapter 34

Alan said good night to her from the doorway and went down the hall to his own room. He lay down, but found he couldn't sleep. The day had been too stressful for him to let go of it. On top of everything else, Tracey was part of his life again, or she seemed to be. Images of her kept falling out of his memory like fumbled photographs: a bare hip, a breast in profile as she turned toward him, her long, slender back. Eventually, he opened his eyes and glanced over at the clock.

It was nearly two. If he wasn't sleeping, he might as well get up and do something.

He was still thinking about what it was he might get up and do when he dropped off to sleep.

He woke to the sound of a woman's voice. He got out of bed and found Tracey on the floor in the living room wearing gym shorts and an exercise bra and mimicking the contortions of the woman on the TV screen.

"Hi," Tracey said, looking up at him through her bare legs.

He nodded at her and, scratching his belly, went and sat on the sofa. After a few more minutes of exercise, Tracey said, "This isn't a spectator sport, you know." She was sweating and slightly breathless.

He raised his shoulders and dropped them.

She turned her head again, both palms on the floor and one leg in the air. "Maybe if I were naked," she said.

He continued to sit and watch her with the dulled expression of early morning, but his mind had made a jump and suddenly naked was all he could see.

He got to work on Friday a little before nine, picking up his mail in the mailroom and carrying it back to his office. He opened a couple of pieces, filed them in the circular file, and picked up the phone to dial the Coleman law firm.

"Harvey Couter, please," he said to the receptionist.

"May I tell him who's calling?"

Alan told her. A few seconds later, he heard Couter's voice.

"Alan, my man!"

It was hard not to despise the guy. "Hi, Harvey."

"What's up, dude?"

"A tax question. I've got a client that runs a closely held corporation, and he's talking to me about how big a salary he can pay himself. He wants salary rather than dividends so he doesn't have to pay taxes on his income twice."

"Sure."

"Didn't you do some work on that, once? It seems like I remember the question coming up back when I was at Coleman Anders."

There was a silence.

"It may have had something to do with that roller rink company," Alan said, thinking surely Harvey wouldn't remember that he had been long gone when the question came up.

"Oh, right. SupeRink." Couter lowered his voice. "Listen, how's it going with Tracey Coleman? I heard you're still handling her case."

"J.P. held her over."

"What did Roger say about that?"

"That I'm a jerk. About what you'd expect."

Couter gave a snort of laughter. "He can't have been surprised, though. She was going to be held over."

"Yeah, it doesn't take much to establish probable cause. So what was the deal with SupeRink? Can you talk about it?"

"I guess so. It's pretty much ancient history."

"Wasn't the president Hugh Royal?" Alan said.

"Yeah, it was. I can't remember how much they were paying him. High six figures. The I.R.S.'s notice of deficiency came while Roger was up in the Panhandle for a month-long trial. I had the memo on his desk when he got back. Couple days later, Roger calls me in and tells me Hugh's decided just to pay the taxes and not to contest the assessment." He snorted. "Twenty-some hours of research down the tubes. It's the kind of thing that'll teach you the value of procrastination."

"I guess so."

"You know what they say: Hard work may pay off some day. Procrastination pays off now." Couter laughed, too loudly considering that it was his own joke.

"SupeRink have a decent argument for calling it salary?" Alan asked.

"I thought so. The weird thing was that Hugh Royal was just a minority shareholder. Dividends weren't really an option, if he was going to be compensated for his work."

"How much money was at stake?"

"Couple hundred thousand in additional taxes, give or take," Couter said.

"You'd think a couple hundred thousand was worth bending over to pick up."

"I run into that kind of thing all the time. The I.R.S. scares people. Some people just won't go up against them."

"Roger couldn't talk Hugh into it?"

"I guess not."

"Do you know if Hugh gave a reason for just rolling over?"

"No. He's a client, and you just never know about clients. That's the one thing I've learned."

"That you never know about clients?"

"You never know."

Alan hung up. He wondered how long it would take Couter to remember that the majority shareholder in SupeRink was Luis Basoalto, the father of the woman Tracey Coleman was accused of killing.

His phone rang.

"That long," he said aloud. He didn't answer it.

Chapter 35

He'd forgotten about Harvey Couter when the phone rang at home that evening, and he picked it up.

"Hello?"

"You son of a bitch. You don't know what the hell you're doing." It was Roger Coleman. "Do you know where she is, at least?"

"She's safe."

"You mean she's staying with you."

Looking across the living room, he could see Tracey in the kitchen.

"Yeah. I guess I do."

"You..." Roger embarked on a string of curses that cast aspersions on Alan's parentage, his mental abilities, and his sexual proclivities. It stunned Alan to hear the expressions coming over the telephone in Roger's voice. He waited for the barrage to subside, but Roger hung up on him abruptly, never giving him the opportunity to respond.

Alan sat numbly on the sofa.

Tracey came out of the kitchen and sat in the recliner opposite him, folding her legs beneath her. "Kitchen's clean," she said.

"I don't think this is going to work."

"What isn't? Who was that on the phone?"

He didn't answer.

"Daddy?"

He shrugged.

"I'm sorry," she said. She came and sat beside him on the couch. When he still didn't say anything, she put a hand on his back and started rubbing.

He stood up. That wasn't going to work either.

It was the weekend, and he spent it at home. Tracey was there, a constant presence, lounging about the house in her nubile young body — which, to be fair, was the only body she had to lounge around in. Alan ran three miles on Saturday morning, wanting to get out of the house, to turn off his mind, to get away from the oppressive aura of sexuality that Tracey radiated like a blast furnace radiated heat. He ran another two miles Saturday evening.

When he was putting on his shoes to go out again Sunday morning, Tracey said, "What's wrong with you?"

He looked up in the midst of tying his shoe. "What do you mean?"

"You can't tell me you're in the habit of running two times a day."

"It helps me clear my head."

"What's wrong with your head?"

"I've got lots to think about."

"Business or personal?"

"I'm not sure there's a difference right now."

She studied him a minute. When he went back to tying his shoe, she stood and kissed him on the top of his head, then went back to her bedroom.

People were going into the St. Peter Claver Catholic Church as he ran past it. He circled the block and stopped, breathing hard as he watched people getting out of their cars, people herding their small children up the sidewalk, people climbing the steps to the entrance. Except for a couple of elderly men, one Latino and one Asian, no one was wearing a suit.

On the other hand, no one was wearing sweats and sneakers either.

He'd never witnessed any negative reaction to the way someone was dressed, though. After a minute's hesitation, he climbed the steps to the entrance, nodded to the man holding the door — Mike Barnes? Someone he should know — and went inside. The woman in front of him dipped her fingers into the font of holy water and crossed herself, the plastic flowers in her hair bobbing on their stems as she ducked her head. Alan dipped his fingers in the font and crossed himself, too, thinking that maybe a sweatshirt was no worse than plastic flowers.

The church filled in virtual silence. Men and women faced the altar and knelt before going into their pews. Once there they sat, or they knelt with their hands folded on the back of the pews in front of them. Alan himself knelt with folded hands as an altar girl in a white surplice went forward to light the candles on either side of the altar. Beyond the altar, high on the wall, Jesus hung on his cross, his head turned partly away. Alan had seen many depictions of the suffering Christ, never a depiction of the angry Christ, though — Christ with whip raised and eyes blazing in his confrontation with the moneychangers in the temple. It was an obvious subject for a work of art, except that maybe the face of an angry God was too much for an artist to contend with.

An empty silver cross and an ornate Bible went forward with the priests. A beautiful woman with wavy, black hair and olive skin led the congregation in the first reading from the missal. After a brief ceremony at the front of the church in which salt was blessed and added to the holy water, a priest walked back down the aisle, dipping an aspergil into a silver bucket carried by the altar girl and throwing holy water out onto the congregation. Alan, standing by the aisle, jerked as he caught a spray of water full in the face. As the priest passed by, Alan stood blinking and looking down at the damp patches on his arms and at his spotted shirt. He felt blessed. There was no accounting for it, but he did.

After the homily, bread and wine went forward and the altar was prepared. The high point of the service came, as it always did for Alan, when the priest quoted Jesus saying, "This is my body," and a tone sounded clear and sweet as, in the belief of everybody present, the substance of the wafers of bread changed into the substance of Christ's body and blood. A little later, "This is my blood, the blood of the covenant, poured out for many for the forgiveness of sins." Again, the tone sounded: *Jesus is in the building.*

As many times as he had been through it, the hair stiffened on Alan's arms. Going to the altar, actually eating the wafer, was almost anticlimactic.

He felt better for having been to church, better able to deal with Tracey and her problems — or so it seemed until he came through the door and Tracey clicked off the TV. "I was waiting for you to take me to breakfast, but I guess it's lunchtime now. How far do you run?"

His head tilted. "Couple miles."

She stood and looked ostentatiously at her watch. She was wearing jeans and a polo shirt, the shirt neatly pressed and the jeans artfully ripped and perforated. "Well, don't get discouraged," she said, "A little more work, and you'll be up to one mile an hour."

"I stopped off for a church service while I was out."

"Dressed like that?"

"It was spur of the moment."

"At least you gave everyone a chance to practice their forgiveness."

"Nice to know I'm good for something."

"Don't take things so personally. Step through the shower, then let's go get a pizza."

About midmorning on Monday Alan went to Jim Angley's office and found him at his desk. "Just out of curiosity, more than anything else," he said from the doorway.

Angley put the letter he was reading down on the short stack of unopened mail. "Yes?"

"How did Hugh Royal and Luis Basoalto come to be in business together? I understand they jointly own their roller-rinks and bowling alleys."

"How do you understand that?" Angley asked.

Alan shrugged. "Scuttlebutt."

"Does this have anything to do with Tracey Royal and Carlotta Basoalto's murder?"

"I don't know. I'm just trying to get some background."

Angley stared at him abstractedly. "Sit down," he said.

Alan sat.

Angley said, "Most of what I know is scuttlebutt, too, you realize. The way I heard it, Hugh was in college when his dad died and left him that rink on the west end of town."

"Skateworld?"

"I guess. It had gotten run-down over the years and needed some major renovations. Hugh needed an investor, and he came up with Luis."

"How?"

"I don't know. Roger would, probably. I think maybe Hugh called Luis cold, sold him on himself and his idea."

Alan nodded.

"Since then, Hugh's run that rink and acquired a bunch more. About ten years ago, they started adding bowling alleys. Luis's collected dividends, and the whole thing's been phenomenally successful."

"I've heard rumors that Luis is some kind of criminal."

"Yeah, maybe. He was indicted once on racketeering charges. It may have been one of the minority of RICO cases that actually had something to do with organized crime. Something happened to the case and the charges were dropped." Angley made a face. "I never heard that any of it had anything to do with Hugh, though. Hugh runs his rinks, and Luis collects his dividends. As far as I know, he's been a completely silent partner."

When Alan got back to his office, he saw that the red light on his phone was lit, meaning he had voice mail. He sat and pushed the necessary buttons.

"Cale Larson," a voice said, and gave a phone number.

Larson was the district attorney. Alan lifted the receiver off its cradle and dialed.

"Larson."

"This is Alan Dougherty."

"Ah. I'm looking for Tracey Coleman's attorney of record, and as near as I can tell you're it."

"I'm it," Alan said.

"The grand jury handed down its indictment this morning. I'm setting the arraignment for one o'clock this afternoon."

Alan looked at his watch. "It's eleven o'clock now," he said.

"Better make it a short lunch. If your client's not there, I'll ask the judge for an arrest warrant." Larson, all of thirty-two, had been the district attorney for three years. So far he was living up to his reputation for arrogance.

"She'll be there," Alan said. "But it's not a lot of notice."

"If you don't mind me asking, Dougherty, why are you doing this? I've asked around about you. This isn't your kind of case."

"It's my kind of client."

"Young, beautiful, falsely accused?"

It made him sound like a Perry Mason wannabe. "For starters," he said.

"From what I hear, her father's gunning for you," Larson said. "I wouldn't be surprised if you got sued for malpractice before all this is over."

"If I get her off, he won't have much of a case."

Larson laughed and hung up on him.

Chapter 36

Tom Mitchell was the district judge who would be trying the case, and the arraignment was set in his courtroom. When Alan got there with Tracey, five minutes early, Larson was standing by the jury box, and the judge was already on the bench. Alan looked at his watch.

Larson smiled at them, showing what seemed to be unusually long teeth. He had started his career as a prosecutor working for the Smith County district attorney. After three years trying misdemeanors and one year in the felony division, he had wrested the Republican nomination from his boss with the financial backing of an old college roommate who had inherited money. He was the first candidate for the office to have spent more than one hundred thousand dollars on his campaign, and, at Alan's age, was probably the youngest district attorney in the state of Texas.

Alan ignored him as he and Tracey walked across the black-and-white tile floor to the defense table. A single sheet of paper lay on the polished mahogany.

It was a copy of the indictment, and it charged Tracey with capital murder as defined in section 19.03 of the Penal Code. The charge was a change from the complaint, which had charged her only with intentional murder, and the difference was critical. Capital murder was punishable by death or life imprisonment with no other options. Under the original charge Tracey could have been sentenced to as little as five years.

Larson was looking at them, a hand on an out-thrust hip. He was two or three inches over six feet in height and had the wiry build of a basketball player.

"Capital murder wasn't charged in the complaint," Alan said.

Larson smiled, again showing them his long, straight teeth. "The grand jury didn't see things the way the arresting officer did."

From the bench, Judge Mitchell cleared his throat. He said, "Everybody ready? Good. The defendant will stand for the reading of the indictment."

Alan stood with her. The critical sentence of the indictment charged that

> *Tracey Ashton Coleman on or about the twenty-fifth day of October and before the presentment of this indictment, in the County of Smith and State of Texas, did then and there intentionally and knowingly cause the death of Carlotta Basoalto, an individual, by shooting said Carlotta Basoalto with a gun, in the course of committing robbery or attempting to commit robbery, against the peace and dignity of the State.*

The prosecution had decided that Carlotta had been robbed. When the judge finished reading the indictment, he put it down and addressed Tracey. "Now then," he said. "We've got some formalities to attend to. You are Tracey Coleman?"

She said she was.

"And you're represented by counsel?"

Alan said, "Yes, sir. Alan Dougherty of Smith, Angley and Waters." Tracey nodded.

The judge said to Tracey, "It's my job to tell you the range of penalties attached to the offense of capital murder. There are only two penalties possible. If convicted, you will be sentenced either to death or to life imprisonment. In a moment I'm going to ask you how you plead to this charge, but before I do, I need to let you know the consequences of a guilty plea. Upon conviction you would have the right only to a limited appeal..." Alan glanced at Tracey, but he couldn't tell how much of the judge's statement she was taking in.

"Now," the judge said, his tone changing. "Has a plea bargain been reached between the state and the defense?"

"No, your honor," Larson said. "There will be no plea bargain."

The judge looked at Larson through the thick lenses of his square-framed glasses. "A simple yes or no will be sufficient, Mr. Larson."

Larson looked as if he might say something, but seemed to think better of it.

"Now," the judge said. "I have in front of me an application for denial of bail."

"Yes, sir," Larson said. "The defendant's bond is currently fifty thousand dollars, clearly inadequate for a capital crime."

"You want the amount raised?"

"I want bail denied altogether."

The judge studied Larson, his seamed face inexpressive of any emotion that Alan could read. It occurred to Alan that Judge Mitchell disliked Larson.

"Your honor," Alan said. "The district attorney is calling this capital murder, and the indictment refers to shooting the decedent in the course of a robbery, but all the evidence at the examining trial indicated that none of the decedent's effects were missing, that no robbery had in fact occurred. I don't think what we have here is a capital crime."

"Mr. Larson?"

"It doesn't matter what the evidence showed at the examining trial. The grand jury wasn't there to consider it, and the grand jury isn't bound by it. Furthermore, it is beyond the authority of this court to consider at this time whether or not the evidence points to a capital crime — or any crime at all, for that matter." Larson paused as if to give the judge a chance to respond, but Mitchell only chewed his lip.

Larson said, "The only matter before the court at present is the matter of bail."

Alan decided to try again. "In the circumstances, the indictment doesn't provide adequate notice of the crime charged. What robbery? The defendant needs to know if she's to prepare a defense."

The judge looked at Larson, who merely smiled. The judge turned back to Alan. "You're free of course to file a motion to quash. And your discovery motions."

Alan hesitated, then nodded. Judge Mitchell looked back and forth between the two lawyers.

"We'll set the bail hearing for noon Wednesday, day after tomorrow," he said.

"Your honor, the state would prefer..."

The gavel cracked, cutting him off. The judge, indifferent to the state's preferences, stood behind his bench and headed for the door.

Larson dropped into the wooden chair behind his table, kicking back to put his feet up, first his left foot, then his right.

Alan put his copy of the indictment into his briefcase. "Let's go," he said to Tracey.

Larson's eyes followed them as they crossed in front of him.

"Counselor?" he said when they were at the door.

Alan turned back to look at him.

"Two rings," Larson said.

"Excuse me?"

"Something seems to have happened to the decedent's rings."

Chapter 37

"So what's next?" Tracey asked as they stood waiting for the elevator.

"I can take you home."

"Don't go domestic on me. I'm counting on you to keep me out of jail."

The elevator doors opened, and they got on. Alan said, "I feel like a lot of what I need to know is already inside your head."

"Such as."

"I don't have much of a feel for the Royals."

"You're on your own there. I don't follow baseball."

He gave her a quick smile to acknowledge the joke, but didn't allow himself to be distracted. "My understanding is that Barry and Tony are cousins, but that they've pretty much grown up together. Barry is Hugh's son. Tony's the nephew."

"That's my understanding, too." The elevator doors opened, and they got off.

He held open the outer door for her. "Is there much rivalry between Barry and Tony?"

"I guess."

She didn't elaborate. At the car, which was parked against the curb, he unlocked her door and held it open for her. "Can you provide any specifics?"

"Nope. Just the general impression." She sat and swung her legs in, and he closed the door. As he crossed behind the car to the driver's side, he saw movement out of the corner of his eye — a man getting into a dark Porsche a few cars behind Alan's.

He opened his own door and swung into the driver's seat. "Carlotta lived in their carriage-house apartment?" he asked.

"Hugh's carriage-house apartment. Barry's renting a loft apartment downtown somewhere. Tony, I don't know about. He doesn't live with his uncle."

Alan found the Porsche in his rearview mirror. "Are they around Hugh's place a lot?"

"A good bit."

The man in the Porsche seemed to be making no effort to get under way. Tracey had an apple green Porsche, but this looked like a newer model.

Tracey said, "I think Tony was sleeping with Carlotta whenever she would let him... What's wrong?" She turned to look behind them.

"Nothing, I hope. What can you tell me about Luis Basoalto?"

"Not much. Luis is Carlotta's father — was her father. He's rich, probably about sixty, sixty-five. Splits his time between Columbia and the United States."

"Is he a U.S. citizen?"

"I don't know. What are you looking at?"

"A man in a Porsche." He backed up enough to clear the car in front of him and shifted into drive. As he started forward, the Porsche pulled out behind them.

"Carlotta had a brother," Tracey said. "Carlos. I've only seen him once."

"What about him?"

"That may be him behind us."

Alan tried to get a better look in his rearview mirror, without success. "Great," he said.

He turned right at the light and, when the Porsche followed suit, turned right again.

"Where are you going?"

"Police station."

But the Porsche crossed the intersection behind them without turning after them.

"So was it following us, or wasn't it?" Tracey said.

"You tell me."

When it started getting dark, sometime before six, Alan went through the house closing window blinds. For the fourth or fifth time he rechecked the doors, which were, of course, locked and bolted. Finally, he got Tracey's gun from his car in the garage and brought it into the house, being careful to keep his finger outside the trigger guard.

"Are we better off with you holding this, or me?" he asked her.

"Judging by the way you're holding it, I'd say me."

He handed it to her, and she set it on the end table nearest her.

"What do you want for dinner?" she asked him. "I take it we're staying in."

"Sandwiches?"

"Your bread was growing mold. I threw it out yesterday." Before he could say anything, she continued, "Fortunately, I went shopping this morning. How about steak and a salad?"

His eyebrows went up. He shrugged.

"I'll take that as an outpouring of gratitude and enthusiasm," she said.

He sat on a barstool as she started pulling things out of the refrigerator and laying them on the counter. "Hugh's not married, is he?" he asked.

"Are we back to that?"

"Better get used to it."

She twisted the top off a bottle of beer and held it out to him, but he shook his head. She took a long pull of it herself, then wiped her mouth with the back of her hand. "He's divorced," she said. "Twice that I know of. Barry's mother ran out on the two of them when Barry was just a toddler. Wife number two — or his most recent wife anyway — is still in town. They've been divorced about five years or so." She found a frying pan and poured a little olive oil in it, then cut the wrap over the steaks.

"Do you know her name?"

"Helen Royal, I think."

"She kept her married name?"

"Her maiden name was really atrocious, Hoopinhammer or something."

"Helen Hoopinhammer?"

She grinned, a little wickedly. "Kind of rolls off the tongue, doesn't it?" The pan having heated to her satisfaction, she laid in the steaks.

"Either Barry or Tony ever been married?"

She shook her head. "Nope."

He was silent.

They were at the kitchen table, halfway through their steaks, when Alan said, "The whole smuggling thing doesn't make sense to me."

She rolled her eyes, letting her knife and fork fall to the table. "Good Lord," she said.

"It's Hugh Royal. Why would a wealthy man involve his relatives and his partner's daughter in smuggling two kilos of cocaine?"

"Maybe he didn't involve them. Maybe they involved him."

"Is that how it happened?"

"I don't know how it happened. I came into the deal late."

After a moment he nodded. She'd said that before.

Chapter 38

The bail hearing depended on what might or might not happen at the sentencing stage, should the case go that far. Because death sentences were subject to automatic review by the Court of Criminal Appeals, there was a lot of relevant case law. He was sitting at the computer in his office scrolling through some of it when Jim Angley stuck his head in.

"Alan, could you join us in the big conference room?"

"Sure." Alan picked up a clean legal pad and followed him, wondering vaguely who "us" was and why they were in the big conference room.

A dozen lawyers sat around the long table, Jordan Conway among them. Everyone stopped talking when Alan came in. Angley took the seat at the head of the table; Alan took the empty chair next to him.

"I think this is it," Angley said. "I understand Tracey Coleman has a bail hearing tomorrow. That right, Alan?"

"Yes."

"And it's capital murder now," Angley said.

"That's right." He could feel his pulse beating in his neck. He had participated in such strategy sessions before. They were the hallmark of a case big enough to affect the firm itself. This was the first time he'd been the guest of honor.

"You ready for it?" Angley asked him.

"I'm getting ready."

"Suppose you tell us what you're expecting from the prosecution. What's going on here? Does Larson really think Tracey's going to hop a plane to Buenos Aires?"

"I don't know. It's possible he's just strutting his stuff, going all out to prove he treats pretty, middle-class white girls just as harshly as he does everyone else. He courted the minority vote hard in the last election, you know, claiming Cummings spent all his time prosecuting blacks and Latinos..."

"And since he's been in office he's spent all his time prosecuting blacks and Latinos," said Ashby Wilson, the senior female partner. She drew some scattered laughter.

Angley said, "Okay, given that he's salivating over the possibility of a high profile prosecution of a middle-class white girl, what's he going to do? What's his angle of attack? Speculate. You must have thought about it."

"Sure." Alan coughed in an effort to clear his throat. "If Larson wants Mitchell to deny bail, he's got two issues to deal with. One, the aggravating circumstances of the murder —"

"As opposed to mitigating circumstances?"

"Right. There aren't any, at least not yet."

"What are the aggravating circumstances?"

"The placement of the bullet through the eye? I don't know. Really, I think he's playing a long-shot." He was hoping to God Larson was playing a long shot. "He's weak on motive before he even gets to aggravating circumstances."

"What about motive?"

"The indictment alleges robbery." He told them about the rings which apparently had disappeared from Carlotta's fingers.

"That's all they've got? Tracey coveting a few pieces of Carlotta's jewelry?"

"Apparently."

"That's going to be a hard sell to a jury," said Brian Corley, a thick-necked lawyer at the other end of the table.

"Yes," Alan agreed, glancing toward him. "Actually, a bail hearing may be in our best interest. If Larson's got something inflammatory to put on, it'll be a lot better to see it now than in the middle of trial."

"You said Larson had two issues to deal with," Angley said. "What was the other?"

"Whether Tracey is likely to commit more acts of criminal violence and would constitute a continuing threat to society."

Someone laughed. Alan didn't see who. "The absence of a record helps there," he said, looking around at them.

Angley and Ashby Wilson exchanged glances. Angley said, "I take it Tracey hasn't told you about being arrested for marijuana possession three or so years ago?"

A chill radiated outward from Alan's spine. "No. She hasn't."

"Cummings was D.A. then. It was less than two ounces, and Roger was able to plead her to a class C misdemeanor, possession of drug paraphernalia, and the judge suspended her sentence."

"So does that make the arrest admissible or not?" Alan asked.

Corley said, "I know it's admissible in the sentencing hearing, so it'll be relevant tomorrow as well. Whether Larson can get it in at trial is problematical."

Everyone was silent. Alan was thinking that, with a prior arrest for possession in Tracey's record, the police and the prosecution would have been looking for drug link from the beginning. He wondered if they'd found it.

"Are you all right for the bail hearing?" Angley asked Alan.

"I think so."

"Do you want someone sitting shotgun?"

He shook his head. "It isn't necessary."

"Would it help?"

"I don't think so. I can carry my own briefcase." No one laughed.

"Roger called today," Angley said. "He's threatening to sue us for malpractice."

"Already? Based on what?"

"Whatever he can come up with. He's going to be watching you like a hawk."

Alan shrugged. "Okay."

"I'm all right with you for the bail hearing," Corley said. "The main trial's a different question. A capital murder trial is the big leagues."

"I'll be okay with Jordan or Jay doing some occasional research to back me up."

But Corley was shaking his head. "Criminal law is its own specialty. You'll need help in the courtroom."

Alan thought about it. "You?" he said.

"No. I've done a couple of felony trials in my time, but never capital murder."

Alan looked at Angley.

"Nobody here has that kind of experience," Angley said. "Brian proposes that we bring Ken Whitaker up from Houston."

"Whitaker?" Alan repeated. He had never thought of Whitaker, though the firm had used him occasionally for criminal defense work. "We don't want Whitaker."

"He's a pro," Corley said. "He's got a score of capital murder trials under his belt."

"Did you read the transcript in the Leadbetter case?"

"That case was lost before it started."

Alan shook his head. "Jay and I worked on the appeal after Whitaker lost it at trial. It could have been close. It should have been, but the jury was out less than an hour."

"Look," Angley said. "You're a good enough trial lawyer — you're an excellent trial lawyer — but you're a civil trial lawyer."

"Go read the Leadbetter transcript," Alan said.

Corley said, "You're saying you could have done better."

"Absolutely."

"Suppose we put you in as second chair?" Angley suggested. "Ken provides the procedural expertise and the overall guidance. You cross-examine some witnesses and contribute in other ways."

"Let him be second chair. I can handle this. I've been going to sleep at night poring over the Code of Criminal Procedure and the Rules of Criminal Evidence."

"That's not the same as trial experience," Corley said. "You should know that."

Angley said, "If it were a pro bono case, we'd let you run with it, but it's not. It's a capital case, and we've got Roger Coleman looking over our shoulders second-guessing everything we do."

Alan opened his mouth, then closed it again. Their minds had been made up before the meeting started.

Jordan Conway spoke up. "Alan's beat three of the best defense lawyers in town, Sandy McCabe and Malcolm Huber over at Gibson Taylor and Jim Bitwell at Dobson and Potts."

Corley said, "Two of those were contract disputes, and one was medical malpractice. What's your point?"

"If he'd done even a couple of felony trials, we might let him handle it," Angley said. "But he's got no experience in criminal defense at all."

"He didn't have any experience for the malpractice case either," Jay Fowler said. "Johnson was his first."

"We're not slighting Alan's courtroom abilities in any way," Angley said, looking at Alan. "I'm sure he knows that."

Alan managed an insincere smile.

Angley pushed back from the table. "Alan, good luck at the bail hearing tomorrow. Let any of us know if you need anything."

Chapter 39

Jordan Conway followed him into his office and shut the door, leaning back against it, her hands behind her. "That was kind of brutal," she said.

"It felt kind of brutal."

"It wasn't really a vote of no confidence, you know. It's your age. To them you're still a kid fresh out of law school. They lose track of time."

"They may be right."

"Jay didn't think so."

"And I appreciate him saying so. You, too. On the other hand, Jay's been here only a year longer than I have."

There was a silence between them. For a week now she'd been avoiding him, he thought. Now here she was.

"You've been busy," he said.

"So have you."

He nodded.

"I heard you put up your house to bail her out," she said.

He shook his head, wondering where she'd heard that. "It was a check from my 401(k)," he said.

"Ah."

"Roger didn't do it because he was afraid Luis Basoalto would be incensed enough to make his own justice for his daughter's death."

"He thought she'd be safer in the county jail than home with him?"

"I guess. Luis seems to have the reputation of being some kind of a crime lord."

"You sure you know what you're getting into?"

"No."

"You may be a week away from Ken Whitaker taking the whole load off your back. That may be a good thing."

"Less stressful, anyway."

"That's the spirit." She gave him a smile, then slipped through the door and was gone.

He put his head back against the headrest and closed his eyes, thinking Jordan evidently did not know Tracey was living with him. That unpleasantness was still ahead of him.

After a few deep, even breaths, he opened his eyes and got his phone book from the desk drawer. He didn't know how much time he had before Whitaker showed up and took charge of the case, but he felt he had to make the most of the time he had. He flipped the pages looking for Helen Royal, who had been, according to Tracey, Hugh's second wife.

He was a little surprised to find her in the book. It seemed too easy. He dialed the number, and a woman answered.

"Hello," he said. "My name is Alan Dougherty. Is Helen Royal available?"

"This is she." The voice sounded cautious.

"I'm the lawyer who represents Tracey Coleman, the girl accused of killing a woman named Carlotta Basoalto."

"What did you say your name was?"

He repeated it.

"I never heard of you, or any of those other people, either." There was something familiar and a little unsettling about her voice.

"Hugh Royal?" he suggested, trying to think of whom she reminded him.

"What about him? What does he have to do with any of this?"

"Carlotta Basoalto was living in his garage apartment and driving one of his cars. I understand that he and her father are business partners."

"I misspoke," she said after a moment. "I meant to say, what does any of this have to do with me?" The ring of familiarity was clearer.

"Nothing to do with you," he said. "I'm trying to fill in the background a little. You were once married to Hugh Royal, I understand. I thought perhaps..."

"You thought wrong."

It was going to drive him nuts if he failed to place her. "I wondered if I could drop by and visit with you a little," he said, afraid she was about to hang up on him. "Or, if it's more convenient, perhaps you could come by the office and see me sometime in the next day or so while you're out and..."

"I don't think it would ever be convenient for me to visit a lawyer's office. I unfortunately had to do a bit of that at one point in my life."

"I understand. And I'd be happy to..."

"Not a lot of good it ever did me. Bob Stott, you know him?"

He hesitated, not wanting to get dragged into a discussion of her dissatisfactions with her divorce lawyer. Nobody liked his divorce lawyer. Divorce law — family practice — was the least satisfying work a lawyer could engage in, in Alan's opinion. A person in the throes of a divorce, with rare exception, could be satisfied with nothing less than seeing his or her spouse stripped of everything and driven naked through the streets on the way to being stoned by a jeering mob. Because that outcome was beyond the reach of even the best attorney, client dissatisfaction was almost a forgone conclusion.

"This Tracey girl's in a lot of trouble if you're no better lawyer than he is," Helen Royal said.

"I'm afraid I'm not."

"Pardon?"

"I'm no more of a magician than Bob Stott. To be successful, I depend on the cooperation of all kinds of people who may or may not be in possession of helpful information. If people like you refuse to talk to me, I'm afraid my client's screwed."

She was silent for several moments, long enough for Alan to decide he had lost her. Then she said, "I don't know whether you're a very good attorney or a very poor one, Mr. Dougherty."

He didn't respond.

"I'm having dinner at the Petroleum Club tonight at seven. If you'd care to meet there a little before then, perhaps I can spare you a few minutes."

"Six-thirty?"

"I'll see you then." She hung up without saying goodbye, and he realized suddenly of whom she reminded him. The quick disconnect was the sort of trick his mother pulled. He didn't believe she'd said goodbye to him more than half-a-dozen times in his life.

Chapter 40

The Petroleum Club occupied the top floor of a bank building that was less than a block away. A cold drizzle had started sometime in the middle of the afternoon, and, when he left his own building shortly after six o'clock, the wind knifed through his suit coat as if it wasn't there. Hands in his pockets and his shoulders hunched against the cold, he trotted stiff-legged across the street.

Oil wasn't the source of wealth in Texas that it had once been. He understood that fifteen years before, with oil under twelve dollars a barrel, there'd been talk of the Petroleum Club closing its doors, though at present, the Petroleum Club seemed to be doing just fine. Its carpets were deep, and chrome and glass were everywhere. Only the occasional Remington replica supplied the requisite southwestern motif, Remington's famous "Bronco Buster" dominating the bar.

Alan was looking, he thought, for a middle-aged woman, once pretty and perhaps still so, but no one at all was at the bar. The bartender, wearing French cuffs and a colorful vest, was watching a small TV with muted sound and closed captioning. Alan stepped up into one of the tall bar chairs.

"What can I get you?" the bartender asked, getting up and stepping toward him. "She's in the ladies room."

"Helen Royal?"

"I guess. She's been here since about five. Said a lawyer was meeting her. Would that be you?"

"I guess it would be. I'll have orange juice."

"Orange juice."

"Please." His mother became irritated if forced to drink alone in the company of others. If Helen Royal was like her in that respect, she would take his failure to order a drink as a personal affront, but a glass of orange juice might be taken for a screwdriver.

He caught movement out of the corner of his eye and turned his head to see a trim woman with frosted hair crossing toward him, just a hint of unsteadiness to her gait. She wore a skirt and matching jacket, earrings and a simple necklace. Alan placed her in her late forties.

Alan slipped out of his chair as she approached.

"Mr. Dougherty?" she asked.

He nodded.

"Well let's get started. Fire away." She ignored his half movement toward one of the tables and stepped into the chair beside him. The bartender lifted a fresh glass of white wine onto the bar.

"Get yourself something," she said. "I'm having dinner later with a gentleman who'll be picking up the tab."

"Thank you." As he spoke, the bartender put a drink in front of him. His orange juice was in a large old-fashioned glass filled with crushed ice and decorated with a small paper umbrella. Alan glanced up, but the bartender had his eyes fixed on the TV.

Helen Royal's eyes moved from Alan's drink to Alan himself, then back to his drink again.

His mouth stretching in a humorless smile, Alan pulled out the umbrella to reveal the blossom of an orchid floating on the surface of his drink.

"I see you've already ordered," Helen Royal said dryly as he plucked out the orchid blossom and laid it next to his glass on the corner of the napkin. Beneath the orchid blossom was a maraschino cherry speared to a wedge of pineapple.

"You'd be surprised how few men have the guts to order one of these," Alan said.

"No, I don't think I would."

He took a sip and was almost surprised to taste nothing but orange juice.

"So what did you want to ask me?"

Though he'd only seen her take a single sip of her wine, somehow she'd managed to consume half the glass. She might have been his mother's own sister, had she had one. "How long were you married to Hugh?" he asked.

"Nine years." She didn't elaborate.

"When?"

"Married June fifteen, nineteen ninety-eight, divorced October twenty, two thousand and seven. Nine years, four months, five days."

"You make it sound like time served."

"Yes."

"Yet you kept his name."

She didn't answer, perhaps because he hadn't really asked a question.

"How old was Barry when you got married?" he asked.

She shrugged. "Thirteen or fourteen. They were both teenagers, Barry and Tony."

"Which one was older?"

"You know, I can't remember. They were within a year of each other."

"You intimated on the phone that the divorce didn't leave you very well off."

"Did I?" She slid her empty glass several inches in the direction of the bartender, and he lifted another one, already poured, onto the bar in front of her. "*Well off* is a relative thing. I came out better financially than I went in. I didn't come out as well as Hugh did, not by a long shot."

"Would you say he lived lavishly, or was he the sort to hoard his money?"

She gave a snort of laughter, and a little wine ran from her nose and dripped on the bar. She was a woman of refinement, and she was a drunk. Alan had grown up with it.

"You tell me," she said. "Hugh drove a Bentley all the time we were married, traded it in every two years. Had to have it taken to Dallas to be serviced — no dealerships here in town. Had that tennis court out back of the house and the swimming pool. Every contraption you could imagine in his house. You've been in Dillard's, I suppose?" She gave him time to nod. "The inside of his house looked a lot like that. Hugh Royal had one of nearly everything that Dillard's did."

"What was his income like in the years you were with him?"

She shook her head. "I doubt if Hugh himself knew. There'd be numbers on the tax returns, of course. I think comfortably in six figures."

"You talk almost as if the numbers didn't have anything to do with his actual income."

"I think that's right. The numbers on the tax returns were just numbers. Everything Hugh bought, he'd pull a big wad of bills out of his pocket and pay cash for it. Except for his cars. He wrote a check for the Mercedes convertible he bought me sometime in 1999 or so."

She was beginning to go beyond the questions he asked her, which was good. It meant he didn't have to know all the right questions. Now he sat sipping his orange juice as the silence spun out around them.

"I never did see how he made all that money," she said musingly, holding up her wine to catch the light. "Have you ever been in one of his skating rinks?"

He shook his head.

"I wasn't in many of the rinks myself, and not often. The times I was in one, there wasn't anyone in there. Same with the bowling alleys, though he didn't have more than a couple of those till right near the end."

This time the silence stretched out until he thought it might become permanent. "Hugh seem worried about his business falling off?" he asked.

She shook her head, pursing her lips around a mouthful of Chardonnay. "If I said anything about business being bad, he'd just smile at me and pat my shoulder."

"Do you think he might have been skimming?"

She gave him a sharp look. "What do you think?" she asked.

"What you've said makes me wonder."

"Let me tell you, there's something special about a roller rink. Bowling alleys, too. Hugh Royal has about the best business in the world for skimming profits, in my opinion."

Alan nodded thoughtfully.

"Think about it," she told him.

He had been thinking about it. "I don't suppose you have copies of any of those old tax returns?"

She shook her head. "Hugh handled all that while we were together. I just signed what he put in front of me. To his credit, none of it's come back to bite me in the fanny."

"Your divorce lawyer would have gotten copies of the old returns."

"I suppose."

"Do you mind if I ask him if he's still got them? He'll probably call you to make sure it's okay to give me copies."

"Ask away."

He took a breath and held it a moment before releasing it. He couldn't think of where else to go with her. "I appreciate your meeting with me," he said. "You've been very helpful."

He took a last slug of his drink as she drained her wine glass. When he put down his glass, she said, "Nothing in that glass but orange juice, was there?"

He hesitated. "No. Just orange juice."

"It takes me awhile sometimes, but I usually get there."

He left the Petroleum Club feeling somehow that he ought to pay his mother a visit. The drizzle had stopped, at least for now, but it seemed colder. He hurried into the lobby of the building that housed his law firm. Helen Royal was right, he reflected as he punched the button for the elevator; there was something special about a roller rink. If instead Hugh were running a hamburger restaurant, then he would have to purchase his hamburger meat and his buns from some supplier, which would produce records available to the I.R.S. in the event of an audit. So much meat made so many hamburgers, which sold for so much apiece. Subtract the cost of the meat and the buns and the rent, and you had your profit. If the profit wasn't there, the I.R.S. would want to know why not and why Hugh wasn't paying taxes on it.

But Hugh rented space. Who would know whether two hundred kids were skating on a given night or whether there were only a hundred and fifty? At the end of the week or a year, who was going to know what the receipts should be? Give each employee limited hours, count the cash yourself, and the setup was very nearly foolproof.

Or maybe not so foolproof. Maybe business had been bad, and he had skimmed too much. Maybe Luis Basoalto had become suspicious of him, and Hugh had had to come up with cash to make up the shortfall. Maybe that was why Carlotta and Tracey were running dope for him.

The doors of the elevator opened on the sixth floor, and he saw Roger Coleman. Though it was not yet seven o'clock, most of the lights on the floor were out, and in the dim light Roger was sitting alone in one of the upholstered chairs in the waiting area. He wasn't reading — just sitting, his hands clasped between his knees, his body hunched.

Alan sat in the chair across from him. "You all right?"

Roger looked up, but his gaze, for a moment, seemed far away. Then his eyes focused, and he was back in the here and now. "Feeling my own mortality," he said, one corner of his mouth starting to rise before the smile collapsed.

Alan nodded, but didn't say anything. It was the first nonhostile encounter he'd had with Roger Coleman in five years. He couldn't imagine what motivated it.

"Jim called me. Told me about bringing in Whitaker."

"Do you know Whitaker?"

"He won the Davenport case about a dozen years ago. You may not remember it. Trophy wife hired some kids to murder her husband. Whitaker got her off. That was the case that made his reputation."

"You think he's good?"

"Yes. There are some things more important than good, though." He met Alan's eyes. "You think she's innocent, don't you?"

"Who, Tracey? Sure." He hesitated. "Don't you?"

Roger's head was bobbing vaguely, but it didn't seem to be in answer to Alan's question. "What I want is for the whole thing to go away," he said at last. "Whatever may have happened in that parking lot, I just want it to go away. Tracey can get over it, go on to build a life for herself. But first it has to go away."

Alan nodded.

"Whitaker's going to assume she's guilty," Roger said. "You're the one who's got to convince him otherwise, ignite a passion for the case in him. Whitaker can do it, but he's got to believe in what he's doing. That's going to have to come from you."

Alan sat looking at him, but Roger stood abruptly. "Time to go home," he said, and his mouth stretched mechanically. "Thanks, Alan."

Alan watched him press the button for the elevator and step into it. The doors slid shut, and Alan stood up. He felt shaken, and he wasn't sure why.

Before leaving for home, he put in a call to Bob Stott and caught him packing his briefcase to go home himself. It turned out that Stott had disposed of everything relating to the Royals' divorce except the papers that had been filed. All the tax returns had been destroyed, as well as everything else that had been obtained in discovery.

"I dispose of everything after five years," Stott said. "Religiously. Every so often I have to disappoint somebody like you, but it saves me all kind of storage problems."

"But it's only just now been five years."

"Religiously," Stott repeated.

"Don't you sometimes find you need something yourself after you've gotten rid of it?"

"Sure. And then I find somebody else who's got it. You know how many times I've needed something I couldn't replace? One time, Alan. One time."

Chapter 41

It was just after seven when he got home. Inside the garage, blocking the door into the house were a couple of gym bags, packed tight, beside them something that looked like a sleeping bag. As he stood looking down at them, Tracey came out wearing a light nylon jacket.

"You're late," she said, slipping cold hands inside the jacket of his suit and rubbing his sides.

"I was working overtime for an important client." He jerked his head toward the bulging gym bags. "What's up?"

"What are your plans for tonight?"

"More of the same."

"What does that mean?"

"More work preparing for your bail hearing." He hefted his briefcase, which was filled with legal pads full of notes and printouts of court opinions he'd found on Lexis.

"How much time have you spent on it so far?"

"Just under twelve hours today, according to my time cards."

"Is more preparation likely to make a difference at this point? Tell the truth."

He broke eye-contact, unwilling to answer.

"Why don't we go camping tonight?"

"Camping?" He laughed hollowly, shaking his head. "We've got to be in court tomorrow at noon."

"Daddy's got some land up near Mineola. If we leave there by ten, we'll be back in time."

"You're not serious."

"I am serious. I feel like this may be my last night of freedom. I want to get out in the open where I can really feel it."

Her unpredictable spontaneity was one reason she had always fascinated him, but there were limits. "You need to find someone to go with you who's not busting his butt to keep you out of jail," he said.

"It's not like you'd be roughing it. There's a cabin out there — a little one, about eight feet square, but it has heat, and a hot plate, and a little dorm-sized refrigerator. We could even take along a TV, if you wanted."

"If we wanted to watch TV, we could just stay here."

"So we won't take the TV. I think I've got you packed. How long would it take you to get ready?"

"Tracey —" He exhaled in a long sigh. He had no idea what the outcome of tomorrow's hearing would be, but for his own peace of mind he had to do everything he could. "I don't want to go camping. Not tonight." An icy breeze was blowing with muted force into the open garage, and he shivered. "Besides, it's cold."

"You're a selfish bastard."

"That's hardly fair, is it?"

"Maybe not," she conceded. "But tomorrow I may very well get locked up again, and, if you can't get me acquitted, I'm likely to stay locked up for a very long time."

"I don't think —"

"Can you guarantee that tomorrow the judge won't revoke my bail?"

He sighed, the air gusting out of him like air from a tired balloon. "There are no guarantees in this business. You know that."

"And yet you begrudge me one last night in the open air."

He thought suddenly of Jim Angley and Brian Corley and the others, calling in high-powered talent from Houston to protect themselves from potential liability — going through the motions when it was results that counted.

Tracey stood looking up at him appealingly.

"Okay," he said. "I don't know that I'm on track to accomplish anything anyway."

"We can go?"

He nodded, and she hugged him, clearly delighted. His own feeling of uneasiness increased suddenly by an order of magnitude.

Roger's land up near Mineola turned out to be eight hundred acres of rocky terrain covered by scraggly, bare-limbed mesquite and persimmon and rusty blackhaw trees. At the entrance, Tracey got out of the car to unlock a massive padlock and to swing back the metal gate. He drove through. She relocked the gate and got back in the car.

As they bounced down the rutted dirt road, the sound of Alan's car was completely masked by a clanking oil-well pump that bobbed its head beside a huge, cylindrical oil tank fifty yards inside the gate.

"Turn here," Tracey shouted.

He turned, and the car bumped over two pipes that lay across the road.

"Speed up. Speed up or you won't make it across that mudhole."

Alan, who had been on the point of braking, sped up, but didn't make it across anyway. The car settled unevenly, its spinning tires throwing water and mud before Alan realized he was just setting the car more deeply. He took his foot off the accelerator and cranked down his window, letting in a gust of cold air that chilled him to the marrow.

"The mud's halfway up the hubcaps," he said looking out.

"That's all right, we can walk from here. Actually, we made it further than I thought we would."

He looked over at her in disbelief.

"Don't get your nose out of joint. I wouldn't have let you get stuck if I couldn't get you out again."

It was possible to get out on Tracey's side of the car without stepping in the mud. Alan worked his way across the gearshift and reached for the two canvas gym bags in the back seat.

The cabin, roughly half a mile further on, had originally been a feed shack, built for storing cattle feed. It was a cube, eight feet on a side, set on cinderblocks. Its plywood siding, grayed by the weather, bore the last flaking remnants of brown paint. Inside, two mattresses were propped against one wall, and across from them was a small sofa that might have come from someone's front curb. By the door was the promised dorm-sized refrigerator with the hot plate sitting on top.

Alan dropped his gym bag onto the sofa. "Whose CD player?" he asked. It sat on a shelf that ran along the back wall.

"Must belong to one of my cousins. They use this place sometimes when they come hunting. Come on back out. The sun's going to set in about twenty minutes, and we've got a way to travel."

"I thought we were staying here."

"We are, but I've got something I want you to see first."

He followed her out.

A lean-to was built onto the back of the cabin. Beneath it was a tarp-covered tractor. "That's how we're going to get your car out," Tracey told him. She dragged away another tarp, uncovering a Yamaha ATV four-wheeler, facing outward. She climbed onto it, and, when she had turned the key, stomped down on the kick-start.

She had to do it twice, and then the engine roared in response. She rolled forward, bouncing over a two-by-four that lay along the ground. "Get on," she shouted over the sound of the engine.

"It's cold," he objected, sounding whiney even to his own ears, "and it'll be dark soon."

"I know. We have to hurry."

When he had climbed on behind her, feeling resigned as well as cold, she popped the clutch, and the front tires lifted off the ground as they jolted forward, the rear tires spitting dirt. Alan clutched at her convulsively to keep from somersaulting off the back.

Already the blue sky had taken on a metallic hue. The sun was an orange ball just above the horizon as they raced along a barbed-wire fence with Tracey's thumb on the throttle. The wind blew Tracey's streaming hair back into Alan's face, and he kept spitting to keep it out of his mouth. On the far side of the barbed wire, vast acres of uncut hay sloped down toward a little lake.

Just as he had begun to relax marginally, she turned the four-wheeler off the track and bounced down a steep embankment toward a rocky stream. She turned as they hit it, and great sheets of water rose up on either side, soaking Alan's left side with icy water.

"Hey," Alan shouted. As she steered upstream over the uneven creek bed, Tracey held her legs straight out in front of her to keep them dry. Alan followed her example, though too late to save his shoes.

"We're taking a short-cut. Have to."

She turned out of the stream onto a slope so steep that the front tires rose off the ground with every surge of power. Alan held onto her, though he expected at any moment that she would lose her grip on the handlebars and they would spill backwards onto the ground.

She didn't, though. They made it to the top, where Tracey picked up another trail, one curving gradually upward. They stopped at the base of a granite outcropping that rose above a clump of sandjack oaks with short trunks, stout, crooked branches, and tree roots twisting in and out of the uneven ground.

On foot Alan followed Tracey up a trail too narrow for the four-wheeler, then took to the rocks behind her. She hopped across a gap about a yard wide, and, as he went across behind her, he looked down into a chasm thirty or forty feet deep.

The goal of their climb was a point of rock with a ledge cut into it, transforming the outcropping into a high throne. Tracey worked her way onto the ledge, sliding along it to make room for Alan. Their legs dangled in space. Hundreds of yards below them ran a river with sandy banks; on the other side of it, pastureland, a white farmhouse, and, beyond it, trees on rising terrain. Far down river, the orange ball of the sun was melting into the horizon.

The wind cut into them, chilling them in their wet clothes, and Tracey pushed against him, working her shoulder into his armpit. The sun was half gone. Alan looked down into Tracey's face, but she was watching the sunset with rapt attention.

In ten minutes the sun was gone, a faint glow marking the sky at the point where it had gone down.

Already the light was fading, leaving them in a ghostly twilight. Alan, cold and shivering, looked back and forth between the land rolling away beneath them and Tracey's intent little face. He was thrilled suddenly, despite his discomfort, all but overcome by a wild exultation.

The darkness was almost total when Tracey said, "We'd better go," and he followed her silently down the rock outcropping to where the four-wheeler sat waiting for them.

Chapter 42

Back in Tyler, a white Corvette turned the corner at a stop sign, went two blocks, thumped over time-smoothed railroad tracks, and turned again. Brick warehouses, their windows boarded over with sheets of graffiti-covered plywood, filled the block on either side, creating an artificial canyon already dark in the twilight. Other than a large oil refinery north of town, Tyler was no longer home to much significant industry, and its warehouse district was a graveyard.

At the end of the street, the Corvette turned left and then left again into a U-shaped loading dock. Three times this week an anonymous caller had phoned to change the meeting place, a business practice typical of Gonzalo Gutierrez, the man Barry Royal was dealing with, but one that irritated Barry profoundly. The last call, in addition to changing the place of the meeting, had moved up the time by a day. It was something he would have ordinarily complained about, because both sides of the transaction had security interests, and the location of the transaction, like the other terms of the contract, should be the subject of negotiation.

This time, however, the only thing that mattered to Barry was collecting his money. The package beside him consisted of two kilos of white powder wrapped in plastic, wrapped again in brown paper. After putting the Corvette in park, Barry's hand went to rest protectively on his merchandise, for which he expected to receive one hundred twenty thousand dollars. He had made the delivery on two previous occasions, working for his father, and he depended on this transaction following form. One way or the other, it would be the last.

Gonzalo's instructions were for Barry to wait inside his car, so Barry waited. He didn't like that either. The floor of the loading dock was higher than the roof of his car, limiting his field of vision in front of him and on both sides. He was immobile, and he was blind. After a minute or so, he turned off the car so the sound of the engine wouldn't render him deaf as well.

Time passed, punctuated only by the clicking of his Corvette's cooling engine. Despite the cold, the armpits of Barry's shirt were soggy with nervous sweat, when a voice called, "Hey, is that you, fatso?"

He opened his car door as far as he could without scraping it on the brick, and he struggled up out of his seat with the merchandise held against his chest like a misshapen football. Gonzalo Gutierrez stood above him with his hands thrust into the pockets of a black trench coat, hanging open to reveal black pants and a pale shirt, buttoned to the throat. Gonzalo had a lean, dark face and a closely trimmed goatee.

"It is you, fatso," Gonzalo said, his breath white in the cold night air. He inhaled through his nose in a productive honk and spat mucous on the concrete floor of the platform. He could afford to be insulting. There were two beefy men with him, one on either wing of the loading platform, and each held a pistol.

Barry held up his free hand in a placating gesture. "I come bearing gifts," he said.

"That the stuff? Put it there on the cement."

The platform surrounding his car was chest high. Barry placed his package gently at Gonzalo's feet and stepped back. Gonzalo knelt beside it.

Barry had never seen either one of the bodyguards before. They, like Gonzalo, were Latino. Their identical crew cuts made them look more than a bit retarded.

"Gotta make sure you don't try to cheat me, eh?" Gonzalo pushed a broad-bladed knife into the bag and drew it out again, carefully, so as not to spill the powder. He took a silver straw from the inside pocket of his jacket and used it to take a snort. After a moment, he said, "I like it," his voice sounding almost wistful.

Barry's lip curled, despite himself. Of course, Gonzalo's quick snort wasn't his only assurance of purity. His real quality control consisted in his willingness to kill people.

"Give him the money," he said.

One of the bodyguards bent to move a small case to the edge of the platform. Barry popped the clasps and opened the lid to reveal two rows of hundred-dollar bills, bundled together in stacks of fifty. Gonzalo remained crouched over his two kilos of merchandise, watching Barry as he counted the stacks. There were twenty-four, making the total one hundred twenty big ones, as agreed. Barry, glancing at Gonzalo, attempted a smile. "Affection beaming out of one eye, calculation shining out of the other," he said as he lifted out one of the stacks to count it. "No offense intended."

"None taken, my friend."

There were fifty bills in the stack, and all of them were hundreds. After replacing the stack in the attaché case, Barry closed the case and stepped back with it.

"A pleasure, as always," he said.

Gonzalo stood. "Ah, my friend."

A car started up not far away.

"Son of a bitch." Feeling a surge of panic, Barry tossed the case with the money through his open door into the passenger seat and swung down into the car, cracking his head on the door-frame in his hurry. The not-so-distant car was approaching fast. His foot was on the accelerator as he turned the key in the ignition, and the big five-point-seven liter engine roared in response.

Too late. A police car turned in behind him, blocking him in. Barry's first instinct was for the gas, but, even as the big car surged backwards, his foot jumped of its own accord to the brake. The Corvette jerked to a stop, throwing his head into the headrest.

Barry stayed where he was for a moment, breathing deeply, then he got out of the car, his hands high and empty. Above him, Gonzalo's hands were already cuffed in front of him. The pistols of the two bodyguards were trained on Barry's forehead.

Uniformed policemen got out of the car behind Barry. They too had pistols drawn.

Gonzalo said, "Sorry, man, I had to deal."

Barry's lip curled. Cross within cross: He had been outdone. "Well, you got me," he said conversationally.

"You have the right to remain silent," one of the uniformed cops said, fumbling for his Miranda card.

Turning his head, Barry saw his brown package still on the loading dock and the scattered powder.

The cop told him about his right to an attorney.

"This is funnier than it looks," Barry said.

"Yeah?" the cop said. "What's funny?" He'd read Barry his rights. Now he was ready to talk.

Barry merely smiled in response.

Chapter 43

Tracey had packed everything but food. It didn't mean they had to go hungry, but what they were eating had been left behind by others. There was a little cheese, rimmed with a white mold that Alan trimmed off with his pocket knife. To drink there was wine. Alan, who hadn't had a glass of wine in five years, found that the astringent taste puckered his mouth.

They ate sitting on a twin-sized mattress, their food between them. The CDs in the shed were all Beethoven. Alone in the middle of hundreds of acres, connected to civilization by a single power line, Alan and Tracey sipped Chablis and ate cheese and stale crackers while listening to the Eroica Symphony.

They finished the cheese, and Alan was refilling their paper cups from the wine bottle when Tracey leaned forward and said, "Kiss me."

His heart went into double time. Tracey waited, eyes closed. After a moment's reflection he leaned forward to peck her on the mouth.

Her eyes opened, and she licked her lips reflectively. "Okay, at least we've got that out of the way," she said.

"Got what out of the way?"

"Our first kiss."

"We've kissed before." He was aware of his pulse as he handed her a cup.

"Not recently."

"No, not recently."

"Things have been pretty strained between us since we got back together."

He started to nod, then stopped himself. Back together?

Tracey eyed him critically. "For you to be any more restrained, you'd have to be wearing a straitjacket," she said.

He looked at her over the edge of his cup and snorted suddenly, spraying the back of his hand liberally with wine. He began to giggle.

Tracey picked up the wine bottle and looked at the label. "I've heard about people like you," she said.

"Like me how?"

"People who get giddy on cough syrup."

"I'm not giddy." But he was. Not from the wine so much as from the sudden release of pent-up stress that until now he hadn't realized he was under. They were back together, and he was okay with that.

"If you say so," Tracey said.

On impulse he leaned toward her again and kissed her cheek, finding it surprisingly soft, almost like a baby's. "Okay?" he said.

She smiled. "Much better," she said.

"You have nice teeth."

She laughed. "I'll have to get you drunk more often."

"I'm not drunk. I've barely had enough wine to wash down these crackers." He kissed her cheek again. It was warm against his cold nose.

She pushed him back. "Okay, that's enough."

"You told me to kiss you."

"I told you once."

"But if we're back together, that suggests more than once. That suggests whenever the mood strikes," he said.

She grabbed his head and held it. The kiss this time had more voltage. As they eased to their sides on the mattress, still locked at the lip, he managed to get the cups and the crackers out of the way, rolling his eyes to see what he was doing. He slipped an arm beneath her, marveling at how fragile she felt — so delicate that her ribs might crack if he squeezed too hard.

Her mouth was touching all over his face: his mouth, his neck, the cartilage of his ear. Then she was above him, kissing and wriggling like a puppy. Her arms went beneath him, and, tucking her face into the base of his neck, she hugged him to her with unexpected strength.

"Just hold me," she breathed, her breath hot on his neck. His arms broke out in goose flesh.

He held her and stroked her hair, and she relaxed slowly against him. When she had been still for several minutes, and he was thinking about what came next, there was a subtle change in her breathing.

"Tracey?" he said softly.

She didn't answer. Her breathing deepened. Her body was completely slack on top of his.

He found it touching. He lay on his back with one arm about her rib cage, his other hand cupping the back of her head. Then he rolled to one side and settled her on the mattress, tucking a pillow beneath her head. The shed was silent, the Beethoven disc having run its course. Her face was soft and innocent in repose.

He switched off the light and lay back, fully clothed, on the other mattress. For a long time his own eyes remained open.

Chapter 44

At seven o'clock the next morning, a deputy sheriff came for Barry and escorted him from his cell to a room furnished with a long wooden table, dented and scarred from hard use, and two heavy wooden chairs that had been similarly abused. There was no one in the room, and when his jailer turned to leave it, Barry said, "What is this crap? I'm supposed to be taken before a magistrate. I should have been taken last night."

"Good for you." The deputy sheriff closed the door on him. Keys jangled briefly, and a deadbolt shot home.

About thirty minutes later, a key sounded again in the lock. The door opened, and a man in uniform entered. He pushed the door shut behind him and pulled the room's remaining chair out from the table.

"You're Barry Royal."

"No. I stole Barry Royal's wallet and had my face superimposed over his on the driver's license."

"And the Sam's Club card," the cop said.

Barry's mouth twitched. "And the Sam's Club card," he conceded. "Though that picture really could be Michael Keaton in *Beetlejuice*, don't you think?"

"My name is Curtis. I'd like you to tell me what you thought you were doing last night. Whoever you are." He smiled, and his teeth gleamed in the fluorescent lighting.

"Shouldn't you be reading me my rights? Or aren't we having this conversation?"

"Are you going to answer the question?"

"About last night? What do you think I was doing?"

"Selling two kilos of cocaine to one Gonzalo Gutierrez."

"Is that really what you think I was doing?"

"Maybe not. Will you concede you were selling something?"

"Sure. I was selling about five pounds of baking powder and powered aspirin in roughly equal amounts."

"You charge a lot for baking powder and aspirin."

Barry grinned. "What can I say?"

"You included the aspirin, I suppose, for its analgesic properties. A little something to numb Gonzalo's nose. But what was the point? Once he found out what you'd done to him, he'd have had to kill you. Unless you killed him first, of course."

"You watch too much TV."

"He's killed people before."

"Can you prove it?"

"Maybe not."

"I never said the package contained cocaine, you know. Last night we were just calling it *stuff*. Gonzalo, I think, was calling it *good stuff*."

"You did tell the arresting officers, 'You got me.' A judge might take that as a confession."

"A confession of what?"

Curtis inclined his head. "Good point. What about the firearm in your glove box? That's a Class A misdemeanor — up to three thousand dollars and a year in jail. You don't have a carry permit."

"I was traveling." It was, under Texas law, a legitimate reason for having a pistol in your glove box.

"Traveling where?" Curtis asked.

"Big D. On my way out of town, I was dropping off some baking powder and aspirin for Gonzalo." He turned his hands palms up. "God knows what he uses the stuff for."

"What were you going to do in Dallas?"

Barry smiled disingenuously. "Hang out. Eat."

"Have a reservation some place?"

"No."

"You think a jury would buy that?"

"I guess we're both gonna find that out."

Curtis shrugged. "It's not my decision. I am curious, though: Did something happen to your source of cocaine, or did you plan to cheat Gonzalo all along?"

"I don't know what you're talking about."

"Gonzalo swears his first two buys from you were the real stuff."

"Gonzalo doesn't know what planet he's on." Barry lowered his voice to a confidential level. "I have a strong suspicion that Gonzalo makes a practice of ingesting mind-altering substances of various types. Not all of them legal." He nodded significantly.

Curtis said, "He says your father was part of the deal."

"My father?"

"Was he?"

"You must think I'm an idiot."

"And Carlotta Basoalto, your father's houseguest, was out of the country last week."

"Ooh, his houseguest spent a week abroad. The man's a felon." Barry understood Curtis's point, though. The cops knew all about the smuggling operation, either knew positively or suspected. "Was she carrying a firearm, too?" Barry asked.

"Gonzalo rolled over too late for us to meet the plane, but we know she was in Colombia. She gets back from Colombia; the next night she's killed."

"Ironic, isn't it? A violent place like Columbia and she's safe enough. As soon as she re-enters the good old U.S. of A..."

"Go figure," Curtis said dryly.

"You're not suggesting her murder had anything to do with her trip to Columbia?"

"It might have left you without cocaine to peddle."

Barry sat back in his chair. "We're back on that again."

"We never left it."

"Look, are you taking me before a magistrate or aren't you? As much as I've enjoyed this little *tête-à-tête*, I have to tell you I've got better things to do than sit around and listen to you blow smoke."

"It's not you we're after. You know that, don't you? Tracey Coleman killed Carlotta Basoalto, and we want to nail her for it."

"So nail her."

"We think she killed Carlotta in a dispute over two kilos of cocaine. What do you think?"

"I don't think."

"If I'm right, Tracey Coleman ripped you off, and she murdered your accomplice."

"So far all you've established is that Carlotta Basoalto was my father's houseguest."

"I don't see why you're protecting Tracey Coleman."

"You're not listening to me. I don't know nothing about nothing."

Curtis shook his head. "Okay," he said, standing. "We'll play it your way."

"Damn straight. It's time to cut me loose or let me call my lawyer."

"Or take you outside and shoot you in the back of the head." Curtis smiled, which silenced Barry.

On that note, Curtis left the room.

Chapter 45

When Alan opened his eyes that morning, he found himself staring up at an unpainted plywood ceiling, and it took a moment for him to remember where he was. Memory flooded back, and he turned his head toward Tracey's mattress. It was empty.

"Tracey?" He ran his fingers through his hair as he got up. He pushed the plywood door open against the spring, and cold air gusted in on him. Arms folded across his chest, he stepped outside, blinking in the sunlight. The door closed behind him with a clap.

There was a fire burning about fifty feet from the cabin. Tracey sat in a lawn chair next to it, reading a book. A big, black pot hung from a frame over the fire, yellow flames licking at it, and a soot-stained kettle sat on a rock just inside the flames.

"You're up," Tracey said, closing the book on her finger. It was a dog-eared, paperback edition of Louis L'Amour's *Bowdrie*. "We keep several dozen of these out here," she said, holding up the book. "I reread one every time I come. It's part of the flavor of the place."

He nodded, shivering and squinting in the sunshine. Steam rose off the pot. Inside bacon sizzled, and its aroma permeated the air.

"There's that for your morning constitutional. Grab you a paperback from the cabin and head on out aways." The *that* she referred to was a toilet seat mounted on a wooden frame. A roll of toilet paper sat on a wooden dowel poking up from the back of it.

He had to go back inside to get his travel kit. When he came back out, Tracey had returned to her book.

"What's in the water kettle?"

She looked up. "Water. I got it from the stream down that way. There's more in the jug there."

"Is it potable?"

"It's not too heavy."

"I meant..."

She smiled. "I know what you meant. No one's gotten sick from it yet."

"You never told me there was water to drink. You said all there was was wine."

She smiled faintly, her eyes on her novel. Sighing, he looked at the ungainly contraption with the toilet seat and, shrugging, hefted it with one arm and carried it off into the brush.

When he got back, she was chopping an onion into the black pot. Two potatoes were cradled in her lap, each sprouting several feet of pale stem. On a nearby plate, bacon lay in a tangled mass, glinting in the sun. She finished with the onion, broke off the stems sprouting from the potatoes, and sliced the potatoes into the pot.

"I'm going to fry these in the bacon grease. I think the water's hot enough for us to have coffee while we wait." She swung the arm holding the pot back over the fire. "It's instant, I'm afraid."

The temperature, beyond the fire, was crisp and cold, and never had he tasted anything as good as that instant coffee. He worked a piece of bacon loose from the pile as he sipped it.

"There was a pound of it up in the freezer compartment of the little refrigerator," Tracey said, watching him consume the bacon in two bites. "The onion and potatoes are a little old ... You don't seem to be saying much. I had the impression you were more of a morning person."

He chased the bacon with a gulp of coffee and grinned at her. "I guess I'm not much of a camping person. I don't think I've been camping more than a couple times in my life."

"Where did you grow up?"

"Philadelphia. There was just Mom and me, and Mom's not the camping type."

"I forgot. Your dad wasn't around much."

"My dad wasn't around."

"How'd you end up in Tyler? Why not a high-octane practice in Dallas — or New York or Chicago for that matter? Isn't Yale in Connecticut?"

He gave her a crooked grin. "I was in love with a girl."

"You came to Tyler for love? I never knew that. What was her name?"

"Emily."

"And?" Tracey said.

"And what?"

"Tell me about her. What did she look like?"

"She was a lawyer. She..." He hesitated. "Actually, she looked a lot like you."

"Like me?"

He shrugged.

"So what happened?"

"Nothing. She moved away. I think she's in Phoenix now."

"And you're stuck in a backwater like Tyler."

"I don't know. The commute's short."

When they had eaten, they tossed their paper plates and napkins onto the fire and watched them burn.

"I'm glad we came," Alan said. "I needed this." He was kneeling by the fire, poking the logs about with a long stick.

"Me, too."

He thought of the jail cell and looked up to meet her eyes. "I bet," he said.

"Wait here. Let's have a little fun." She disappeared into the shed and came back with a big revolver and a box of ammunition. "This is a .45. It's a little more gun than I'm used to, but it's all right. My favorite is the Walther you've got back at your house."

"It's in my car."

"It is?"

"Back under the driver's seat. Do you have targets?"

"No, but there're some sticks poking up out there we can put empty soda cans on. There's a sack of them in the lean-to. Get it, will you?"

He did, and they walked out into the brush. Fifteen yards or so beyond the fire they found five sticks, three standing up and two leaning over. Alan righted the two that needed it, working them into the ground, and Tracey slipped the cans onto the ends. Then they walked back to the fire.

"You first," she said, pushing the cartridges into the cylinder and rotating the cylinder back into place. "It's got double-action, so you can just pull the trigger."

He took the gun from her. It was a Smith and Wesson with a rubberized grip. He pointed the gun at the Dr. Pepper can on the far left. At fifteen yards, the can did not seem very big, little more than a glint amid the tall brown grass.

"It would be better if we had a target," she said. "If you miss the can, you're not going to have any idea whether you're shooting high and left, or low and right, or what."

He squeezed the trigger. The gun kicked in his hand, and the explosion deafened him. The can didn't move.

Tracey said, "We really could use ear protection. I saw a ripple in the grass. I think maybe you're low."

He clenched his teeth and fired again.

"Still low." After his third shot, she said, "You're still not hitting it. Try left a little."

His ears ringing, he fired three more shots. He handed the gun to Tracey, and they walked out to inspect the damage. There were two holes in the Dr. Pepper can, opposite each other.

"I think you got it on that fourth shot," Tracey said. "I thought I saw it spin a little."

He himself hadn't seen a thing. They walked back, Tracey shucking the empty casings and reloading. She turned toward the targets. As she raised the gun, Alan backed hastily away.

She looked apologetic. "We really do need ear protection." She fired the gun twice. He saw the Dr. Pepper can jump and fall to the ground. The next four shots were spaced about a second apart.

The Dr. Pepper can, lying on the ground, had been torn nearly in two. The other four cans all had holes in them.

"You're good," he said.

She grinned, clearly pleased with herself. She dumped the spent cartridges and replaced them with fresh ones. "Point at something," she said.

"Huh?"

"Anything. Point at something, and I'll hit it."

His eyes scanned the area. He pointed. "See that squirrel over there? About halfway up that tree by the shed." The tree was perhaps a hundred feet away, more than twice the range of their target practice, and its gray bark was approximately the same color as the squirrel.

"I see it," she said. "Halfway up, head down."

He jumped as the gun went off, and the squirrel dropped from the tree. He felt a little sick as they walked toward it. A smear of blood marked the tree where the squirrel had been, a hole in the midst of the smear where the bullet had entered the tree. The squirrel at the base of the tree was a bloody carcass.

Tracey turned it with the toe of her shoe.

"Don't do that," he said, and she looked up, surprised. "I feel bad about this all of a sudden," he said.

"You don't hunt?"

He shook his head. He'd never killed anything.

"There's a lot you don't do," Tracey told him. "I wonder sometimes whether I'd be attracted to you if you weren't such a fox."

When they finished hauling his car out of the mud, it was just nine o'clock. They took the four-wheeler out again, taking a more leisurely tour of the land than they had the night before. The trees and the high brush limited visibility less than the uneven terrain. They splashed through two different creeks, each more than once. Everywhere were the signs of oil extraction: pumps and tanks and pipes laid along the ground. In some places the trees thinned unexpectedly, and they rode through yellow grass as high as their shoulders. They saw two deer, one of them a doe that stood frozen for a moment before turning to make an elegant leap over a deadfall and disappear into the trees.

They ended up at the outcropping of rock that rose above the river. The white clapboard farmhouse looked tiny and far away, but the sight of it transported Alan backward in time to the world of

John Steinbeck, to pickups with narrow truck beds and union suits hanging among the clothes on the clothesline.

He looked down at Tracey and was startled to find her looking not at the scenery but at him.

"What are you thinking?" she asked.

He shook his head. "Nothing." He sighed, looking out again over the river.

From where they were, they could hear the faint ripple of moving water and the raucous caw of a mockingbird in the trees behind them. After several minutes of listening to the relative quiet, Tracey said, "So what's wrong?"

"How did you get involved in all this?"

"Carlotta's murder?"

"No. The murder weapon was registered to you. That's really the only connection. That and your being in the same place at the same time."

"Along with a couple hundred other people," Tracey said.

"I mean the smuggling thing."

"I told you about that."

"You didn't tell me why."

She didn't answer immediately, and he darted a glance at her. Her eyes were on the river below them.

"Excitement," she said finally. "Mom died when I was twelve. For a long time after that I felt dead myself. Then came you. I was alive again. The romance, the secrecy, the illicitness seemed to give me the spark I needed. This smuggling lark was kind of the same. I was in Mexico City when Carlotta broached the idea, and I just couldn't resist it." She met his eyes and gave him an uncertain smile. "I know, it sounds really stupid."

He shook his head.

"It had everything the affair with you had. Except sex, of course."

Their time was running out. After a few minutes of silence, he said, "We've got to go."

"Yeah, I know." But they both felt strangely reluctant, and they continued to sit.

"Can you keep me out of jail?" she asked him.

"I don't know," he said. "We'll find out."

Chapter 46

Lieutenant Curtis and Cale Larson were in the prosecutor's office, Curtis standing, Larson sitting back in his antique swivel-chair. "So what are you telling me?" Larson said. "Are you telling me I've got nothing?"

"We can put Carlotta and Tracey in Mexico City together the week of the murder. We can show that they came back together, but separated at the airport, Carlotta making the connecting flight, Tracey renting a car."

"Even though she also had a ticket on the connecting flight."

"Even though she also had a ticket. We think they entered the country with a large quantity of cocaine, but it's pure speculation at this point. You'll have to tell me if it's something you want to take before a judge."

Larson's lip curled. "Not ideally, no."

"You've got the prior drug arrest."

"The prior's not diddly-squat. To win this bail hearing, I need some kind of ongoing criminal activity, and right now I haven't even got a motive for the murder."

"You've got the rings."

"And a boyfriend who's almost positive she had them on that night."

"They haven't turned up on Carlotta's beside table or her bathroom counter or anything."

"They weren't found in Tracey Coleman's possession, either. I don't think I've made it past reasonable doubt, do you?" Larson sat drumming his fingers on the desktop. He didn't have any doubts himself, but he was a good enough lawyer to know that there was a difference between what he believed and what he could sell to a judge.

Curtis turned to go.

"Damn it to hell," Larson said behind him.

Larson was already in the courtroom when Alan and Tracey got there. He was sitting slumped behind one of the tables, watching the doorway over tented fingers, and as they came in, he gave them a nod. They crossed to the defense table without responding.

"I hoped you could make it," Larson said sardonically.

The bailiff called the court into session as the judge entered the courtroom. Alan and Larson and Tracey Coleman all stood up. The judge sat down. The courtroom was empty, and Alan wondered at the absence of reporters. Larson was a notorious publicity hound.

"Mr. Larson," the judge said. "We're here to consider your application for denial of bail. If you have an opening statement, I would like it to be brief. State the facts on which you feel I should base my denial, and name the witnesses you propose to call to prove each fact. Understood?"

Larson nodded. "Thank you, your honor." He paused. "Actually, your honor, one of the witnesses the state expected to call has failed to materialize. One of the key witnesses."

"Who?"

"While we feel that fifty thousand dollars is ridiculously low for a capital crime, we find ourselves unable to pursue our application for denial of bail at this time."

Judge Mitchell studied him.

"For the reasons I've stated, the state respectfully withdraws its application," Larson said.

Judge Mitchell frowned at him. He started to say something, then shrugged and looked toward the defense table. "Any objection?"

The obvious answer was no, perhaps a mere shake of the head, but, on the other hand, Larson was in retreat. If Alan pressed his advantage, he might learn something useful. He stood.

"Your honor, I'm grateful that the state has elected not to pursue a groundless application, but it looks as if the state never intended to pursue it. The defense's preparation for trial on the merits of the case has been sidetracked for two days."

"It also makes you wonder about the basis for upgrading the charge to a capital crime," the judge said.

Larson said, "Your honor, the grand jury...," but Mitchell raised a hand to silence him.

"I know. Beyond the authority of this court."

Alan said, "Your honor, the prosecution is under some obligation to explain this maneuvering. Who is this key witness the prosecution planned to present, and how long did the state know it wouldn't proceed with today's hearing?"

"Mr. Larson?"

"The state is not obligated to provide the defense with an account of its continuing investigation or of its developing strategy," Larson said.

Alan said, "A person's life is at stake here. This is not an appropriate forum for posturing or for anything else not related to the merits of the case. We want to know the name of that witness."

"You get the witnesses I call, not the ones I decide not to."

"Two days ago—"

But the judge banged his gavel to cut them off. He leaned forward to peer at them through his thick lenses. "Play fair, boys, can't you?"

When neither said anything, he banged his gavel again and rose from behind his bench.

Chapter 47

"That was kind of a letdown," Tracey said.

He glanced at her, then turned his attention back to the road as the light ahead changed and the car ahead of him hit its brakes. "We won," he said.

"By default."

"Yeah. It's not the same, is it?"

She didn't say anything, and they drove in silence until he turned the car into the alley that led to his driveway.

"So what's next?" Tracey asked.

"For me, not much."

"What are you talking about?"

He pulled into the garage and looked over at her. "I don't guess anybody's told you about Ken Whitaker."

"Who?"

He sighed. "In a week or so, a lawyer named Ken Whitaker will be here to take over your case. He's a specialist in criminal defense. My firm's bringing him in."

"What about you?"

"I'll be helping him out."

She looked utterly exasperated. "That's horse-crap," she said.

"Maybe. On the other hand, I've never handled a criminal jury trial, never done any criminal defense work except for working on an appellate brief a couple of years ago. The firm didn't think a capital murder case was the place for me to start."

"Don't I have anything to say about this?"

"Theoretically, yes. You're the client."

"But practically?"

"The firm can't control you, but it can control me. If I'm going to work on your case, it can dictate the terms."

She was silent, her mouth compressed in a grim line. Then she got out of the car.

"That sucks," she said as she banged the car door shut.

She went into the house, banging that door, too.

He found her in the living room, sitting rigidly on the sofa. "Are you all right?"

She looked up at him and blew at the strand of hair that hung in front of her flushed face. "Daddy had something to do with this, didn't he?"

"Only indirectly. If you're convicted, Jim Angley's expecting him to sue us for malpractice."

"So he didn't have anything to do with selecting Whitaker specifically."

Alan shook his head.

"So tell me about him," she said. "Is he any good?"

"He's got a reputation."

Tracey rolled her eyes. Alan glanced at his watch. It was ten minutes to five.

"Do you mind if I make a quick call?" he asked.

She got up and stomped back to her bedroom. The door slammed, and he fished out his iPhone. Steve Booker's cell was on his speed-dial.

"Alan!"

"Hey, Steve. Do you have a minute? I have a question for you."

"Shoot."

"In a hypothetical case, could a bank examiner come up with a list of banks where a given person has loans?"

"A bank examiner like me, for instance?"

"For instance."

"A given person like..."

"Hugh Royal, or one of his corporations."

"Are we ignoring what's legal for the moment?"

"Yes, for the moment."

"Then the answer is maybe. Among the work papers we have on each bank we examine, we have a card on each of the big loans."

"What constitutes a big loan?"

"It depends on the size of the bank."

"Could you check them for me?"

"Hypothetically, you mean?"

Alan was silent.

"What good's it going to do you anyway?" Steve said. "Are you in a position to subpoena bank records?"

"No."

"Then we might as well put the legalities back into the equation, don't you think?"

Alan sighed. "I guess."

"You sound depressed."

"It was just a wild hare. I guess I'm getting desperate."

"Aren't we all," Steve said.

Chapter 48

The walls of Hugh Royal's study were paneled in oak, and six rifles hung on the gun rack behind his desk. Across from it, beneath a twelve-foot ceiling, the head of a deer with an eight-point rack loomed over the doorway. Hugh had shot the buck himself when it wandered into his camp twenty years before.

Though he had the pretensions of an inveterate sportsman, the work he did in his study consisted primarily of receipts and ledgers, of credits and debits. He had an accountant's compulsion to order. At the moment, his desk was clear but for a small antique globe on one corner and a single enameled pen just to the right of center.

Standing behind his desk, Hugh glared across it at his son, Barry, who had been released from police custody scant hours before. "Do you realize," Hugh asked him, "that Luis Basoalto has informants in the police department? If he finds out that a member of my family has been arrested for peddling cocaine — cocaine he knows nothing about — he is going to be pretty damn pissed."

"It wasn't cocaine."

"And we can't afford to get Luis pissed at us," Hugh said. "That could be fatal."

"It wasn't cocaine, and no charges were filed."

"An arrest was made."

"And I was released because I wasn't selling cocaine."

Hugh dropped down into the high-backed chair, which was upholstered in oxblood leather. "You put all of us in danger, most obviously from Gonzalo. We don't have to deal with him now, of course, but Luis is still a concern."

"Who could have known Gonzalo'd turned stool-pigeon? That's what would have destroyed us if we'd actually had cocaine to peddle. As it was, we found out about it fairly painlessly."

"What the hell did you think you were doing anyway? Gonzalo would have killed you, if he didn't kill Tony or me first."

Barry shrugged. "Making a score."

"Making yourself a hundred-twenty big ones," Tony said, sitting with his chair tipped back against the wall by the door. Barry turned to glare at him.

"Is that what this is all about?" he said, turning back to his father. "You think I was going to stiff you?"

"You were going to get us killed," Tony said.

Hugh said, "You were starting a turf war in Luis Basoalto's back yard, Barry."

"Gonzalo would've been dead before anybody knew," Barry said. "He's a user. He's falling apart, and his organization is falling apart with him. Mr. B would hardly notice if someone put a bullet in his head."

"Who was going to do that?" Hugh asked. "You?"

"It doesn't matter now. The police got to him first."

Hugh sat looking at him.

"I wanted to come to you with a fait accompli, okay? You've made a lot of money as Mr. B's bookkeeper, but you always wanted to be a player yourself. My idea was that we'd take Gonzalo's money, kill him, and take over his organization. Mr.

B would have accepted it. He'd see Gonzalo needed to be replaced."

"It was risky."

"No more risky than the original plan involving two kilos of actual cocaine. Less risky than trying to build an organization from the ground up. Trying to do that has involved you with every two-bit hood in Tyler."

Hugh pushed himself out of his chair, paced to the wall, and turned. "Ah, you may be right."

"Except for Carlotta," Tony said. "Now we can't afford to have anything to do with drugs or smuggling or anything else illegal. Mr. B finds out we were working his daughter..."

Barry twisted in his chair. "You shut up."

"Tony's part of this," Hugh said.

Barry heaved himself out of his chair. "Fine," he said.

"Sit down. We're not done yet."

"I think we are. I've explained what I was doing, and you've made your point." He headed for the door.

"Barry!"

Barry stopped in the doorway.

"We need to stay clean, okay?"

Barry gave him a curt nod and went out.

Chapter 49

On Friday morning, Alan had breakfast at The Greasy Spoon, a restaurant that had opened during World War II and still served breakfast and lunch in an atmosphere in which the faint smell of stale cigarette smoke still mingled with cooking odors years after smoking had been made illegal. He had finished eating and was sipping his orange juice as he read through the *Rules of Criminal Evidence* for the fourth or fifth time, paying special attention to the associated commentary.

"Alan?"

He looked up. "Jordan?" She was dressed for the office, wearing a tailored, navy dress with a white collar. As always, since Tracey had come back into his life, he felt a twinge of guilt on seeing her.

She smiled. "Do you doubt the evidence of your own eyes?"

"No, I —"

"May I sit down, or are you expecting someone?" The waitress set a heavy porcelain mug in front of her and filled it with steaming coffee while she stood there. At the Greasy Spoon, those who didn't want coffee with their breakfast had to speak up fast.

"No, sit, please," Alan said. "It's been a while since I've seen you to talk to."

"Yes." She slipped into the chair across from him.

"I've missed it."

"Me, too." She nodded toward his *Rules*. "How's it going?"

"So far she's staying out of jail. Ken Whitaker's supposed to show up some time next week, and then I'm mostly out of it."

"Except that Tracey's living with you."

His heart stopped.

The waitress came back, and Jordan ordered the special — bacon, eggs, toast, and coffee. Alan's heart started beating again.

"We're not..." He realized that denial was pointless. "Oh, hell."

"Not sleeping together?" Jordan sipped her coffee.

"For what it's worth," he said.

He pulled out of the parking lot and followed Jordan's Mustang to the parking garage across from the office. She seemed to know what was going on in his house as well as if she were living there herself. More incomprehensible to him was that she was still speaking to him. "Women," he muttered as he killed his engine.

Jordan's legs flashed as she got out of her car. She smiled brilliantly at him, and he grimaced in return. They crossed the street together. On the elevator, it was just the two of them. Jordan laughed suddenly and punched his arm. "Poor Alan," she said.

He raised his eyebrows, but she only laughed and shook her head.

He spent the morning on Tracey's case, ignoring his other cases as far as he could. At one o'clock he had a docket call in the first RICO case he had ever filed, so after lunch he walked down the block to the courthouse to announce ready for trial. Congress had passed RICO in an effort to weaken organized crime, but Alan was suing a small bank in Mount Pleasant rather than a criminal syndicate. If he won, the RICO statute would give him triple damages and attorney fees, and a simple fraud claim would give him neither.

"We'd like a continuance," the lawyer for the bank said.

"I can see by the docket number you're entitled," said the judge, and Alan carried the folder back to his office and gave it to the office manager to enter the new date into the master schedule.

At about three o'clock, he called home, and Tracey answered.

"How'd you like to go roller-skating tonight?" he asked.

There was a pause. "What kind of date is roller skating?" she asked.

"It's not a date exactly."

"What is it?"

"Hugh Royal owns the rink."

"And?"

"It might be important."

"Important how?"

"No idea."

She was silent a moment. "Good thing you're not in sales," she said.

"Does that mean you don't want to go?"

"Oh, I want to go all right. What time are you coming home?"

Chapter 50

Only about a score of cars were on Skateworld's lot, all clustered as close to the building as the handicapped parking spaces would allow. Alan didn't know how many disabled people went skating on a given night, but to judge by the number of spaces, Skateworld expected at least a dozen.

Alan parked, and he and Tracey got out.

"So what is it we're going to do?" she said as they walked through the cold mist toward the door. She had her fingers pushed as far as they would go into the pockets of jeans that fit her slender thighs like sausage skins.

"I don't know about you," he said. "I'm planning to get my heart rate up into my target range, and keep it there for twenty minutes."

"High expectations," she said.

The rink was a cavernous warehouse of a building with yellow cinderblock walls. The music was loud and sassy, young black voices chanting to a hip-hop beat.

"I thought rap was as dead as disco," he said as they stood in line to get their skates, speaking loudly to be heard over the pounding music.

"As what?"

He raised his voice. "I guess I'm showing my age."

"You probably expected Gregorian chants," she said.

He shook his head. "Too new-fangled."

They sat on the carpet-covered blocks outside the rail to put their skates on. Alan shouted, "Everyone's so young." The music throbbed in his head like a rotten tooth. At some point in the last decade, he and popular music seemed to have parted ways.

"You look like you're in pain," Tracey yelled in his ear.

"What happened to Gloria Estefan and Paula Abdul?"

"Who?" She grinned and punched his arm. "I'm kidding. Come on, Grandpa."

He felt more natural on the skates than he had expected to, and he found the beat of the music less irritating when he was moving to it. A tall, skinny kid whizzed by him, crouching, one pole-like leg extended in front of him. A boy and a girl went by in a clutch, the girl skating backwards with her eyes closed and a spaced-out expression on her round, pimpled face. Alan was the oldest skater on the rink by a full decade.

He skated faster, making the turn smoothly, picking up speed on the straightaway. Tracey came up behind him and caught his hand. "Don't try so hard. What have you got to prove?"

"Someone once told me ... a man hits middle-age in his early thirties. I never really believed it until now."

"What?"

"I could come out here every night for a year; I'd never skate like that." He pointed.

"He's probably been out here every night for a year." She dropped his hand and turned to skate backwards into the turn, her slim legs working.

Fifteen minutes later, a buzzer sounded and suddenly everybody was coming back at him. Alan looked around wildly for an explanation, dodging skaters and trying to make his way to the rail.

On the wall, a sign blinked, "Reverse."

He slammed into the rail and clutched at it.

At nine-thirty, there were still no more than fifty skaters in the building, roughly half of them skating and the other half eating and talking and going in and out of the restrooms. If it had cost each of them eight-fifty for admission and skate rental, then that was fifty skaters times eight-fifty . . . Four hundred twenty-five dollars. If they got that every night of the year, they might gross one hundred fifty thousand dollars or so. Plus the concessions.

"And this is Friday night," Alan told Tracey. "You've got to figure this is one of their big nights."

"One of them. Tuesday night is half-price night, though, and Wednesday night is skating-to-the-oldies. You know — Gloria Estefan and Paula Abdul."

"But half-price doesn't help. If it makes Tuesday night as busy as Friday night, it's still half the revenue."

Later, when they were getting slices of pizza at the snack bar, Alan said to the man behind the counter, "Not many people here for a Friday night."

The man shrugged. He was middle-aged with dark hair, a mustache, and a layer of fat that softened his features.

"Saturday much busier?" Alan asked.

His question garnered him a sour expression as the man handed over their Cokes. "Help you?" he said to the kid behind them.

Alan moved on. According to the schedule by the door, the rink was closed on Mondays. Subtract fifty-two days' worth of revenues.

SupeRink controlled nineteen rinks, two of them through TyleRink. Hugh could not possibly be skimming cash. If Hugh skimmed anything, then the remaining revenues, meager enough to begin with, would be insufficient even to cover overhead and expenses, much less a salary in the high six-figures for Hugh and dividends for his majority shareholder.

It had begun to rain. On the drive back, Tracey sat with her back against the passenger door, her gaze alternating between Alan and the wet road. "So where are we going now?" she asked.

"I don't know."

"You seem depressed."

"Not really. I'm just kind of lost." He turned onto Rosemont and stopped the car.

"Where are we? Isn't this Hugh Royal's house?"

He looked up the sloping lawn at the big, two-story colonial. "Yeah."

"Are we ... here for a visit?" she asked.

He shook his head, but continued to stare at the house.

"What were you hoping to discover at Skateworld anyway?"

"Evidence of criminal activity."

"A lot of under-age smoking going on in the women's room."

He nodded, and she reached across the car to pat his leg. "Cheer up. You'll come up with something."

"What makes you say that?"

"A desire to cheer you up."

He laughed. "That's not what you're supposed to say. You're supposed to say, 'You always —'" He jumped as a tap sounded on the window beside him. A bulky figure crouched beside his car, the light from a distant streetlamp glinting from a wet slicker.

"Open that window," a voice said. "I want to see some ID." The man shone his flashlight into the car, illuminating his face, then Tracey's, then the backseat.

Alan lowered his window about an inch, his heart pounding. "I'd like to see some myself," he said.

The man pressed a badge against the glass: Tyler Police Department.

Alan fished his driver's license out of his billfold and handed it out.

"Alan Dougherty," the man read, shining a flashlight on the license. "You live around here, Mr. Dougherty?"

"No."

"What are you doing here?"

"I was about to kiss a girl."

"You're going to have to pucker up to reach her there on the other side of the car. What is it you do for a living, Mr. Dougherty?"

"I'm a lawyer."

The light returned to his face. "A lawyer," the cop repeated.

"That's right. Do you have probable cause to search the car? Perhaps you'd like to conduct a *Terry* frisk." He released the doorlatch, intending to get out, but the cop pushed the door shut again with his hip.

"I don't want to frisk you, counselor. Why don't you just move along?"

Alan put the car in gear and pulled away from the curb.

"What was that about, do you think?" Tracey asked him.

"I don't know. Either an off-duty cop doing security for Hugh Royal..."

"Why would —"

"I don't know. Or else the police are keeping an eye on Hugh's house for some reason."

She chewed at her lower lip. "You think Hugh's a suspect in Carlotta's death, as well as me?"

"I wouldn't think so. Once the police have made their arrest, they're not likely to go looking for evidence that might implicate other people."

"Then why would the police be watching his house?"

He shook his head. "Maybe he is just providing security."

"Can cops do things like that when they're off-duty?"

"I think so."

Chapter 51

Ken Whitaker arrived in Tyler on Sunday. He called Alan to ask him to meet him at his hotel that evening to start going over Tracey's case. The trial was set to begin the week after Thanksgiving, three weeks from Monday.

"What's your room number?" Alan asked Ken.

"Oh, hell. Hotel rooms are so damn depressing. How about just meeting at the bar in the lobby? Say eight o'clock?"

So at eight Alan parked his car in front of the Sheraton. The lobby was a huge, glass-ceilinged atrium with marble walkways running between palm trees and fern beds, sage and agave and Texas milkweed. Immediately inside the lobby were the cashier and registration desk. The bar was halfway back, almost lost in the foliage, a gleaming square of brass and polished wood ringed with high stools.

Ken Whitaker raised a hand as Alan approached. He was a big man with snow-white hair, a florid complexion, and a booming voice. "Alan! Good to see you again."

"Hi, Ken." Alan took the stool beside him. The bartender, a woman wearing black trousers and a black vest over a ruffled shirt, walked down the bar to take his order.

"What can I get you?" Her face was pretty, though her features were dwarfed by the great mass of yellow hair that billowed around her head.

257

Alan hesitated, and his eyes went to the drink in front of Ken. "Do you have any bottled water?" he asked.

"Perrier?"

Alan nodded.

"Designer water," Ken said, shaking his head. His own glass was filled with an amber fluid so deep in color that it might have been straight bourbon.

"School night," Alan said.

Ken put back his head and laughed. "Okay," he said and slapped Alan on the back. "Business before pleasure. I got the papers you faxed to me: indictment, autopsy report, transcript of the examining trial. Looks like we've got a fight on our hands."

Alan shrugged, nodded. The bartender placed a cocktail napkin on the bar in front of him and set a collins glass on it filled with sparkling water.

Alan picked up the glass and took a sip. "What did you think of my discovery motions?" he asked. "Okay to file them?"

"Sure, sooner the better. Need to see what the prosecution's got. What I want to hear from you tonight is our best line of defense. How do you see it?"

"Tracey's apartment was burglarized the night before the murder, and one of the items she reported missing was the murder weapon. I was with her when she entered the apartment the next morning and found it ransacked. Her father showed up, then the police."

"Then that night, the handgun was used in a murder. That would be Saturday night."

"Right."

"I'd like it better if the murder victim was a stranger to Tracey."

"Yeah," Alan said.

"And if Tracey hadn't been at the crime scene the night of the murder."

"In the area anyway."

"You say you were with her Saturday morning. Where did she spend Friday night? Not with you."

Alan took another drink of his water. "With me," he said.

Ken's white, caterpillar eyebrows rose onto his ruddy forehead.

"It's kind of a long story."

"How about the next night, the night of the murder? She spend that with you, too?"

"Not really. We didn't go to the symphony ball together. I saw her there, Carlotta, too. Then both of them disappeared. After everything was over, Carlotta was discovered murdered, and nobody saw Tracey again until she turned up on my couch the next morning."

"You don't know when she got there?"

Alan shook his head.

"How did she get in? She have a key?"

"There was a spare key on the porch."

"Do you think she killed Carlotta Basoalto?"

"No."

"Did you think about giving her an alibi?"

"I wasn't alone when I got home."

"Your date with you?"

Alan moved his head equivocally. "She didn't stay long."

"You could have said Tracey showed up right after she left," Ken said.

"I had another house guest."

Again Ken's shaggy eyebrows climbed his forehead.

"An old college buddy," Alan said. "He was waiting for me when I got home from the party that evening."

"I was beginning to think you were the man in the world I most admired." Ken drained his whiskey and signaled the bartender for another one. "This burglary thing is weak, I got to tell you." He put his hands to the small of his back and stretched. "Unless we can establish who did it — and establish that it was someone with a connection to Carlotta Basoalto — the jury just ain't gonna buy it."

"Maybe not."

"The next couple of weeks we'll have our own experts go over the physical evidence — ballistics, autopsy report, and so forth. Something might turn up there."

"Something might."

"But you doubt it."

"If there's a weakness in the prosecution's case, it's probably in the area of motive. They're reaching on that."

"The indictment said robbery." Ken took a large swallow of his whiskey, and it brought tears to his reddened eyes.

"All that was missing were some rings," Alan said.

"Valuable rings? Diamond solitaire, that sort of thing?"

"I don't know. Apparently valuable, but Carlotta wasn't married."

"You don't like the robbery motive, I take it."

"No. If robbery was the motive, why wasn't Carlotta's wallet touched? Or her other jewelry? What was Tracey going to do with another woman's rings? Fence them? Wear them? Either way, why haven't they been found?"

"So what the prosecution has is the defendant's gun as the murder weapon, the defendant's presence at the civic center where the murder occurred, no explanation of the defendant's whereabouts...Why don't you think she did it, other than you're sleeping with her?"

"I'm not..." Alan broke off, perceiving the futility of denial.

Ken eyed him. "No answer," he said. "Okay."

Alan shrugged.

"You know what I think?" Ken said. He emptied his glass and pushed it along the bar for a refill.

"What's that?"

"I think I don't drink nearly enough. Have yourself another water, on me. Here's what else I think: If the prosecution comes up with a real motive for your girlfriend, a rational one, then she's headed for death row. Ain't one damn thing you or I or anybody else can do about it."

Chapter 52

On Monday Alan filed his discovery motions, and Ken Whitaker set about hiring his experts and arranging for them to examine the physical evidence the prosecution would be introducing at trial.

Alan found himself with free time, and he tried to use it to work on other matters. There were any number of files overflowing his desktop. Every time he got in the middle of something, though, a potential legal issue in Tracey's case would occur to him and he would spend an hour or two on Lexis trying to clarify it. It seemed incredible to him that Tracey's life or death, her freedom or lifetime incarceration, would be determined in a courtroom in less than three weeks' time, and almost intolerable that he himself would have little to do with the outcome.

Ken Whitaker had an office just down the hall from Alan. Though he put in full days, he spent his evenings in the hotel bar, drinking and joking with the bartender with the great mass of yellow hair. Each night Alan met him there, and they talked for twenty or thirty minutes before the topic of the upcoming trial was exhausted. Then Whitaker settled in for some serious drinking, and Alan went home to Tracey and his volumes on criminal procedure and trial tactics.

On Thursday evening, when he returned from the Sheraton, Tracey was sitting at the kitchen table, nursing a glass of iced tea.

"What do you think of him?" she asked.

Alan shook his head. "I don't know."

"You've been working with him four days now. What do you mean, you don't know?"

He shrugged. "I haven't been working with him that closely."

"Is he the great lawyer everybody says he is?"

"Does everybody say that?"

"Everybody I've talked to at Daddy's office."

"What does your father say?"

"He says he's good."

"But?"

"I don't like the way he says it."

Alan's mouth twitched. He pulled out a chair and dropped into it.

"So I want to know what you say. What kind of lawyer is he?"

He took a moment to answer. "He may have been really good once. At this point in his career, I'd say he's competent."

Tracey rolled her eyes. "Great," she said.

That Monday night, only two weeks before trial, Whitaker met Alan in his hotel suite to go over developments. They went through the entire stack of accumulating reports and documents, making notes and talking out ideas. When Alan got home at close to two in the morning, he was tired, but feeling better about the case.

He looked in on Tracey and found her asleep in her bed, lying on her stomach. The bedclothes trailed off the bed so that the sheet covered only her left leg. As near as he could tell from the doorway, she was sleeping in nothing but her panties. It made his heart hurt, somehow.

The prosecution's witness list came on Tuesday afternoon, giving them the names of everyone the prosecution expected to call at trial: Lieutenant Curtis and the other witnesses who had testified at the examining trial as well as perhaps a dozen others. All three of the Royals were listed, Hugh and Tony and Barry. Also listed were Harvey Couter and Charles Danvers, one presently and the other formerly of the Coleman law firm.

"What's Couter going to testify to?" Ken asked Alan.

Alan shook his head. "He sat next to her empty chair all evening. He talked to her earlier."

"How about Danvers?"

"He was at the symphony ball along with a few hundred others."

"So you have no idea?"

"There's some history between Danvers and Roger Coleman, and a lot of animosity. He might have seen Tracey and Carlotta go out into the lobby together. Somebody must have. I don't know why they'd use him for that, though, unless he was the only one who saw it. Danvers had a lot to drink that night. He ended up falling asleep at his table."

"Huh," Whitaker said.

"I really have no idea about Danvers. For that matter, why are the Royals on the list?"

"Hugh and Tony found the body. Probably they're part of the *res gestae*."

Alan nodded. The *res gestae* were the incidental matters surrounding the crime: the time Carlotta arrived at the party, the nature of her relationship to the defendant, and that sort of thing. "Tony and Carlotta actually rode to the party together," he said.

"Who is this Marty Harding?" Ken asked, underlining the name with a yellowed thumbnail.

"I don't know."

"How about this one, Dale Calaway?"

Alan shook his head.

"Hal Green?"

"He's one of the cops who responded to the burglary at Tracey's place."

"So they're going to put on the burglary evidence themselves, steal our thunder."

"Maybe."

"Maybe they plan to show the burglary was staged."

"It looked real to me."

Ken shoved the list across the desk at him. "Call and make an appointment to see Cale Larson. Tell him you and he need to go over the witness list."

"Okay."

"On the way back from the courthouse, you can stop by my hotel and pick up my other briefcase. I left my cell phone in it, and I'm lost without it." Ken thumped his cardkey on the desktop, and Alan took it. He was no longer merely second chair in the upcoming trial. He was now officially Ken's gofer.

Chapter 53

Alan didn't get very far with Larson, who conducted the interview with his chair tilted backwards and one leg hooked over the corner of his desk. "Look, Dougherty," he said at last. "I gave you the names like I'm supposed to. Under *Gaskin*, I don't have to give you their statements until after they've testified on direct. You're entitled to read the statements before cross, but that's all you're entitled to. You don't get a couple of weeks to think about it."

"You've at least got to tell me who they are."

"You've got their names and addresses."

"I've got a Marty Harding with an Arlington address. No suggestion of who he is in relation to the case." He knew the response to that one: Call him and ask him.

"Look, didn't I hear Ken Whitaker was trying this case?" Larson said. "Why the hell am I talking to you?"

"I'm also counsel of record."

"You like carrying Whitaker's briefcase for him?"

"Why wouldn't I? I get to come have these nice chats with you."

A faint flush mounted Larson's cheeks, but his sneer remained intact.

Alan said, "What is it? Is it the Angley law firm in general, or is it something personal?"

"It's all you guys."

"Lawyers?"

"Criminal defense lawyers. Winning is everything for you. You don't care who you're keeping out of jail and on the streets, just so you get the chance to make a name for yourselves. Now, if you've finished wasting my time —"

"Not yet." Alan was surprised at Larson's passion. He would have made much the same assessment of Larson, that he was interested less in achieving justice than in making a name for himself. Alan said, "I want to know who Dale Calaway is — not what he said in his statement to the police, just who he is in relation to this case. If I can't find him or get him on the phone, I'll file a motion. Judge Mitchell will give me that much."

Larson tilted his head back, looking down at Alan along his bony nose. "Dale Calaway is the owner of the Southern Gun Shop here in Tyler," he said at last.

"Marty Harding?"

"Marty Harding is employed by the Hertz Corporation."

"He —"

"He works at their counter at DFW."

Before going back to the office, he headed for the Sheraton to pick up Ken's briefcase. He felt numb. Larson had Marty Harding on his witness list, which meant he thought it significant that Tracey was with Carlotta in Mexico City. He knew about the drugs.

It was more than Ken Whitaker knew. A light turned red in front of him, and Alan braked hard, throwing himself against the shoulder harness. A pickup crossed the intersection in front of him. The light turned green, and a horn sounded behind him, but he didn't move. A big SUV whipped around him, and a woman's voice shouted.

At last he moved his foot from the brake to the accelerator. He made it to the Sheraton, driving clumsily, trying to think. He took a glass-sided elevator up to Ken's floor and used the card key to let himself into Ken's suite. The briefcase was by the love seat in the sitting area off the bedroom. He picked it up and went out.

Ken was on the phone when Alan looked into his office, but he nodded at Alan and waived for him to put the briefcase down by the file cabinet. "Uh huh," he said into the phone. Alan gave him a nod and went out.

He had to come clean with Whitaker, tell him everything. If Larson knew about the cocaine Tracey and Carlotta had smuggled into the country, the prosecution had a good start on motive. Back in his own office, Alan handwrote his notes on his copy of the witness list: Dale Calaway, Southern Gun Shop, Tyler; Marty Harding, Hertz counter, DFW Airport.

In the discussion of his annotated list, everything would come out. Whitaker would be furious with him, and justifiably so, but there was no helping it. He picked up the list and headed back down the hall to get it over with.

Whitaker wasn't in his office, and, seeing the empty desk chair, Alan found himself more relieved than disappointed. Tonight at the Sheraton would be soon enough, he told himself. He ought to talk to Tracey first anyway.

Chapter 54

Tracey wasn't home when he got there, though. He tried her cell, and it shunted him directly to her voice mail. He made himself a sandwich while he waited, but she didn't show. When it came time for him to leave for the Sheraton, he called her cell phone again and this time left a message on her voice mail: "Tracey, it's eight o'clock. What's going on? I haven't seen you. Call me on my cell."

At eight-thirty, he pulled into a parking space at the Sheraton. He half expected to find Ken at the bar, drinking his whiskey straight and talking to the bartender with the throaty voice and the mass of blonde hair, but neither Ken nor the blonde bartender was there.

"What can I get you?" called the bartender, slapping a napkin down in front of Alan.

He was a small man with red hair and a turned-up nose, not nearly as attractive as the woman he'd replaced. Alan shook his head and turned in the direction of the elevators.

Ken didn't answer Alan's knock. Alan was about to leave when he remembered the cardkey Ken had given him that morning. He hesitated, then fished it out and slipped it into the lock.

"Ken?" he said as he pushed open the door. There was no answer. He smelled whiskey and the ashy smell of a cigar, along with a more exotic scent that he couldn't put a name to. "Ken?"

He stepped into the room. The door snicked shut behind him, and the hair at the nape of his neck stirred. Hardly aware that he was holding his breath, he stepped softly past the closets and the open bathroom door.

The bedclothes were on the floor in knots, but the king-sized bed was empty. An empty bottle of Jack Daniels, its cap off, stood on the bedside table beside an ashtray containing ash and a cigar butt. Alan exhaled slowly, his eyes on the open door that led into the suite's adjoining room.

Taking another breath, he eased forward.

They were in the sitting room. Ken Whitaker lay face down on the floor in front of the love seat. He was naked, with one knee caught between his chest and the coffee table. Another bottle of whiskey, not yet empty, lay on its side by Ken's head, its top off, the carpet stained dark beneath the mouth of the bottle. Ken's mouth was open, his fleshy face puckered from its weight against the carpet.

The woman on the love seat was also naked. One foot trailed off the love seat, the instep resting on Ken Whitaker's bare buttocks. Her head was thrown back against the cushioned arm.

She looked a lot like Tracey Coleman. He thought she was Tracey, then he thought she wasn't, but he couldn't bring himself to take the necessary step toward her to be sure. He became conscious of the puff of her breathing, and his eyes were drawn to the rise and fall of her chest. He leaned toward the loveseat, his eyes straining; a half step, and suddenly he was sure.

"Tracey," he breathed. A wave of emotion swept over him, dizzying him, and his vision went dark around the edges. He felt pain so intense that it was almost physical, and he blocked his mind against it.

He looked down at Ken, who, from all outward appearances, was dead. He dropped to his knees beside him, resting a hand on the bare back, which, though warm, was utterly still. Alan got down in Ken's face to study the thick, ruddy features. Even nose to nose with him, Alan could feel no breath against his own face. He peeled back an eyelid with his thumb, expecting to find Ken's eyes rolled back in his head, but the pupil was facing out and moving jerkily.

"Ken?"

There was no answer, but the rapid eye movements continued. He was alive, then. Alan got unsteadily to his feet. There was an ashtray near Tracey on the coffee table, in it a few conical stubs of a home-rolled product among the ashes. Marijuana was his guess. It would explain the vaguely exotic scent mingling with the odors of cigar smoke and booze.

He stumbled toward the door, then saw the smart phone sitting on an end table in the corner, and he wondered. Picking it up, he pushed the home button, swept his thumb across the screen, tapped it. A photo appeared, showing a lamp, only half in the frame; the top of Ken Whitaker's head. He swept his thumb to the right to reveal Ken standing back-lighted and naked against the window, his head back as he drained one of the square-based bottles of whiskey. Alan's heartbeat picked up the tempo, and he swept his thumb across the screen again. Tracey Coleman sat propped against the pillows at the head of a bed, probably the bed in the next room, sucking on the last embers of one of the home-rolled cigarettes, holding it clamped between a couple of car keys.

Behind him Tracey snorted explosively, and Alan's heart lurched against the wall of his chest. His head whipped toward her, but she lay just as she had before, her head thrown back and her mouth open. She had started to snore.

Chapter 55

The next morning, Alan sat on a stool at the counter at the Greasy Spoon, sipping orange juice and eyeing the cooling plate of eggs in front of him. He had eaten the bacon and found it was all he had any stomach for. His iPhone hung heavily in his shirt pocket, hanging all the heavier for the photographs he had texted to himself. The one he had open showed Tracey's naked body only partially obscured by a long, bony foot with a yellow toenail. It was that foot he kept seeing as he sipped his juice, kept seeing despite all his efforts to blot it out.

"Hey, Alan."

Alan turned as Ken slipped onto the stool beside him.

"I got your message." Ken cleared his throat, or tried to; the sound was like the grinding of a car ignition. He squinted against the light.

"It's after ten," Alan said.

"I know. Sorry." He winced as he said it. His big voice was gone; what was left had a whispery quality.

"I came by to see you last night. I still had your cardkey. Here." He laid the cardkey on the counter. "You can imagine what I found." Dread seemed to squeeze his abdominal cavity as he said it.

Ken winced again, but didn't say anything. The waitress came by.

"What can I get you, hon?" she asked, turning over his cup and pouring his coffee.

Ken's smile was more like an expression of pain. "This will do it."

When the waitress was gone, Alan fished his iPhone from his shirt pocket, unlocked it, and laid it face-down on the counter. Ken picked it up, looked at the photograph, and put it back down. The waitress brought his coffee.

Ken sipped it before he spoke. "I don't guess it would do any good to tell you I'm sorry. I know you're in love with her."

"No. Sorry won't do it," Alan said.

"So what do you want?"

"I want you to drop the case and go back to Houston."

Ken took another sip of his coffee. The silence stretched out between them. "You know," Ken said at last, "these out-of-town trips aren't good for me. When I'm home, I'm all right. I moderate my drinking; I'm in control of things. It's when I'm on the road..."

He trailed off, but Alan didn't say anything.

"What's my alternative?" Ken asked him. "If I don't go back to Houston, you've got a bunch of dirty pictures you're going to show Jim Angley?"

"I wasn't planning to bring him in on it. Do I need to?"

"Are you that anxious to be lead counsel in a big murder case?"

"I'm anxious to have what's best for Tracey Coleman."

"And that's you, you think."

"It's not you."

"We didn't sleep together, if it makes you feel any better. We didn't get any more sexual than..."

"Than taking off your clothes."

Ken's mouth stretched in a pained grimace.

"It doesn't change what you need to do," Alan said.

"You realize your partners don't think you're up to the job, don't you? That's why I'm here."

"I think you're here so that when Tracey goes to Huntsville everybody can tell themselves, 'We did all we could for her. We hired experience; we hired a reputation. We paid top dollar.'"

"You're a real prick, aren't you?" He put down his coffee and pushed it away. "I used to have your cockiness. Now, so often, I feel like I'm just going through the motions." He got out a five-dollar bill and tucked it beneath his saucer. "Have you thought of an excuse for me to give Jim Angley?"

"No."

"Not a lot of help, are you?"

"You don't need my help."

"That's where you're wrong, kid." He put a hand on Alan's shoulder as he got off his stool. "I need all kinds of help."

He walked away, leaving Alan alone at the counter.

THREE

TRIAL & ITS INCIDENTS

All persons are presumed to be innocent and no person may be convicted of an offense unless each element of the offense is proved beyond a reasonable doubt. The fact that he has been arrested, confined, or indicted for, or otherwise charged with, the offense gives rise to no inference of guilt at his trial.

—Texas Penal Code § 2.01.

Everyone, perhaps, felt from the first that the case was beyond dispute, that there was no doubt about it, that there could be really no discussion, and that the defense was only a matter of form, and that the prisoner was guilty, obviously and conclusively guilty.

—F. Dostoevsky, *The Brothers Karamazov.*

Chapter 56

Jury selection started twelve days later. Alan Dougherty sat behind the defense table with Tracey on his left, closest to the empty jury box. Out in the gallery, a panel of sixty prospective jurors sat in rows of ten.

The bailiff called the court into session, and everyone stood. "Oyez! Oyez! The court for the one hundred sixty-first judicial court is now in session, the honorable Judge Tom Mitchell presiding."

Judge Mitchell entered the courtroom. He paused behind the bench, sweeping his gaze across the courtroom, then sank abruptly into his high-backed chair. Those in the courtroom settled down into their own chairs with a sound like a collective sigh.

The spectators sat opposite the prospective jurors on one side of the gallery, Roger Coleman among them. Sitting directly beside him was an elderly man with cottony hair and skin dark and leathery from years of exposure to a tropical sun.

"We're here in the case of *State versus Tracey Coleman*," the judge said. "Is counsel for the state prepared for trial?"

Larson stood. "The people are ready, your honor."

"The defense?"

"Ready." Alan dropped back into his seat. As the judge greeted the prospective jurors, Alan leaned toward Tracey to ask, "Who's that with your father? Do you know him?"

She turned her head enough to study them without seeming to. "Carlotta's father and brother," she said.

"Luis and Carlos? Carlos is the ferret-faced guy on the other side of the old man?"

She half smiled. "That's him."

"What are they doing with your father?" Why would the father of the victim be sitting next to the father of the accused?

"Don't know," she said.

Alan frowned. The judge was telling the prospective jurors that the proceeding in which they might be called upon to serve was a trial on the charge of capital murder. "I am Judge Mitchell. On your right is the prosecutor, Mr. Caleb Larson. On your left are the defendant, Tracey Coleman, and her lawyer, Mr. Alan Dougherty.

"Our job today and for the next several days is to select from your number twelve jurors and two alternate jurors to hear the case. We will choose the jurors by asking questions, some of them designed to discover possible bias, others designed merely for us to get acquainted." He bared his yellowed teeth in what was probably meant as a smile.

He began asking questions, some of individual jurors, sometimes just asking for a show of hands. Do any of you know the defendant? Did any of you know the victim? Do you know either of the lawyers? What have you read or heard about this case in the media? Have you formed any conclusions about this defendant's guilt or innocence? He went on to matters of law: the presumption of innocence, the burden of proof, reasonable doubt. He asked the jurors if they would follow the law as he gave it to them.

By the time he was done, it was twelve-thirty, and the judge dismissed them for lunch. When they came back, he told the panel that in the next phase of *voir dire*, the jury selection process, each panelist would be questioned individually, apart from the rest of the panel. "Now this isn't designed to scare you or intimidate you," the judge said. "With everybody here, some of you may not feel free to speak and you need to feel free to speak. Furthermore, at this stage it is the lawyers who will be asking the questions, and they need to feel free to ask tough questions and to challenge members of the panel they feel might be a problem for them. So if all of you will follow the bailiff there, all of you except for...Mr. Livermore. Mr. Livermore, you stay here. Come on up and have a seat there in the jury box."

Mr. Livermore was about sixty, with a tanned, seamy face and slicked-down hair. He wore sun-faded Wranglers and a flannel shirt neatly buttoned at the wrists. As he took his seat in the jury box, Cale Larson got up from behind his table and smoothed the jacket of his suit. "Mr. Livermore," he said. "Charles Livermore?"

"That's right."

"Mr. Livermore, have you ever been a witness to or a victim of a crime?"

Mr. Livermore chewed briefly at his lower lip. "I reckon I have," he said.

"What was it?"

Mr. Livermore gave them the details. In response to further questions, he indicated he didn't know how the case was handled once it got to court and had no strong feelings as to how it should have been handled.

"Has anyone in your circle of friends or relatives ever been charged with a crime?"

"No, I can't say that they have."

Larson spent roughly forty-five minutes questioning Mr. Livermore. "This juror is acceptable to the prosecution," he told the judge when he had finished.

Judge Mitchell nodded at Alan. "Counselor."

Alan got up. He introduced himself again, then introduced Tracey. "Mr. Livermore, are you aware by this time that the defendant doesn't have to prove anything during the course of this trial and, in fact, doesn't have to present any evidence whatsoever?"

Mr. Livermore hesitated. "I guess I am," he said.

"How do you feel about that?"

Alan was done with him in thirty minutes. "Mr. Livermore is acceptable to the defense," he said. At roughly three o'clock, they had their first juror.

By the end of the day, the defense and the prosecution had each used one of their fifteen peremptory challenges to get rid of an undesirable panelist: The judge refused to excuse either for cause.

"How's it going?" Tracey asked as they left the courthouse.

"Okay. I think we're getting an impartial jury."

"You don't think we're getting an edge on the prosecution?"

"We can hope. We're also educating the jury. None of them have ever served on a jury in a criminal case before. I've been doing what I can to bring them up to speed."

"If you say so."

He opened the car door for her and watched as she sat and swung her legs in and adjusted her skirt. As he walked around the car, a sour expression settled on his face. He'd worn that expression a lot since finding her in Ken Whitaker's hotel room.

They rode home in silence, just as they'd spent the past week in silence. Midweek she'd given up and gone to her father's for Thanksgiving and the day after. Saturday she'd reappeared, and he'd been unable to escape her since.

He parked the car in his garage, and they went inside, Tracey first, Alan following. He got some ice water from the refrigerator and stood at the counter with it.

Tracey got her own water.

"It's not every lawyer who takes his client home at the end of the day," she said, smiling.

Alan sipped his water, and she dropped the smile.

"I had to get rid of him, you know."

Alan put down his water carefully. "Get rid of whom?"

"You know whom."

"We don't have to talk about it."

"Yes, we do, or I do anyway. We can't keep just ignoring it."

"What is there to talk about?" He went to the table, pulled out a chair, and sat down.

"I hurt you..."

"No, you didn't."

"Don't be a jackass. I hurt you, and I'm sorry."

"The jackass accepts your apology." He got up again and went into the living room. She followed him.

"You said we'd be better off without him," she said. "I didn't know how else to do it. Look at me, damn it."

He took a breath, then met her gaze. "What?" he said.

"Nothing happened between us. You know that, don't you?"

"How could I possibly know that?"

"Ken was drinking whiskey like it was water. In ten minutes he wasn't interested in anything else."

Her casual use of Whitaker's first name stabbed deep. The image came to him of the man's naked body, sprawled on the floor. He turned away from her, heading for his bedroom.

"You didn't know how to get rid of him," she said from the living room, raising her voice. "You know you didn't. I gave you what you needed."

He tugged savagely at his tie, pulling it free.

"I don't like whiskey myself. I had a couple of sips and shared a joint with him. By that time he was gone."

He came out of the bedroom toward her, but image of the photograph, of her body and that long, bony foot, came to him so strongly that it obscured her face. He turned and went back into his room.

"I expected you to knock on the door a couple of times and go away, not walk right in," she said. "I thought I'd be texting you the photos, and I could be selective about what you saw. A couple of photos that gave you the ammunition you needed without...without so much pain."

He looked toward the door, eyes suddenly burning, but she hadn't followed him as far as the doorway.

From the hallway she continued, "When I heard you coming in, I didn't know what to do. All I could think of was to lie down and close my eyes so you wouldn't be any more embarrassed than you had to be."

He gave a roar of frustration, turning and jerking up his pillow and slamming it down on the bed. Then she was there in the bedroom, and he was holding her, and he cried into her hair.

Chapter 57

Opening arguments began on Friday morning. As Cale Larson was making eye-contact with each member of the jury, Alan looked out over the gallery and saw that Carlotta's father and brother were still with them, still sitting beside Roger Coleman as they had been throughout jury selection.

"Members of the jury," Larson said. "The facts of the case are these. Carlotta Basoalto was shot through the eye on the evening of Saturday, October twenty-fifth, sometime between nine-forty and ten-fifty-five p.m. This occurred in a Volkswagen Touareg, the decedent's car, in the parking lot of the Harvey Convention Center, here in Tyler.

"The Tyler Symphony Orchestra was having its annual ball that evening. The murder victim, Carlotta Basoalto, was at the party. She went wearing several items of jewelry, among them two rings, one of them mounted with a five-carat garnet." That, Alan had learned, was one reason Tony Royal was on the witness list. He had given her one of the rings and could testify as to its value.

"Also at the reception was the defendant, Tracey Coleman. The two women were seen going out into the lobby of the convention center together at some time between nine-thirty and ten o'clock. Roughly three hours later, Carlotta's body was discovered in the Touareg. Carlotta had been shot cleanly through the eye with a .25 caliber Davis derringer." He turned to look at Tracey Coleman a moment before continuing, and the jurors looked with him.

"The defendant's rings, which had a total value in excess of ten thousand dollars, all had been removed. The murder weapon was found in the car, partially concealed beneath the body. It is registered to the defendant, Tracey Coleman, who has a permit to carry a concealed weapon, and who owns a number of other handguns in addition to the murder weapon. She is an expert shot. None of these facts can be reasonably disputed."

Alan watched Larson in his peripheral vision, feigning boredom, but feeling a growing anger.

Larson said, "The very day of the murder, mere hours before it, the defendant reported the murder weapon stolen, evidence that she was already planning —"

Alan stood up, interrupting Larson. "Your honor, he's arguing his case."

"Sustained." Arguments were improper in an opening statement, which was supposed to be limited to the facts to be introduced at trial. The place to argue conclusions, inferences, and the relative credibility of the witnesses was closing argument.

Alan said, "He has the fact of the burglary, and he has the fact of a gun left at the murder scene."

"Sustained."

"When he suggests a causal connection, he's going beyond any evidence he can possibly be planning to introduce."

Larson said, "Now he's arguing his case."

"Gentlemen, shut up!"

Alan sat down, and Larson turned back to the jury. He took a breath. "Allow me to rephrase," he said. "On Saturday afternoon, the defendant reported a .25 caliber Davis derringer stolen from her apartment, and a police officer will testify to that. She also reported three other handguns stolen, though none of them have been recovered. Nothing else was missing, just the three handguns. On Saturday evening, one of the handguns reported stolen fired the bullet that killed Carlotta Basoalto. That handgun, the derringer, was left at the scene." He turned to look at Alan, raising his eyebrows.

Alan didn't respond. He would have his chance to present his own theory of the case, the theory that the burglar who had taken the handguns — Barry or Tony Royal — had murdered Carlotta. It would be nice to have some evidence of that, but under the Constitution it was the prosecution's job to prove Tracey's guilt, not his job to prove her innocence.

Larson returned to the heinous nature of the crime, describing it in meticulous, gory detail. "Who is responsible for this act of brutality?" he asked. "This defendant," he said. "This Tracey Coleman. When all the evidence is in and you twelve citizens of the state of Texas have had the opportunity to deliberate, you will know it beyond any reasonable doubt. You will know it, and you will find her guilty of capital murder as charged. Thank you." He sat down.

Judge Mitchell looked at Alan Dougherty. "Counselor?"

Alan stood in front of the jury, his hands in his pockets. "Carlotta's rings have never been found," he said. "If they were stolen, if they weren't merely lost or misplaced, there is no evidence at all suggesting it was Tracey Coleman who took them. The police have looked for evidence, of course. They have searched Tracey, and they've searched her apartment, and they've searched her car." He shook his head. "Nothing. We don't know what happened to the rings. The prosecution can present not one single, slender shred of evidence as to what happened to them — and yet, Mr. Larson here is going to ask you to find beyond a reasonable doubt that Tracey Coleman took them.

"Mr. Larson has suggested that there was no burglary of the defendant's apartment on the night before the murder. That Tracey Coleman busted open her own front door and ransacked her apartment herself, all for the purpose of drawing attention to a handgun she proposed to use to commit a murder. Why did she do this? According to the prosecution, because she planned to commit a murder with it, and it was registered to her, so she had to get it out of her possession. Why? Because after she committed her crime, she planned to leave the handgun at the scene. Why?" He held out his hands. "There can be no answer to that. It—"

"Your honor," Larson said, interrupting him. "I think he's arguing his case."

"I think he is, too," the judge said.

Alan nodded. After a moment, he continued. "What about the other three handguns that were 'stolen?'" He formed the quotation marks in the air. "Where are they? Did the police find them on the person of Tracey Coleman when they searched her? Did they find them in her apartment when they searched it? Did they find them in her car, in her father's house?" He shook his head. "Again, the prosecution doesn't know what happened to those handguns, but what evidence you will hear indicates that they are not in the possession of Tracey Coleman. You will hear no evidence at all that the defendant faked the burglary of her apartment.

"The prosecutor has referred to you as citizens, and so you are. And so is Tracey Coleman. The laws of this country and of the state of Texas weave a cocoon of protection around its citizens. Its citizens can't be put away, they can't be executed, until every piece of that cocoon of protection is peeled away. It requires more than a couple of incriminating circumstances and a little speculation. It requires proof. It requires the elimination of every reasonable doubt."

Alan walked back to his table and stood by Tracey. "Carlotta Basoalto has been murdered. Two hours elapsed between the murder and the discovery of the body, maybe more. During that time, more than two hundred people passed through the parking lot where the car sat unlocked. Whoever the killer was, he or she was not the last person with the opportunity to remove a ring or anything else from the decedent's body. If the prosecutor cannot eliminate every other reasonable possibility for what happened to those rings, he cannot establish that the killer murdered Carlotta in the course of stealing her rings. He cannot establish that the murder of Carlotta Basoalto was a capital crime. He cannot ask you to put anyone to death. A murder occurred here, beyond any doubt, but only speculation can make it capital murder. Not only does the prosecution have the wrong defendant here, but it has charged the defendant with the wrong crime — overreaching its evidence, trying to turn a murder case into capital murder even when the evidence doesn't support it. It's up to you twelve to correct it, you twelve to keep the prosecution honest."

He walked back to the jury box and stood with his hands on the rail. "The state has awesome power. It can arrest people, literally snatching them off the streets, and it can lock them away forever. In certain circumstances it can put them to death. To balance that awesome power, the Constitution of the United States appoints..." Alan raised a finger and leveled it at the jurors. "You. You alone stand between the unbridled power of the state and someone — anyone — charged with a crime. It is an awesome responsibility.

"The prosecution has several tricks — to be charitable we'll call them techniques — which he will use to encourage you to abdicate that responsibility." Alan expected another objection, but none came. "One of the techniques will be to show you a host of pictures, gory, bloody, awful pictures with no purpose other than to inflame your passions. Carlotta Basoalto is dead, and Tracey Coleman does not dispute that. You don't need to see photographs of her corpse to convince you she's dead — but you will see them. She was killed by a .25 caliber slug that entered her brain through her right eye. It makes a messy wound, and you can bet you will see it, though it's unnecessary to establish any fact in dispute."

He took a breath. It was time to deal with what he had dismissed as a couple of incriminating circumstances. He said, "On the night of the murder, Tracey Coleman attended the Symphony Ball along with the murder victim and two hundred other people, none of whom have been charged with a crime. Tracey Coleman was seen talking to the murder victim. So were a number of other people, none of whom have been charged with a crime. What distinguishes the defendant from everyone else is one fact, and one fact alone. The gun used to commit the crime was registered to her. That's it. It is on the basis of that one fact that the prosecution wants you to sentence this woman to death."

He continued for another thirty minutes, returning again and again to his central theme: It was the jury's job to force the prosecution to prove its case, to force the prosecution to eliminate every other reasonable interpretation of the evidence. By the time he was done, he had several of the jurors nodding at him, and he sat down feeling that Tracey Coleman still had a shot at a fair hearing, that he had done his job.

Chapter 58

Larson called his first witness on Monday, Corporal William Jenkins, who, along with his partner, was the first policeman to arrive at the crime scene. The testimony went very much as it had at the examining trial. Corporal Jenkins identified his inventory of the crime scene, and it was introduced into evidence.

After about 45 minutes of testimony, Larson extracted a set of sixteen-by-twenty inch photographs from a large vinyl case. "Corporal Jenkins, was there a police photographer present at the crime scene?"

"There was."

"Did he take any pictures of the scene before the body was moved?"

"He did."

"I want to show you certain photographs and to ask you..."

Alan got to his feet. "Your honor, the defense will stipulate that the decedent is in fact dead and to the nature of the wounds that killed her." Normally, this was the sort of objection you made outside the presence of the jury, but Alan thought he had prepared them sufficiently in his opening statement.

Larson said, "The prosecution will not accept the stipulation."

Alan looked at the jury. They looked at him, and he raised his eyebrows. *See what he's doing?*

"Mr. Dougherty?" the judge said.

Alan turned to the judge. "Your honor, with those stipulations, the photographs are irrelevant. The prosecution can't prove any more than what I've stipulated to already. Mr. Larson values the photographs only for their inflammatory nature."

"They show the position of the murder weapon," Larson said.

"We'll stipulate..."

"I don't have to accept any stipulations," Larson said. "I'm entitled to prove my case."

The judge nodded. "All right," he said. He looked at Alan. "I think you've made your point."

Alan sat down.

As the first photograph was held up before the witness in plain view of the judge and jury, Alan glanced out across the gallery. Beside Roger Coleman, Luis Basoalto, the decedent's father, was sitting rigidly, his eyes on Larson. As Larson turned the photograph toward the defendant and the gallery, they all saw Carlotta's body crumpled in the knee-well of her car, her skirt bunched about her hips, her head hanging, her hair so disheveled that it covered her face completely.

The second picture was at closer range, bringing into prominence the dark blood staining the car seat and an out-flung hand. The third picture was of the face with its staring, sightless eye, blood running from the crusted socket. Alan stood up. "Your honor, is this really necessary? The victim's family is in the courtroom." He glanced toward the leathery old man on the back row, and the judge and jury followed his gaze. For a long moment there was silence.

Larson turned the photograph face down. "We won't submit this one, your honor."

"The jury's seen it," Alan said. "It needs to be in evidence."

The photograph was introduced and made a part of the record. Alan sat down. Larson hesitated with his remaining photographs. Alan, glancing again across the gallery, noticed with a start that Luis Basoalto was looking at him with eyes so unblinking as to appear lidless.

"Your witness," Larson said.

Alan stood. He did not dispute the circumstances of the crime; he had said so. With the inventory in evidence, he could wait until his closing argument to point out all the valuable items that remained at the crime scene — the necklace and earrings and gold bracelets and cash. Robbery was not the motive, he could argue; the crime, whoever committed it, was not a capital crime. "No questions," he said.

The prosecution's next witness was Dr. Quillen, the assistant medical examiner. The gun had been fired at a distance from the entrance wound of two inches to three feet. The bullet had entered the cranium at an upward angle of approximately thirty degrees. And so on. Larson was still asking him questions at noon, when the judge recessed for lunch.

Roger Coleman came to the rail.

"Hi, Daddy."

"I'd like to take you to lunch." He was looking at Tracey.

Tracey looked at Alan, who shrugged. "I've got some work to do," he said. "I'll see you back here."

There was a message from Steve Booker waiting for Alan at the office. He dialed Steve's cell.

"Hey, Alan," said a familiar voice. "I didn't want to call your cell in case you were in court and had forgotten to silence it.

"What are you doing in town?"

"Examining banks, what else? I'm at Citizens and Farmers. You available for dinner tonight?"

"Sure."

At one-thirty he was in the law firm's parking lot, bending over to insert the key in his car door, when a giant's reflection loomed behind his, a giant with dark hair and dusky skin. Alan tried to turn, but the giant was already turning him. Another man was with him, equally as large.

Alan's briefcase hit the asphalt. "Hey," he said. Each man pressed one of Alan's arms against the frame of Alan's Corolla, and one of them drove his fist into Alan's abdomen. Alan's knees buckled, but the two men held him up, one powering his right fist into Alan's solar plexus, then leaning out to give the other man room enough to hit him with his left. The world darkened.

When they stepped away, Alan fell forward onto his hands and knees, blood dripping from his mouth as he fought to breathe. He fell to his side, gaping soundlessly, his diaphragm temporarily paralyzed.

The Latin giants were gone.

Alan made a croaking sound as he sucked in his first breath of air. A dark Jaguar sedan turned out of the alley and stopped beside him. The window slid downward, revealing Luis Basoalto's dark face and cottony hair. The old man looked down at him, his black eyes expressionless. He didn't speak.

Alan closed his eyes, and, when he opened them, Jordan Conway was kneeling over him.

"Alan?" The midday sun formed a halo about her light brown hair. The Mercedes was gone.

He reached out to touch her face, but it shifted on him, mirage-like, and his hand dropped without having reached her.

"What happened?" she asked. "Are you all right? Can you move?"

As he shifted, pain lanced through him, intense enough to make him wonder about internal injuries. "Help," he gasped. With Jordan's support, he managed to sit up enough to lean against the front wheel of his car.

"I'm okay," he said, breathing hard.

"What happened? Were you mugged?"

"I think I bit my lip." He touched his lip gingerly with his index finger. He could taste the coppery flavor of the blood.

"Did you fall? Were you hit by a car?"

"Two thugs..." He broke off, shocked to find himself suddenly on the verge of tears. "They..." His voice cracked, and it was nearly a minute before he could go on. "They held me up against the car and..." He couldn't continue.

Her expression was dark. "I'll call the police," she said. She reached for the purse lying on the asphalt.

"No. Let me think a minute. Help me up." As he struggled to get to his feet, she slipped an arm beneath his shoulder to help him.

"Who was it?" she asked. "Anyone you recognized? Was it..." She broke off. A careless breath had stabbed deep and left him gasping shallowly. She said, "I'm taking you to the hospital."

"I don't see my keys. Can you help me find my keys?"

"They're in the car door," Jordan said.

"Oh." He opened the door and braced a hand in the seat as he reached beneath it for Tracey's Walther PPK. He eased down into the low seat and laid the gun in the passenger seat, within easy reach.

Jordan, her eyes on the gun, said, "Care to explain that?"

"No."

"Didn't do you a lot of good, did it?"

"No."

"You can't take it into court with you, you know."

He did. The metal detector would pick it up as he entered the courthouse. He pressed his eyes tightly shut for a few moments, then opened them again.

Jordan was holding onto the door. "I don't like this," she said.

"Me either." It was all he could do to breathe.

"We need to call the police."

"Not yet." He reached out to pull the door shut, but fell back into his seat without reaching the handle.

"Why not?"

He didn't answer. "When this trial is over, I'm done," he said. "This is my last criminal trial."

"Maybe I should drive you to the courthouse. I can park your car and walk back."

He wished she'd mentioned it sooner, but it would be harder to get out and walk around to the passenger side than just to drive the car himself. "I'm okay," he said.

She studied him a moment, then shut his door for him. He let his head roll back against the headrest for a few moments before putting the car in gear. Then, using his rearview mirror, he backed out of his parking space.

Thirty minutes later he sat beside Tracey at the defense table. Without moving his head, he let his eyes move over the gallery, scanning it for Carlotta's father and brother. He didn't see them, but couldn't shake the feeling that they were there, just outside his field of vision.

"What did your father want?" he said to Tracey.

"Father-daughter time. Nothing specific. What happened to your face?"

"What do you mean?"

"Your lip's swelling."

He felt of it with his tongue. "I bit it."

"Dork." She smiled at him as if to show she didn't mean it.

The judge came in, and everyone stood, Alan making it to his feet by degrees. When the rear doors opened, and Luis and Carlos Basoalto entered the gallery, Alan was seized by a sudden terror that made him sway on his feet. The court was called to order, and everyone sat down.

Larson said, "The state has no further questions of Dr. Quillen, your honor."

"Mr. Dougherty?"

Alan stood, the muscles in his legs quivering. He turned his head toward the gallery to look at Luis Basoalto, who returned his gaze unsmiling.

He turned back to the judge.

"Well, Mr. Dougherty? Any questions for Dr. Quillen?"

"No questions."

Bending his knees, keeping his torso as upright as possible, he lowered himself into his seat.

"Are you all right?" Tracey whispered.

"I'm all right."

He didn't sound all right, he knew. Tracey nodded, but she continued to eye him.

Chapter 59

He told her about the assault on the way home.

"That's why you didn't have any questions for Dr. Quillen?"

"No. I didn't have any questions for Corporal Jenkins either, remember? I didn't have any broken ribs then."

"You were in better shape to exercise good judgment."

"What would you have asked Dr. Quillen? Did your father have any ideas?"

She shrugged. "He didn't mention any."

"Well, if he never brings it up, you can be pretty sure I did all right." He pulled the car up to the curb in front of his house, right behind her Porsche. "I've got to let you out here. I'm having dinner with Steve Booker tonight."

"What?"

She was clearly offended, but he left her standing on the sidewalk.

When he got to the restaurant, Steve's new Mercedes was in the parking lot, parked diagonally across two parking spaces near the door. The only space Alan could find was beside the dumpster in the rear of the building. He tucked Tracey's pistol into the side pocket of his jacket before getting out of the car.

Steve already had a drink in front of him — a margarita on the rocks, tequila being his liquor of choice. "Hey, buddy," Steve said as he sat down. "I started to order you a drink, but they were out of Kool-Aid."

"Did anyone ever tell you you were a butthead?" Alan said.

"Sure, all the time, but I don't let it get to me. What happened to your lip?"

"I bit it when two big guys were hitting me in the stomach." He picked up the menu.

"Okay, fine. Don't tell me."

The waitress approached for his drink order, and he asked for iced tea.

"Caffeine," Steve observed. "You're going to be a wild man tonight."

"Why are you in such a good mood? I hate it when you're in a good mood."

The waitress came back with the tea. Steve ordered soft tacos, and, after a moment's hesitation, Alan followed suit.

"I didn't know you were going to be in Tyler," Alan said.

"That's because I didn't tell you."

"You staying with Susan? Things heating up there?"

"I'm staying with her. The temperature's under control, thank you."

"Why fight it? This could be the beginning of something beautiful."

Steve made a face at him, and Alan felt the dull stirrings of sadistic pleasure.

"Something permanent," he said.

"Now cut that out. You remember what you promised me."

"No. What did I promise you?"

"If I ever tell you I'm getting married, you whack me in the head with a two-by-four and keep me locked in the trunk of my car until I come to my senses."

Alan's laughter turned into a prolonged gasp.

"Don't laugh," Steve said. "You made me a promise, and I expect you to keep it."

For dessert Alan had fried ice cream, and Steve ordered the Mexican coffee, which came mixed with tequila and an espresso liqueur and was topped with whipped cream.

"Someday we're not going to be able to eat like this," Alan said.

"Why not?"

"Our bellies will start to lap over our belts."

"And that's a problem why?"

"Did you have something to tell me?" Alan asked. "Or was Susan just not available for dinner?"

Steve leaned across the table, and Alan leaned forward expectantly. "See those two guys sitting just behind you and to your left?" Steve asked in a low voice. "Eight o'clock."

Frowning, Alan turned his head enough to take them in. They looked like college kids, both of them skinny, one sporting a downy goatee. Each had a beer mug in front of him.

Steve said, "Now watch them when that waitress comes by."

The waitress had the build of a gymnast and a girl-next-door sort of face. She was carrying a tray of food above her shoulder, and, as the hem of her skirt brushed the top of the college kids' table, they seemed actually to stop breathing.

"Man," one of them said, taking a slug of his beer and wiping his mouth with the back of his hand. "Man."

Steve sat back, grinning widely. Alan rolled his eyes.

"Ten years ago, that was you and me, buddy," Steve said.

"Were you the one with the scraggly goatee or the other one?"

"Oh, it hardly matters, does it? You want to know why we're here. I have a present for you." He brought out a leather portfolio which had been propped against the leg of the table by his chair. Unzipping it, he extracted a large manila envelope and placed it on the table beside Alan's now empty ice cream dish.

"What is it?"

"SupeRink has a construction loan with Citizens and Farmers, and Hugh personally has a one hundred thousand dollar line of credit. In the envelope are four years' worth of corporate and personal tax returns, and three years' worth of financial statements."

Alan opened the envelope and peered into it at the stack of papers.

"Jackpot, buddy," Steve said.

"I thought you..."

"After I saw the loan cards, I had myself assigned to Citizens and Farmers, citing romantic necessity."

"I thought you said this would be illegal as hell."

"I did. I never said I wouldn't do it."

Alan closed the envelope and slid it off the table onto his lap.

"Just think of a good story about where you got it," Steve said.

Chapter 60

The prosecution got its own break that night, not much later. Three kids were working 6th Street for car radios, two of the kids about eighteen years old, the other younger, maybe fourteen. He was the one with the slim jim. It wouldn't open every car on the block — some required other tools or other techniques — but he knew from long experience which cars to pass by and which were susceptible to his special expertise.

He paused beside each car for the barest moment it took him to slide the flat piece of steel down between the glass and the rubber gasket, to catch the rods connected to the lock mechanism, and to lift or slide as necessary to unlock the door. He did the whole block, then started back to rejoin his buddies, who by that time had the stereo out of the first car.

"Here, take this," one of the older kids said to him, thrusting the components at him. The components included a CD-player and a graphic equalizer, sprouting wires. The boy pulled a canvas bag from where it was tucked into the back of his pants, and he thrust the components down into it, following them to the next vehicle. It was a Chevy Cobalt, not much of a car, but one with a fairly good radio/CD-player.

"Here."

The boy took the unit and pushed it into his bag. They skipped the next car; its radio was crap.

Two plainclothesmen were watching from an unmarked car. "They just pulled their third one, Lieu," said one of them, speaking into the radio handset. "You want we should let them take the whole row?"

Curtis, standing behind the dispatcher, leaned forward. "I do if you think their fence is Hugh Royal."

"I only know what our informant said," said the plainclothesman.

"Let 'em fill their pockets."

"You got it." Though of course the boys weren't filling their pockets, they were filling a canvas bag, a big one.

It was full after nine cars, but the boys took a couple more radios for good measure, carrying them openly back down the street with no more concern than if they'd been carrying groceries. Their own car was an ancient Camaro with patches of rust. It lurched away from the curb and turned right at the corner with a brief squeal of the suspension.

"Here we go." The cop turned the key in the ignition and pulled away from the curb. He didn't worry too much about keeping the Camaro in sight, because he thought he knew where it was going. Given what was at stake, it was better to be wrong than to get spotted.

Hugh's house was on Rosemont. When the unmarked police car turned onto it, the Camaro was nowhere to be seen.

"Try the alley."

They saw the Camaro as soon as they made the turn. It was parked against the fence, its lights on and its motor running. Only two of the kids seemed to be in it.

"We got 'em," said the cop in the passenger's seat, pressing the button on his handset. "One of them is inside the house now."

Curtis looked at the magistrate, who sat waiting in a chair by the door. She nodded.

"I've got the warrant, and I'm on my way. Go for it."

Hugh Royal lived in a two-story colonial with a porch supported by white, fluted columns. Curtis and a uniformed patrolman pulled into the driveway, and another marked car pulled in behind them. Curtis waited until everyone was out of the cars, then led the way up the sidewalk to the house. He took the three steps up to the slate-floored porch, rang the doorbell and tried the latch. It wasn't locked, so he opened the door and went in, the others crowding in behind him.

The house had twelve-foot ceilings and hardwood floors largely covered with massive Oriental carpets. To the left of the doorway, the living room opened off the entrance hall; to the right, the dining room. Both entrances were flanked by fluted columns similar to those along the front of the house. Straight ahead was a wide staircase going up to the second floor.

Curtis stopped, seeing no one. He jerked his head left and right, and the police officers with him fanned out through the house.

"Here, what is this?" said a voice from the head of the stairs. "What are you doing in my home?"

It was Hugh Royal. "We have a warrant to search the house, Mr. Royal," Curtis said.

"That's ridiculous. Let me see it." He came down the stairs with a hand extended, and he snatched the document from Curtis's grasp.

"Buying stolen property!" Hugh said. "Who made this up? There has to be some basis for what it says in a warrant. You can't just put down anything you want."

A door opened in the back of the house. Tony Royal appeared, along with a pimple-faced teenager and the two plain-clothed police officers. Hugh's eyes widened fractionally. He glanced at the canvas sack one of the police officers was carrying, bulging with hard, irregularly shaped objects, then back at Tony.

Tony said, "This boy came to the door wanting to use the telephone. These guys, these police officers, are saying the bag he was carrying had a bunch of stolen stuff in it."

After the merest flicker of hesitation, Hugh turned to Curtis. "So arrest the kid. We're not responsible for what he might be hauling around with him."

"We found them in the mud room, Lieu," said one of the plainclothesmen. "Automotive stereo components spread all over a piece of carpet. The kid had a hundred dollar bill in his pocket."

Curtis smiled at Hugh. "I believe we're going to search your house, Mr. Royal." To the plainclothesman, he said, "I want to talk to the boy in the kitchen."

The kid sat slumped in a chair beside a table decorated with an intricate wood inlay. He had narrow shoulders and a thin chest, and it was hard to tell whether he was tall or merely skinny. Patches of acne marked his face like a rash.

"What's your name?" Curtis asked him.

The boy didn't answer. Curtis fished a driver's license out of the boy's oversized canvas wallet.

"William Addison." He had turned eighteen just the week before. "They call you Will?" Curtis asked him.

"I ain't saying nothing."

"We'll stick with William, then." Curtis extracted a card from his shirt pocket. Reading, he said, "William, you have the right to remain silent. If you give up that right, anything you say can and will be used against you in a court of law. You have the right to an attorney..." When he had finished, he asked, "Do you understand the rights I've just read to you?"

William Addison watched him without expression.

Curtis gave the other police officer in the room a glance, then pulled up a chair and straddled it, his forearms resting on the back of the chair.

"Let me tell you what we've got, William," he said. "We've got two witnesses, both of them police officers, who watched you steal all that stereo equipment you had in the bag. If the total value of that equipment exceeds seven hundred and fifty dollars, and I'm betting it will, then it's a third degree felony, the penalty for which is confinement in a penitentiary for not more than ten years, nor less than two."

Curtis waited, but the boy's only response was a shrug of his shoulders. His eyes remained on the floor.

Curtis said, "You'll hardly believe it, but this is your lucky day."

The boy's eyes cut toward him.

"We don't want you. We want him." Curtis pointed back toward the dining room.

"Tony?"

"His father, Hugh. You give us Hugh Royal, and you won't be prosecuted."

"I ain't never done business with the old guy but once. And you're a liar; you can't promise nothing. It's all up to the D.A."

Everyone these days was a jailhouse lawyer.

"You're right," Curtis said. "And you don't have to say anything until the D.A. confirms the deal. All I need to know now is, if he gives you immunity, will you testify?"

The boy thought about it. "They'll call me a snitch."

"Weigh that against two to ten in the state penitentiary."

No response.

Curtis stood up. "Last chance, William. If the D.A. gives you immunity, will you testify?"

The boy shrugged. "I guess."

"I'll need you to say that one more time, then we'll take you down to the courthouse to make our deal." Curtis got up and walked toward the door to the dining room. When he swung it open, Hugh and Tony and two uniformed cops turned to look.

Curtis looked back into the kitchen. "I need to know now, William. If the D.A. offers you immunity from prosecution, will you testify?"

"Sure." His voice was clearly audible in the next room.

Chapter 61

The latest tax return showed that Skateworld, in Tyler, had grossed just under six hundred thousand dollars, more than three times what Alan had estimated as the skating rink's maximum potential. The combined revenues of SupeRink's nineteen skating rinks and five bowling alleys came to roughly nine million dollars.

SupeRink had little debt. All but one of the rinks was owned outright. Expenses, including Hugh Royal's six-figure salary, came to one million, nine hundred thousand dollars and change, leaving profits of about seven million dollars. SupeRink had the highest profit margin of any business Alan had ever heard of, though perhaps interest expense would have eaten up some of the profit had the business not been so strongly capitalized.

All SupeRink sold, really, outside of a few concessions, was space. It was the ideal opportunity to under-report income — but if that was happening, then SupeRink was even more profitable than the tax returns indicated, which was hard to believe, even impossible.

The copies Steve had made for Alan were scattered across the kitchen table. Tracey, sitting across from Alan, glanced at this page and that one, but without any real interest or apparent comprehension.

Alan was hardly aware of her. Hugh's net worth was . . . He found it. Four-point-five million dollars — not surprising given the profitability of the businesses he ran, perhaps even on the low side. But then, his ex-wife had said he lived extravagantly.

"He's not an embezzler," Alan said to Tracey.

"And that matters why?"

"I don't know, but it makes me think maybe the drugs you took from Carlotta were somebody else's. Not Hugh's."

"Barry and Tony's?"

"I don't know." He wondered if he were putting too much faith in what Tracey had told him about the whole affair, though he wasn't ready to say so.

He got up and walked into the living room, where he dropped into the recliner. Tracey came in and stood watching him as he thought.

"It's more interesting if you turn it on."

"What?"

She jerked her head at the TV.

"Oh, yeah." He laughed without meaning it. He was involved with his puzzle. Pieces of it were scattered through his mind like the pieces of a giant jigsaw puzzle.

Tracey went to bed. At midnight Alan went to bed himself.

When his alarm went off at six the next morning, he had the answer. He didn't know what to do with the answer, but he knew at last what was going on. It was embarrassing to him that he hadn't thought of it before.

If it was possible for Hugh to understate his income and get away with it, it was possible for him to overstate it as well. Hugh wasn't an embezzler; he was a money launderer. That was why he kept starting new rinks: every skater could have two or maybe three imaginary friends skating beside him, but not ten. As Hugh had more and more money to launder, he had to have more and more plausible sources for it. At each of the twenty-four rinks and bowling alleys, Hugh and Luis Basoalto piled cash into the receipts drawer, and they paid taxes on it. That allowed them to spend their money without the I.R.S. nailing them for tax evasion the way it had Al Capone.

Alan started to laugh.

Tracey appeared wide-eyed in his doorway. "What's wrong?"

"I've got it," he said. "I now understand Hugh Royal."

"And it's funny?"

"No. It's simple, really. Hugh's a money launderer."

She waited.

"Don't you see? It explains everything," he said.

"And it helps me? How?"

His smile faded. "I don't know," he admitted.

"Uh huh. Well, congratulations on your breakthrough."

Hugh Royal spent the night in a cell. Early the next morning, a deputy sheriff came and got him, leading him down the hall to a conference room where a number of people were waiting for him: Cale Larson, the district attorney, one hip propped on a corner of the table; the lawyer Hugh had called, a man named Charlie Duff; Lieutenant Curtis; and another uniformed policeman, who was seated at the table with a pen and a yellow pad. There was a tape recorder on the table.

"Hello, Hugh," Larson said. "Did you have a nice night?"

"I'm not talking to you. I want to talk to my lawyer here, and I want to be taken before a magistrate. You're not going to hold me five minutes."

"Maybe not," Larson said. "You've been charged with receiving stolen property worth more than seven hundred fifty dollars, which is a third degree felony. The magistrate will tell you all about the range of penalties associated with that. Before we go, though, I want Lieutenant Curtis to read you your rights again, this time in the presence of your attorney."

Curtis read Hugh his rights. When he got to Hugh's right to an attorney, Hugh's eyes cut to his lawyer. Charlie Duff had done the occasional bit of legal work for him before, but he wasn't Roger Coleman. It was unfortunate that, in the circumstances, Roger Coleman wouldn't do.

Larson said, "When we searched your house, we found something of an arsenal, which might interest the Federal Bureau of Alcohol, Tobacco, and Firearms."

"I'm not making any statement," Hugh said. He looked at Duff and jerked his head in Larson's direction, inviting him to interfere.

"Also," Larson continued. "We found what the Texas Penal Code refers to as a chemical laboratory apparatus: condensers, distilling equipment, a vacuum dryer, and an encapsulating machine."

"So?"

"Equipment adapted to the manufacture of a controlled substance. Unless you have a transfer permit — and the Department of Public Safety says you don't — that's a Class A misdemeanor, which carries penalties of its own. And that's if the equipment's clean. Do you know what the consequences will be if we find a particle of a controlled substance adhering to a test tube or beaker? Even one particle? Depending on what the controlled substance is, we might have you on a first degree felony, which means the possibility of life imprisonment."

"I'm not making any statement," Hugh repeated —but fine beads of perspiration had appeared on his forehead.

"I'm not asking you to make a statement. I just want you to listen to one."

"Come on, Charlie," Hugh said to his attorney. "End this and get me out of here."

"I think you'd better listen to him, Hugh."

Hugh glared at him, then turned his gaze on Larson. "Fine," he said. "Make your statement."

Larson was swinging his leg. "I'm prepared to prosecute you for the third-degree felony and the Class A misdemeanor," he said. "I think I can see to it you serve time, a minimum of two years in the penitentiary. If our chemists get a break, we may be able to put you away for the rest of your life. You can confer with your lawyer on that. Maybe he disagrees with me and thinks you can walk away from it all, I don't know. Whether you walk or not, yours is the kind of case that is going to generate publicity. Lots of publicity." Larson smiled for a long moment, then he dropped the smile and leaned forward. "Fortunately for you, we're not after you. We're after Tracey Coleman, and we think you can give her to us."

Hugh looked from Larson to his lawyer and back again.

"Here's what we think," Larson said. "We think that Carlotta Basoalto and Tracey Coleman smuggled a fair amount of cocaine into the country the week before the murder. We're guessing two kilos, because that was the quantity of powdered aspirin and baking soda your son tried to palm off on

Gonzalo Gutierrez a week later. The problem with our smuggling theory is that we can't prove it. We have some circumstantial evidence, but probably not enough to get before a jury. We need your testimony to do that."

Hugh moistened his lips with his tongue, but said nothing.

"What's in it for me, you ask?" Larson said. "Immunity on the smuggling charge —"

"Transactional immunity," Hugh's lawyer said.

Larson inclined his head. "Transactional immunity. No prosecution whatsoever on the smuggling charge."

"You haven't got me on any smuggling charge," Hugh said. "So far you're offering squat."

"Good point. What we have you on is a felony theft charge. Among other things. We're prepared to reduce all of it to a Class A misdemeanor."

"No."

"Are you sure you're in a position to bargain?"

Hugh wasn't sure, evidently; his breathing was clearly audible in the overcrowded room. But he said, "I can't implicate myself in the smuggling charge."

"They're offering you immunity," his lawyer said.

"It doesn't matter. You all know who Carlotta's father is. You all know Luis Basoalto. If he hears me admit I was using his daughter as a mule to bring drugs into the country..."

"Like he's pure as the driven snow," Larson said.

Hugh shook his head. "The man loves his daughter. If I used her as a mule, I'm a dead man."

"We'd protect you."

"I'll take my chances on life imprisonment." But he was sweating profusely now, and his face shone.

Larson studied him. "So we can't deal."

"Here's what I can do. Carlotta went home to Columbia for a visit a couple of weeks before she died. While she was there, she called to ask me to lend her thirty thousand dollars." He stopped.

"And?"

Hugh swallowed. "She wanted me to wire transfer the money to her." He paused, his eyes moving from face to face. "She said she was picking up some stuff, some...artifacts and stuff. Some of it was kind of awkward to handle, and Tracey was meeting her in Mexico City to help her with it."

"But she never said cocaine."

"Not until later. Not until Tracey had run off with it at the airport."

"Ah."

"She told me all about it then."

There was a silence. "Can you provide us with documentary evidence of the wire transfer?" Larson asked.

Hugh hesitated, then nodded.

Curtis said, "That wasn't smart."

"It isn't illegal to transfer money."

Larson shook his head. "I'm not sure I understand how this helps you with Luis Basoalto," he said. "It makes you look like an idiot — sending off money with no idea what it was for."

"It makes me look like an accommodating idiot. I was trying to help Carlotta."

For roughly a minute nobody said anything. All eyes were on Cale Larson. Charlie Duff asked, "What about it? Is it enough?"

Larson took a while to answer. "It might be, assuming I can get in Tracey Coleman's prior arrest for possession."

"So we have a deal?" Hugh said.

Larson nodded. "I think so. I think we have a deal."

Chapter 62

Later that morning Lieutenant Curtis was on the witness stand, his uniform pressed and clean, his manner intelligent and forthright. He gave the results of the ballistics tests and testified that the Davis derringer in question was registered to the defendant, Tracey Coleman.

"Are these photostatic copies of the registration papers?"

Curtis examined the papers Larson handed him. "They are."

"Move for admission."

"No objection," Alan said.

"Your witness."

Alan Dougherty had time for no more than a few questions on cross-examination before the noon recess. The prosecution's case was shaping up very much as it had in justice court. It had the same strengths and the same glaring weakness, the absence of motive. Alan glanced at Tracey as he loaded his papers into his briefcase. How close was the prosecution to any real evidence of a criminal conspiracy, he wondered? What were they going to do with Marty Harding, the Hertz employee at DFW?

That afternoon he cross-examined Curtis about the fingerprints found in the car. "I don't remember, did you say there were fingerprints in the car?"

"I didn't, but there were. Both the decedent, Carlotta Basoalto, and Tony Royal left fingerprints."

"Tony Royal?"

"They came to the symphony ball together."

"Who drove? Could the fingerprints tell you that?"

"There were no fingerprints on the steering wheel, if that's what you're getting at."

"None at all? Not even Carlotta's?"

"No."

"Smudges?"

"No."

"So the steering wheel had been wiped clean?"

"Evidently."

"Were there any other surfaces that appear to have been wiped clean of prints?"

"The door-handle on the driver's side."

"Were the fingerprints of Tracey Coleman anywhere on or in the car?"

"No."

"Nowhere in the car?"

"No."

"Not even on the murder weapon?"

"No. There were no fingerprints on the murder weapon."

"Smudges?"

"No."

"Suggesting that at some point the gun had been wiped clean — and afterwards handled only with gloves?"

"Possibly."

"Because the murderer expected the gun to be found."

Curtis smiled briefly. "I have no way of knowing what the murderer expected."

"But if the weapon were never found, fingerprints would be irrelevant. Or they could have been wiped off later. The murderer wiped off his prints to avoid being connected in any way to the murder weapon. From your perspective, that's the whole point of fingerprints, isn't it? To connect a suspect to the murder weapon?"

"They help."

"So if the murderer were Tracey Coleman as you suppose, there is no point to wiping off fingerprints. The gun is registered to her."

"Maybe she didn't intend to drop it."

"Then why wipe off the prints?" Alan held up a hand. "Never mind, lieutenant. You don't need to answer that. No further questions."

Larson stood up. "I'd like you to answer that last question, lieutenant."

"It is inconsistent," Curtis said. "People under stress are often inconsistent."

"And that would include murderers?"

"Objection," Alan said. "Leading."

"No further questions."

The judge looked at Alan.

"No further cross," Alan said.

"Call Hugh Royal," Larson said.

With some apprehension, Alan watched him come forward. Hugh Royal was the first of the witnesses from whom he didn't know what to expect.

After identifying himself, Hugh acknowledged being at the Tyler Symphony Orchestra's Boot-scootin' Ball.

"Did you go alone?" Larson asked him.

"No. I picked up my son Barry on the way."

"How about your nephew, Tony Royal?"

"No, he came with Carlotta."

"That's Carlotta Basoalto, the victim in this case?"

"Yes."

"What was *your* relationship to Carlotta?"

Hugh shifted, his eyes going to Luis Basoalto, who was sitting with his son Carlos in the gallery. "Landlord-tenant," he said. "She stayed in the apartment over my garage."

"When did you see her last?"

"Alive? She left the ball with Tracey Coleman."

"And never came back?"

"No."

In the jury box, several jurors changed position.

"When Carlotta left the ball with the defendant that evening, did she seem agitated or excited?"

"Tense, perhaps. Tracey and Carlotta had just returned from Mexico City the day before the murder. They'd had a falling out."

Alan glanced at Tracey.

"Had Carlotta been anywhere else outside the country?" Larson asked.

"To Colombia, where she's from. She stopped in Mexico City on her way back, and Tracey Coleman met her there."

Alan stood up. "Before Mr. Royal answers any more questions about this trip, I'd like to establish the source of his knowledge."

Larson asked Hugh, "Did Carlotta call you from Colombia to ask you to wire-transfer some funds to her?"

"Yes. Thirty thousand dollars."

"Objection," Alan said. "Relevance."

"And did you subsequently learn that Carlotta and the defendant Tracey Coleman —"

"Objection!" Alan shouted, loudly enough to cut Larson off. In the sudden silence of the courtroom, he drew an audible breath. "I want a ruling from the court before you ask any more questions."

Larson opened his mouth, but Judge Mitchell jabbed a finger at him. "Wait." His eyes moved back and forth between the two lawyers. "I think we'd better continue this conversation in chambers."

Hanging in an ornate silver frame on the wall behind Judge Mitchell's desk was a black-and-white photograph of a young woman in a simple bridal gown. It was, as everyone knew, Mitchell's wife as the beauty she had been in 1970. Nobody Alan knew had seen her in recent years.

"What's this about, counselors?" Judge Mitchell said as he dropped back into his padded leather chair. The stenographer sat against the wall with her Stenograph.

Larson spoke. "Evidence has come into our possession that the defendant and the murder victim smuggled a large quantity of cocaine into this country on the day before the murder."

"What evidence?" Alan demanded.

"Hugh Royal supplied the necessary money for the transaction. He —"

Alan interrupted. "Your honor, obviously Hugh Royal has made some sort of statement to the prosecution. The critical question, though, is whether Hugh himself had any direct communication with Tracey Coleman. If he didn't, then Mr. Larson has him on the stand to recite to us a lot of things that Carlotta may or may not have said to him. That's hearsay, and it's inadmissible."

The judge asked Larson, "When is it that the two women are supposed to have brought this contraband into the country? October twenty-fourth. And the murder occurred on the night of the twenty-fifth. I take it you're claiming there's some sort of connection."

Alan didn't give Larson time to answer. "Your honor, if Hugh Royal has made a statement to the prosecution, I would very much like to see it."

The judge looked at Larson.

"People in hell would very much like some ice water," Larson said.

The judge scowled, but before he could respond, Larson added, "Under *Gaskin* I don't have to produce Mr. Royal's statement until the conclusion of my direct examination," he said. "I haven't concluded my direct examination."

"I think you have," Alan said.

The judge said, "Maybe we'd better have a copy of that statement."

"Your honor," Larson said in protest. "There was a conspiracy here, and before her death the murder victim made a number of statements during the course and in furtherance of the conspiracy. Rule 801(e) excludes such statements from the definition of hearsay."

Alan said, "We need to see that statement."

The judge sighed. "Mr. Larson, produce the statement."

Larson's lower lip protruded, and for a moment Alan thought he would refuse. "I'll have to get it. It's in the courtroom."

When he had gone, Alan began, "I think —," but the judge cut him off.

"Wait until he gets back."

It didn't take long. Larson came in with two copies of the statement, each four sheets of paper filled with single-spaced type. He presented one to each of them.

The judge said, "Now be quiet, both of you, while I read this."

Alan scanned his own copy as a clock ticked on the wall. The statement had everything. Tracey had double-crossed Carlotta by absconding with two kilograms of cocaine, and Carlotta had drawn her away from the Harvey Convention Center for a confrontation from which she had never returned. By providing a motive for the murder, a strong one, Hugh's testimony transformed the prosecution's case. When Alan had finished reading, he looked up and saw that the judge was watching him.

He swallowed. "I was right, your honor. All of this refers to a single occasion of smuggling —"

"Which doesn't prevent it from being a conspiracy," Judge Mitchell said.

"Not if it were true, but Hugh Royal's only knowledge of it came from Carlotta. Mr. Larson's got nothing to offer us but statements she supposedly made to Hugh."

"During the course and in furtherance of the conspiracy," Larson said. "First, to acquire financing, then to recover the contraband after Tracey double-crossed her. The statements she made to Hugh fall under the exception to the hearsay rule."

Alan said, "I deny that it does. You've got to show the existence of a conspiracy by independent evidence."

"I have independent evidence," Larson said. "I have documents showing the wire transfer of funds. I have..."

"Diddly-squat," Alan said. "Everything you've got could have any number of innocent explanations. Without the hearsay, none of it adds up to criminal conspiracy." He turned to the judge. "He can't offer hearsay evidence unless he can show there's a conspiracy, and the only evidence he has of a conspiracy is that same hearsay evidence. Which is inadmissible." A smile touched the judge's lips, but Alan pressed on. "Give me until tomorrow morning, your honor. I can bring you cases out the ying-yang that hold the conspiracy has to be established by independent evidence."

"Do you have any cases to cite, Mr. Larson?" the judge asked.

"Not off the top of my head."

"I think Mr. Dougherty is likely right. Would you care to have until tomorrow to brief the issue?"

Larson looked angry.

Mitchell said, "Fine, then. We'll return to the courtroom and recess until ten o'clock tomorrow morning. I'll want your briefs by eight a.m. We'll meet in here again at nine-thirty." The judge stood. "And Mr. Larson —"

Larson turned, his hand already on the doorknob.

"I'll expect cases out the ying-yang from both of you." He grinned broadly at them, exposing glints of dark metal in his yellow teeth.

Alan called the office as he walked down the corridor of the courthouse basement. "Jay Fowler, please."

Jay was in court.

"This is Alan Dougherty," he told the receptionist. "Where is he really?"

"I think he had a dentist appointment. He said he wouldn't be back."

Alan took a breath. He had a brief to write tonight, and he was going to need help with the research.

"Can I get you anyone else?" the receptionist asked.

"Jordan Conway."

"One moment, please."

There was a click on the line and, after a pause, another click. "Hi, Alan," Jordan said. "How's it going over there?"

"I need a favor."

"Uh oh."

"A big favor."

"Is there any other kind?"

He took that as a go-ahead. "Are you familiar with the co-conspirator exception to the hearsay rule in..." He held up his paperback edition of *Texas Criminal Procedure*, which he carried folded open in the same hand as the handle of his briefcase. "...Rule 801(e)(2)(E) of the Rules of Criminal Evidence?" He lowered the book and briefcase.

"Oh, right," she said. "Rule 801(e)(2)(E). I was thinking about that this morning at breakfast."

"Good," he said, ignoring the sarcasm. He pushed through the swinging door at the end of the hall, passing into the late-afternoon shadow of the courthouse. It was cold. "It seems like I remember from my evidence class in law school..."

"Oh, great."

"...that a criminal conspiracy has to be proven by independent evidence before an out-of-court statement by a co-conspirator — Carlotta in this case — becomes admissible. It has to be true, or there'd be an easy end-run around the hearsay rule."

"'It has to be true' — is that the argument you gave the judge?"

"No. I told him I could get him cases out the ying-yang."

She laughed shortly. "Now I gather you don't think you can deliver."

"Not without help. I have to have it by tomorrow morning."

"Figures."

"If you could get started on it, I'll join you as soon as I can. Are you in the middle of anything?"

"No. I was just sitting here with folded hands, waiting for the phone to ring."

"So you'll do it?"

She exhaled audibly. "I'll get started. But you get over here as soon as you can."

"Thanks, Jordan. I owe you."
"Don't think I won't collect."

Chapter 63

He pocketed his phone, turned the corner, and walked right into a man big and beefy enough to be hanging in a meat locker.

"Excuse me," Alan said. He spun away and ran full into the man's twin, who was coming up behind him. Arms as long and muscular as a gorilla's closed around him, pinning one arm and squeezing the breath out of him in a single gust. His briefcase hit the sidewalk with a clap, and his copy of *Texas Criminal Procedure* fell open beside it. He struggled, but his feet left the ground, his rising knee caught only a hip, and the pressure on his ribcage increased to the limits of his endurance.

"Relax, mi compañero." But it evidently didn't matter to his attackers whether he relaxed or not. A hand went into his pants pocket and came out with his keys. "El jefe, theese time he wants only to talk to you."

"Okay," Alan gasped. "Okay." The pressure on his chest eased, and he drew in air. "I'll talk to el jefe."

"Come."

The two men turned him. As he walked down the sidewalk between them, his heart was pounding. At the end of the sidewalk loomed a dark Jaguar sedan, where a thin, sallow man swung open a rear door to reveal an empty back seat.

Alan decided he didn't want to go where they were taking him. He leaped forward, but a grab at the sleeve of his jacket sent him staggering forward off-balance. He recovered. The Jaguar was blocking his escape, but he took two running steps and tried to go over it, belly-flopping on the car's roof and scrambling in an effort to get across it before a hand caught the heel of his shoe and dragged him back.

He landed unsteadily, his nose hitting the top of the open door to numb his face. Hands on his shoulder and the top of his head pushed him downward and into the car, where he sprawled on the leather upholstery.

"Esta tranquilo." A man pushed into the backseat beside him.

"My keys," Alan said, panting. "My briefcase."

"Later."

The other giant pushed into the backseat from the other side, wedging Alan upright between them.

Alan's knees were nearly against his chest, his feet propped on the hump over the drive shaft. "I'm going to need my briefcase," he said.

"You will have it."

"And my keys?" Their shoulders were so broad that he had no room to lean back, and he had to twist his neck to see either of them.

The man laughed and slapped the back of Alan's head. "Què bromista, this one," he said.

Alan found himself examining the tightly laced wingtips that had been his undoing. If he'd worn other shoes, he'd have gotten away, poorer by a penny-loafer and a set of car keys, but free.

"Seriously," the big man said. "The chances of our keeling you today..." Alan turned his head, and the man smiled, exposing crooked teeth. "Very small," he said.

The Jaguar headed out Route 155 through increasingly bleak country. Thirty minutes down the road it came to Teaselville, or at least to the Texaco

Foodmart that represented the heart of Teaselville's business district, and turned right. It was nearly six o'clock, and the quality of the sunlight was beginning to change as the Jaguar turned south on the road that circled Lake Palestine. A half-mile further on, the car turned into a short drive that ended in a wrought-iron gate.

There was a tiny gatehouse beside the gate, in it a thin man with a black, drooping moustache. He nodded and waved, and the gate swung inward.

Beyond the gate the ground sloped steeply upward. At the top of the slope sat a building that looked less like a house than a spaceship, being disk-shaped and sided with what might have been crumpled green aluminum.

Craning his neck as they drove upward, Alan saw dust rising off the road behind them and the gate swinging slowly shut.

The driver parked the Jaguar in front of the alien spacecraft. The double front doors looked like they belonged on a submarine, being convex rather than flat. In the center of each, in lieu of the conventional doorknob, was a four-spoked wheel about a foot in diameter.

The men on either side of Alan reached for the door handles, and the car doors sprang outward with the release of pressure. As the men pushed out of the car, Alan drew his first full breath since the trip began.

"Get out," said one of them, and Alan scrambled awkwardly to the edge of the seat.

They pushed Alan along the sidewalk that circled the house, bypassing the front doors. The driver walked behind them. As they rounded a corner, Alan saw that the spaceship wasn't a full disk, but a half-disk. The back wall was a vast expanse of dark glass through which he could see, faintly, a living area on the first floor and a rail overlooking it from the floor above.

The men turned on him abruptly.

"Hey! Hey, let go."

They handled him roughly but not cruelly, throwing him casually against a stone buttress that protruded from the house at the edge of the crumpled green aluminum. One reached around him to run a practiced hand over his chest and around his waist, then down each of his legs.

"This isn't necessary," Alan said, supporting himself with his hands. "I'm not armed." It was true. They had taken him from the courthouse, and courthouse security had made sure that he was unarmed and helpless.

"Forgive us please for not taking you at your word."

They let him off the wall and watched with apparent amusement as he straightened his clothes. In the moment allowed him, Alan's eyes moved over the area in back of the house, taking in the in-ground pool and the patio furniture sitting around it on the terrazzo tile. A stone wall overlooked the lake below, where dark water reflected a few wispy bits of fluff that floated in a sky that was darkening to the color of blued steel.

"Are you ready, poco?" There was no mistaking the note of amusement.

Alan nodded.

"This way." The man opened a door of dark glass. Alan hesitated for a moment, then ducked his head and walked past him into the house.

Luis Basoalto was at the wet bar making himself a drink, his black shirt open at the throat to reveal curling chest hair of the same snowy white as the hair on his head. He stirred his drink, the glass stirring-rod clinking against the ice, and, when he had finished, he came around the bar toward them.

"Mr. Dougherty," he said. "So." He wore white cotton slacks and leather sandals.

"So," Alan said, his mouth suddenly dry.

"I wish to apologize for the insistent nature of my invitation. Welcome to my abode."

Alan inclined his head.

The old man crossed to a white leather sofa and sat down. "Can Raul get you something from the bar?" He gestured to one of Alan's broad-shouldered escorts.

"No, thank you." He cleared his throat.

"Tequila perhaps? A beer?"

"I don't drink."

"Very commendable on your part, I'm sure. I myself find that I abuse the alcohol almost daily."

Alan felt rather than heard the door open behind him.

"Ah, here he is. I don't know whether you've had the pleasure of meeting my son Carlos."

Carlos Basoalto entered the house from the patio. He carried Alan's briefcase to the coffee table, laid it flat and dropped Alan's keys on top of it.

Alan's eyes returned to Luis.

"I want to compliment you on your skills in the courtroom," Luis said. "You are, I think, an effective advocate for your client."

"Is that why I'm here?"

Luis smiled. "You are direct. Very good. There is a subject which I felt it would be to our mutual advantage to discuss privately."

"What?"

"There is again the direct approach: 'What?' Okay. I want to know the nature of the testimony which Hugh Royal seemed so anxious to give this afternoon and which you seemed equally anxious to exclude."

"Have you talked to Hugh?"

Luis's mouth stretched in an expression no one would have mistaken for a smile. "Hugh Royal's appearance on the witness stand came as a surprise to me. While Mr. Larson and you were in chambers together, it occurred to me that a conversation with Hugh would be in order, but Hugh, regretfully, had made himself, eh..." He waved a hand.

"Scarce?"

"Scarce, yes. I cannot talk to Hugh Royal this afternoon. I will talk to him, of course, but I will talk to Mr. Dougherty first, I tell myself. Perhaps he can give me a perspective that is useful to me, no?"

Alan stood looking at him. After a moment, he reached into his suit coat. Raul, standing at one end of the sofa, reached into his own jacket, and Alan froze without withdrawing his hand.

"I want to show Mr. Basoalto some papers," Alan said, addressing Raul.

"You may show me some papers. Raul, you searched him, did you not?"

His eyes on Raul, Alan drew out Hugh's typewritten statement, and he stepped forward to hand it to Luis.

Everyone waited in silence while the old man read the first page and flipped it back, read the second and flipped it back, read the third. When he had finished the statement, Luis looked up. His face was curiously immobile. "This makes me most unhappy with my friend Hugh Royal," he said. "It seems he would implicate my daughter publicly in the smuggling of drugs."

"Yes."

"But, Mr. Dougherty, it seems also that you represent a woman who has killed my daughter."

"No. I represent a woman who is accused of killing your daughter."

"Evidently a legal technicality at this point." He rattled Hugh's statement.

"No," Alan said. He swallowed. "Tracey Coleman is innocent."

"Yes? You know who is guilty then?" His eyes were hard and disbelieving.

"No. Not yet. This statement of Hugh's — it's mingled fact and fiction. It makes you unhappy with Hugh Royal. Ask yourself: Why would Hugh say all this? Especially knowing that you would be there in the courtroom to hear him. It must be that the truth is worse for Hugh than what he says."

"What is the truth?"

Alan took a breath. "Mr. Basoalto, Hugh Royal was using your daughter as a carrier to smuggle illegal drugs into this country. He was using Tracey, too, which is what makes his testimony useful to the prosecution. He admits in his statement that he supplied the money to buy the cocaine. You know him. Is it reasonable that he would wire thirty thousand dollars to Columbia without knowing what the money was for?"

"Go on."

"Tracey told me that Hugh was going to pay Carlotta and her five thousand dollars for their part in bringing the cocaine through customs. On the way back to the States from Mexico City, Carlotta and Tracey decided Hugh was taking advantage of them, giving them all the risk for very little of the profit. The two of them decided on a plan..."

He told the story very much the way Tracey had told it when she was sitting beside him in the holding cell at the Smith County Police Department. Tracey and Carlotta had decided to double-cross Hugh Royal, with Tracey keeping the cocaine until she, speaking through Carlotta, could demand more money, but the plan started going wrong almost immediately. First, Tony and Barry acted too quickly in breaking into Tracey's apartment on Friday night to recover the cocaine...

Luis interrupted him. "Mr. Dougherty, this is a fairy tale; it means nothing to me. My daughter was killed with a bullet fired from your client's own handgun —"

"Which was in Tracey Coleman's apartment on the night the Royal boys broke into it to get the cocaine."

"You're saying that Tony and Barry Royal killed my daughter?"

"One of them, or someone else who had access to the gun they took that night. Again, why would Hugh tell this story to the police? It makes him look like a fool at best. His testimony makes it pretty clear that he used your daughter in a criminal enterprise. Despite what he says, he's implicating himself in the smuggling."

There was a silence. Finally, Luis said, "Very well, Mr. Dougherty, perhaps you should tell me. Why would Hugh tell the police this story?"

"Because the police have something on Hugh. They're threatening him with prosecution."

Luis's mouth twisted. "What could they have on Hugh Royal? The man runs a roller rink."

"I don't know. Maybe they've got him on the smuggling, maybe something else. He's telling this story as part of a deal, a plea bargain."

A thought started Alan's mind in a new direction. "Actually, I don't think it could be the smuggling," he said. "If it were, then the prosecution knows he's lying when he denies any knowing involvement, and Larson's suborning perjury. I don't think he'd do that, not like this. Too many people would know about it."

"But if it is not smuggling...," Luis began.

"If a man like Hugh is engaged in smuggling, he's engaged in other illegal activities as well. I've uncovered evidence of one of them myself." He reached for his briefcase, which was on the coffee table, pausing at a movement from Raul. "May I?" he asked Luis.

Luis glanced at Raul, then gave Alan a nod. "Please."

Alan pocketed his keys, which Carlos had left on the briefcase, then opened the briefcase and reached into it for the envelope he'd gotten from Steve Booker. Withdrawing its contents, he placed the papers on the glass coffee table in front of Luis.

"These are the tax records and financial statements from one of Citizen and Farmer's loan files on Hugh Royal," Alan said.

Luis leaned forward to spread the papers across the coffee table, pushing at them with a brown finger.

Alan said, "You'll note that they deal not only with Hugh personally but with SupeRink, Inc., a corporation in which you are the majority stockholder."

Luis looked up at Alan with eyes so dark as to be nearly black.

Alan pushed on. "I've done some investigating. The operating profits SupeRink reports on these tax returns are far in excess of its actual profits." Of course, other than a single evening spent at one of its roller rinks, he had no evidence at all as to SupeRink's actual profits, but he knew what he knew. "Mr. Basoalto, Hugh Royal is using your company to launder money, perhaps money from his own illegal operations, perhaps money from the illegal operations of others."

Luis gaze was unblinking, and Alan returned it with a face as free from guile as he could manage.

"Are you threatening me, Mr. Dougherty?" Luis's voice was soft.

Drops of sweat dripped cold against Alan's sides. "You?" He gave a laugh that sounded disastrously false to his own ears. "You're one of Hugh's victims. Hugh, though, is involved in criminal activity up to his kiester. Whatever the police have on him, to get out of it Hugh's willing to implicate your daughter in drug activity and my client in a murder she didn't commit. Possibly he's willing to implicate others as well."

For too long nobody said anything.

"To whom have you told these lies?" Luis jerked his chin at the documents on the table.

"To nobody." Alan smiled mechanically. "Nobody outside the lawyers of my firm. Smith, Angley..."

"And Waters. Yes, I know of them." He studied Alan across the coffee table, clicking his thumbnail with the nail of his middle finger. "What happens tomorrow when Hugh Royal testifies?" he said at last.

Alan exhaled audibly. "I don't know. I have some hope I can keep him from testifying at all."

"How is that?"

"The prosecutor and I are meeting with the judge at nine-thirty tomorrow morning to argue the point. If I lose the argument, Hugh goes on the witness stand at ten. I'll cross-examine him — and I'll have to ask him, among other things, about his use of your business as a front for illegal activities. I'll..." Alan stopped, realizing he had just threatened Luis Basoalto.

"It is fortunate for you that we have this opportunity to talk privately," Luis said.

"Is it?" Alan took a breath. He was aware of beads of sweat rolling past his hairline and onto his forehead, but he dared not draw attention to them by wiping them away. "Suppose you tell me not to use this information, and in the interests of my client I feel I have to do it anyway?"

"How would asking questions about SupeRink serve the interests of your client?"

"If the jury believes Hugh's testimony linking Tracey and Carlotta to illegal smuggling and criminal conspiracy, then Tracey's heading for death by lethal injection. If I can show the jury Hugh Royal is a crook and can destroy his credibility..."

"Though what he says about the criminal conspiracy is true, you say."

Alan hesitated. "Yes."

Luis Basoalto studied him for perhaps a minute. "I share your desire to keep Hugh Royal from testifying," he said at last. "I am an old man. My daughter, my only daughter, is dead, and I have no wish to see Hugh Royal desecrate her memory. Tell me, what do you believe are your chances of keeping Hugh from testifying tomorrow?"

"Good. Better than even."

"That does not sound so good to me, not with the stakes involved. But perhaps if you cannot keep him from testifying, I will be able to do so."

"How?"

Luis smiled grimly.

"No," Alan said, shaking his head.

"No?"

"Mr. Basoalto...The D.A.'s gotten hold of this smuggling thing, and for the rest of the trial he's going to be doing his best to get it into evidence. Hugh's only one possible avenue for him. If Larson succeeds, then everything's going to come out into the open, with or without Hugh Royal."

"I cannot allow him to say these things about my daughter."

"Mr. Basoalto, if you kill Hugh Royal..." Alan stopped, unable to continue either with threat or prediction.

"I understand your problem, I think," Luis said. "I understand, and I will think what I can do to help you."

Carlos Basoalto spoke for the first time. "We have to do something about Hugh Royal, regardless."

Luis looked up into the eyes of his son and gave him a small nod. "Yes. Mr. Dougherty tells us many troubling things about our friend Hugh. You, Carlos, will talk to our friend in the Tyler Police Department to find out just what they have on him and why we have heard nothing about it until now. Raul, you —"

"Mr. Basoalto," Alan said, interrupting.

Luis Basoalto raised a hand. "As for you, it is enough. As you say in the law —" He smiled, showing white, strong teeth. "We have a meeting of the minds."

Alan shook his head. "No, I don't think we do."

"You will see me tomorrow when you come out of the judge's chambers," Luis said. "If you have succeeded with your argument, then tell me it is a good morning. If you have not —"

"Mr. Basoalto, I can't be a party to —" But he was a party to it. He was, and he knew it.

"Remove him from my house," Luis said, jerking his head at Raul.

Alan started, but Raul had him by the arm, dragging him toward the patio doors like a recalcitrant child, his resistance and stumbling of no more effect than a four-year-old's. In his other hand, Raul carried Alan's briefcase. As the door closed behind them, Alan heard a remark in Spanish from inside the house and a burst of laughter.

The sun had just dropped below the horizon beyond the lake, and the sky was red.

"I can walk," he said to Raul, reaching for his briefcase and trying to twist away. "You don't..."

Raul released the briefcase and shoved him forward. Alan staggered along the sidewalk and stopped.

His car was there, parked beside the dark Jaguar. He went to it, pulled at the door handle and got in. He felt numb.

The gate was swinging toward him as he drove down the hill, and he slowed to allow it to open all the way.

Chapter 64

It was just after eight-thirty when he got to the office. Jordan's Mustang was still in the lot, and he found her in her office, her desk and the floor around it littered with print-outs.

"What have you got?" he asked her.

"A headache. I thought you were going to help with this."

"I got detained."

"Well, I haven't had any dinner. If I ever find out you spent the evening playing footsies with Tracey Coleman, you're going to be one sorry S.O.B."

"Other than no dinner, how's it going?" He gestured at the desktop.

She exhaled. "It's going okay. Turned out you were right. I did find cases out the ying-yang." She tapped the screen of her computer. "Got the brief right here, all ready to print."

"It's done?"

"All done, no thanks to you."

"That's good." He flopped into one of her client chairs and ran his hand backward through his hair.

"What's wrong?"

He shook his head. "I thought commercial litigation was tough. It's nothing compared to this."

"Because Tracey goes to Huntsville if you blow it?"

"And even if she doesn't go to Huntsville, we're likely to end up in a field somewhere with bullets in the backs of our heads."

Jordan turned her chair toward him. "Luis Basoalto?"

"Yep."

"I hope to hell you know what you're doing."

"So do I."

She stood abruptly. "I've sent the brief to the printer. Take that stack of cases on the corner of the desk, and we'll go make the copies."

"Just this stack?" He pushed at it.

"I cited twenty-four cases in the brief. Those eight are the most important. If they don't do it for you, then I'm afraid you are out of luck. Or Tracey is."

He sighed again and heaved himself up out of his chair.

He read her brief as it came off the printer, and it was even better than he had hoped. A depression settled on him as he drove home, though, a weariness of mind and body so great that he had difficulty keeping his car on the road. By the time he passed his house to circle around to the alley, even his death-grip on the steering wheel was failing to control the tremor in his hands. He parked his car in the garage.

Tracey was in the living room, and the television was on.

"Where you been?" she said, muting the volume.

"At the firm. Research."

"I didn't see you after the judge called you into chambers."

"No. He assigned us briefs to write."

"And you couldn't come back into the courtroom long enough to let me know what was going on? It's a good thing I had my own car."

"I was detained."

"What does that mean?"

He dropped onto the sofa. He glanced at the television and saw two women and a guy all in their underwear. He frowned. "I saw Luis Basoalto this evening," he said. "I was at his house on Lake Palestine."

Her eyes widened. "Why?"

"He kind of insisted. Like you, he wanted to know what went on in the judge's chambers. He was especially interested in what Hugh Royal was going to be testifying to."

"What did you tell him?"

"That Hugh's going to say you and Carlotta were smuggling Colombian cocaine into the country." He glanced again at the TV. There was a black bar blanking out the guy's hips, suggesting he'd lost his boxers. The girls were still there, both still in bra and panties. "What is this?" he asked.

"Reality TV." She killed the picture. "Were you telling the truth? The police know about the cocaine?"

"Everyone knows about the cocaine. Here." He reached into his suit jacket. "No, Luis kept my copy."

"Copy of what?"

"Hugh's statement. Hugh claims that you and Carlotta were smuggling cocaine into the country, but that he didn't know anything about it until you ran off with it. She was going to confront you at the reception, but he lost sight of you — and her, too, until he found her in her car."

"That's not good."

"No, it's not. If he testifies, you'll be convicted. If I get you acquitted by excluding Hugh's testimony, father Luis shoots you in the head. Me, too, maybe."

"Unless we can convince him I didn't do it."

Alan nodded morosely.

"What did you tell him?"

"That you and Carlotta were smuggling drugs, but that you were doing it for Hugh. That you and she tried to pull a scam on Hugh to get a bigger share of the profits. That Hugh's boys broke into your apartment to recover their cocaine and, while they were at it, stole a .25 caliber Davis derringer from your underwear drawer. It's a good story, even if you did make it up."

Her face tightened. "Sometimes I could jerk your hair out by the roots."

He studied her. "That was out of line," he conceded. "I'm sorry."

"Did he believe you? Luis?"

"I don't know what he believed. He'll look into it, he said."

"Look into it how?"

"I don't know. It would be nice if there were corroborating evidence of some kind, something to tie Barry and Tony into either the smuggling or Carlotta's murder. Then I think maybe Luis would buy it."

"Maybe there is something."

He eyed her. "What?"

"I don't know, but they are tied into the smuggling *and* the murder. There has to be evidence of it somewhere."

Chapter 65

Larson, as it turned out, hadn't written much of a brief. The only cases he cited were for general principles of law not directly related to the admissibility of a co-conspirator's out-of-court statement. He argued essentially from the language of the hearsay exception: It said what it said, and it meant it.

"I'm not going to let Hugh Royal testify as to anything Carlotta told him," Judge Mitchell said when they met again at nine-thirty. "What he's said so far will be stricken from the record, and the jury will be admonished to disregard it. I don't want to hear anything further about a trip to Mexico City until such time as you can prove the existence of a criminal conspiracy by independent evidence."

"I have the wire transfer," Larson said. "All kinds of circumstantial evidence."

"I've looked at your circumstantial evidence. None of it adds up to criminal conspiracy, either by itself or taken all together."

Alan, who had opened his mouth to respond, closed it promptly. When you had the judge arguing your case for you, it was time to shut up.

Larson said, "Tracey Coleman rented a car at DFW and drove it home alone — even though she had a ticket to Tyler on the same plane as Carlotta. Why would she do that?"

Judge Mitchell looked at him.

"She has a prior arrest for —"

"That's enough," Mitchell said, raising a hand to cut him off. "You know better than that."

"The evidence is circumstantial, but it all points in one direction. It's enough that reasonable jury could conclude..."

"No, Mr. Larson."

"But —"

"That's enough, I said. I'll see you both in court in thirty minutes."

Hugh Royal was in the offices of the district attorney, waiting for Larson as instructed, when Larson swept scowling into the reception area.

"Come on back," he snapped, and Hugh got up to follow him into Larson's cluttered office.

Larson tossed his leather portfolio onto the top of his desk and dropped into his chair. "Well, you did it," he said. "You really did it."

"The judge is going to let me testify?"

"No, as matters stand, the judge is not going to let you testify."

"Then —"

"You just couldn't implicate yourself in the smuggling thing, could you? You know and I know you were in it up to your eyebrows, but now it's too late for you to say so."

Hugh didn't say anything.

Larson said, "If you yourself were part of the conspiracy, there'd be no question of your testifying. You could testify to your own activities and to any contact you had with Tracey, either directly or through an intermediary."

"You mean Carlotta?"

"Now, though, any testimony along those lines would contradict your sworn testimony that you yourself were Mr. Clean in the smuggling affair. So what I've got is a dead co-conspirator who supposedly made a lot of statements to you just prior to her death — and a judge who isn't going to let you repeat those statements unless I can come up with more evidence that a conspiracy existed in the first place."

"So I won't be testifying?"

Larson brought his hand down on his desk. "No, you won't be testifying. Haven't you been listening? I can't use you unless and until I come up with something else on the smuggling conspiracy."

Hugh stood. "I can go?"

Larson cocked his head, looking up at Hugh with obvious distaste. "You be where I can reach you tonight," he said. "We're gonna come up with something. If I have to drag it out of you with a pair of pliers, we're gonna come up with something."

Coming out of the judge's chambers, Alan turned the corner toward the restroom and fell back, rebounding off the chest of Raul or his twin. Luis stood just beyond them in front of the restroom door.

"And how are we today, Mr. Dougherty?" Luis asked, his hands in the pockets of his topcoat.

Alan felt his heart go into double time. "I'm okay," he said. He looked from Luis to his bodyguards and back again. "Good morning."

He ducked his head as he pushed past them into the restroom. When he realized they weren't going to follow him, he began to shake. It was more than a minute before he could attend to business without being in danger of making a mess of himself.

Chapter 66

In the courtroom, Larson declined to recall Hugh Royal to the stand for further questions. The judge told the jury to disregard any statements Hugh Royal had made about anything that might or might not have been said to him by Carlotta Basoalto. "Ms. Basoalto can neither confirm nor deny such statements, and, even if she made them, we have no way to judge her honesty or to ask for clarification. Anything that somebody says she told them is outside of the evidence that the law permits us to consider."

Larson called Dale Calaway to the stand. Calaway had blond hair and glasses with tortoise-shell frames. "State your name and occupation for us, please."

"Dale Calaway. I own and manage the Southern Gun Shop here in Tyler."

"In the course of business, have you come into contact with the defendant Tracey Coleman?"

"She's a customer."

"She's purchased guns from you? Did she purchase a .25 caliber Davis derringer from you, serial number..." He lifted a paper from the lectern and read it to him.

"Yes. She did."

"When?"

Calaway checked his list and gave them the date.

"You have a shooting range at your establishment?" Larson asked him.

"I do."

"Has the defendant ever used it for target practice?"

"Yes."

"How often?"

"A few times."

"Is she any good?"

"She's competent."

"Has she practiced with different types of pistols?"

"Sure. I think so."

"How many types of pistol? The derringer?"

"Oh, I doubt it. The derringer's not a target pistol."

Larson turned to walk back to his table, the eyes of the jurors tracking him. Turning back, he asked, "How many pistols has Tracey Coleman purchased from you over the years? Do you know?"

Calaway's eyes went briefly to Tracey. "Six," he said.

"How many were purse guns like the Davis derringer?" he asked.

"Just the one."

Larson smiled. "Thank you, Mr. Calaway. Your witness."

Alan stood, wondering about that last question: How many purse guns. What was the significance of that?

"When you say the derringer isn't a target pistol," he asked, "what exactly do you mean?"

"It's not a target pistol. No one would ever use it for that."

"Why not?"

"It's too small to fit comfortably in the hand, and the barrel's too short for consistent accuracy."

Alan hesitated. Dr. Quillen had said the range was two inches to three feet, far less than target range. Larson had left him with nowhere to go. "Thank you," he said at last, and, to the judge, "No further questions."

Judge Mitchell looked at Larson. "Mr. Larson?" he said.

"Call Charles Danvers."

The disgraced lawyer, formerly of Coleman, Anders and Davis, stood and pushed through the bar.

Chapter 67

Hugh Royal was ebullient. He'd expected to spend the day in the witness box, sweat beaded on his forehead as he worked to give the district attorney what he wanted without compromising himself fatally with Luis Basoalto. Instead he was on the links, watching Luis stroke through the ball at the first hole, Luis's club finishing behind his back as the ball lifted high in the air.

The ball drifted slightly to the right and landed in the rough about twenty yards off the green.

"Good drive, Mr. B.," Hugh said. "That was a hell of a carry."

Luis Basoalto had stopped him at the door of the courtroom. "I cannot go into the courtroom today, Hugh," he had said. "All the testimony, it weighs on my spirits. I feel suddenly I cannot sit in that courtroom any longer. The prosecution, it finished with you yesterday, did it not? The weather is nice. Why don't we take in a few holes this morning, you and I?"

It was the most that Hugh could have wished for. Now, at the first hole, Luis flashed him a white smile as he carried his driver back to his golf bag. "A hell of a carry," Hugh said again, and in high spirits he clasped Luis's shoulder.

Carlos made a bad drive, his ball falling short of the green. The meaty Raul did worse still, the divot he gouged from the turf flying high in the air. Hugh's own drive, though, was perfect, his ball landing on the apron just short of the green and bouncing onto it. The four men gathered their bags and walked down the hill. The air was crisp and clean, the sky clear, the weather fine.

Carlos overshot the green on his next shot. Hugh and Luis and Carlos waited for Raul to hit his ball out from the trees, then, when he had rejoined them, they walked along to Luis's ball. Luis used a wedge to chip it onto the green.

Hugh made a birdie on the first hole, one under par.

He was a full seven strokes ahead of Luis when they reached the ninth hole at the farthest corner of the links. The conversation was easy, and everyone was smiling.

"Why don't you tee-off first on this hole, Hugh, and let me take the last spot," Luis said. "Maybe it will change my luck."

As Hugh bent to jab his tee into the soft turf and to place his ball on it, Luis said, "I had an interesting talk yesterday with the young lawyer who is representing Tracey Coleman. What is his name? Dougherty, I think." The tone was friendly, but Hugh stiffened. As he straightened, his gaze flickered to Luis's face and away.

"He came to my home." Luis shook his head with a rueful smile. "I was sorely tempted, I will tell you. There in my own house is the man representing this person who has killed my daughter. Ah, I will be silent. Forgive me, Hugh. I wish to allow you to concentrate."

Hugh hunched over his ball, waiting stiffly for some further comment. When none seemed to be forthcoming, he began his backswing. His ball plopped in the lake, short and far to the left of the green.

"You pulled your shot, I think. Carlos, Raul, we have our chance to close the gap a little."

But Carlos sliced his ball into the trees, and Raul put his into the lake with Hugh's.

"Ah, too bad," Luis said. "At least I have a chance to improve my own position." One foot came off the ground slightly as he bent to place his ball. "This lawyer, he also tells me that Carlotta has been engaged in smuggling cocaine. You can imagine how seriously this offends me. My own daughter serving as a mule to bring drugs into the country." He made a few practice swings toward the distant green. "Of course I do not believe such lies. I could kill a man, he stands in my own house saying such things about my daughter.

"Ridiculous!" Mr. Basoalto exclaimed. He whipped his club up onto his shoulder as he walked around his ball.

Hugh was mesmerized.

"Imagine my surprise when in support of his allegations he produces a signed statement which my good friend Hugh Royal has given to the police." Luis shook his head, allowing the head of his club to fall forward.

"I investigate, of course. I have to prove that the statement with which he has presented me is a fabrication. The statement and its signature look genuine, yes, but why would Hugh Royal sign such a thing?" Luis made a few little practice swings, one-handed, in the direction of the ball. "You know, of course, what I find, heh?" He glanced up briefly, then returned his eyes to the ball. It looked as if Luis was teeing up in the direction of Hugh Royal, but Hugh stood transfixed, unable even to blink.

Luis said, "First, I find my friend Hugh has been arrested on the charge of receiving stolen property. I cannot imagine why he would be engaged in such conduct, but the arrest tells me something about the signed statement I have not known before. It tells me why."

He swept the club down, and the golf ball flew short and straight into Hugh's chest, sending him staggering backwards, wide-eyed, one hand to his chest, the other stretched wide.

Hugh fell to sitting position.

"My friend Hugh has made this statement to protect himself from prosecution," Luis said. "I investigate further. I make some calls to friends of mine in Columbia, and I discover that Hugh has been supplying my daughter with money to buy cocaine, that he is using the daughter I have entrusted to his care as a mule. What is it with Hugh Royal, I wonder? What is going on with him?"

Hugh, looking up, could only shake his head.

Luis said, "He has only to run a small string of roller rinks and bowling alleys — to run them badly, I might add — and to do a little creative bookkeeping. I find that so careless has he been that this young lawyer, this Mr. Dougherty, knows about this as well."

Luis fished another golf ball from his pocket and dropped it onto the grass.

His tone, which had been conversational, almost playful, became deadly serious. "I don't know who has killed my daughter," he said, "but I am beginning to wonder. And I tell you this, Hugh: I will find out. If any action of yours is responsible for her death..."

Abruptly, Luis swung, chopping at the ball, and it hit Hugh right at the hairline, bouncing high in the air as Hugh fell onto his back.

Luis approached him. "If it is so, it would be better for you to gouge out your eyes, to mutilate your own body, than to face what it is that I have planned for you," Luis said. His head, seemingly too large for his body, then too small, briefly superimposed itself on the cloudless sky. It went away.

"Another ball, please, Carlos. We will finish the course."

There was the swish of the club cutting through the air, the smack of it connecting with the ball. Voices, receding.

Hugh lay without moving, his eyes open. A flock of crows flew overhead, filling his field of vision.

Chapter 68

Charles Danvers swore to tell the truth, the whole truth, and nothing but the truth. He stepped up into the witness box and sat down.

"Your name?"

"Charles Danvers."

"Your occupation?"

"Unemployed." He cleared his throat. "Until a few years ago I was a partner in the law firm of Coleman, Anders and Davis."

"On the night of October twenty-fifth, did you attend a fundraiser for the Tyler Symphony Orchestra? The Boot-scootin' Ball?"

"I did."

"And the Boot-scootin' Ball was held where?"

"In the Harvey Convention Center."

"Did you see the defendant Tracey Coleman at the ball?"

"Yes. I saw her talking to Alan Dougherty, the man now acting as her attorney."

"The man seated beside her there?" Larson pointed at Alan, his tone one of apparent surprise. Alan didn't know what was coming, but he couldn't imagine that it was anything good.

"Yes," Danvers said.

"Did you have occasion to speak to them?"

"No. I saw them standing together between her table and his."

"What happened?"

"I tripped on the strap of a purse that was hanging on the back of a chair."

"Whose purse was this?"

"Later I saw Tracey Coleman with it."

"So it was her purse?"

"It was a small rectangular purse made of fabric of some kind, gold in color. It matched her dress."

"Was this the purse?" Larson reached into a big litigator case and lifted out what looked like the purse Tracey had carried that night.

"It looks like it."

"What happened with the purse that night?"

"It was a small purse with a long strap. I tripped on it, like I said, and the purse fell to the floor. I picked it up."

"So you were holding it?"

"Yes. I had the purse in my hands, and it had come open. Inside was a small pistol."

Alan felt as if a horse had kicked him. His head had gone numb.

"A small pistol," Larson was saying. He crossed to the table holding the exhibits and picked up the .25 caliber Davis derringer.

"This pistol?" he asked.

"I don't know. It was about that size. Truthfully, the purse wouldn't have held a gun much larger than that."

Larson turned to the table that held his briefcase and picked up a thin stack of typed pages. He turned back to Danvers. "No more questions," he said. He crossed to the defense table and dropped Danvers's written statement onto the table in front of Alan. "Your witness," he said.

Alan stared at the top page of single-spaced type.

"We'll take a thirty minute recess," the judge said.

Alan looked up sightlessly. The judge banged his gavel and swept out of the courtroom. In the gallery, everybody started talking at once.

"Why didn't you tell me?" Alan said.

"Tell you what?"

"That you had the gun. That you killed her."

"I didn't kill her."

They were in a conference room just off the courtroom. Both were standing.

"I still would have represented you," Alan said. "And I could have done a better job of it. This sucker punch wouldn't have come out of nowhere to knock me on my butt."

"You're not listening to me. I didn't kill her."

"But you did have the murder weapon that night."

"No."

"What happened to it, Tracey? What's your story this time? It had better be a good one, because, whatever it is, in less than thirty minutes I have to go back out there and sell it to the jury."

Tracey grabbed his arm. "Stop pacing," she said.

He glared at her. "Danvers just put you on death row. Do you realize that?"

"He will have if you don't calm down. Take a breath, will you?"

He jerked away from her. "I don't need a breath."

"You sure need something. You're not hearing a word I say."

"I'll tell you what I need."

"What's that?"

"The truth, Tracey. I could really use a nice, strong dose of the truth."

"Then sit down. Sit down, and I'll give it to you."

He jerked out a chair and dropped down into it. He crossed his ankle over his knee and folded his arms across his chest. "I'm sitting."

"I didn't have the derringer at the reception that night," Tracey said. "Charles Danvers is making it up. He's just completely making it up."

"I thought you said the truth."

"He hates Daddy. Daddy destroyed him professionally, and his profession was all he had. He's made up this story to get back at him."

"Hating the man who fired you and committing perjury to get a young woman sentenced to death are two different things."

"Daddy sued him for fraud, misapplication of funds, embezzlement...He ruined his reputation in the community and drove him into bankruptcy."

"Yes, but..."

"Why is Danvers such an angel all of a sudden? He engaged in self-dealing at the expense of a really vulnerable group of people. He's a small, broken man filled with hatred."

"Your dad has sued a lot of people, Tracey. How many..."

"How many have daughters who attempted suicide?"

"Suicide!"

She stared at him. "You don't know? You don't read the papers? Or watch the local news?"

"I've been in the middle of a big murder trial."

"Four weeks ago, Danvers' sixteen-year-old daughter Kelsey got into a bathtub of warm water with a couple of single-edged razor blades. She's still at East Texas Regional."

Alan jerked up Danvers's written statement from where it lay on the conference room table. He flipped to the last page and saw the date.

Just over three weeks ago, the day before Larson sent over his witness list.

—

"Counselor?"

Alan stood.

"Do you have any questions of this witness?"

"Your honor, Mr. Danvers's statement is dated twenty-three days ago. I would like to know whether Mr. Danvers made any prior statements to the police." He specifically wanted to know whether Danvers's statement had changed after his daughter's suicide attempt.

Larson stood. "This is the only statement we have, your honor."

The judge looked at Alan.

"Is it the only statement the prosecution has ever had?"

"It is, your honor," Larson said.

"How much did the statement change after you first talked to him? Twenty-three days ago, you presented him with a transcript of what he had said to you. How substantially did Danvers edit it before he signed it?"

"I'm not a witness in this case," Larson said.

"Your honor, I'd like to see a transcription of everything this witness has said to the police."

"Your honor, that's ridiculous. He's asking for attorney work product."

Alan held up Danvers's statement. "Is that what this is? Is the district attorney saying he had a hand in developing this witness's testimony?"

"That's slander," Larson said. "Your honor, that's —"

The gavel cracked. "That's enough," the judge said. "Mr. Dougherty, do you have any questions for this witness, or don't you?"

Alan hesitated.

"Well?"

"Did you rule on my motion?"

The judge studied him. "What was your motion exactly? You want everything Mr. Danvers here has ever said to the police?"

"Yes, your honor."

"That would be highly unusual. I may have you and Mr. Larson brief the issue for me. Right now, though, I want to know if you're planning to cross-examine this witness."

"I am, your honor."

"Then get on with it."

"Thank you." Alan took a breath. "Mr. Danvers," he said. "Let me see if I have your story straight. You tripped on the defendant's purse, is that right?"

"That's right."

"Did you fall?"

"No. I may have staggered a bit until I regained my balance."

Alan paused, calculating his approach. "Mr. Danvers, you'd been drinking at the time of this incident, hadn't you?"

"I think I'd had a drink."

"In fact, you had a glass in your hand at the moment you tripped on the strap of the purse. You put your drink down before you bent to pick the purse up off the floor, didn't you?" This wasn't something Alan remembered. He was guessing, couching his guesses in the style of a typical cross-examination, with him asking questions in a way that required assent or contradiction.

"I may have," Danvers said.

"You think you'd had a drink, and you might have put your glass down. Just how clear is your memory of this occasion, counselor?"

"Clear enough."

"What is it you were drinking?"

"Bourbon and water, I think."

Alan raised his eyebrows. "You think. You think you were holding a bourbon and water when you tripped on this purse. Is that right?"

"Yes."

"This was about nine o'clock in the evening, wasn't it?"

"About."

"And the ball began at eight. This wasn't your first drink, was it?"

"I don't remember."

"You have a convenient memory, Mr. Danvers. Very detailed as to certain particulars, very vague as to others."

Danvers flushed almost imperceptibly, but he said nothing.

"Okay. You were drinking bourbon and water. You tripped on the purse-strap, and the purse fell to the floor. Is that right so far?"

"Yes."

"Did anything spill out of it?"

"No."

"No gun slipped out onto the floor where anyone else could see it?"

"No."

"Or protruded from the purse even by a little bit?"

"Not that I remember."

Alan smiled, looking at Danvers until Danvers shifted position.

"Nothing else fell out of the purse, did it?" Alan said. "No lipstick, no hairbrush, no compact."

"No."

"This small, rectangular purse hit the floor, and nothing protruded from it and nothing fell out. Everything was consistent with a purse that had not come open."

Danvers didn't answer, but Alan hadn't asked a question.

"So you put down your drink...On Tracey's table, the table where her purse was hanging?"

"I think so."

"And you picked up the purse. You had the body of the purse in your hands for how long? At most a fraction of a second, isn't that true?"

"I don't know. It wasn't long."

"The purse wasn't really open, was it, Mr. Danvers?"

"It was. I was holding it — like this — and I could feel the gun. The mouth of the purse was open slightly, and I could see it."

"Ah. You felt it. You felt something hard in the purse, and now, when you get to thinking about it, weeks after the event in question, you think to yourself that it must have been a gun."

"No."

"And just twenty-three days ago you went down to the prosecutor's office to sign a statement that you'd seen a gun."

"I'd already told them about the gun."

"When you'd hung the purse back on the chair, you picked up your drink. Then you went immediately to get another one, didn't you?"

Danvers looked away.

"And you continued to drink."

"I...guess I did."

"And, later in the evening, you passed out at your table, didn't you?"

"No."

"You went to sleep with your head resting on your folded arms. People saw you."

"Sleeping isn't the same as passed out."

"Not a very good image to present, is it? A lawyer sleeping with his head on his arms in the middle of a party."

"I don't guess I have to worry about my image much anymore, do I?"

"Good point. You're not a lawyer anymore. You've been disbarred."

Danvers' voice was steady. "That's right."

"The State Bar of Texas took your license away from you, and you can no longer practice law."

"Yes."

"How long ago was this?"

"Eighteen months or so."

"Why was it the state bar revoked your license?"

The skin reddened around Danvers's eyes, and for an awful moment Alan thought he would break down.

"It was the result of a grievance filed against you by Roger Coleman on behalf of several of his clients, wasn't it?"

"That's right." Danvers's eyes were bloodshot.

"On behalf of several people who used to be your clients."

Danvers didn't speak, though his breathing had become audible.

"A couple of years ago you were a partner in the law firm of Coleman, Anders and Davis, weren't you?" Alan asked him.

"Yes."

"But Roger Coleman and your other partners threw you out, accused you of defrauding a group of children and young adults you were supposed to be taking care of, accused you of embezzling funds. Isn't that right?"

"Yes." The word was almost inaudible.

"Roger Coleman, the man who fired you, who pursued you into bankruptcy, who got you disbarred, is the father of Tracey Coleman, the defendant in this case." Alan gestured in Tracey's direction. Danvers didn't say anything.

"Isn't he?"

Danvers mumbled something Alan couldn't make out.

"You hate him, don't you? You'd like to see him pay for what he's done to you."

"No. I don't hate anyone."

"Yet you claim that on the evening of October twenty-fifth — an evening on which you drank until you were unconscious — for the barest fraction of a second, you caught a glimpse of a .25 caliber Davis derringer."

"I saw the gun," Danvers said. "I felt it through the fabric of the purse, and I saw it."

"Here you sit giving testimony that could send Roger Coleman's only child to death row, testimony that could lead ultimately to her death by lethal injection."

"Objection," Larson said.

"Sustained."

Alan's eyes were locked on those of Charles Danvers. "This hasn't affected just you, has it? It's affected your whole family."

Danvers mouth had come open, but he didn't speak.

Alan continued in a softer tone, "Four weeks ago, five days before you signed your statement, your daughter attempted suicide."

Danvers was gasping.

"You're lashing out at whoever you can," Alan said, his tone almost sympathetic. "And right now, the only person you can get to is Tracey Coleman."

"No. No, I..." It was all he could manage. He started to cry.

Alan turned away, then stopped short. The gaze of every juror in the box was locked on him, and their angry faces seemed turned to stone.

FOUR

JUDGMENT & SENTENCE

It is essential to the idea of a law, that it be attended with a sanction; or, in other words, a penalty or punishment for disobedience.

—The Federalist No. 15 (A. Hamilton).

Whoever sheds the blood of man, by man shall his blood be shed.

—Genesis 9:6.

Chapter 69

Barry Royal, mounting the stairs to his apartment over the tobacco shop, saw that his door was open several inches. He stopped and stood looking up, listening. From the street below, he heard the sound of an approaching car, the squeal of its brakes as it stopped at the traffic light. From above him, nothing. Cautiously, he shifted his weight to the outer edge of the next higher tread. The step creaked softly. Holding his breath, he took another step upward.

When he got to the landing, he stood for several minutes, his eyes on the crack between door and jamb, on the wedge of the living room visible beyond. Finally he reached out a hand and pushed at the door.

It swung inward, expanding his wedge of vision without showing him anything out of the ordinary. The cushions were on his sofa. The chrome floor lamp was upright. His magazines were stacked neatly on the coffee table.

Cautiously he stepped over the threshold, wincing at the creak of the heart pine flooring. The apartment was, in essence, all one big room. From where he stood, he could see his bed, neatly made, and his clothes, hanging on the exposed rods. Absolutely nothing was other than as it should have been. He walked through the apartment, glancing behind the kitchen counter, looking behind the door of the bathroom, raking back the shower curtain. There was no one.

He walked slowly back toward the front door, still uneasy, but if anyone had ever been there, he had left no sign. There was no sign of injury to either door or jamb. Except for a few scratches around the keyhole that he imagined he himself was responsible for with his thrusting key, the lock was in pristine condition.

He turned the thumb latch to secure the door, then went to the refrigerator and pulled the cork from an unfinished bottle of white zinfandel. As he poured himself a glass of wine, he paused and his gaze again strayed over the apartment, looking for something, anything that was out of place. There was nothing.

He took his glass over to the sofa and sank down onto it. He had not left his door standing open; therefore, someone had unlocked it, and whoever had done it was good. Someone that good would have left the door standing ajar deliberately or not at all. It was a kind of calling card, albeit a blank one. The implications were deeply unsettling.

Barry's first impulse, as he sipped his wine, was to disappear for a while. Get out of Tyler. A drastic response to finding his door ajar, but then, he dealt with some drastic people.

Carlos Basoalto and Raul were at that moment inside Tony Royal's townhouse, each wearing paint-stained coveralls. Carlos was seated at the desk in the second bedroom, going through the files on Tony's computer. There was an empty paint can sitting beside him. Tony was not at home.

"Boss?"

Carlos looked over his shoulder. Raul's big frame filled the doorway.

"I think I find something."

Carlos got up without a word and followed him across the upstairs landing into Tony's bedroom, which was dominated by a king-size bed with dark, rumpled sheets. The walls were littered with paintings and sketches, a few in frames, but most held in place with push-pins.

"You think he did these?" Carlos said to Raul, jerking his head at the largest of the paintings. "I don't see his name on any of them."

"Here," Raul said, ignoring the question, and he pulled down the drop front of a walnut secretary that stood in front of the room's only window. He shone his penlight on his find.

Carlos stared. "Sweet Mother Mary." He pulled a handkerchief from his pocket and laid it over the rings, the garnet solitaire and the diamond cluster, that had once belonged to his sister. Picking up the rings with the handkerchief, he folded it twice and returned it to his pocket.

"Have we found your sister's killer, you think?" Raul asked.

"Yes, I think," Carlos answered.

"Then we should leave," Raul said. "We been here too long already."

They were on Broadway, a mile from Tony's townhouse, when Carlos pointed out a man crossing the park. "It's him."

It was dusk, and they could see him only in silhouette, but there was no mistaking his tall frame and athletic gait as he walked along the jogging track at the top of the embankment. He had a small paper sack in one arm.

"It is him," Carlos said again. "Don't let him get away."

Punching the accelerator, Raul swung the wheel. A horn blared as their car crossed the path of approaching headlights to bounce over the curb and onto the grassy hill. The car mounted the embankment, its tires spinning on the grass here and there as their quarry retreated, one step, then two, his head swiveling left and right as if in search of a way of escape.

He threw down his paper sack and started to run.

"Tony," Carlos called through his open window. "Tony Royal." He had his pistol out and in his lap as the car reached the top of the hill and swung in pursuit of the man who was on the path now less than fifty yards ahead of them.

He was running hard, and he didn't look back.

The big car accelerated, its tires spitting dirt. "We have him," Carlos said to Raul. "We have him." He lifted his pistol, pointing the barrel of the gun through the open window.

It was not necessary to shoot. Their quarry staggered, evidently the result of a low spot in the path, and the car caught him. At the last instant he dove sideways, and the car's bumper caught his heel, spinning him as he hit the ground.

The car skidded as Raul turned it, its tires chewing up the turf, and already their prey had lunged from the ground and started running in the opposite direction. He was limping, but his head was down as he devoted all his energy to forward speed.

The car plowed into him from behind, throwing him up onto the windshield. Raul brought the car skidding to a stop, and the body slid down the hood, landing heavily on the hard ground.

"Child's play," Carlos said, and he and Raul got out of the car.

The body lay face down, its head in a spreading pool of blood that in the twilight looked black against the grass. Raul turned the body with his foot.

"Damn," Carlos said.

Raul said nothing.

"It sure looked like him," Carlos said. "You thought it was him, didn't you?"

"I sure did, boss."

It had been a natural mistake in the darkness.

Chapter 70

When Alan got home a little later, he dropped his briefcase on the floor and fell into his recliner. For a long time he didn't move. Days were left in the trial, but there was no longer any question in his mind about the ultimate outcome. It was over, and he had lost.

"Are you all right?" Tracey asked, standing in the archway to the hall.

"No."

She came into the room and sat in his lap, putting her arms around his neck. He rested his head against hers. She was the real loser. Her life was over at twenty-three.

He continued to sit, holding her. He ought to be doing something, but he didn't know what. All he could think about was what a mistake it had been to bring up Danvers's daughter.

She kissed him, and his arms tightened about her. What choice had he had, he asked himself? Danvers blamed Roger Coleman for destroying his daughter, so he got on the stand to destroy Roger's. It had an almost literary symmetry. Alan had used Danvers' daughter and his professional misfortunes in an attempt to break him, and the jury hated him for it, hated him and Tracey both.

The doorbell rang, and they both went still. It rang again.

"Jordan," Tracey breathed into his ear, but the hammering of his heart told him different.

He pushed her off his lap and got to his feet. She took a couple steps toward the kitchen and stopped. They both jumped when a knock sounded.

He jerked his head in the direction of the kitchen, then went to the door and opened it.

On the stoop were Luis Basoalto's beefy bodyguards; behind them on the sidewalk, Luis himself, wearing a gray overcoat, his hands in the pockets.

"May we come in, Mr. Dougherty?" Luis said in his lilting speech. Behind him, light from the lamp at the end of the sidewalk gleamed on the dark skin of the big car parked against the curb.

Alan hesitated, then stepped aside. The three men filed past him, bodyguards first, then Luis. Alan followed them into the living room, where everyone remained on his feet. The living room seemed suddenly very small.

"Do I get beat up this time?" Alan said, his gaze moving from one to another of them. "Or are we having another conversation?"

Luis smiled. "I like you, counselor. You have cojones."

"So what's this about?"

"Things do not look so good for your client," Luis said. "I was not in court this afternoon, but I heard how it went."

"Danvers is lying," Alan said.

"Knowing a thing and proving it are two different things."

"What do you want?"

"I have a proposition for you. You say your client did not kill my daughter Carlotta. For reasons of my own, I believe you. I find also that I am in a position to clear Miss Coleman of the charges against her."

"How?"

"Does it matter, Mr. Dougherty?"

"It might."

Luis shook his head. "I'm sorry. I cannot tell you that."

"Why come here then? If you have evidence, turn it over to the police."

"Ah, but what is it to me if your client lives or dies?"

"You want your daughter's murderer brought to justice."

"He will be brought to justice; of that you may be certain."

Alan looked into Luis Basoalto's expressionless eyes and felt a shudder work its way along his spine. "You said you had a proposition for me," he said finally.

"Yes. I clear your client of the charges against her. In exchange, you cease your investigations into Hugh Royal and his roller rinks."

Alan waited. "That's it?"

Luis held his hands out, palms up. "That is all. You simply cease your activities. You turn over to me no documents. You destroy no evidence."

"I just stop."

"Could anything be easier?"

Alan smiled crookedly. A desperate recklessness came over him. "I haven't got anything on Hugh Royal, you know," he said. "Not really. It's all supposition and innuendo. There isn't really any investigation to stop."

"You have shown me tax returns and financial statements."

"Public documents, all on file with Hugh's bank — some of them with the I.R.S. as well. They're not going anywhere."

"No. They are harmless without your, how do you say it, your supposition and innuendo."

"It would be more accurate just to say that they're harmless."

"So we have a deal, you and I?"

Alan went to the front door and, opening it, turned back into the room. "I have nothing with which to deal." He stood holding the door. His heart was pounding, and he could feel his pulse in both hands.

After a moment, Luis smiled. "I think I like you, counselor," he said. He jerked his head at Raul, who pushed a bulging Tyvek envelope against Alan's chest.

He didn't take it. "What's this?" he said. Raul continued to hold the package against him.

"I believe you have the basis for an assault charge against two of my employees. I wish to settle the claim."

Alan shook his head. "It isn't necessary."

"If you do not take it, how can I be sure we have a meeting of the minds?"

Alan hesitated, and he felt sweat prickle suddenly on his forehead. "You can't," he said.

Luis moved toward him. "You and I are reasonable men," he said quietly. "Do not disappoint me." Menace seemed to radiate from the old man's skin.

"I can't take your money."

"You must, or how can I trust you?"

"You'll kill me." He cleared his throat. "You'll kill me if I...keep looking into things."

"That is true, you know."

Alan nodded. "I know it. You know it. It is enough."

After a long moment, Luis said, "Very good." He gestured with his chin, and Raul tucked the Tyvek envelope away again inside his top coat.

Chapter 71

It was just before seven o'clock the next morning when Barry Royal let himself into his cousin's townhouse. "Tony?" he said.

He turned the corner into the galley-style kitchen and saw him on the tiled floor in the eating area beyond it, his face a ruin, what was left of his head resting in a puddle of dark, coagulating gore. A twelve-gauge shotgun lay nearby, and it looked as if Tony had been seated at the table when the gun went off: His hips rested on the back of the overturned chair, one leg still hooked over the seat. Already the body had a ripe smell, and Barry kept his face buried in the crook of his arm as he moved to look down at the corpse, as he craned his neck to read what was written on the notepad still on the table.

At the top was Tony's name, pre-printed in a *sans serif* font. Scrawled on the top page: *I'm going to do it this time. I'm sorry about Carlotta. I didn't mean to do what I did. I loved her, and I wouldn't have hurt...* It was Tony's handwriting, which, never the best, deteriorated markedly toward the bottom of the page.

Barry lifted the top sheet, but there was nothing underneath — no conclusion, no signature. Had Tony been too overcome with despair when he reached the bottom of the page to flip to the next? He shook his head, his gaze going back to Tony's body. Only one eye remained intact, the socket torn away around it so that it stared unblinking upward like an egg frying slowly on the sidewalk in the morning sun. The left hand was clenched, the arm outflung.

Barry squatted over the body to work a finger into the midst of the stiffened fist, prying at it until he caught the gleam of white gold.

"You screwed-up bastard," he said, softly. "You stupid, screwed-up bastard."

He went into the living room, out of sight of the body, trying to think, but thinking was difficult. Shockwaves of violence seemed to ripple outward from the death-scene with tangible force. His thoughts shifted randomly, images in a kaleidoscope.

In the dim light of dawn that filtered through the curtained windows, his mind took inventory of the furniture about him, noting the upright floor lamp, the undisturbed sofa, the absence of any signs of struggle. There was nothing to suggest that the scene in the other room was anything other than what it appeared to be — a suicide.

He was still thinking it through when the doorknob on the front door moved stealthily. A soft knock sounded on the door. Barry hesitated, then moved as quietly as possible to the door. Through the peephole, he saw his father Hugh, his face against the door, distorted by the peephole's small lens, his skin almost yellow in the artificial light of the bulb in the brass fixture above the townhouse door.

His heart beating hard from a sudden surge of adrenalin, Barry turned the knob and pulled the door open.

His father was wild-eyed. A strong body-odor emanated from him, and a line of crusted blood ran from his hairline. He walked past his son, staggering almost blindly. "Thank God," he said, turning into the kitchen. "Thank God." He came up short at the sight of the ruined body of his nephew sprawled on the floor.

Barry was at his shoulder. "What happened to you? What's been going on?"

"Tony?" Hugh said to the corpse in a quavering voice. "Tony?"

"Was it Luis?"

Hugh stumbled forward through the kitchen and fell to his knees beside Tony's body.

After listening to his gasping breath for perhaps a half-minute, Barry said, "He has her rings clenched there in his left fist. Carlotta's."

Hugh lifted the hand. Between the fingers, the hint of a gem sparkled in the overhead light. Barry picked up the pad of paper from the table and held it down where Hugh could see it.

"He killed her," Hugh said, his voice shaking. "He killed her, and he killed himself." He looked up to meet his son's eyes, but Barry shook his head.

"No," he said. He took a long breath, released it. "He didn't kill himself. He may have killed Carlotta, but he didn't kill himself."

"The note —" Hugh struggled to his feet, clutching at the pad. "It's his handwriting. It looks like his."

"He was compelled to write it, I think."

"Compelled," Hugh repeated.

"They tortured him."

"Torture... There's no sign—"

"Look at the face, Dad."

"The shotgun —"

"Exactly," Barry said. "All signs of torture have been carefully erased."

Hugh got up and began opening cabinet doors until he came upon a bottle of Old Thompson whiskey. His shaking hands were so palsied that

Barry took the bottle from him and poured a couple of fingers of the whiskey into the bottom of a water glass.

"You can't get drunk," Barry said as he handed Hugh the glass. He felt calm returning to him almost in proportion as his father's lack of it. Hugh's look was one of shell-shocked wonder.

"Can't get drunk? Why the hell not?" With a jerk of his head, Hugh tossed back the whiskey.

"Because a lot's going to happen today. By the end of it, either you and I will both be dead..."

"We're already dead." He grappled for the whiskey bottle, but Barry held onto it.

"Five people are a danger to us," he said. "Luis, Carlos, Raul, Juan, and Alejandro. Think. Is it possible that we could take out all five of them before they got to us?"

Lunging, Hugh tore the bottle loose from Barry's grasp.

"We'd not only save our lives, we might just find ourselves in control of the whole operation."

Hugh's head was back, his throat working as he drank directly from the mouth of the bottle. "You're nuts," he said as he wiped away the whiskey dripping from his chin. "We're both walking corpses, and you know it."

"We are if we panic."

"No, we just are." He gestured with the bottle. "What, you think you're Wyatt Earp? You think I'm Doc Holliday? We're not even Kirk Douglas and Burt Lancaster. We go after them, they'll shoot us down like dogs."

"Have another look at your nephew there. That's what doing nothing gets us."

Hugh pushed past him. "See you in hell, Barry," he said, and he staggered for the door.

"Wait!"

Hugh paused in the doorway, but only for a moment. "For what?" he asked. He belched, and the door closed, and he was gone. He'd taken the whiskey with him.

Barry was again alone with his cousin's corpse.

Chapter 72

The number of spectators in the courtroom gallery had increased markedly over the day before. A hanging crowd, Alan thought, drawn by news of Danvers's devastating testimony. As he and Tracey sat waiting for the judge and jury, Alan kept his eyes on the table. He became aware of Tracey watching him, and, when he looked up, he saw that Cale Larson was watching him, too.

Alan raised an eyebrow, but Larson looked away. The jury began to file in.

The bailiff called the court into session, and the judge swept in. "Be seated," he said, sitting himself as if in example. "Now where were we?" His eyes fell on his notes. "Oh, yes. Mr. Larson, you may call your next witness."

Larson got to his feet, but for a long moment didn't speak.

"Mr. Larson?"

Larson expelled his breath in a long sigh. "Your honor, the state requests a twenty-four-hour recess to evaluate certain new evidence that has come to its attention."

Alan's head swung toward him.

The judge was shaking his head. "Mr. Larson, you know I can't —"

"Perhaps this is something best discussed *in camera*, your honor."

Judge Mitchell looked surprised. After a moment, he said, "Very well. Both counsel in my chambers. Court is recessed for thirty minutes."

"Now what's this about?" the judge asked Larson. "Why is he here?" He jerked his head.

"Lieutenant Curtis is here to present the new evidence."

Curtis withdrew an eight-by-ten print from a manila folder. Judge Mitchell recoiled. "That's ghastly," he said. "What is it?"

"Tony Royal, dead in his townhouse apartment."

A chill went down Alan's spine in a cascade of shaved ice.

Larson said, "A neighbor called the police at about seven-thirty this morning complaining about an explosion that had jolted her out of bed some hours before."

"What time?" the judge asked.

"She doesn't know; she didn't look at the clock. First she thought it was an earthquake, then some sort of chemical explosion. After she got up, she saw some wild-looking man staggering around outside Tony Royal's apartment, and finally she called us."

"Who was the wild man?"

"At this point, we have no idea. Two more items of interest." A yellow envelope came out of the folder. Curtis opened it and tipped it carefully over the judge's desk. Inside the plastic bag that slid out, metal glinted and a gem sparked in the light from the desk lamp.

"Carlotta's rings?" Mitchell asked.

"We think so, but we haven't been able to locate anyone who can confirm it. The rings were clutched in the left hand of Tony Royal."

"You said two items of interest."

"Yes, well." Curtis handed across a sheet of paper. "This is a photocopy of a note that was on a table inside Royal's apartment, just in front of the body."

"Suicide note."

"And apparent confession."

The judge studied it.

"The handwriting seems to match other examples of handwriting we found in the apartment. We're still making comparisons."

After a long moment, Mitchell said, "I guess that about wraps it up."

"Just now we're not sure what it does. All this came to my attention less than an hour ago. We need that twenty-four-hour recess to give us a chance to evaluate everything."

"Do you think twenty-four hours will be enough?"

Larson nodded. "I think so. By tomorrow morning, we should know whether we want to proceed with the prosecution against Tracey Coleman or dismiss the charges."

"Counselor?"

"No objection," Alan said.

He ignored Tracey's questioning look until the jury had been dismissed and had exited the courtroom. She pulled at his arm to make him look at her. "What?" she said. "What's going on?"

He tried to smile at her. "Tony Royal has confessed to Carlotta's murder," he said.

"He's in jail?"

"Dead. Apparent suicide."

Tracey was silent for a long moment. "It's over then?" she said.

"Not quite. Larson wants until tomorrow to think about it. They found the body only hours ago, if that. He wants to be sure everything is what it appears to be."

"But it will be over."

He nodded. "I think so."

"Well, don't look so happy for me."

"I'm sorry." He shook his head and managed an apologetic smile.

"I don't see Daddy," she said, looking around the courtroom. "We need to find him and tell him the good news."

"You need to find him. Your father doesn't want to see me."

"Take me home then. I need to get my car."

Chapter 73

Home. Take me home, she had said, and he hadn't questioned it. His house was her home. After she had left, he sat in the living room with a glass of tea he had gotten from the refrigerator. One leg was over the arm of the upholstered chair. His collar was unbuttoned; and his tie was at half-mast.

Home, he mused as he sipped his tea. He had set up housekeeping with Tracey Coleman, the girl who had almost brought him to ruin five years ago. Then, their love had been dominated by hormones and a wild recklessness. This time, so far, they had been celibate. Then, they had been deliriously happy. This time he at least was miserable. "God doesn't care whether we're happy so much as He cares that we are good," Alan said aloud. Where had he read that?

The phone rang, and he reached for it. "Hello."

"Alan? It's Tracey."

"Yes, what is it?" He sat up, alarmed by the quiet tenseness in her voice.

"It's Daddy. He..." Her voice broke, and for a few seconds he could make out nothing but the sound of her breathing.

"Yes? Is he all right?"

"I've called 9-1-1. There's an ambulance on its way."

"What happened? Is he alive?" Alan asked.

"Uh huh."

"I'll meet you at the hospital."

Her breathing became more ragged, and the connection ended abruptly.

Alan was outside the emergency room when the ambulance pulled up to it. The paramedics came around and opened the rear doors. As they dragged out the gurney, the retractable wheels popped down as the stretcher cleared the bumper. On the stretcher lay Roger, his hair looking wild and oily beneath the straps of an oxygen mask that obscured his face.

Tracey's apple green Porsche jerked to a stop in a parking space labeled "Emergency Vehicles Only," and she got out, leaving the driver's door open and the car running. She caught up with the gurney as it went through the automatic doors.

"I'll park your car," Alan called to her, but she didn't answer.

He changed his mind; he wanted to get inside to Tracey and Roger. He killed the Porsche's engine, leaving the key in the ignition, then closed the doors and sprinted for the entrance. A woman checked him at the swinging doors to the ER proper.

"You can't go back there." She wore a garish print smock over solid slacks, and the tag hanging from her neck identified her as Wendy Ward, R.N.

"I'm with Roger Coleman," Alan said. "The man who was just wheeled through here."

"Family?"

"Son-in-law. My fiancé... Well, future son-in-law. My wife — fiancé's — in there with him."

She looked at him closely, and he wondered why that particular lie had been the one to spill out of him.

"Why don't you wait in there," she said, and she pointed to the waiting room. "I'll check for you and let you know in a minute what's going on."

Tracey appeared in the doorway. "Alan? We need you in here."

Alan looked at the nurse, raising his eyebrows, and she nodded her consent.

Roger Coleman's face was bruised at the left temple, black and purple at the perimeter, an ugly yellow in the center. His lips were chapped and a little swollen.

A doctor, a thin man who looked to be in his early thirties despite a receding hairline, opened Roger's shirt to reveal more deep bruising, including a bruise that had split and was crusted with dark blood. There was a rigid quality to Roger's body. Pain, Alan thought.

"What do you think happened?" Tracey asked softly.

"I don't know, but I'd say somebody beat the crap out of this man. He your father?" Raising his voice, the doctor called, "Ruby!"

A nurse appeared.

"Let's hang a bag of saline." He scrawled something on a clipboard and handed it to her. "And give him 2 cc's of Demerol."

Roger's eyes had opened, and Tracey leaned over him. "It's okay, Daddy. We're here."

But Roger was looking past her at Alan. "You're okay," he said weakly.

Alan laid a hand on Roger's. "I'm fine."

The nurse hung a bag of saline and deftly inserted the needle into Roger's arm.

Roger closed his eyes as the nurse secured the needle with a strip of Coban. "Some things aren't...safe to look into," he said.

Tracey looked up at Alan. He met her gaze and shrugged very slightly.

"SupeRink," Roger said without opening his eyes. He coughed, and then caught his breath in apparent pain.

"Who did this to you?" Alan asked.

"You knew too much. Luis said...my fault."

Tracey said, "Luis Basoalto did this to you?"

"I'll be...okay. Just needed my lesson." He made an effort to smile, but the effect was ghastly.

For a moment Tracey stood rigid, looking down at her father. Then she spun away, avoiding Alan's grasp, and she disappeared through the opening in the curtain. Alan turned to go after her, but Roger gripped his wrist.

"I'm counting on you," he said. "To take care of her. You're..." He had to take a couple of shallow breaths. "You're a good man." He let go of Alan's hand.

Alan hesitated, not sure whether to stay with him or go after Tracey. Roger's neck relaxed, and his head rolled a little to one side. Alan hesitated a moment longer, then pushed through the curtains and half-walked, half-ran for the swinging doors.

Chapter 74

Tracey's Porsche was already gone when Alan got outside. He ran across the parking lot to his own car. Though he didn't know where she had gone in such a hurry, he had a suspicion that was enough to make him sick. He turned out of the parking lot onto the Loop and, keeping his foot heavy on the gas pedal, weaved recklessly in and out of traffic, once running a traffic light as it turned red, once drawing the irate blast of a car horn. He made it to Frankston Highway and turned south.

There was less traffic south of the Loop. No sign of Tracey's Porsche. He had misjudged her, he thought. She was reckless sometimes, but she wasn't insane. Still, he increased his speed until the pedal was on the floor. At just under a hundred miles per hour, the Corolla developed an unpleasant shimmy that suggested it couldn't hold that speed for long.

The road dipped, and suddenly he saw her, saw the back end of her Porsche topping the next rise perhaps a mile ahead. He honked, knowing it was too far for her to hear him, but not knowing what else to do to get her attention. When he reached the top of the rise, he saw only a flash of light on the horizon, and then nothing. She was gone.

What was she doing? Was she still rational, or had she come unhinged?

At the Texaco in Teaselville, he made the turn toward Lake Palestine and pushed his speed back up to eighty-five. One more turn, suspension squealing, and he was coming up on Luis Basoalto's gatehouse.

He slowed. There were two cars parked at the gate, a Bentley and Tracey's Porsche, both apparently abandoned.

He pulled in behind them and stopped. As he got out of the car, he saw dark-panted legs sticking out through the door of the gatehouse. The gate finished closing and stopped.

He stooped and reached back inside his car for the Walther PPK beneath his seat. As he ran toward the gatehouse, he tucked it into his waistband at the small of his back.

The guard's body was slumped against the legs of an overturned stool, and Tracey was kneeling beside it. She looked up at Alan, and her eyes were empty.

"It wasn't me," she said. Blood welled up in the hole in the guard's forehead and began to run.

"Tracey," Alan said, and he heard the despair in his voice.

She tugged the pistol from the guard's shoulder holster as she stood. "Don't be an idiot. I didn't even have a gun. Look."

Through the window at the back of the gatehouse, they saw Hugh Royal walking unsteadily up the graveled road toward the house. Alan realized that the Bentley outside the gatehouse was his.

"Come on," Tracey said. She pushed into him, driving her shoulder into his solar plexus, moving him out of the doorway.

"Wait —" But she was already past him and climbing the gate. *Murder's been done,* he tried to say. *It's being done.* "We have no business here," he called to her, but she paid no attention to him. She dropped to the ground on the far side of the gate and began running gracefully up the gravel drive.

"Hell." He ran to the gate, rattled it, then gave up and climbed over. As he landed inside the fence, a gunshot sounded in the distance, followed by another.

The house looked more than ever like an alien space craft perched on top of the hill, and the sun glinting from the green aluminum blinded him as he ran. Tracey seemed to have disappeared behind the house. When he hit the sidewalk, Alan turned to go around it after her.

He almost ran into her as he rounded the corner. On the terrazzo nearby, a man lay on his back gazing sightlessly upward. A big man. No wound was visible, but seeping blood gave his body a dark outline.

The sun shone on the black panes of glass covering the inside profile of the half-disk of the house. Tracey stood stock-still, looking toward the pool, the pistol hanging by her right leg. Beyond her, Hugh Royal was standing on the pool's near side, a pistol in his hand and pointing. On the other side of the pool, Luis Basoalto sat shirtless on a lounge chair upholstered in green and white. His right hand held a collins glass.

Luis Basoalto raised his drink. On this unseasonably warm day, he was wearing only a brightly colored bathing suit, and his dry, leathery skin was taut over a tidy gut. "To you, Hugh," Luis said. "A true James Bond. Who's that behind you? Did you bring guests?"

As Hugh's head turned, a shot crashed from high inside the house. A pane of glass shattered, and Hugh staggered sideways, the barrel of his gun whipping in wild circles. From his open mouth came a useless gurgle, and a spreading stain showed where the bullet had taken him high in the chest. For a moment he teetered at the edge of the pool, his arms going up and his pistol plopping into the water. Then he died and fell, hitting the water with a splat that threw up a wall of water, and blood mushroomed from his body in a dark cloud.

Through the dark glass of the house, the shape of a man was just visible on the balcony. Tracey's gun went off in a jarring explosion that sent Alan staggering away from her. Her gun went off again, the bullet starring the glass as it punched through.

"Got him," she said with calm satisfaction, but Alan could see only the reflection of the sun in the shards of dark glass.

"Impressive," Luis Basoalto said from the far side of the pool. "Very impressive." He had put down the collins glass and now held an automatic pistol in one brown fist.

When Tracey's head turned, she saw the gun and hesitated.

"You are not that good," Luis Basoalto said. "Drop the weapon."

It clattered onto the terrazzo.

"Now gently, with the toe of your shoe, kick it into the pool."

She glanced at Alan, and he saw in her eyes a flash of despair. He had a momentary vision of a bullet bursting from the side of her head, her body beginning to fall even as the crash of Luis's pistol reached him. "Do what he says."

She moved her foot so that the toe of her shoe was touching the gun. She kicked, lofting it toward the pool.

Plop.

"Now what?" Alan said to Luis.

"Walk forward and sit at the edge of the pool while we think how best to handle what has happened. You, Mr. Dougherty, I believe to be an intelligent man. I hope you are not so foolish as to come armed to my house."

Conscious of the gun at the small of his back, Alan held up empty hands, palms outward, as he started forward. Tracey was just behind him. From the front of the house came the sound of footsteps crunching on gravel. Running footsteps.

"Move quickly," Luis said. "If I feel I have to shoot you, I will."

Carlos and Raul rounded the corner of the building. Alan saw the glint of a weapon, then felt a small, strong hand in the middle of his back and a tug at his waistband as he was shoved forward. He overbalanced on the edge of the pool and went over.

Tracey fired the first shot into Luis Basoalto even before Alan hit the water, dropping to her knees on the rough tile and squeezing the trigger, then rolling onto her back as Alan plunged into the icy water and firing between her knees at Carlos and the beefy Raul.

The water in the pool was cold enough to squeeze the breath from Alan in a single contraction as he went deep, almost to the pool's bottom. He heard the sounds of distant thunder as he struggled upward in wide-eyed desperation. He tangled with arms and legs that were not his own and, as he struggled to free himself, came face to face with Hugh Royal, whose gaping expression was partly obscured by the dark mist floating upward from the wound in his chest.

Alan kicked, and his head broke the surface of the water. He reached for the edge of the pool and pulled up onto it, gasping. A silence reverberated in his water-logged ears, and moisture dripped from his face and chin to spot the surface of the pool-side terrazzo. When he could, he rolled onto his back, drawing his cold legs up out of the water.

Tracey was sitting on the ground not two feet away, to all appearances examining a scraped knee. The Walther she had taken from his waistband was no longer in her hand, nor was it on the tile beside her.

"What —" Alan said, raising his head to look about them. Luis Basoalto sat motionless in his lounge chair, his head hanging forward and his face in shadow, his taut belly punctured and shrunken like a partially deflated balloon. In the other direction, Carlos and Raul lay not far from the corner of the house, the body of one crossing over the legs of the other. "Are they—"

"Dead. All dead."

"How?" Despair blossomed inside him like a deadly rose. "How did you—"

"They were in motion, running. You can't hit anything when you're running." She pulled a shard of tile out of her leg and held it up, blood tipped. "They came close though, got me with a chip of tile."

"Why, Tracey? Why did you come here?"

She shook her head. "I don't want to think about it."

He lowered his head again to the terrazzo. Above him, the sky was clear — china blue and serene.

Chapter 75

"We do need to decide what to do next, though," Tracey said. "Do we call the police, or do we get the hell out of here?"

"We call the police. We have to; that gun you took from me was your own Walther."

"What gun?"

"What do you mean, what gun?" he said.

She shrugged. "Look over the wall."

"What?" He got to his feet and walked across the terrazzo to the stone wall. On the other side of it, the drop-off was so steep that no plants or soil had managed to cling to the bare rock. A hundred yards below lay the slate-gray waters of Lake Palestine.

He turned back to meet Tracey's wide-eyed gaze. "You didn't," he said flatly. The cold breeze blowing off the lake tugged at his wet clothing, and his teeth chattered briefly. He clenched his jaw to still them.

She smiled at him, and he was suddenly furious.

"You little idiot. Ballistics tests are going to show the guns here don't account for all the bullets."

"A Columbian gangster and his bodyguards die in a bloodbath. Who's going to come looking for us?"

"You think nobody's going to glance over that wall and maybe speculate a little? They'll dive for the gun, and a hundred to one they'll find it. They'll check the registration and, when they do, they'll want some answers."

"Not from me. The guy who gave it to me picked it up at a flea market."

He stared at her, his expression incredulous. "I can't believe you."

"So. Do we get the hell out of here?"

"I don't know." His eyes passed over the bodies around them: Hugh in the pool, Luis slumped beside it, Raul, Carlos, and the other man. Plus the guard down at the gatehouse and the guy Tracey had shot through the plate glass window. Seven corpses. Tracey was responsible for four of them — killing three with the Walther he himself had brought to the house. About all you could plead was self-defense, and self-defense was a hard sell when you'd killed a man sunbathing beside his pool.

"Alan?"

He looked at her, but his eyes were slow to focus.

"We have to decide," she said.

He took a breath, expelled it. "Let's get the hell out of here," he said.

Whether because of his wet clothes or because of some deeper chill, he began to shake uncontrollably as he backed his car onto the road. His muscles were clenched as tightly as he could clench them, and still his arms and legs trembled and his teeth rattled in his head. He put the heater on high. Temporary insanity, he thought. She'd seen what Luis had done to her father. She'd snapped.

Her Porsche pulled ahead of him. He was afraid she'd roar back into Tyler at the same speed she left it, but she kept the speedometer on the conservative side of seventy-five. In forty minutes they pulled into his driveway from the alley behind his house. Tracey got out of her Porsche. "Are you all right?"

"No," he said. "Are you?" Seven men had died, violently. He would feel better himself if she weren't all right, if she weren't all right at all.

Her eyes drifted from his, and she didn't answer.

As they entered the kitchen, she said, "You better get out of those clothes. I wouldn't be surprised if you're feverish, the way you're shivering."

"I've got to get something hot going first." He bent to open the cabinet door nearest the refrigerator and started shoving through the jumbled sauce pans and frying pans and cookie sheets.

"What?" he said, unable to make out something she had said over all the clatter.

"I said, 'God, what a racket,'" she shouted. "What the hell are you after?"

He rocked back on his heels, dragging out his coffeemaker. "I want to get this going before I get in the shower," he said, as he spooned the coffee into the filter.

"I wish you had some booze to go in that."

He opened another cabinet and pulled out a bottle of José Cuervo, unscrewing the top and taking a swig directly from the bottle before handing it to her, shuddering as the fiery liquid slipped down his throat. There was an explosion of warmth when it hit his stomach, and he felt the first easing of his rigid muscles.

She held the bottle without drinking from it. "Who are you anyway?"

He laughed shortly, pressing the switch to turn on the coffee-maker. "Steve left it. Let's go take a shower."

Her eyebrows went up. "It's going to be that kind of shower, is it?"

"Why not? Even hell has its compensations, surely."

"Hell? I'm not sure I like this."

They went through the archway into the living room, and there in the leather recliner sat Barry Royal with a pistol in his lap, his hand loosely on the Packmahr grip. Alan stopped, and Tracey bumped into him.

"Sorry to turn your little tête-à-tête into a ménage à trois," Barry said.

It took Alan a moment to say anything. "What do you want?" he asked belligerently.

"To the point. 'Why meet we on the bridge of time to exchange one greeting and to part?'"

"It wasn't a philosophical question."

Tracey took a step away from him, and Barry raised the pistol. The movement seemed almost casual, but it focused the business-end of the gun on her breastbone. Tracey stopped moving.

"It's just as well," Barry said to Alan. "The answer isn't philosophical, either. I've come for the two kilos of cocaine that your girlfriend stole from us six weeks ago."

"You've already got it."

Barry raised his eyebrows in an expression of polite disbelief.

"You broke into her apartment later that same day."

"But she escaped out the window using her chain-ladder fire escape."

"Leaving you in possession."

"Of the apartment, yes, but unfortunately for all of us, she took the cocaine with her."

A sudden doubt sent a ripple of unease through Alan's midsection. His gaze flickered in Tracey's direction before returning to Barry.

"Go on, ask her," Barry told him. Abruptly, he swung the pistol toward Alan and pulled the trigger, the gun jerking in his hand as the crack of the gunshot bounced off the walls and the brass casing arched high in the air. Alan lurched violently, but Tracey remained stock-still, not so much as flinching. The ringing in their ears masked the following silence.

"Tell her your life depends on a straight answer," Barry said to Alan. "Because it does."

To Alan's right and slightly to his rear, a puff of white powder hung in the air near the spot where the slug had punched into the sheetrock. In front of him, the barrel of the pistol loomed like a dark tunnel.

"Tracey?" he said.

"It's behind the bookcase."

Alan's eyes followed the jerk of her head to his antique sectional bookcase.

Barry was smiling at him. "A deceitful little bitch, isn't she?" His eyes cut to Tracey. "Get it," he said.

Her eyes cut toward Alan. "Tony took it that night they flushed me out of my apartment. He put it back a couple of days ago. I don't know why he was planting it on me, but I had to move it somewhere before he sprung his trap. You understand that, don't you?"

"The next one blows your boyfriend's brains out the back of his head," Barry said to her. "I don't know if that matters much to you — does it?"

She crossed in front of Alan on her way to the bookcase. Two sets of eyes tracked her as she knelt to shift it away from the wall. It was heavy with all the books on it, and she tipped it too far in moving it. Its glass doors flapped open as it fell forward, the glass shattering as the bookcase hit the floor and books spilled forward. For a moment, the TV remote reverberated on the coffee table, then everything stopped.

Behind the space where the bookcase had stood, a piece of sheetrock had been cut raggedly from the wall and then forced back into place.

Tracey knelt by the wall, prying at the insert with her slender fingers. When she got it out, she reached into the hole to pull at something that was hidden inside, an irregularly shaped bundle of white powder packaged in Saran wrap. She stood, holding it with both hands in front of her chest.

Barry pushed to his feet, his pistol shifting so that it pointed slightly downward at a spot halfway between Alan and Tracey.

"Butthead," Tracey said. She used both hands to chest-pass the package to Alan, and, as Barry's gun followed automatically, she charged him.

The gun went off, and the TV exploded into fragments as Alan caught the package of cocaine against his chest. He reacted instinctively, swinging the package against the side of Barry's head even as Barry threw Tracey back onto the wreckage of the antique bookcase. The package ruptured, and, as cocaine rose in a cloud about his head, Barry staggered, gasping, sucking enough white powder into his mouth and nose to coat his tongue and throat and nasal passages. He cried out, and the gun fell to the carpet as his hands went to his eyes, his body twisting, his every muscle rigid, his fingers clawing deep gashes in his face. The cocaine settled in his hair and eyebrows, and it bleached his skin. He fell to his knees, choking and gasping and sobbing unintelligibly.

Alan stood watching in stupefied awe.

Barry fell to his side as his muscles locked, and he went into full-scale convulsions, thrashing and stirring up the cocaine that blanketed him into a low-hanging cloud. Tracey, on her feet now, stood beside Alan, looking down. Alan was in shock, staring, unaware of Tracey reaching for his hand.

"You did it," she said. "You got him."

He turned toward her with a dazed expression. "We've got to call an ambulance."

She didn't say anything.

"An ambulance," he said again, and he stumbled toward the phone.

Chapter 76

They could hear sirens in the distance. "That doesn't look like his gun," Alan said, noticing it by Barry's hand.

"Doesn't it?"

"His had some kind of rubberized grip." He bent over Barry, staying as much as possible out of the cocaine that shrouded Barry and the floor around him. "It's a Walther."

"We need a story," she said.

"What?"

"How about this. We got Daddy to East Texas Regional. He went to sleep, and we went for a walk in that park that's across the street from the hospital."

"What are you talking about?"

"You were horsing around and fell in the creek, so we had to come back here for you to change clothes. When we got here, we surprised Barry Royal in the act of planting two kilos of cocaine in the wall behind your bookcase."

"Is that your Walther or isn't it?"

"It would be nice if it were, because it would tie Barry Royal into that shoot-out down at Lake Palestine."

"You said you threw it in the lake."

"Okay, I lied to you, I'm sorry. I had to get you out of there. It was for your sake as much as mine."

The doorbell rang.

"Get it," Tracey said. "And don't worry. Everything will be fine."

Barry Royal was pronounced dead at the scene. The ambulance took him away, and the police stayed asking questions for most of the afternoon. Alan followed the script that Tracey had outlined to him, but without embellishments. How long had they been at the park? He didn't know. No, he couldn't even estimate. At which end of the park had he fallen into the stream? It could have been at the south end. Or maybe the north end. He didn't know; it could have been somewhere in the middle. Tracey's fertile imagination would no doubt supply the details, and he wasn't about to contradict her.

It was over an hour before Alan got to change into dry clothes. Lieutenant Curtis showed up at the house, and eventually Cale Larson. Tracey was in the kitchen, going over everything for perhaps the fourth or fifth time, when Larson came out and took a seat on the sofa across from Alan.

"Hell of a thing, isn't it?" Larson asked rhetorically. "What we had was a court case, and now what we have are a couple of corpses."

He was referring of course to Tony and Barry. He didn't yet know about the Lake Palestine massacre.

"When court reconvenes tomorrow," Larson said, "we're going to ask the judge to dismiss the case against Tracey Coleman. I just wanted you to know." He gave Alan a lopsided smile. "It's kind of ironic, isn't it?"

"What is?"

"It turns out you were one of the good guys."

Chapter 77

When they had gone — when all of them had gone, including Tracey, who had left to check on her father even before the last of the police — Alan finally got to take his shower. He made it hot enough to scald, and he dressed in warm dry clothes.

His living room was a disaster area. The bookcase lay where it had fallen, glass strewn among the jumbled books. The 50-inch panel TV had a hole in it ringed with glass teeth. Only the cocaine had been cleaned up. The police had vacuumed it up and taken it with them.

Alan stacked the four sections of the bookcase, doing his best to avoid the scattered glass. The old mahogany was splintered and cracked, giving the whole thing a sideways list, and one of the doors hung crookedly. Still, he picked up each of the fallen books and returned it to a shelf.

Near the sofa he found a picture of himself and Jordan Conway, both smiling easily at the camera. He sat down, transfixed by it, and time slipped past at an uncertain rate.

The doorbell rang, and he looked up, startled to note that the room had darkened appreciably. He heard the door open.

"Alan?" It was Jordan's voice. He sensed her in the doorway, silhouetted against the twilight sky, just outside his field of vision.

He looked down again at the photograph he held, glancing up only when she sat beside him. She took the small frame from him and studied the photograph, though the images were now hardly discernible in the darkened room.

"That was a good time for us," she said.

He nodded, his eyes fixed on the pale crescent of her captured smile.

"But hey, complications happen," she said.

"I've heard it put differently."

"I heard about what happened here. I'm sorry."

"Me, too."

"They've found some more bodies near Teaselville at the home of Luis Basoalto. It was on the radio."

He looked at her. After a long moment, he said, "Maybe you could move a little closer, and I could put my arm around you. Maybe we could sit like that for a while."

She smiled. "Maybe we could." She shifted toward him, accepted his arm about her, and worked her shoulder against him.

It was quite dark when he said, "Jordan?"

"Hmm?"

"Did you ever think about getting in the car and just driving away from it all? Doesn't it seem like life would be a lot simpler in Alaska?"

"I don't know. I'm not licensed to practice law in Alaska."

"Maybe life would be simpler working in a lumberyard or something."

"I might rather teach Business Law at a community college. You could work in the lumberyard."

He sighed.

"I'm sorry," she said. "This is your fantasy. We can work in the lumberyard."

"Huh. I think I could fall in love with you, Jordan."

She moved her head away from him far enough to look at him. "I don't know if I could fall in love with you or not," she said seriously. "You're a difficult boyfriend."

"I might could do better."

"You might could. We'll have to see."

Chapter 78

When court reconvened at ten o'clock the next morning, the courtroom was crowded and the judge's gavel was needed to silence the spectators. From that point, the proceedings went forward as if rehearsed — as indeed they had been, beginning an hour earlier with Larson and Alan Dougherty both in the judge's chambers.

Judge Mitchell looked at the district attorney and said, "Mr. Larson, I believe you have a motion to make."

Larson, on his feet, said, "Yes, your honor. New evidence has come to our attention that strongly suggests the defendant Tracey Coleman is innocent of the crime charged in the indictment. The state asks the court's permission to dismiss the action against her."

"You have an order for me to sign?"

"I do." Larson presented the judge with one copy, Alan with another. The top page was a Judgment of Dismissal, typed and ready for the judge's signature. Beneath it was a document detailing the state's reasons for its request.

"Very well," Judge Mitchell said, flapping through the pages for a brief look at what they contained. Dropping them to the bench, he waited for stillness and got it. He said, "The action of *State of Texas versus Tracey Coleman* is dismissed. The bail is discharged." He lifted his gavel and dropped it. As a muted hubbub erupted in the courtroom, he looked down at Tracey Coleman and smiled.

People crowded forward from the gallery, shaking hands and slapping shoulders. Several members of the jury stopped by the defense table to congratulate Tracey and to shake Alan's hand. "If I ever need a lawyer, you're the one I'm going to," said one of them. At the prosecutor's table, Cale Larson stood in relative isolation, but he nodded solemnly when Alan caught his gaze.

An older woman with perm-damaged hair told Tracey, "You look like such a sweet thing. I never could believe you'd done anything bad."

Tracey smiled shyly at her in answer and ducked her head.

Tracey and Alan left the courthouse together, crossing the street toward the town square where both of them had left their cars. "Is this it?" she asked. "It's over?"

"This is it."

"They can't change their minds and indict me again tomorrow?"

"No. The Fifth Amendment won't allow it."

"You mean double jeopardy? But they never finished the trial. The jury never returned its verdict."

"Doesn't matter. Jeopardy attached when the jury was empanelled and sworn."

"So no matter what comes up later, they can't prosecute me," she said.

"Not for the murder of Carlotta Basoalto. You could confess, you could take out a full-page ad in the paper, and still you couldn't be prosecuted."

"So it's over."

"It's really over."

She took a breath and released it slowly.

"So how do you feel?" he asked her. He tried to put some emotion in his voice, but he felt emotionally flat, perhaps from a sense of anticlimax, perhaps from something deeper. "Pretty good?"

"Pretty wonderful. Daddy's better. I'm going to be all right. Everything's great."

He was almost surprised to hear that good things happened to people anymore. Tracey opened the door of her Porsche and called to Alan across the top of her car, "I don't figure Tony Royal really committed suicide, do you?"

He flinched, then glanced warily about them to see who had overheard. There was no one. "No, I don't figure he did."

"I figure it was the rings," Tracey said. "Don't you?"

"What?"

"After you put Luis onto the Royal boys, he searched until he found his daughter's rings. That's when he came to visit you with his deal: Tony confesses; you stop looking into the money laundering arrangement."

Alan leaned over the roof of the car that separated him from Tracey. "We ought never to talk about this," he said earnestly. "We ought to pretend it never happened."

She smiled at him. "Okay, boss. As of now, I am in denial."

Her dark hair swung as she got into her car.

He got into his own car. Revelation hit him, and he held onto the steering wheel in an effort to keep his hands from shaking.

Nothing about the rings had appeared in the newspaper. Nothing about them had been said in open court. *I just wish there were some corroborating evidence,* he had said once to Tracey. *Something to tie Barry and Tony into either the smuggling or Carlotta's murder, at least in Luis's mind.*

Maybe there is something. It was after she had said that that the rings had been discovered.

And how does she know about those rings, he asked himself, unless she planted them? And how did she come to have the rings in the first place, unless she herself...

"Guilty knowledge," he muttered, struggling to adjust to the weight of this newest revelation, to find his equilibrium.

The door on the other side of the car opened, and Tracey dropped into the passenger seat.

Chapter 79

"I blew it, didn't I?" Tracey said. "I'm not supposed to know about the rings." Her eyes, when she glanced at him, were bright and clear, as always.

She said, "I can see the horror in your face. Tracey killed Carlotta, you think. She took Carlotta's rings, and she planted them on Tony to get him killed, too — tortured and killed." She sighed, and her gaze went to her bare left knee, which still showed the cut she had gotten by the pool at the house of Luis Basoalto. "It isn't true."

"You planted the rings," Alan said hoarsely, then stopped to clear his throat with a sound like the grinding of gears. He continued, just as hoarsely: "There's no other possible explanation."

"No other explanation you can think of," she corrected. She sighed again. "Yes, I planted the rings on Tony. I didn't get them from Carlotta, though." She glanced at him again, gave him a half-smile that was more an expression of pain. "I found them in the trap under my bathroom sink. Tony put them there. When you think about it, I was only returning them."

"You're saying he planted them on you."

"Yes, when he planted the cocaine." She laughed, but there was no mirth in it. "I see you still don't believe me about the cocaine. It's true, though. About a week ago, a day or two before Luis Basoalto kidnapped you and hauled you out to his place, I saw Tony pulling out of my apartment complex, and I turned in to see what he'd been doing there. I found the cocaine behind the target over my bed, inside the wall where a piece of wallboard had been cut out and fitted in again."

"Is that why you..."

"Sure. I did the same thing at your place, just to have somewhere to stash it until I thought what to do."

She let him chew on that a minute before giving him more to digest. "I'd shot Barry, remember, that night he and Tony had forced their way into my apartment, but I left the cocaine in plain sight, thinking they'd take it and leave me alone. Barry passed out when he tried to follow me out the window, and Tony took it, either then, or when he came back for it later. I don't know what he told Barry — I guess that I'd taken it with me. Or maybe Barry reeled through the apartment and never saw the Saran-wrapped package at all."

"Who wrecked your apartment?"

"I guess Tony did to make it look like he'd searched everywhere and hadn't found the cocaine. And he put the cocaine back in my apartment because it was getting too hot to handle. He could get rid of the cocaine, frame me, put everything to rest. He did kill Carlotta, you know. He was one sick puppy."

"And the rings?"

"I was lucky there. Evidently he knocked over the tray of cosmetics by my sink. He put it back, but the bottles and stuff weren't arranged the way I keep them. If it weren't for that, I'd have thought I'd found everything there was to find when I found the cocaine." She stopped, opened her mouth to continue, then shrugged her slender shoulders again and let it go.

After a while Alan said, "You don't know how much I'd like to believe you."

"You don't know how sorry I am to have squandered all my credibility."

His lips drew back.

"I guess I have, though, haven't I? At this point, it would take a supernatural power to convince you I was telling the truth."

He opened his mouth to agree when a tone sounded, clear and sweet, and she fished her iPhone from a pocket in her skirt. "It's from Daddy," she said. Seeing his face, she clicked off her phone without answering it. "What?" she asked Alan. "What is it?"

His mouth had remained open as a shiver worked its way up his back and the hair stiffened on his arms and at the back of his neck. The tone was the same as the one he'd heard so often at the St. Peter Claver Catholic Church: *Jesus is in the building*. "I believe you," he said in strangled tones.

"What? Really?"

He managed a nod. Tears welled in her eyes, overflowing the lower lid on one eye and sliding down her cheek.

"That means everything to me," she said. She laid the backs of her fingers against the side of his face. "It's almost redemptive."

Both her cheeks were wet now. Tears were streaming down his face, too.

Chapter 80

Alan was nearly home when his doubts rose up once again to assail him, and he worked to push them back. It was no good. How often had Tracey lied to him before? How many times was he going to fall for it? "Lord, I believe," he muttered. "Help thou mine unbelief."

But it was no good. He took a right, then a mile later turned into Tracey's apartment complex. He parked badly, his car angled across two spaces, and got out. As he went up the sidewalk to her building, his breath began coming to him in great gulps, and darkness clouded his vision. He had to stop at the bottom of her stairs and bend over until his head cleared. If he didn't get away from Tracey soon, he thought, she was going to kill him.

At the top of the stairs, the door of her apartment stood closed and locked. A reinforcing brass plate surrounded the doorknob, part of the repair done by the landlord. He stood looking down at it, still breathing heavily, then stepped back and, raising his knee to his chest, kicked out at the door, hitting it just above the knob. The door shivered, and he kicked it again. Then he backed up two more steps and ran at it, lowering his shoulder and slamming into the door with a guttural cry that seemed to come all the way from his toes. This time the deadbolt and the tongue of the lock tore through the inner molding around the door, and the door vibrated open.

In another moment he was in the bedroom, and the target was off the wall. There was a hole in the sheetrock. He pulled the bed away from the wall, and there on the floor behind the headboard was a rectangular piece of sheetrock. This time, Tracey had told the truth.

He sat abruptly on the bed, laughing giddily, but he broke off when he saw Tracey in the bedroom doorway. A short-barreled revolver — yet another gun he had never seen before — was in her right hand, though it was pointed downward. In her left hand was a splintered piece of molding from the doorframe.

"Trust but verify, huh?" she said dryly.

"I —" Words failed him, and he turned his hands over so that they lay on his lap, palms upward.

"I know," she said. "It's important to me that you believed me, if only for a while. And that it mattered to you whether I was telling the truth." She looked back toward her broken doorframe, held up the broken piece of molding. "Mattered to you quite a lot."

She crossed to the bed and sat down beside him. Neither spoke. At last she said, "Poor Alan."

He looked at her.

"You deserve to be whole and at peace," she said.

"Deserve?"

"Maybe not deserve," she conceded. "But you could be at peace. You should be." She took his hand, intertwining her fingers with his, bouncing their joined hands on his leg. Then she released him and stood. "Go find Jordan," she said. "I'm your past. She's your future."

He felt the truth of that and with it the stirrings of hope. "What will you do?" he asked.

"Me? I need to be at peace, too." Her smile was sad. "For right now, I'm going home to Daddy."

ABOUT THE AUTHOR

Michael Monhollon took out a semester in college to write science fiction stories and collect rejection slips. His first book sale, a legal thriller, came at the age of 31 at about the time *The Firm* was coming out in paperback. Its sales fell short of *The Firm*'s, though, and he continues to work for a living. For a dozen years he practiced law. Currently, he is a professor of business law at a small liberal arts college in Abilene, Texas.

www.ingramcontent.com/pod-product-compliance
Lightning Source LLC
Chambersburg PA
CBHW072105250626
47159CB00007B/2313